# THE SPEED OF DARK

# THE SPEED OF DARK

## ELIZABETH MOON

BALLANTINE BOOKS • NEW YORK

A Ballantine Book
Published by The Ballantine Publishing Group

www.ballantinebooks.com

Library of Congress Cataloging-in-Publication Data
Moon, Elizabeth.
The speed of dark / Elizabeth Moon.
p.     cm.
ISBN 0-345-44755-7
1. Autism—Patients—Fiction. I. Title.
PS3563.O557 S64 2002
813'.54—dc21

Text design by Holly Johnson

Manufactured in the United States of America

First Edition: January 2003

1 3 5 7 9 10 8 6 4 2

For Michael, whose courage and joy are a constant delight, and for Richard, without whose love and support the job would have been 200 percent harder. And for other parents of autistic children, in the hope that they also find that delight in difference.

# ACKNOWLEDGMENTS

Among the people who had helped most in research for this book were the autistic children and adults and the families of autists who over the years have communicated with me—by their writings, in person, on the Internet. In the planning stages of this book, I distanced myself from most of these sources (unsubscribing from mailing lists and news groups, et cetera) to protect the privacy of those individuals; a normally spotty memory made it unlikely that any identifiable details would survive several years of noncontact. One of those individuals chose to stay in e-mail contact; for her generosity in discussing issues related to disability, inclusion, and the perception of nonautistic persons I am always in her debt. However, she has not read this book (yet) and is not responsible for anything in it.

Of the writers in this field, I am most indebted to Oliver Sacks, whose many books on neurology are informed with humanity as well as knowledge, and Temple Grandin, whose inside view of autism was invaluable (and especially accessible to me since my lifelong interest in animal behavior overlaps her expertise). Readers who are particularly interested in autism might want to look at the reading list on my Web site.

J. Ferris Duhon, an attorney with extensive experience in employment law, helped me design a plausible near-future business and legal climate as it related to employment of persons labeled disabled; any remaining legal pratfalls are my fault, not his. J.B., J.H., J.K., and K.S. contributed insights into the corporate structure and the internal politics of large multinational corporations and research institutions; for obvious reasons they preferred not to be identified more fully. David Watson provided expert advice on fencing, historical re-creation organizations, and the protocol of tournaments. Again, any errors in any of this are my fault, not theirs.

My editor, Shelly Shapiro, provided exactly the right blend of freedom and guidance, and my agent, Joshua Bilmes, sustained the effort with his belief that I could actually do this.

QUESTIONS, ALWAYS QUESTIONS. THEY DIDN'T WAIT FOR the answers, either. They rushed on, piling questions on questions, covering every moment with questions, blocking off every sensation but the thorn stab of questions.

And orders. If it wasn't, "Lou, what is this?" it was, "Tell me what this is." A bowl. The same bowl, time after time. It is a bowl and it is an ugly bowl, a boring bowl, a bowl of total and complete boring blandness, uninteresting. I am uninterested in that uninteresting bowl.

If they aren't going to listen, why should I talk?

I know better than to say that out loud. Everything in my life that I value has been gained at the cost of not saying what I really think and saying what they want me to say.

In this office, where I am evaluated and advised four times a year, the psychiatrist is no less certain of the line between us than all the others have been. Her certainty is painful to see, so I try not to look at her more than I have to. That has its own dangers; like the others, she thinks I should make more eye contact than I do. I glance at her now.

Dr. Fornum, crisp and professional, raises an eyebrow and shakes her head not quite imperceptibly. Autistic persons do not understand these signals; the book says so. I have read the book, so I know what it is I do not understand.

What I haven't figured out yet is the range of things *they* don't understand. The normals. The reals. The ones who have the degrees and sit behind the desks in comfortable chairs.

I know some of what she doesn't know. She doesn't know that I can read. She thinks I'm hyperlexic, just parroting the words. The difference between what she calls parroting and what she does when she reads is imperceptible to me. She doesn't know that I have a large vocabulary. Every time she asks what my job is and I say I am still working for the pharmaceutical company, she asks if I know what *pharmaceutical* means. She thinks I'm parroting. The difference between what she calls parroting and my use of a large number of words is imperceptible to me. She uses large words when talking to the other doctors and nurses and technicians, babbling on and on and saying things that could be said more simply. She knows I work on a computer, she knows I went to school, but she has not caught on that this is incompatible with her belief that I am actually nearly illiterate and barely verbal.

She talks to me as if I were a rather stupid child. She does not like it when I use big words (as she calls them) and she tells me to just say what I mean.

What I mean is the speed of dark is as interesting as the speed of light, and maybe it is faster and who will find out?

What I mean is about gravity, if there were a world where it is twice as strong, then on that world would the wind from a fan be stronger because the air is thicker and blow my glass off the table, not just my napkin? Or would the greater gravity hold the glass more firmly to the table, so the stronger wind couldn't move it?

What I mean is the world is big and scary and noisy and crazy but also beautiful and still in the middle of the windstorm.

What I mean is what difference does it make if I think of colors as people or people as sticks of chalk, all stiff and white unless they are brown chalk or black?

What I mean is I know what I like and want, and she does not, and I do not want to like or want what she wants me to like or want.

She doesn't want to know what I mean. She wants me to say what other people say. "Good morning, Dr. Fornum." "Yes, I'm fine, thank you." "Yes, I can wait. I don't mind."

I don't mind. When she answers the phone I can look around her office and find the twinkly things she doesn't know she has. I can move my head back and forth so the light in the corner glints off and on over there, on the shiny cover of a book in the bookcase. If she notices that I'm moving my head back and forth she makes a note in my record. She may even interrupt her phone call to tell me to stop. It is called stereotypy when I do it and relaxing her neck when she does it. I call it fun, watching the reflected light blink off and on.

Dr. Fornum's office has a strange blend of smells, not just the paper and ink and book smell and the carpet glue and the plastic smell of the chair frames, but something else that I keep thinking must be chocolate. Does she keep a box of candy in her desk drawer? I would like to find out. I know if I asked her she would make a note in my record. Noticing smells is not appropriate. Notes about noticing are bad notes, but not like bad notes in music, which are wrong.

I do not think everyone else is alike in every way. She has told me that Everyone knows this and Everyone does that, but I am not blind, just autistic, and I know that they know and do different things. The cars in the parking lot are different colors and sizes. Thirty-seven percent of them, this morning, are blue. Nine percent are oversize: trucks or vans. There are eighteen motorcycles in three racks, which would be six apiece, except that ten of them are in the back rack, near Maintenance. Different channels carry different programs; that would not happen if everyone were alike.

When she puts down the phone and looks at me, her face has that look. I don't know what most people would call it, but I call it the I AM REAL look. It means she is real and she has answers and I am someone less, not completely real, even though I can feel the nubbly texture of the office chair right through my slacks. I used to put a magazine under me, but she says I don't need to do that. She is real, she thinks, so she knows what I need and don't need.

"Yes, Dr. Fornum, I am listening." Her words pour over me, slightly irritating, like a vat of vinegar. "Listen for conversational cues," she tells me, and waits. "Yes," I say. She nods, marks on the record, and says, "Very good," without looking at me. Down the hall somewhere, someone starts walking this way. Two someones, talking. Soon their talk tangles with hers. I am hearing about Debby on Friday . . . next time . . .

going to the Did they? And I told her. But never bird on a stool . . . can't be, and Dr. Fornum is waiting for me to answer something. She would not talk to me about a bird on a stool. "I'm sorry," I say. She tells me to pay better attention and makes another mark on my record and asks about my social life.

She does not like what I tell her, which is that I play games on the Internet with my friend Alex in Germany and my friend Ky in Indonesia. "In real life," she says firmly. "People at work," I say, and she nods again and then asks about bowling and miniature golf and movies and the local branch of the Autism Society.

Bowling hurts my back and the noise is ugly in my head. Miniature golf is for kids, not grownups, but I didn't like it even when I was a kid. I liked laser tag, but when I told her that in the first session she put down "violent tendencies." It took a long time to get that set of questions about violence off my regular agenda, and I'm sure she has never removed the notation. I remind her that I don't like bowling or miniature golf, and she tells me I should make an effort. I tell her I've been to three movies, and she asks about them. I read the reviews, so I can tell her the plots. I don't like movies much, either, especially in movie theaters, but I have to have something to tell her . . . and so far she hasn't figured out that my bald recitation of the plot is straight from a review.

I brace myself for the next question, which always makes me angry. My sex life is none of her business. She is the last person I would tell about a girlfriend or boyfriend. But she doesn't expect me to have one; she just wants to document that I do not, and that is worse.

Finally it is over. She will see me next time, she says, and I say, "Thank you, Dr. Fornum," and she says, "Very good," as if I were a trained dog.

Outside, it is hot and dry, and I must squint against the glitter of all the parked cars. The people walking on the sidewalk are dark blots in the sunlight, hard to see against the shimmer of the light until my eyes adjust.

I am walking too fast. I know that not just from the firm smack of my shoes on the pavement, but because the people walking toward me have their faces bunched up in the way that I think means they're worried. Why? I am not trying to hit them. So I will slow down and think music.

Dr. Fornum says I should learn to enjoy music other people enjoy. I do. I know other people like Bach and Schubert and not all of them are autistic. There are not enough autistic people to support all those orchestras and operas. But to her *other people* means "the most people." I think of the *Trout Quintet*, and as the music flows through my mind I can feel my breathing steady and my steps slow to match its tempo.

My key slides into my car's door lock easily, now that I have the right music. The seat is warm, cozily warm, and the soft fleece comforts me. I used to use hospital fleece, but with one of my first paychecks I bought a real sheepskin. I bounce a little to the internal music before turning on the engine. It's hard to keep the music going sometimes when the engine starts; I like to wait until it's on the beat.

On the way back to work, I let the music ease me through intersections, traffic lights, near-jams, and then the gates of the campus, as they call it. Our building is off to the right; I flash my ID at the parking lot guard and find my favorite space. I hear people from other buildings complain about not getting their favorite space, but here we always do. No one would take my space, and I would not take anyone else's. Dale on my right and Linda on my left, facing into Cameron.

I walk to the building, on the last phrase of my favorite part of the music, and let it fade as I go through the door. Dale is there, by the coffee machine. He does not speak, nor do I. Dr. Fornum would want me to speak, but there is no reason. I can see that Dale is thinking very hard and doesn't need to be interrupted. I am still annoyed about Dr. Fornum, as I am every quarter, so I pass my desk and go on into the minigym. Bouncing will help. Bouncing always helps. No one else is there, so I hang the sign on the door and turn good bouncing music up loud.

No one interrupts me while I bounce; the strong thrust of the trampoline followed by weightless suspension makes me feel vast and light. I can feel my mind stretching out, relaxing, even as I keep perfect time with the music. When I feel the concentration returning and curiosity drives me once more toward my assignment, I slow the bouncing to tiny little baby bounces and swing off the trampoline.

No one interrupts me as I walk to my desk. I think Linda is there, and Bailey, but it doesn't matter. Later we may go for supper, but not now. Now I am ready to work.

The symbols I work with are meaningless and confusing to most people. It is hard to explain what I do, but I know it is valuable work, because they pay me enough to afford the car, the apartment, and they supply the gym and the quarterly visits to Dr. Fornum. Basically I look for patterns. Some of the patterns have fancy names and other people find them hard to see, but for me they have always been easy. All I had to do was learn the way to describe them so others could see that I had something in mind.

I put headphones on and choose a music. For the project I'm on now, Schubert is too lush. Bach is perfect, the complex patterns mirroring the pattern I need. I let the place in my mind that finds and generates patterns sink into the project, and then it is like watching ice crystals grow on the surface of still water: one after another, the lines of ice grow, branch, branch again, interlace. . . . All I have to do is pay attention and ensure that the pattern remains symmetrical or asymmetrical or whatever the particular project calls for. This time it is more intensely recursive than most, and I see it in my mind as stacks of fractal growth, forming a spiky sphere.

When the edges blur, I shake myself and sit back. It has been five hours, and I didn't notice. All the agitation from Dr. Fornum has gone, leaving me clear. Sometimes when I come back I can't work for a day or so, but this time I got back into balance with the bouncing. Above my workstation, a pinwheel spins lazily in the draft of the ventilation system. I blow at it, and after a moment—1.3 seconds, actually—it spins faster, twinkling purple-and-silver in the light. I decide to turn on my swiveling fan so all the pinwheels and spin spirals can spin together, filling my office with twinkling light.

The dazzle has just started when I hear Bailey calling from down the hall, "Anyone for pizza?" I am hungry; my stomach makes noises and I can suddenly smell everything in the office: the paper, the workstation, the carpet, the metal/plastic/dust/cleaning solution . . . myself. I turn off the fan, give a last glance at the spinning and twinkling beauty, and go out into the hall. A quick flick of a glance at my friends' faces is all I need to know who is coming and who is not. We do not need to talk about it; we know one another.

We come into the pizza place about nine. Linda, Bailey, Eric, Dale, Cameron, and me. Chuy was ready to eat, too, but the tables here hold only six. He understands. I would understand if he and the others were ready first. I would not want to come here and sit at another table, so I know that Chuy will not come here and we will not have to try to squeeze him in. A new manager last year did not understand that. He was always trying to arrange big dinners for us and mix us up in seating. "Don't be so hidebound," he would say. When he wasn't looking, we went back to where we like to sit. Dale has an eye tic that bothers Linda, so she sits where she can't see it. I think it's funny and I like to watch it, so I sit on Dale's left, where it looks like he's winking at me.

The people who work here know us. Even when other people in the restaurant look too long at us for our movements and the way we talk— or don't—the people here don't ever give us that go-away look I've had other places. Linda just points to what she wants or sometimes she writes it out first, and they never bother her with more questions.

Tonight our favorite table is dirty. I can hardly stand to look at the five dirty plates and pizza pans; it makes my stomach turn to think of the smears of sauce and cheese and crust crumbs, and the uneven number makes it worse. There is an empty table to our right, but we do not like that one. It's next to the passage to the rest rooms, and too many people go by behind us.

We wait, trying to be patient, as Hi-I'm-Sylvia—she has that on her name tag, as if she were a product for sale and not a person—signals to one of the others to clean up our table. I like her and can remember to call her Sylvia without the Hi-I'm as long as I'm not looking at her name tag. Hi-I'm-Sylvia always smiles at us and tries to be helpful; Hi-I'm-Jean is the reason we don't come in on Thursdays, when she works this shift. Hi-I'm-Jean doesn't like us and mutters under her breath if she sees us. Sometimes one of us will come to pick up an order for the others;

the last time I did, Hi-I'm-Jean said, "At least he didn't bring all the other freaks in here," to one of the cooks as I turned away from the register. She knew I heard. She meant me to hear. She is the only one who gives us trouble.

But tonight it's Hi-I'm-Sylvia and Tyree, who is picking up the plates and dirty knives and forks as if it didn't bother him. Tyree doesn't wear a name tag; he just cleans tables. We know he's Tyree because we heard the others call him that. The first time I used his name to him, he looked startled and a little scared, but now he knows us, though he doesn't use our names.

"Be done in a minute here," Tyree says, and gives us a sidelong look. "You doin' okay?"

"Fine," Cameron says. He's bouncing a little from heel to toe. He always does that a little, but I can tell he's bouncing a bit faster than usual.

I am watching the beer sign blinking in the window. It comes on in three segments, red, green, then blue in the middle, and then goes off all at once. Blink, red. Blink, green, blink blue, then blink red/green/blue, all off, all on, all off, and start over. A very simple pattern, and the colors aren't that pretty (the red is too orange for my taste and so is the green, but the blue is a lovely blue), but still it's a pattern to watch.

"Your table's ready," Hi-I'm-Sylvia says, and I try not to twitch as I shift my attention from the beer sign to her.

We arrange ourselves around the table in the usual way and sit down. We are having the same thing we have every time we come here, so it doesn't take long to order. We wait for the food to come, not talking because we are each, in our own way, settling into this situation. Because of the visit to Dr. Fornum, I'm more aware than usual of the details of this process: that Linda is bouncing her fingers on the bowl of her spoon in a complex pattern that would delight a mathematician as much as it does her. I'm watching the beer sign out of the corner of my eye, as is Dale. Cameron is bouncing the tiny plastic dice he keeps in his pocket, discreetly enough that people who don't know him wouldn't notice, but I can see the rhythmic flutter of his sleeve. Bailey also watches the beer sign. Eric has taken out his multicolor pen and is drawing tiny geometric patterns on the paper place mat. First red, then purple, then blue, then green, then yellow, then orange, then red again. He likes it when the food arrives just when he finishes a color sequence.

This time the drinks come while he's at yellow; the food comes on the next orange. His face relaxes.

We are not supposed to talk about the project off-campus. But Cameron is still bouncing in his seat, full of his need to tell us about a problem he solved, when we've almost finished eating. I glance around. No one is at a table near us. "Ezzer," I say. *Ezzer* means "go ahead" in our private language. We aren't supposed to have a private language and nobody thinks we can do something like that, but we can. Many people have a private language without even knowing it. They may call it jargon or slang, but it's really a private language, a way of telling who is in the group and who is not.

Cameron pulls a paper out of his pocket and spreads it out. We aren't supposed to take papers out of the office, in case someone else gets hold of them, but we all do it. It's hard to talk, sometimes, and much easier to write things down or draw them.

I recognize the curly guardians Cameron always puts in the corner of his drawings. He likes anime. I recognize as well the patterns he has linked through a partial recursion that has the lean elegance of most of his solutions. We all look at it and nod. "Pretty," Linda says. Her hands jerk sideways a little; she would be flapping wildly if we were back at the campus, but here she tries not to do it.

"Yes," Cameron says, and folds the paper back up.

I know that this exchange would not satisfy Dr. Fornum. She would want Cameron to explain the drawing, even though it is clear to all of us. She would want us to ask questions, make comments, talk about it. There is nothing to talk about: it is clear to all of us what the problem was and that Cameron's solution is good in all senses. Anything else is just busy talk. Among ourselves we don't have to do that.

"I was wondering about the speed of dark," I say, looking down. They will look at me, if only briefly, when I speak, and I don't want to feel all those gazes.

"It doesn't have a speed," Eric says. "It's just the space where light isn't."

"What would it feel like if someone ate pizza on a world with more than one gravity?" Linda asks.

"I don't know," Dale says, sounding worried.

"The speed of not knowing," Linda says.

I puzzle at that a moment and figure it out. "Not knowing expands faster than knowing," I say. Linda grins and ducks her head. "So the speed of dark could be greater than the speed of light. If there always has to be dark around the light, then it has to go out ahead of it."

"I want to go home now," Eric says. Dr. Fornum would want me to ask if he is upset. I know he is not upset; if he goes home now he will see his favorite TV program. We say good-bye because we are in public and we all know you are supposed to say good-bye in public. I go back to the campus. I want to watch my whirligigs and spin spirals for a while before going home to bed.

CAMERON AND I ARE IN THE GYM, TALKING IN BURSTS AS WE bounce on the trampolines. We have both done a lot of good work in the last few days, and we are relaxing.

Joe Lee comes in and I look at Cameron. Joe Lee is only twenty-four. He would be one of us if he hadn't had the treatments that were developed too late for us. He thinks he's one of us because he knows he would have been and he has some of our characteristics. He is very good at abstractions and recursions, for instance. He likes some of the same games; he likes our gym. But he is much better—he is normal, in fact—in his ability to read minds and expressions. Normal minds and expressions. He misses with us, who are his closest relatives in that way.

"Hi, Lou," he says to me. "Hi, Cam." I see Cameron stiffen. He doesn't like to have his name shortened. He has told me it feels like having his legs cut off. He has told Joe Lee, too, but Joe Lee forgets because he spends so much of his time with the normals. "Howzitgoin'?" he asks, slurring the words and forgetting to face us so we can see his lips. I catch it, because my auditory processing is better than Cameron's and I know that Joe Lee often slurs his words.

"How is it going?" I say clearly, for Cameron's benefit. "Fine, Joe Lee." Cameron breathes out.

"Didja hear?" Joe Lee asks, and without waiting for an answer he rushes on. "Somebody's working on a reversal procedure for autism. It worked on some rats or something, so they're trying it on primates. I'll bet it won't be long before you guys can be normal like me."

Joe Lee has always said he's one of us, but this makes it clear that he has never really believed it. We are "you guys" and normal is "like me." I wonder if he said he was one of us but luckier to make us feel better or to please someone else.

Cameron glares; I can almost feel the tangle of words filling his throat, making it impossible for him to speak. I know better than to speak for him. I speak only for myself, which is how everyone should speak.

"So you admit you are not one of us," I say, and Joe Lee stiffens, his face assuming an expression I've been taught is "hurt feelings."

"How can you say that, Lou? You know it's just the treatment—"

"If you give a deaf child hearing, he is no longer one of the deaf," I say. "If you do it early enough, he never was. It's all pretending otherwise."

"What's all pretending otherwise? Otherwise what?" Joe Lee looks confused as well as hurt, and I realize that I left out one of the little pauses where a comma would be if you wrote what I said. But his confusion alarms me—being not understood alarms me; it lasted so long when I was a child. I feel the words tangling in my head, in my throat, and struggle to get them out in the right order, with the right expression. Why can't people just say what they mean, the words alone? Why do I have to fight with tone and rate and pitch and variation?

I can feel and hear my voice going tight and mechanical. I sound angry to myself, but what I feel is scared. "They fixed you before you were born, Joe Lee," I say. "You never lived days—one day—like us."

"You're wrong," he says quickly, interrupting. "I'm just like you inside, except—"

"Except what makes you different from others, what you call normal," I say, interrupting in turn. It hurts to interrupt. Miss Finley, one of my therapists, used to tap my hand if I interrupted. But I could not stand to hear him going on saying things that were not true. "You could hear and process language sounds—you learned to talk normally. You didn't have dazzle eyes."

"Yeah, but my brain works the same way."

I shake my head. Joe Lee should know better; we've told him again and again. The problems we have with hearing and vision and other senses aren't in the sensory organs but in the brain. So the brain does not work the same if someone doesn't have those problems. If we were computers, Joe Lee would have a different main processor chip, with a different instruction set. Even if two computers with different chips do use the same software, it will not run the same.

"But I do the same work—"

But he doesn't. He thinks he does. Sometimes I wonder if the company we work for thinks he does, because they have hired other Joe Lees and no more of us, even though I know there are unemployed people like us. Joe Lee's solutions are linear. Sometimes that's very effective, but sometimes . . . I want to say that, but I can't, because he looks so angry and upset.

"C'mon," he says. "Have supper with me, you and Cam. My treat."

I feel cold in the middle. I do not want to have supper with Joe Lee.

"Can't," Cameron says. "Got a date." He has a date with his chess partner in Japan, I suspect. Joe Lee turns to look at me.

"Sorry," I remember to say. "I have a meeting." Sweat trickles down my back; I hope Joe Lee doesn't ask what meeting. It's bad enough that I know there is time for supper with Joe Lee between now and the meeting, but if I have to lie about the meeting I will be miserable for days.


GENE CRENSHAW SAT IN A BIG CHAIR AT ONE END OF THE TABLE; Pete Aldrin, like the others, sat in an ordinary chair along one side. Typical, Aldrin thought. He calls meetings because he can be visibly important in the big chair. It was the third meeting in four days, and Aldrin had stacks of work on his desk that wasn't getting done because of these meetings. So did the others.

Today the topic was the negative spirit in the workplace, which seemed to mean anyone who questioned Crenshaw in any way. Instead, they were supposed to "catch the vision"—Crenshaw's vision—and concentrate on that to the exclusion of everything else. Anything that didn't fit the vision was . . . suspect if not bad. Democracy wasn't in it: this was a business, not a party. Crenshaw said that several times. Then he pointed to Aldrin's unit, Section A as it was known in-house, as an example of what was wrong.

Aldrin's stomach burned; a sour taste came into his mouth. Section A had remarkable productivity; he had a string of commendations in his record because of it. How could Crenshaw possibly think there was anything wrong with it?

Before he could jump in, Madge Demont spoke up. "You know, Gene, we've always worked as a team in this department. Now you come in here and pay no attention to our established, and successful, ways of working together—"

"I'm a natural leader," Crenshaw said. "My personality profile shows that I'm cut out to be a captain, not crew."

"Teamwork is important for anyone," Aldrin said. "Leaders have to learn how to work with others—"

"That's not my gift," Crenshaw said. "My gift is inspiring others and giving a strong lead."

His gift, Aldrin thought, was being bossy without having earned the right, but Crenshaw came highly recommended by higher management. They would all be fired before he was.

"These people," Crenshaw went on, "have to realize that they are not the be-all and end-all of this company. They have to fit in; it's their responsibility to do the job they were hired to do—"

"And if some of them are also natural leaders?" Aldrin asked.

Crenshaw snorted. "Autistics? Leaders? You must be kidding. They don't have what it takes; they don't understand the first thing about how society works."

"We have a contractual obligation . . . " Aldrin said, shifting ground before he got too angry to be coherent. "Under the terms of the contract, we must provide them with working conditions suitable to them."

"Well, we certainly do that, don't we?" Crenshaw almost quivered with indignation. "At enormous expense, too. Their own private gym, sound system, parking lot, all kinds of toys."

Upper management also had a private gym, sound system, parking lot, and such useful toys as stock options. Saying so wouldn't help.

Crenshaw went on. "I'm sure our other hardworking employees would like the chance to play in that sandbox—but they do their jobs."

"So does Section A," Aldrin said. "Their productivity figures—"

"Are adequate, I agree. But if they spent the time working that they waste on playtime, it would be a lot better."

Aldrin felt his neck getting hot. "Their productivity is not just *adequate*, Gene. It's outstanding. Section A is, person for person, more productive than any other department. Maybe what we should do is let other people have the same kinds of supportive resources that we give Section A—"

"And drop the profit margin to zero? Our stockholders would love that. Pete, I admire you for sticking up for your people, but that's exactly why you didn't make VP and why you won't rise any higher until you learn to see the big picture, get the vision. This company is going places, and it needs a workforce of unimpaired, productive workers—people who don't need all these little extras. We're cutting the fat, getting back to the lean, tough, productive machine . . ."

Buzzwords, Aldrin thought. The same buzzwords he had fought in the first place, to get Section A those very perks that made them so productive. When the profitability of Section A proved him right, senior management had given in gracefully—he thought. But now they'd put Crenshaw in. Did they know? Could they not know?

"I know you have an older brother with autism," Crenshaw said, his voice unctuous. "I feel your pain, but you have to realize that this is the real world, not nursery school. Your family problems can't be allowed to make policy."

Aldrin wanted to pick up the water pitcher and smash it—water and ice cubes and all—onto Crenshaw's head. He knew better. Nothing would convince Crenshaw that his reasons for championing Section A were far more complex than having an autistic brother. He had almost refused to work there because of Jeremy, because of a childhood spent in the shadow of Jeremy's incoherent rages, the ridicule he'd had from other kids about his "crazy retard" brother. He'd had more than enough of Jeremy; he'd sworn, when he left home, that he would avoid any reminders, that he would live among safe, sane, normal people for the rest of his life.

Now, though, it was the difference between Jeremy (still living in a group home, spending his days at an adult day-care center, unable to do more than simple self-care tasks) and the men and women of Section A that made Aldrin defend them. It was still hard, sometimes, to see what they had in common with Jeremy and not flinch away. Yet working with them, he felt a little less guilty about not visiting his parents and Jeremy more than once a year.

"You're wrong," he said to Crenshaw. "If you try to dismantle Section A's support apparatus, you will cost this company more in productivity than you'll gain. We depend on their unique abilities; the search algorithms and pattern analysis they've developed have cut the time from raw data to production—that's our edge over the competition—"

"I don't think so. It's your job to keep them productive, Aldrin. Let's see if you're up to it."

Aldrin choked down his anger. Crenshaw had the self-satisfied smirk of a man who knew he was in power and enjoyed watching his subordinates cringe. Aldrin glanced sideways; the others were studiously not looking at him, hoping that the trouble landing on him would not spread to them.

"Besides," Crenshaw went on. "There's a new study coming out, from a lab in Europe. It's supposed to be on-line in a day or so. Experimental as yet, but I understand very promising. Maybe we should suggest that they get on the protocol for it."

"New treatment?"

"Yeah. I don't know much about it, but I know someone who does and he knew I was taking over a bunch of autistics. Told me to keep an eye out for when it went to human trials. It's supposed to fix the fundamental deficit, make them normal. If they were normal, they wouldn't have an excuse for those luxuries."

"If they were normal," Aldrin said, "they couldn't do the work."

"In either case, we'd be clear of having to provide this stuff—" Crenshaw's expansive wave included everything from the gym to individual cubbies with doors. "Either they could do the work at less cost to us or, if they couldn't do the work, they wouldn't be our employees anymore."

"What is the treatment?" Aldrin asked.

"Oh, some combination of neuro-enhancers and nanotech. It makes the right parts of the brain grow, supposedly." Crenshaw grinned, an unfriendly grin. "Why don't you find out all about it, Pete, and send me a report? If it works we might even go after the North American license."

Aldrin wanted to glare, but he knew glaring wouldn't help. He had walked into Crenshaw's trap; he would be the one Section A blamed, if this turned out bad for them. "You know you can't force treatment on anyone," he said, as sweat crawled down his ribs, tickling. "They have civil rights."

"I can't imagine anyone *wanting* to be like that," Crenshaw said. "And if they do, that's a matter for a psych evaluation, I would think. Preferring to be sick—"

"They aren't *sick*," Aldrin said.

"And damaged. Preferring special treatment to a cure. That would have to be some kind of mental imbalance. Grounds for serious consideration of termination, I believe, seeing as they're doing sensitive work, which other entities would love to have."

Aldrin struggled again with the desire to hit Crenshaw over the head with something heavy.

"It might even help your brother," Crenshaw said.

That was too much. "Please leave my brother out of this," Aldrin said through his teeth.

"Now, now, I didn't mean to upset you." Crenshaw smiled even wider. "I was just thinking how it might help. . . ." He turned away with a casual wave before Aldrin could say any of the devastating things colliding in his mind and turned to the next person in line. "Now, Jennifer, about those target dates your team isn't meeting . . ."

What could Aldrin do? Nothing. What could anyone do? Nothing.

Men like Crenshaw rose to the top because they were like that—that is what it took. Apparently.

If there were such a treatment—not that he believed it—would it help his brother? He hated Crenshaw for dangling that lure in front of him. He had finally accepted Jeremy the way he was; he had worked through the old resentment and guilt. If Jeremy changed, what would that mean?

CHAPTER TWO

MR. CRENSHAW IS THE NEW SENIOR MANAGER. MR. Aldrin, our boss, took him around that first day. I didn't like him much—Crenshaw, that is—because he had the same false-hearty voice as the boys' PE teacher in my junior high school, the one who wanted to be a football coach at a high school. Coach Jerry, we had to call him. He thought the special-needs class was stupid, and we all hated him. I don't hate Mr. Crenshaw, but I don't like him, either.

Today on the way to work I wait at a red light, where the street crosses the interstate. The car in front of me is a midnight-blue minivan with out-of-state plates, Georgia. It has a fuzzy bear with little rubber suckers stuck to the back window. The bear grins at me with a foolish expression. I'm glad it's a toy; I hate it when there's a dog in the back of a car, looking at me. Usually they bark at me.

The light changes, and the minivan shoots ahead. Before I can think, No, don't! two cars running a red light speed through, a beige pickup with a brown stripe and an orange watercooler in the back and a brown sedan, and the truck hits the van broadside. The noise is appalling, shriek/crash/squeal/crunch all together, and the van and truck spin, spraying arcs of glittering glass. . . . I want to vanish inside myself as the grotesque shapes spin nearer. I shut my eyes.

Silence comes back slowly, punctuated by the honking horns of those who don't know why traffic stopped. I open my eyes. The light is green. People have gotten out of their cars; the drivers of the wrecked cars are moving, talking.

The driving code says that any person involved in an accident should not leave the scene. The driving code says stop and render assistance. But I was not involved, because nothing but a few bits of broken glass touched my car. And there are lots of other people to give assistance. I am not trained to give assistance.

I look carefully behind me and slowly, carefully, edge past the wreck. People look at me angrily. But I didn't do anything wrong; I wasn't in the accident. If I stayed, I would be late for work. And I would have to talk to policemen. I am afraid of policemen.

I feel shaky when I get to work, so instead of going into my office I go to the gym first. I put on the "Polka and Fugue" from *Schwanda the Bagpiper*, because I need to do big bounces and big swinging movements. I am a little calmer with bouncing by the time Mr. Crenshaw shows up, his face glistening an ugly shade of reddish beige.

"Well now, Lou," he says. The tone is clouded, as if he wanted to sound jovial but was really angry. Coach Jerry used to sound like that. "Do you like the gym a lot, then?"

The long answer is always more interesting than the short one. I know that most people want the short uninteresting answer rather than the long interesting one, so I try to remember that when they ask me questions that could have long answers if they only understood them. Mr. Crenshaw only wants to know if I like the gym room. He doesn't want to know how much.

"It's fine," I tell him.

"Do you need anything that isn't here?"

"No." I need many things that aren't here, including food, water, and a place to sleep, but he means do I need anything in this room for the purpose it is designed for that isn't in this room.

"Do you need that music?"

That music. Laura taught me that when people say "that" in front of a noun it implies an attitude about the content of the noun. I am trying to think what attitude Mr. Crenshaw has about that music when he goes on, as people often do, before I can answer.

"It's so difficult," he says. "Trying to keep all that music on hand. The recordings wear out. . . . It would be easier if we could just turn on the radio."

The radio here has loud banging noises or that whining singing, not music. And commercials, even louder, every few minutes. There is no rhythm to it, not one I could use for relaxing.

"The radio won't work," I say. I know that is too abrupt by the hardening in his face. I have to say more, not the short answer, but the long one. "The music has to go through me," I say. "It needs to be the right music to have the right effect, and it needs to be music, not talking or singing. It's the same for each of us. We need our own music, the music that works for us."

"It would be nice," Mr. Crenshaw says in a voice that has more overtones of anger, "if we could each have the music we like best. But most people—" He says "most people" in the tone that means "real people, normal people." "Most people have to listen to what's available."

"I understand," I say, though I don't actually. Everyone could bring in a player and their own music and wear earphones while they work, as we do. "But for us—" For us, the autistic, the incomplete. "It needs to be the right music."

Now he looks really angry, the muscles bunching in his cheeks, his face redder and shinier. I can see the tightness in his shoulders, his shirt stretched across them.

"Very well," he says. He does not mean that it is very well. He means he has to let us play the right music, but he would change it if he could. I wonder if the words on paper in our contract are strong enough to prevent him from changing it. I think about asking Mr. Aldrin.

It takes me another fifteen minutes to calm down enough to go to my office. I am soaked with sweat. I smell bad. I grab my spare clothes and go take a shower. When I finally sit down to work, it is an hour and forty-seven minutes after the time to start work; I will work late tonight to make up for that.

Mr. Crenshaw comes by again at closing time, when I am still working. He opens my door without knocking. I don't know how long he was there before I noticed him, but I am sure he did not knock. I jump when he says, "Lou!" and turn around.

"What are you doing?" he asks.

"Working," I say. What did he think? What else would I be doing in my office, at my workstation?

"Let me see," he says, and comes over to my workstation. He comes up behind me; I feel my nerves rucking up under my skin like a kicked throw rug. I hate it when someone is behind me. "What is that?" He points to a line of symbols separated from the mass above and below by a blank line. I have been tinkering with that line all day, trying to make it do what I want it to do.

"It will be the . . . the link between this"—I point to the blocks above—"and this." I point to the blocks below.

"And what are they?" he asks.

Does he really not know? Or is this what the books call instructional discourse, as when teachers ask questions whose answers they know to find out if the students know? If he really doesn't know, then whatever I say will make no sense. If he really does know, he will be angry when he finds out I think he does not.

It would be simpler if people said what they meant.

"This is the layer-three system for synthesis," I say. That is a right answer, though it is a short one.

"Oh, I see," he says. His voice smirks. Does he think I am lying? I can see a blurry, distorted reflection of his face in the shiny ball on my desk. It is hard to tell what its expression is.

"The layer-three system will be embedded into the production codes," I say, trying very hard to stay calm. "This ensures that the end user will be able to define the production parameters but cannot change them to something harmful."

"And you understand this?" he says.

Which this is this? I understand what I am doing. I do not always understand why it is to be done. I opt for the easy short answer.

"Yes," I say.

"Good," he says. It sounds as false as it did in the morning. "You started late today," he says.

"I'm staying late tonight," I say. "I was one hour and forty-seven minutes late. I worked through lunch; that is thirty minutes. I will stay one hour and seventeen minutes late."

"You're honest," he says, clearly surprised.

"Yes," I say. I do not turn to look at him. I do not want to see his face. After seven seconds, he turns to leave. From the door he has a last word.

"Things cannot go on like this, Lou. Change happens."

Nine words. Nine words that make me shiver after the door is closed.

I turn on the fan, and my office fills with twinkling, whirling reflections. I work on, one hour and seventeen minutes. Tonight I am not tempted to work any longer than that. It is Wednesday night, and I have things to do.

Outside it is mild, a little humid. I am very careful driving back to my place, where I change into T-shirt and shorts and eat a slice of cold pizza.

AMONG THE THINGS I NEVER TELL DR. FORNUM ABOUT IS MY sex life. She doesn't think I have a sex life because when she asks if I have a sex partner, a girlfriend or boyfriend, I just say no. She doesn't ask more than that. That is fine with me, because I do not want to talk about it with her. She is not attractive to me, and my parents said the only reason to talk about sex was to find out how to please your partner and be pleased by your partner. Or if something went wrong, you would talk to a doctor.

Nothing has ever gone wrong with me. Some things were wrong from the beginning, but that's different. I think about Marjory while I finish my pizza. Marjory is not my sex partner, but I wish she were my girlfriend. I met Marjory at fencing class, not at any of the social events for disabled people that Dr. Fornum thinks I should go to. I don't tell Dr. Fornum about fencing because she would worry about violent tendencies. If laser tag was enough to bother her, long pointed swords would send her into a panic. I don't tell Dr. Fornum about Marjory because she would ask questions I don't want to answer. So that makes two big secrets, swords and Marjory.

When I've eaten, I drive over to my fencing class, at Tom and

Lucia's. Marjory will be there. I want to close my eyes, thinking of Marjory, but I am driving and it is not safe. I think of music instead, of the chorale of Bach's *Cantata no. 39.*

Tom and Lucia have a large house with a big fenced backyard. They have no children, even though they are older than I am. At first I thought this was because Lucia liked working with clients so much that she did not want to stay home with children, but I heard her tell someone else that she and Tom could not have children. They have many friends, and eight or nine usually show up for fencing practice. I don't know if Lucia has told anyone at the hospital that she fences or that she sometimes invites clients to come learn fencing. I think the hospital would not approve. I am not the only person under psychiatric supervision who comes to Tom and Lucia's to learn to fight with swords. I asked her once, and she just laughed and said, "What they don't know won't scare them."

I have been fencing here for five years. I helped Tom put down the new surface on the fencing area, stuff that's usually used for tennis courts. I helped Tom build the rack in the back room where we store our blades. I do not want to have my blades in my car or in my apartment, because I know that it would scare some people. Tom warned me about it. It is important not to scare people. So I leave all my fencing gear at Tom and Lucia's, and everyone knows that the left-hand-but-two slot is mine and so is the left-hand-but-two peg on the other wall and my mask has its own pigeonhole in the mask storage.

First I do my stretches. I am careful to do all the stretches; Lucia says I am an example to the others. Don, for instance, rarely does all his stretches, and he is always putting his back out or pulling a muscle. Then he sits on the side and complains. I am not as good as he is, but I do not get hurt because I neglect the rules. I wish he would follow the rules because I am sad when a friend gets hurt.

When I have stretched my arms, my shoulders, my back, my legs, my feet, I go to the back room and put on my leather jacket with the sleeves cut off at the elbow and my steel gorget. The weight of the gorget around my neck feels good. I take down my mask, with my gloves folded inside, and put the gloves in my pocket for now. My épée and rapier are in the rack; I tuck the mask under one arm and take them out carefully.

Don comes in, rushed and sweating as usual, his face red. "Hi, Lou," he says. I say hi and step back so he can get his blade from the rack. He is normal and could carry his épée in his car if he wanted without scaring people, but he forgets things. He was always having to borrow someone else's, and finally Tom told him to leave his own here.

I go outside. Marjory isn't here yet. Cindy and Lucia are lining up with épées; Max is putting on his steel helmet. I don't think I would like the steel helmet; it would be too loud when someone hit it. Max laughed when I told him that and said I could always wear earplugs, but I hate earplugs. They make me feel as if I have a bad cold. It's strange, because I actually like wearing a blindfold. I used to wear one a lot when I was younger, pretending I was blind. I could understand voices a little better that way. But feeling my ears stuffed up doesn't help me see better.

Don swaggers out, épée tucked under his arm, buttoning his fancy leather doublet. Sometimes I wish I had one like that, but I think I do better with plain things.

"Did you stretch?" Lucia asks him.

He shrugs. "Enough."

She shrugs back. "Your pain," she says. She and Cindy start fencing. I like to watch them and try to figure out what they're doing. It's all so fast I have trouble following it, but so do normal people.

"Hi, Lou," Marjory says, from behind me. I feel warm and light, as if there were less gravity. For a moment I squeeze my eyes shut. She is beautiful, but it is hard to look at her.

"Hi, Marjory," I say, and turn around. She is smiling at me. Her face is shiny. That used to bother me, when people were very happy and their faces got shiny, because angry people also get shiny faces and I could not be sure which it was. My parents tried to show me the difference, with the position of eyebrows and so on, but I finally figured out that the best way to tell was the outside corners of the eyes. Marjory's shiny face is a happy face. She is happy to see me, and I am happy to see her.

I worry about a lot of things, though, when I think about Marjory.

Is autism contagious? Can she catch it from me? She won't like it if she does. I know it's not supposed to be catching, but they say if you hang around with a group of people, you'll start thinking like them. If she hangs around me, will she think like me? I don't want that to happen to her. If she were born like me it would be fine, but someone like her shouldn't become like me. I don't think it will happen, but I would feel guilty if it did. Sometimes this makes me want to stay away from her, but mostly I want to be with her more than I am.

"Hi, Marj," Don says. His face is even shinier now. He thinks she is pretty, too. I know that what I feel is called jealousy; I read it in a book. It is a bad feeling, and it means that I am too controlling. I step back, trying not to be too controlling, and Don steps forward. Marjory is looking at me, not at Don.

"Want to play?" Don says, nudging me with his elbow. He means do I want to fence with him. I did not understand that at first. Now I do. I nod, silently, and we go to find a place where we can line up.

Don does a little flick with his wrist, the way he starts every bout, and I counter it automatically. We circle each other, feinting and parrying, and then I see his arm droop from the shoulder. Is this another feint? It's an opening, at least, and I lunge, catching him on the chest.

"Got me," he says. "My arm's really sore."

"I'm sorry," I say. He works his shoulder, then suddenly leaps forward and strikes at my foot. He's done this before; I move back quickly and he doesn't get me. After I get him three more times, he heaves a great sigh and says he's tired. That's fine with me; I would rather talk to Marjory. Max and Tom move out to the space we were using. Lucia has stopped to rest; Cindy is lined up with Susan.

Marjory is sitting beside Lucia now; Lucia is showing her some pictures. One of Lucia's hobbies is photography. I take off my mask and watch them. Marjory's face is broader than Lucia's. Don gets between me and Marjory and starts talking.

"You're interrupting," Lucia says.

"Oh, sorry," Don says, but he still stands there, blocking my view.

"And you're right in the middle," Lucia says. "Please get out from between people." She flicks a glance at me. I am not doing anything wrong or she would tell me. More than anyone I know who isn't like me, she says very clearly what she wants.

Don glances back, huffs, and shifts sideways. "I didn't see Lou," he says.

"I did," Lucia says. She turns back to Marjory. "Now here, this is where we stayed on the fourth night. I took this from inside—what about that view!"

"Lovely," Marjory says. I can't see the picture she's looking at, but I can see the happiness on her face. I watch her instead of listening to Lucia as she talks about the rest of the pictures. Don interrupts with comments from time to time. When they've looked at the pictures, Lucia folds the case of the portable viewer and puts it under her chair.

"Come on, Don," she says. "Let's see how you do with me." She puts her gloves and mask back on and picks up her épée. Don shrugs and follows her out to an open space.

"Have a seat," Marjory says. I sit down, feeling the slight warmth from Lucia in the chair she just left. "How was your day?" Marjory asks.

"I almost was in a wreck," I tell her. She doesn't ask questions; she just lets me talk. It is hard to say it all; now it seems less acceptable that I just drove away, but I was worried about getting to work and about the police.

"That sounds scary," she says. Her voice is warm, soothing. Not a professional soothing, but just gentle on my ears.

I want to tell her about Mr. Crenshaw, but now Tom comes back and asks me if I want to fight. I like to fight Tom. Tom is almost as tall as I am, and even though he is older, he is very fit. And he's the best fencer in the group.

"I saw you fight Don," he says. "You handle his tricks very well. But he's not improving—in fact, he's let his training slide—so be sure you fight some of the better fencers each week. Me, Lucia, Cindy, Max. At least two of us, okay?"

*At least* means "not less than." "Okay," I say. We each have two long blades, épée and rapier. When I first tried to use a second blade, I was always banging one into the other. Then I tried to hold them parallel.

That way they didn't cross each other, but Tom could sweep them both aside. Now I know to hold them at different heights and angles.

We circle, first one way, then the other. I try to remember everything Tom has taught me: how to place my feet, how to hold the blades, which moves counter which moves. He throws a shot; my arm rises to parry it with my left blade; at the same time I throw a shot and he counters. It is like a dance: step-step-thrust-parry-step. Tom talks about the need to vary the pattern, to be unpredictable, but last time I watched him fight someone else, I thought I saw a pattern in his nonpattern. If I can just hold him off long enough, maybe I can find it again.

Suddenly I hear the music of Prokofiev's *Romeo and Juliet*, the stately dance. It fills my head, and I move into that rhythm, slowing from the faster movements. Tom slows as I slow. Now I can see it, that long pattern he has devised because no one can be utterly random. Moving with it, in my personal music, I'm able to stay with him, blocking every thrust, testing his parries. And then I know what he will do, and without thought my arm swings around and I strike with a *punta riversa* to the side of his head. I feel the blow in my hand, in my arm.

"Good!" he says. The music stops. "Wow!" he says, shaking his head.

"It was too hard I am sorry," I say.

"No, no, that's fine. A good clean shot, right through my guard. I didn't even come close to a parry on it." He is grinning through his mask. "I told you you were getting better. Let's go again."

I do not want to hurt anyone. When I first started, they could not get me to actually touch anyone with the blade, not hard enough to feel. I still don't like it. What I like is learning patterns and then remaking them so that I am in the pattern, too.

Light flashes down Tom's blades as he lifts them both in salute. For a moment I'm struck by the dazzle, by the speed of the light's dance.

Then I move again, in the darkness beyond the light. How fast is dark? Shadow can be no faster than what casts it, but not all darkness is shadow. Is it? This time I hear no music but see a pattern of light and shadow, shifting, twirling, arcs and helices of light against a background of dark.

I am dancing at the tip of the light, but beyond it, and suddenly feel

THE SPEED OF DARK

that jarring pressure on my hand. This time I also feel the hard thump of Tom's blade on my chest. I say, "Good," just as he does, and we both step back, acknowledging the double kill.

"Owwww!" I look away from Tom and see Don leaning over with a hand to his back. He hobbles toward the chairs, but Lucia gets there first and sits beside Marjory again. I have a strange feeling: that I noticed and that I cared. Don has stopped, still bent over. There are no spare chairs now, as other fencers have arrived. Don lowers himself to the flagstones finally, grunting and groaning all the way.

"I'm going to have to quit this," he says. "I'm getting too old."

"You're not old," Lucia says. "You're lazy." I do not understand why Lucia is being so mean to Don. He is a friend; it is not nice to call friends names except in teasing. Don doesn't like to do the stretches and he complains a lot, but that does not make him not a friend.

"Come on, Lou," Tom says. "You killed me; we killed each other; I want a chance to get you back." The words could be angry, but the voice is friendly and he is smiling. I lift my blades again.

This time Tom does what he never does and charges. I have no time to remember what he says is the right thing to do if someone charges; I step back and pivot, pushing his off-hand blade aside with mine and trying for a thrust to his head with the rapier. But he is moving too fast; I miss, and his rapier arm swings over his own head and gives me a whack on the top of the head.

"Gotcha!" he says.

"You did that how?" I ask, and then quickly reorder the words. "How did you do that?"

"It's my secret tournament shot," Tom said, pushing his mask back. "Someone did it to me twelve years ago, and I came home and practiced until I could do it to a stump . . . and normally I use it only in competition. But you're ready to learn it. There's only one trick." He was grinning, his face streaked with sweat.

"Hey!" Don yelled across the yard. "I didn't see that. Do it again, huh?"

"What is the trick?" I ask.

"You have to figure out how to do it for yourself. You're welcome to my stump, but you've just had all the demonstration you're going to get. I will mention that if you don't get it exactly right, you're dead meat to an opponent who doesn't panic. You saw how easy it was to parry the off-hand weapon."

"Tom, you haven't showed me that one—do it again," Don said.

"You're not ready," Tom said. "You have to earn it." He sounds angry now, just as Lucia did. What has Don done to make them angry? He hasn't stretched and gets tired really fast, but is that a good reason? I can't ask now, but I will ask later.

I take my mask off and walk over to stand near Marjory. From above I can see the lights reflecting from her shiny dark hair. If I move back and forth, the lights run up and down her hair, as the light ran up and down Tom's blades. I wonder what her hair would feel like.

"Have my seat," Lucia says, standing up. "I'm going to fight again."

I sit down, very conscious of Marjory beside me. "Are you going to fence tonight?" I ask.

"Not tonight. I have to leave early. My friend Karen's coming in at the airport, and I promised to pick her up. I just stopped by to see . . . people."

I want to tell her I'm glad she did, but the words stick in my mouth. I feel stiff and awkward. "Karen is coming from where?" I finally say.

"Chicago. She was visiting her parents." Marjory stretches her legs out in front of her. "She was going to leave her car at the airport, but she had a flat the morning she left. That's why I have to pick her up." She turns to look at me; I glance down, unable to bear the heat of her gaze. "Are you going to stay long tonight?"

"Not that long," I say. If Marjory is leaving and Don is staying, I will go home.

"Want to ride out to the airport with me? I could bring you back by here to pick up your car. Of course, it'll make you late getting home; her plane won't be in until ten-fifteen."

Ride with Marjory? I am so surprised/happy that I can't move for a long moment. "Yes," I say. "Yes." I can feel my face getting hot.

ON THE WAY TO THE AIRPORT, I LOOK OUT THE WINDOW. I FEEL light, as if I could float up into the air. "Being happy makes it feel like less than normal gravity," I say.

I feel Marjory's glance. "Light as a feather," she says. "Is that what you mean?"

"Maybe not a feather. I feel more like a balloon," I say.

"I know that feeling," Marjory says. She doesn't say she feels like that now. I don't know how she feels. Normal people would know how she feels, but I can't tell. The more I know her, the more things I don't know about her. I don't know why Tom and Lucia were being mean to Don, either.

"Tom and Lucia both sounded angry with Don," I say. She gives me a quick sideways glance. I think I am supposed to understand it, but I don't know what it means. It makes me want to look away; I feel funny inside.

"Don can be a real heel," she says.

Don is not a heel; he is a person. Normal people say things like this, changing the meaning of words without warning, and they understand it. I know, because someone told me years ago, that *heel* is a slang word for "bad person." But he couldn't tell me why, and I still wonder about it. If someone is a bad person and you want to say that he is a bad person, why not just say it? Why say "heel" or "jerk" or something? And adding "real" to it only makes it worse. If you say something is real, it should be real.

But I want to know why Tom and Lucia are angry with Don more than I want to explain to Marjory about why it's wrong to say Don is a real heel. "Is it because he doesn't do enough stretches?"

"No." Marjory sounds a little angry now, and I feel my stomach tightening. What have I done? "He's just . . . just mean, sometimes, Lou. He makes jokes about people that aren't funny."

I wonder if it is the jokes or the people that aren't funny. I know about jokes that most people don't think are funny, because I have made some. I still don't understand why some jokes are funny and why mine aren't, but I know it is true.

"He made jokes about you," Marjory says, a block later, in a low voice. "And we didn't like it."

I don't know what to say. Don makes jokes about everybody, even Marjory. I didn't like those jokes, but I didn't do anything about it. Should I have? Marjory glances at me again. This time I think she wants me to say something. I can't think of anything. Finally I do.

"My parents said acting mad at people didn't make them act better."

Marjory makes a funny noise. I don't know what it means. "Lou, sometimes I think you're a philosopher."

"No," I say. "I'm not smart enough to be a philosopher."

Marjory makes the noise again. I look out the window; we are almost to the airport. The airport at night has different-colored lights laid out along the runways and taxiways. Amber, blue, green, red. I wish they had purple ones. Marjory parks in the short-term section of the parking garage, and we walk across the bus lanes into the terminal.

When I'm traveling alone, I like to watch the automatic doors open and close. Tonight, I walk on beside Marjory, pretending I don't care about the doors. She stops to look at the video display of departures and arrivals. I have already spotted the flight it must be: the right airline, from Chicago, landing at 10:15 P.M., on time, Gate Seventeen. It takes her longer; it always takes normal people longer.

At the security gate for "Arrivals," I feel my stomach tightening again. I know how to do this; my parents taught me, and I have done it before. Take everything metallic out of your pockets and put it in the little basket. Wait your turn. Walk through the arch. If nobody asks me any questions, it's easy. But if they ask, I don't always hear them exactly: it's too noisy, with too many echoes off the hard surfaces. I can feel myself tensing up.

Marjory goes first: her purse onto the conveyor belt, her keys in the little basket. I see her walk through; no one asks her anything. I put my keys, my wallet, my change into the little basket and walk through. No buzz, no bleep. The man in uniform stares at me as I pick up my keys, my wallet, my change and put them back in my pockets. I turn away, toward Marjory waiting a few yards away. Then he speaks.

"May I see your ticket, please? And some ID?"

I feel cold all over. He hasn't asked anyone else—not the man with the long braided hair who pushed past me to get his briefcase off the conveyor belt, not Marjory—and I haven't done anything wrong. You don't have to have a ticket to go through security for arrivals; you just have to know the flight number you're meeting. People who are meeting people don't have tickets because they aren't traveling. Security for departures requires a ticket.

"I don't have a ticket," I say. Beyond him, I can see Marjory shift her weight, but she doesn't come closer. I don't think she can hear what he is saying, and I don't want to yell in a public place.

"ID?" he says. His face is focused on me and starting to get shiny. I pull out my wallet and open it to my ID. He looks at it, then back at me. "If you don't have a ticket, what are you doing here?" he asks.

I can feel my heart racing, sweat springing out on my neck. "I'm . . . I'm . . . I'm . . ."

"Spit it out," he says, frowning. "Or do you stutter like that all the time?"

I nod. I know I can't say anything now, not for a few minutes. I reach into my shirt pocket and take out the little card I keep there. I offer it to him; he glances at it.

"Autistic, huh? But you were talking; you answered me a second ago. Who are you meeting?"

Marjory moves, coming up behind him. "Anything wrong, Lou?"

"Stand back, lady," the man says. He doesn't look at her.

"He's my friend," Marjory says. "We're meeting a friend of mine on Flight Three-eighty-two, Gate Seventeen. I didn't hear the buzzer go off. . . ." There is an edge of anger to her tone.

Now the man turns his head just enough to see her. He relaxes a little. "He's with you?"

"Yes. Was there a problem?"

"No, ma'am. He just looked a little odd. I guess this"—he still has my card in his hand—"explains it. As long as you're with him . . ."

"I'm not his keeper," Marjory says, in the same tone that she used when she said Don was a real heel. "Lou is my friend."

The man's eyebrows go up, then down. He hands me back my card and turns away. I walk away, beside Marjory, who is headed off in a fast walk that must be stretching her legs. We say nothing until after we arrive at the secured waiting area for Gates Fifteen through Thirty. On the other side of the glass wall, people with tickets, on the departures side, sit in rows; the seatframes are shiny metal and the seats are dark blue. We don't have seats in arrivals because we are not supposed to come more than ten minutes before the flight's scheduled arrival.

This is not the way it used to be. I don't remember that, of course—I was born at the turn of the century—but my parents told me about being able to just walk right up to the gates to meet people arriving. Then after the 2001 disasters, only departing passengers could go to the gates. That was so awkward for people who needed help, and so many people asked for special passes, that the government designed these arrival lounges instead, with separate security lines. By the time my parents took me on an airplane for the first time, when I was nine, all large airports had separated arriving and departing passengers.

I look out the big windows. Lights everywhere. Red and green lights on the tips of the airplanes' wings. Rows of dim square lights along the planes, showing where the windows are. Headlights on the little vehicles that pull baggage carts. Steady lights and blinking lights.

"Can you talk now?" Marjory asks while I'm still looking out at the lights.

"Yes." I can feel her warmth; she is standing very close beside me. I close my eyes a moment. "I just . . . I can get confused." I point to an airplane coming toward a gate. "Is that the one?"

"I think so." She moves around me and turns to face me. "Are you all right?"

"Yes. It just . . . happens that way sometimes." I am embarrassed that it happened tonight, the first time I have ever been alone with Marjory. I remember in high school wanting to talk to girls who didn't want to talk to me. Will she go away, too? I could get a taxi back to Tom and Lucia's, but I don't have a lot of money with me.

"I'm glad you're okay," Marjory says, and then the door opens and people start coming off the plane. She is watching for Karen, and I am watching her. Karen turns out to be an older woman, gray-haired. Soon we are all back outside and then on the way to Karen's apartment. I sit quietly in the backseat, listening to Marjory and Karen talk. Their voices flow and ripple like swift water over rocks. I can't quite follow what they're talking about. They go too fast for me, and I don't know the people or places they speak of. It's all right, though, because I can watch Marjory without having to talk at the same time.

When we get back to Tom and Lucia's, where my car is, Don has gone and the last of the fencing group are packing things in their car. I remember that I did not put my blades and mask away and go outside to collect them, but Tom has picked them up, he says. He wasn't sure what time we would get back; he didn't want to leave them out in the dark.

I say good-bye to Tom and Lucia and Marjory and drive home in the swift dark.

CHAPTER THREE

M Y MESSAGER IS BLINKING WHEN I GET HOME. IT'S Lars's code; he wants me to come on-line. It's late. I don't want to oversleep and be late tomorrow. But Lars knows I fence on Wednesdays, and he doesn't usually try to contact me then. It must be important.

I sign on and find his message. He has clipped a journal article for me, research on reversal of autistic-like symptoms in adult primates. I skim it, my heart thudding. Reversing genetic autism in the infant or brain damage that resulted in autisticlike syndromes in the small child has now become common, but I had been told it was too late for me. If this is real, it is not too late. In the last sentence, the article's author makes that connection, speculating that the research might be applicable to humans and suggesting further research.

As I read, other icons pop up on my screen. The logo of our local autistic society. Cameron's logo and Dale's. So they've heard about it, too. I ignore them for the time being and go on reading. Even though it is about brains like mine, this is not my field and I cannot quite understand how the treatment is supposed to work. The authors keep referring to other articles in which the procedures were spelled out. Those articles aren't accessible—not to me, not tonight. I don't know what "Ho and Delgracia's method" is. I don't know what all the words mean, either, and my dictionary doesn't have them.

When I look at the clock, it is long after midnight. Bed. I must sleep. I turn everything off, set the alarm, and go to bed. In my mind, photons chase darkness but never catch up.

AT WORK THE NEXT MORNING, WE ALL STAND IN THE HALL, NOT quite meeting one anothers' eyes. Everybody knows.

"I think it's a fake," Linda says. "It can't possibly work."

"But if it does," Cameron says. "If it does, we can be normal."

"I don't want to be normal," Linda says. "I am who I am. I'm happy." She does not look happy. She looks fierce and determined.

"Me, too," Dale says. "What if it works for monkeys—what does that mean? They're not people; they're simpler than we are. Monkeys don't talk." His eyelid twitches more than usual.

"We already communicate better than monkeys," Linda says.

When we are together like this, just us, we can talk better than any other time. We laugh about that, about how normal people must be putting out a field that inhibits our abilities. We know that's not true, and we know the others would think we were paranoid if we told that joke around them. They would think we were crazy in a bad way; they would not understand that it is a joke. When we do not recognize a joke, they say it is because we are literal-minded, but we know that we cannot say that about them.

"I would like to not have to see a psychiatrist every quarter," Cameron says.

I think of not having to see Dr. Fornum. I would be much happier if I did not have to see Dr. Fornum. Would she be happy not to have to see me?

"Lou, what about you?" Linda asks. "You're already living partly in their world."

We all are, by working here, by living independently. But Linda doesn't like doing anything with people who are not autistic, and she has said before she thinks I shouldn't hang around with Tom and Lucia's fencing group or the people at my church. If she knew how I really felt about Marjory she would say mean things.

"I get along. . . . I don't see why change." I hear my voice, harsher than usual and wish it didn't do that when I get upset. I'm not angry; I don't want to sound angry.

"See?" Linda looks at Cameron, who looks away.

"I need to work," I say, and head for my office, where I turn on the little fan and watch the twinkles of light. I need to bounce, but I don't want to go in the gym, in case Mr. Crenshaw comes in. I feel like something is squeezing me. It is hard to get into the problem I'm working on.

I wonder what it would be like to be normal. I made myself quit thinking about that when I left school. When it comes up, I push the thought away. But now . . . what would it be like to not be worried that people think I'm crazy when I stutter or when I can't answer at all and have to write on my little pad? What would it be like to not carry that card in my pocket? To be able to see and hear everywhere? To know what people are thinking just by looking at their faces?

The block of symbols I'm working on suddenly looks densely meaningless, as meaningless as voices used to sound.

Is that it? Is this why normal people don't do the kind of work we do? Do I have to choose between this work I know how to do, this work I'm good at, and being normal? I look around the office. The spin spirals suddenly annoy me. All they do is turn around, the same pattern, over and over and over. I reach to turn the fan off. If this is normal, I don't like it.

The symbols come alive again, rich with meaning, and I dive into them, submerging my mind in them so I don't have to see the sky overhead.

When I emerge again, it is past lunchtime. I have a headache from sitting too long in one place and not eating lunch. I get up, walk around my office, trying not to think about what Lars told me. I can't help it. I am not hungry, but I know I should eat. I go to the kitchenette in our building and get my plastic box from the refrigerator. None of us like the smell of the plastic, but it does keep our food separate, so that I don't have to smell Linda's tuna fish sandwich and she doesn't have to smell my jerky and fruit.

I eat an apple and a few grapes, then nibble on the jerky. My stomach feels unsettled; I think about going into the gym, but when I check,

Linda and Chuy are in there. Linda is bouncing high, her face set in a scowl; Chuy is sitting on the floor, watching colored streamers blow from the fan. Linda catches sight of me and turns around on the trampoline. She does not want to talk. I do not want to talk, either.

The afternoon seems to last forever. I leave right on time, striding out to my car in its spot. The music is all wrong, loud and pounding in my head. When I open the door of my car, superheated air puffs out. I stand by the car, wishing for autumn and cooler weather. I see the others come out, all showing tension in one way or another, and avoid their gaze. No one speaks. We get in our cars; I leave first because I came out first.

It is hard to drive safely in the hot afternoon, with the wrong music in my head. Light flashes off windshields, bumpers, trim; there are too many flashing lights. By the time I get home, my head hurts and I'm shaking. I take the pillows off my couch into the bedroom, closing all the shades tightly and then the door. I lie down, piling the pillows on top of me, then turn off the light.

This is something else I never tell Dr. Fornum about. She would make notes in my record about this; I know it. As I lie there in the dark, the gentle, soft pressure gradually eases my tension, and the wrong music in my mind empties out. I float in a soft, dark silence . . . at rest, at peace, uninvaded by the fast-moving photons.

Eventually I am ready to think and feel again. I am sad. I am not supposed to be sad. I tell myself what Dr. Fornum would tell me. I am healthy. I have a job that pays pretty well. I have a place to live and clothes to wear. I have a rare high-status permit for a private automobile so that I do not have to ride with anyone else or take the noisy, crowded public transit. I am lucky.

I am sad anyway. I try so hard, and it is still not working. I wear the same clothes as the others. I say the same words at the same times: good morning, hi, how are you, I'm fine, good night, please, thank you, you're welcome, no thank you, not right now. I obey the traffic laws; I obey the rules. I have ordinary furniture in my apartment, and I play my unusual music very softly or use headphones. But it is not enough. Even as hard as I try, the real people still want me to change, to be like them.

They do not know how hard it is. They do not care. They want me to change. They want to put things in my head, to change my brain. They would say they don't, but they do.

I thought I was safe, living independently, living like anyone else. But I wasn't.

Under the pillows, I'm starting to shake again. I don't want to cry; crying might be too loud and my neighbors might notice. I am hearing the labels crowding in on me, the labels they put in my record when I was a child. Primary diagnosis Autistic Spectrum Disorder/autism. Sensory integration deficit. Auditory processing deficit. Visual processing deficit. Tactile defensiveness.

I hate the labels; they make me feel sticky, where they are stuck to me with professional glue I can't pry off.

All babies are born autistic, one of our group said once. We laughed nervously. We agreed, but it was dangerous to say so.

It takes a neurologically normal infant years to learn to integrate the incoming sensory data into a coherent concept of the world. While it took me much longer—and I readily admit that my sensory processing is not normal even now—I went at the task much the same way as any other infant. First flooded by ungated, unedited sensory input, protecting myself from sensory overload with sleep and inattention.

You might think, reading the literature, that only neurologically damaged children do this, but in fact all infants control their exposure—by closing their eyes, averting their gaze, or simply falling asleep when the world is too much. Over time, as they make sense of this data chunk and then that, they learn what patterns of retinal excitation signal what events in the visible world, what patterns of auditory excitation signal a human voice—and then a human voice speaking their native tongue.

For me—for any autistic individual—this took much longer. My parents explained it to me, when I was old enough to understand: for some reason, my infant nerves needed a stimulus to persist longer before it would bridge the gap. They—and I—were lucky that techniques were available to provide my neurons this needed duration of signal. Instead of being labeled with an "attention deficit" (which used to be quite common), I was simply given stimuli to which I *could* attend.

I can remember the time before I was exposed to the computer-assisted primary language-learning program . . . when the sounds that came from people's mouths seemed as random—no, more random—than a cow mooing and moaning in the field. I couldn't hear many consonants—they didn't last long enough. Therapy helped—a computer stretched the sounds out until I could hear them, and gradually my brain learned to capture briefer signals. But not all of them. To this day, a fast-talking speaker can lose me, no matter how I concentrate.

It used to be much worse. Before the computer-assisted language-learning programs, children like me might never learn language at all. Back in the mid–twentieth century, therapists thought autism was a mental illness, like schizophrenia. My mother had read a book by a woman who had been told she had made her child crazy. The idea that autistic people are, or become, mentally ill persisted right through the end of the twentieth century, and I even saw an article about that in a magazine a few years ago. That is why I have to visit Dr. Fornum, so that she can be sure I am not developing a mental illness.

I wonder if Mr. Crenshaw thinks I am crazy. Is that why his face gets shiny when he talks to me? Is he frightened? I don't think Mr. Aldrin is frightened of me—of any of us. He talks to us as if we were real. But Mr. Crenshaw talks to me as if I were a stubborn animal, one he had a right to train. I am often scared, but now, after the rest under the pillows, I am not.

WHAT I WISH IS THAT I COULD GO OUT AND LOOK UP AT THE stars. My parents took me camping in the Southwest; I remember lying there and seeing all the beautiful patterns, patterns that went on and on forever. I would like to see the stars again. They made me feel calm when I was a child; they showed me an ordered universe, a patterned universe, in which I could be a small part of a large pattern. When my parents told me how long the light had traveled to reach my eyes—hundreds, thousands, of years—I felt comforted though I could not say why.

I cannot see the stars from here. The safety lights in the parking lot next to our building are sodium vapor lights emitting a pinkish yellow light. They make the air seem fuzzy, and the stars can't show through the blurry black lid of sky. Only the moon and a few bright stars and planets show at all.

Sometimes I used to go out in the country and try to find a spot to look at the stars. It is hard. If I park on a country road and turn off the lights of the car, someone could run into me because he can't see me. I have tried parking beside the road or in some unused lane that leads to a barn, but someone who lives nearby may notice and call the police. Then the police will come and want to know why I'm parked there late at night. They do not understand wanting to see the stars. They say that is just an excuse. I don't do this anymore. Instead, I try to save up enough money that I can take my vacations where there are stars.

It's funny about the police. Some of us have more trouble than others. Jorge, who grew up in San Antonio, told me if you are anything but rich, white, and normal they think you are a criminal. He had been stopped many times when he was growing up; he didn't learn to talk until he was twelve and even then couldn't talk very well. They always thought he was drunk or on drugs, he said. Even when he wore a bracelet that explained who he was and that he couldn't talk, they'd wait until they'd taken him to the station to look at it. Then they'd try to find a parent to take him home, rather than taking him back across town themselves. Both his parents worked, so he usually had to sit there for three or four hours.

That didn't happen to me, but sometimes I've been stopped for no reason I can understand, like with the security man at the airport. I get very scared when someone speaks harshly to me and sometimes I have trouble answering. I practiced saying, "My name is Lou Arrendale; I am autistic; I have trouble answering questions," in front of a mirror until I could say it no matter how scared I am. My voice sounds harsh and strained when I do it. They ask, "Do you have identification?" I know I'm supposed to say, "In my pocket." If I try to get my own wallet out, they may be scared enough to kill me. Miss Sevier in high school told us the police think we have knives or guns in our pockets and that they have killed people who were just trying to get out their IDs.

I think that is wrong, but I read where the court decided it was all right if the police were really scared. Yet if anybody else is really scared of the police it's not all right for the scared person to kill a policeman.

This does not make sense. There is no symmetry.

The policeman who visited our class in high school said the police were there to help us and that only people who had done wrong would be scared of them. Jen Brouchard said what I was thinking, that it was hard not to be scared of people who yelled at you and threatened you and could make you lie facedown on the ground. That even if you hadn't done anything, having a big man waving a gun at you would scare anyone. The policeman got red in the face and said that attitude didn't help. Neither did his, I thought, but I knew better than to say so.

Yet the policeman who lives in our building has always been pleasant to me. His name is Daniel Bryce, but he says to call him Danny. He says good morning and good evening when he sees me, and I say good morning and good evening. He complimented me on how clean I keep my car. We both helped Miss Watson move when she had to go to Assisted Living; we each had one end of her coffee table carrying it downstairs. He offered to be the one to go backward. He doesn't yell at anyone that I know of. I do not know what he thinks about me, except that he likes it that my car is clean. I do not know if he knows that I am autistic. I try not to be scared of him, because I have not done anything wrong, but I am, a little.

I would like to ask him if he thinks people are scared of him, but I do not want to make him angry. I do not want him to think I am doing something wrong, because I am still scared a little.

I tried watching some police shows on TV, but that scared me again. The police seemed tired and angry all the time, and the shows make it seem that this is all right. I am not supposed to act angry even when I am angry, but they can.

Yet I do not like to be judged by what others like me do, and I do not want to be unfair to Danny Bryce. He smiles at me, and I smile back. He says good morning and I say good morning back. I try to pretend that the gun he carries is a toy, so that I do not sweat too much when I am around him and make him think I am guilty of something I did not do.

Under the blankets and pillows, I am sweaty now as well as calm. I crawl out, replace the pillows, and take a shower. It is important not to smell bad. People who smell bad make other people angry or scared. I do not like the smell of the soap I use—it is an artificial scent, too strong—but I know it is an acceptable smell to other people.

It is late, after nine, when I get out of the shower and dress again. Usually I watch *Cobalt 457* on Thursdays, but it is too late for that now. I am hungry; I put water on to boil and then drop some noodles into it.

The phone rings. I jump; no matter which of the choice of ringers I use, the phone always surprises me, and I always jump when I am surprised.

It is Mr. Aldrin. My throat tightens; I cannot speak for a long moment, but he does not go on talking. He waits. He understands.

I do not understand. He belongs at the office; he is part of the office cast. He has never called me at home before. Now he wants to meet with me. I feel trapped. He is my boss. He can tell me what to do, but only at work. It feels wrong to hear his voice on the phone at home.

"I—I did not expect you to call," I say.

"I know," he says. "I called you at home because I needed to talk to you away from the office."

My stomach feels tight. "For what reason?" I ask.

"Lou, you need to know before Mr. Crenshaw calls you all in. There's an experimental treatment that may reverse adult autism."

"I know," I say. "I heard about it. They have tried it on apes."

"Yes. But what's in the journal is over a year old; there's been . . . progress. Our company bought out the research. Crenshaw wants all of you to try the new treatment. I don't agree with him. I think it is too early, and I think he is wrong to ask you. At least it should be your choice; no one should pressure you. But he is my boss, and I can't keep him from talking to you about it."

If he cannot help, why is he calling? Is this one of those maneuvers I have read about normal people doing when they want sympathy for doing wrong because they could not help it?

"I want to help you," he says. I remember my parents saying that wanting to do something was not the same thing as doing . . . that trying was not the same thing as doing. Why doesn't he say, "I will help you," instead?

"I think you need an advocate," he says. "Someone to help you negotiate with Crenshaw. Someone better than me. I can find that person for you."

I think he does not want to be our advocate. I think he is afraid Crenshaw will fire him. This is reasonable. Crenshaw could fire any of us. I struggle with my stubborn tongue to get the words out. "Shouldn't . . . wouldn't it . . . I think . . . I think I—we—should find our own person."

"Can you?" he asks. I hear the doubt in his voice. Once I would have heard only something other than happiness and I would have been afraid he was angry with me. I am glad not to be like that anymore. I wonder why he has that doubt, since he knows the kind of work we can do and knows I live independently.

"I can go to the Center," I say.

"Maybe that would be better," he says. A noise starts at his end of the telephone; his voice speaks, but I think it is not for me. "Turn that down; I'm on the phone." I hear another voice, an unhappy voice, but I can't hear the words clearly. Then Mr. Aldrin's voice, louder, in my ear: "Lou, if you have any trouble finding someone . . . if you want me to help, please let me know. I want the best for you; you know that."

I do not know that. I know that Mr. Aldrin has been our manager and he has always been pleasant and patient with us and he has provided things for us that make our work easier, but I do not know that he wants the best for us. How would he know what that is? Would he want me to marry Marjory? What does he know of any of us outside work?

"Thank you," I say, a safe conventional thing to say at almost any occasion. Dr. Fornum would be proud.

"Right, then," he says. I try not to let my mind tangle on those words that have no meaning in themselves at this time. It is a conventional thing to say; he is coming to the end of the conversation. "Call me if you need any help. Let me give you my home number . . ." He rattles off a number; my phone system captures it, though I will not forget. Numbers are easy and this one is especially so, being a series of primes, though he probably has never noticed it. "Good-bye, Lou," he says at the end. "Try not to worry."

Trying is not doing. I say good-bye, hang up the phone, and return to my noodles, now slightly soggy. I do not mind soggy noodles; they are soft and soothing. Most people do not like peanut butter on noodles, but I do.

I think about Mr. Crenshaw wanting us to take the treatment. I do not think he can make us do that. There are laws about us and medical research. I do not know exactly what the laws say, but I do not think they would let him make us do it. Mr. Aldrin should know more about this than I do; he is a manager. So he must think Mr. Crenshaw can do it or will try to do it.

It is hard to go to sleep.

ON FRIDAY MORNING, CAMERON TELLS ME THAT MR. ALDRIN called him, too. He called everyone. Mr. Crenshaw has not said anything to any of us yet. I have that uncomfortable sick feeling in my stomach, like before a test that I do not expect to pass. It is a relief to get on the computer and go to work.

Nothing happens all day except that I finish the first half of the current project and the test runs all come out clean. After lunch, Cameron tells me that the local autism society has posted a meeting at the Center about the research paper. He is going. He thinks we should all go. I had not planned anything this Saturday other than cleaning my car, and I go to the Center almost every Saturday morning anyway.

On Saturday morning, I walk over to the Center. It is a long walk, but it is not hot this early in the morning and it makes my legs feel good. Besides, there is a brick sidewalk on the way, with two colors of brick—tan and red—laid in interesting patterns. I like to see it.

At the Center, I see not only people from my work group but also those who are dispersed elsewhere in the city. Some, mostly the older ones, are in adult day care or sheltered workshops with a lot of supervision and live in group homes. Stefan is a professor at the smaller university here; he does research in some area of biology. Mai is a professor at the larger university; her field is in some overlap of mathematics and biophysics. Neither of them comes to meetings often. I have noticed that the people who are most impaired come most often; the young people who are like Joe Lee almost never show up.

I chat with some of the others I know and like, some from work and some from elsewhere, like Murray, who works for a big accounting firm. Murray wants to hear about my fencing; he studies aikido and also hasn't told his psychiatrist about it. I know that Murray has heard about the new treatment, or for what reason would he be here today, but I think he does not want to talk about it. He doesn't work with us; he may not know it is near human trials. Maybe he wants it and wishes it were. I do not want to ask him that, not today.

The Center isn't just for autistic people; we see a lot of people with various other disabilities, too, especially on weekends. I do not know what all of the disabilities are. I do not want to think about all the things that can be wrong with someone.

Some are friendly and speak to us, and some do not. Emmy comes right up to me today. She is nearly always there. She is shorter than I am, with straight dark hair and thick glasses. I do not know why she has not had eye surgery. It is not polite to ask. Emmy always seems angry. Her eyebrows bunch together, and she has tight little wads of muscle at the corners of her mouth, and her mouth turns down. "You have a girlfriend," she says.

"No," I say.

"Yes. Linda told me. She's not one of us."

"No," I say again. Marjory isn't my girlfriend—yet—and I do not want to talk about her to Emmy. Linda should not have told Emmy anything, and certainly not that. I did not tell Linda Marjory was my girlfriend because she is not. It was not right.

"Where you go to play with swords," Emmy says. "There's a girl—"

"She is not a girl," I say. "She is a woman, and she is not my girlfriend." Yet, I think. I feel heat on my neck, thinking of Marjory and the look on her face last week.

"Linda says she is. She's a spy, Lou."

Emmy rarely uses people's names; when she says my name it feels like a slap on the arm. "What do you mean, 'spy'?"

"She works at the university. Where they do that project, you know." She glares at me, as if I were doing the project. She means the research group on developmental disabilities. When I was a child, my parents took me there for evaluation and for three years I went to the special class. Then my parents decided that the group was more interested in doing research papers to get grant money than in helping children, so they put me in another program, at the regional clinic. It is the policy of our local society to require researchers to disclose their identity; we do not allow them to attend our meetings.

Emmy works at the university herself, as a custodian, and I suppose this is how she knows Marjory works there.

"Lots of people work at the university," I say. "Not all are in the research group."

"She is a spy, Lou," Emmy says again. "She is only interested in your diagnosis, not in you as a person."

I feel a hollow opening inside me; I am sure that Marjory is not a researcher, but not that sure.

"To her you are a freak," Emmy says. "A subject." She made *subject* sound obscene, if I understand *obscene*. Nasty. A mouse in a maze, a monkey in a cage. I think about the new treatment; the people who take it first will be subjects, just like the apes they tried it on first.

"That's not true," I say. I can feel the prickling of sweat under my arms, on my neck, and the faint tremor that comes when I feel threatened. "But anyway, she is not my girlfriend."

"I'm glad you have that much sense," Emmy says.

I go on to the meeting because if I left the Center Emmy would talk to the others about Marjory and me. It is hard to listen to the speaker, who is talking about the research protocol and its implications. I hear and do not hear what he says; I notice when he says something I have not heard before, but I do not pay much attention. I can read the posted speech on the Center Web site later. I was not thinking about Marjory until Emmy said that about her, but now I cannot stop thinking about Marjory.

Marjory likes me. I am sure she likes me. I am sure she likes me as myself, as Lou who fences with the group, as Lou she asked to come to the airport with her that Wednesday night. Lucia said Marjory liked me. Lucia does not lie.

But there is liking and liking. I like ham, as a food. I do not care what the ham thinks when I bite into it. I know that ham doesn't think, so it does not bother me to bite into it. Some people will not eat meat because the animals it came from were once alive and maybe had feelings and thoughts, but this does not bother me once they are dead. Everything eaten was alive once, saving a few grams of minerals, and a tree might have thoughts and feelings if we knew how to access them.

What if Marjory likes me as Emmy says—as a thing, a subject, the equivalent of my bite of ham? What if she likes me more than some other research subject because I am quiet and friendly?

I do not feel quiet and friendly. I feel like hitting someone.

The counselor at the meeting does not say anything we have not already read on-line. He cannot explain the method; he does not know where someone would go to apply to be in the study. He does not say that the company I work for has bought up the research. Maybe he does not know. I do not say anything. I am not sure Mr. Aldrin is right about that.

After the meeting the others want to stay and talk about the new process, but I leave quickly. I want to go home and think about Marjory without Emmy around. I do not want to think about Marjory being a researcher; I want to think about her sitting beside me in the car. I want to think about her smell, and the lights in her hair, and even the way she fights with a rapier.

It is easier to think about Marjory while I am cleaning out my car. I untie the sheepskin seat pad and shake it out. No matter how careful I am, there are always things caught in it, dust and threads and—today— a paper clip. I do not know where that came from. I lay it on the front of the car and sweep the seats with a little brush, then vacuum the floor. The noise of the vacuum hurts my ears, but it is quicker than sweeping and less dust gets up my nose. I clean the inside of the windshield, being careful to go all the way into the corners, then clean the mirrors. Stores sell special cleaners for cars, but they all smell very bad and make me feel sick, so I just use a damp rag.

I put the sheepskin back on the seat and tie it snugly in place. Now my car is all clean for Sunday morning. Even though I take the bus to church, I like to think of my car sitting clean in its Sunday clothes on Sunday.

*I TAKE MY SHOWER QUICKLY, NOT THINKING ABOUT MARJORY,* and then I go to bed and think of her. She is moving, in my thoughts, always moving and yet always still. Her face expresses itself more clearly to me than most faces. The expressions stay long enough that I can interpret them. When I fall asleep, she is smiling.

CHAPTER FOUR

*F*ROM THE STREET TOM WATCHED MARJORY SHAW AND Don Poiteau walk across the yard. Lucia thought Marjory was becoming attached to Lou Arrendale, but here she was walking with Don. Granted, Don had grabbed her gear bag from her, but—if she didn't like him, wouldn't she take it back?

He sighed, running a hand through his thinning hair. He loved the sport of fencing, loved having people over, but the constant burden of the interpersonal intrigues of the group exhausted him more as he got older. He wanted his and Lucia's home to be a place where people grew into their potential, physical and social, but sometimes it seemed he was stuck with a yardful of permanent adolescents. Sooner or later, they all came to him with their complaints, their grudges, their hurt feelings.

Or they dumped on Lucia. Mostly the women did that. They sat down beside her, pretending an interest in her needlework or her pictures, and poured out their troubles. He and Lucia spent hours talking about what was going on, who needed which kind of support, how best to help without taking on too much responsibility.

As Don and Marjory came closer, Tom could see that she was annoyed. Don, as usual, was oblivious, talking fast, swinging her bag in his enthusiasm for what he was saying. Case in point, Tom thought. Before the night was out, he was sure he'd hear what Don had done to annoy Marjory and from Don he'd hear that Marjory wasn't understanding enough.

"He has to have his stuff in exactly the same place every time, can't put it anywhere else," Don was saying as he and Marjory came within earshot.

"It's tidy," Marjory said. She sounded prissy, which meant she was more than just annoyed. "Do you object to tidy?"

"I object to obsessive," Don said. "You, my lady, exhibit a healthy flexibility in sometimes parking on this side of the street and sometimes on that and wearing different clothes. Lou wears the same clothes every week—clean, I'll give him that, but the same—and this thing he has about where to store his gear . . ."

"You put it in the wrong place and Tom made you move it, didn't he?" Marjory said.

"Because Lou would be upset," Don said, sounding sulky. "It's not fair—"

Tom could tell Marjory wanted to yell at Don. So did he. But yelling at Don never seemed to do any good. Don'd had an earnest, hard-working girlfriend who put eight years of her life into parenting him, and he was still the same.

"I like the place tidy, too," Tom said, trying to keep the sting out of his voice. "It's much easier for everyone when we know where to find each person's gear. Besides, leaving things all over the place could be considered just as obsessive as insisting on having the same place."

"C'mon, Tom; *forgetful* and *obsessive* are opposites." He didn't even sound annoyed, just amused, as if Tom were an ignorant boy. Tom wondered if Don acted that way at work. If he did, it would explain his checkered employment history.

"Don't blame Lou for my rules," Tom said. Don shrugged and went into the house to get his equipment.

A few minutes of peace, before things started. . . . Tom sat down beside Lucia, who had begun her stretches, and reached for his toes. It used to be easy. Marjory sat on Lucia's other side and leaned forward, trying to touch her forehead to her knees.

"Lou should be here tonight," Lucia said. She gave Marjory a sideways look.

"I wondered if I'd bothered him," Marjory said. "Asking him to come with me to the airport."

"I don't think so," Lucia said. "I'd have said he was very pleased indeed. Did anything happen?"

"No. We picked up my friend; I dropped Lou back here. That was all. Don said something about his gear—"

"Oh, Tom made him pick up lots of the gear, and Don was going to just shove it in the racks anyhow. Tom made him do it right. As many times as he's seen it done, he ought to have the way of it by now, but Don . . . he just will not learn. Now that he's not with Helen anymore, he's really backsliding into the slapdash boy we had years back. I wish he'd grow up."

Tom listened without joining in. He knew the signs: any moment now Lucia would tackle Marjory about her feelings for Lou and for Don, and he wanted to be far away when that happened. He finished stretching and stood up just as Lou came around the corner of the house.

AS HE CHECKED THE LIGHTS AND MADE A FINAL SWEEP OF THE area for possible hazards that might cause injury, Tom watched Lou stretching . . . methodical as always, thorough as always. Some people might think Lou was dull, but Tom found him endlessly fascinating. Thirty years before, he might well never have made it in the ordinary way; fifty years before, he would have spent his life in an institution. But improvements in early intervention, in teaching methods, and in computer-assisted sensory integration exercises had given him the ability to find good employment, live independently, deal with the real world on near-equal terms.

A miracle of adaptation and also, to Tom, a little sad. Younger people than Lou, born with the same neurological deficit, could be completely cured with gene therapy in the first two years of life. Only those whose parents refused the treatment had to struggle, as Lou had done, with the strenuous therapies Lou had mastered. If Lou had been younger, he'd not have suffered. He might be normal, whatever that meant.

Yet here he was, fencing. Tom thought of the jerky, uneven movements Lou had made when he first began—it had seemed, for the longest time, that Lou's fencing could be only a parody of the real thing. At each stage of development, he'd had the same slow, difficult start and slow, difficult progression . . . from foil to épée, from épée to rapier, from single blade to foil and dagger, épée and dagger, rapier and dagger, and so on.

He had mastered each by sheer effort, not by innate talent. Yet now that he had the physical skills, the mental skills that took other fencers decades seemed to come to him in only a few months.

Tom caught Lou's eye and beckoned him over. "Remember what I said—you need to be fencing with the top group now."

"Yes. . . ." Lou nodded, then made a formal salute. His opening moves seemed stiff, but he quickly shifted into a style that took advantage of his more fractal movement. Tom circled, changed direction, feinted and probed and offered fake openings, and Lou matched him movement for movement, testing him as he was tested. Was there a pattern in Lou's moves, other than a response to his own? He couldn't tell. But again and again, Lou almost caught him out, anticipating his own moves . . . which must mean, Tom thought, that he himself had a pattern and Lou had spotted it.

"Pattern analysis," he said aloud, just as Lou's blade slipped his and made a touch on his chest. "I should have thought of that."

"Sorry," Lou said. He almost always said, "Sorry," and then looked embarrassed.

"Good touch," Tom said. "I was trying to think how you were doing what you were doing, rather than concentrating on the match. But are you using pattern analysis?"

"Yes," Lou said. His tone was mild surprise, and Tom wondered if he was thinking, Doesn't everyone?

"I can't do it in real time," Tom said. "Not unless someone's got a very simple pattern."

"Is it not fair?" Lou asked.

"It's very fair, if you can do it," Tom said. "It's also the sign of a good fencer—or chess player, for that matter. Do you play chess?"

"No."

"Well . . . then let's see if I can keep my mind on what I'm doing and get a touch back." Tom nodded, and they began again, but it was hard to concentrate. He wanted to think about Lou—about when that awkward jerkiness had become effective, when he'd first seen real promise, when Lou had begun reading the patterns of the slower fencers. What did it say about the way he thought? What did it say about him as a person?

Tom saw an opening and moved in, only to feel the sharp thud on his chest of another touch.

"Shoot, Lou, if you keep doing this we'll have to promote you to tournaments," he said, only half joking. Lou stiffened, his shoulders hunching. "Does that bother you?"

"I . . . do not think I should fence in a tournament," Lou said.

"It's up to you." Tom saluted again. He wondered why Lou phrased it that way. It was one thing to have no desire for competition but another to think he "shouldn't" do it. If Lou had been normal—Tom hated himself for even thinking the word, but there it was—he'd have been in tournaments for the past three years. Starting too early, as most people did, rather than keeping to this private practice venue for so long. Tom pulled his mind back to the bout, barely parried a thrust, and tried to make his own attacks more random.

Finally, his breath failed and he had to stop, gasping. "I need a break, Lou. C'mon over here and let's review—" Lou followed him obediently and sat on the stone ledge bordering the patio while Tom took one of the chairs. Lou was sweating, he noticed, but not breathing particularly hard.

TOM FINALLY STOPS, GASPING, AND DECLARES HIMSELF TOO tired to go on. He leads me off to one side while two others step onto the ring. He is breathing very hard; his words come spaced apart, which makes it easier to understand them. I am glad he thinks I am doing so well.

"But here—you're not out of breath yet. Go fight someone else, give me a chance to catch mine, and we'll talk later."

I look over at Marjory sitting beside Lucia. I saw her watching me while Tom and I fought. Now she is looking down and the heat has brought more pink into her face. My stomach clenches, but I get up and walk over to her.

"Hi, Marjory," I say. My heart is pounding.

She looks up. She is smiling, a complete smile. "Hi, Lou," she says. "How are you tonight?"

"Fine," I say. "Will you . . . do you want to . . . will you fence with me?"

"Of course." She reaches down to pick up her mask and puts it on. I cannot see her face as well now, and she will not be able to see mine when I'm masked; I slide it back over my head. I can look without being seen; my heart steadies.

We begin with a recapitulation of some sequences from Saviolo's fencing manual. Step by step, forward and sideways, circling and feeling each other out. It is both ritual and conversation, as I balance parry against her thrust and thrust against her parry. Do I know this? Does she know that? Her movements are softer, more tentative, than Tom's. Circle, step, question, answer, a dialogue in steel to music I can hear in my head.

I make a touch when she does not move as I expect. I did not want to hit her. "Sorry," I say. My music falters; my rhythm stumbles. I step back, breaking contact, blade tip grounded.

"No—a good one," Marjory says. "I know better than to let down my guard. . . ."

"You're not hurt?" It felt like a hard touch, jarring the palm of my hand.

"No . . . let's go on."

I see the flash of teeth inside her mask: a smile. I salute; she answers;

we move back into the dance. I try to be careful, and through the touch of steel on steel I can feel that she is firmer, more concentrated, moving faster. I do not speed up; she makes a touch on my shoulder. From that point, I try to fence at her pace, making the encounter last as long as it can.

Too soon I hear her breathing roughen and she is ready to stop for a rest. We thank each other, clasping arms; I feel giddy.

"That was fun," she says. "But I've got to quit making excuses for not working out. If I'd been doing my weights, my arm wouldn't hurt."

"I do weights three times a week," I say. Then I realize she might think I am telling her what to do or boasting, but all I meant was that I do weights so my arms don't hurt.

"I should," she says. Her voice sounds happy and relaxed. I relax too. She is not unhappy that I said I do weights. "I used to. But I'm on a new project and it's eating my time."

I picture the project as something alive gnawing at a clock. This must be the research Emmy mentioned.

"Yes. What project is that?" I can hardly breathe as I wait for the answer.

"Well, my field is neuromuscular signal systems," Marjory said. "We're working on possible therapies for some of the genetic neuromuscular diseases that haven't yielded to gene therapy." She looks at me, and I nod.

"Like muscular dystrophy?" I ask.

"Yes, that's one," Marjory says "It's how I got involved in fencing, actually."

I feel my forehead wrinkling: confusion. How would fencing and muscular dystrophy be connected? People with MD don't fence. "Fencing . . . ?"

"Yes. I was on my way to a departmental meeting, years ago, and cut through a courtyard just as Tom was giving a fencing demo. I had been thinking of good muscle function from a physician's perspective, not from a user's perspective. . . . I remember I was standing there, watching people fence and thinking of the biochemical behavior of muscle cells, when Tom suddenly asked me if I'd like to try it. I think he mistook the look on my face for interest in fencing when it was the leg muscles I'd been watching."

"I thought you fenced in college," Lou said.

"That was college," Marjory said. "I was a grad student at the time."

"Oh . . . and you've always worked on muscles?"

"In one sense or another. With the success of some gene therapies for pure muscle diseases I've shifted more toward neuromuscular . . . or my employers have, I should say. I'm hardly a project director." She looks at my face a long time; I have to look away because the feeling is too intense. "I hope you didn't mind my asking you to ride with me to the airport, Lou. I felt safer with you along."

I feel myself getting hot. "It's not . . . I didn't . . . I wanted—" A gulp and a swallow. "I am not upset," I say when I get my voice under control. "I was glad to go with you."

"That's good," Marjory says.

She says nothing more; I sit beside her feeling my body relax. If it were possible, I would just sit here all night. As my heart slows, I look around at the others. Max and Tom and Susan are fencing two-on-one. Don is slouched in a chair across the patio; he is staring at me but looks away when I look at him.

TOM WAVED GOOD-BYE TO MAX, SUSAN, AND MARJORY, WHO all walked out together. When he turned around, Lou was still there. Lucia had gone inside, trailed as usual by those who wanted to talk.

"There's research," Lou said. "New. A treatment, maybe."

Tom listened more to the jerkiness of Lou's voice, the strain obvious in the pitch and tonality, than to the actual words. Lou was frightened; he sounded like this only when he was anxious.

"Is it still experimental, or is it available?"

"Experimental. But they, the office, they want—my boss said . . . they want me to . . . to take it."

"An experimental treatment? That's odd. Usually those aren't open to commercial health plans."

"It's—they—it is something developed at the Cambridge center,"

Lou said, his voice even more jerky and mechanical. "They own it now. My boss says his boss wants us to take it. He does not agree, but he cannot stop them."

Tom felt a sudden desire to slam his fist into someone's head. Lou was scared; someone was bullying him. He's not my child, Tom reminded himself. He had no rights in this situation, but as Lou's friend, he did have responsibilities.

"Do you know how it's supposed to work?" he asked.

"Not yet." Lou shook his head. "It just came out on the Web this past week; the local autism society had a meeting about it, but they didn't know. . . . They think it's still years from human use. Mr. Aldrin—my supervisor—said it could be tested now, and Mr. Crenshaw wants us to take it."

"They can't make you use experimental stuff, Lou; it's against the law to force you—"

"But they could take my job—"

"Are they threatening to fire you if you don't? They can't do that." He didn't think they could. They couldn't at the university, but the private sector was different. That different? "You need a lawyer," he said. He tried to think of lawyers he knew. Gail might be the right lawyer for this, Tom thought. Gail had done human rights work for a long time and, more than that, had made it pay. He would think about who might help, rather than his own increasing desire to smash someone's head in.

"No . . . yes . . . I do not know. I am worried. Mr. Aldrin said we should get help, a lawyer—"

"That's exactly right," Tom said. He wondered if giving Lou something else to think about would be a help or not. "Look, you know I mentioned tournaments to you—"

"I am not good enough," Lou said quickly.

"Actually, you are. And I'm wondering if maybe fighting in a tournament would help you with this other problem—" Tom scrambled through his own thoughts, trying to clarify why he thought it might be a good idea. "If you end up needing to go to court against your employer, that's kind of like a fencing match. The confidence you get from fencing could help."

Lou just looked at him, almost expressionless. "I do not understand why it would help."

"Well . . . maybe it wouldn't. I just thought having some other experience, with more people than us, might."

"When is a tournament?"

"The next one locally is a couple of weeks away," Tom said. "Saturday. You could ride with us; Lucia and I would be around to back you up, make sure you met the nice people."

"There are not-nice people?"

"Well, yes. There are not-nice people everywhere, and a few always manage to get into the fencing groups. But most of them are nice. You might enjoy it." He shouldn't push, even though he felt more and more that Lou needed more exposure to the normal world, if you could call a bunch of historical re-creation enthusiasts normal. They were normal in their everyday lives; they just liked to wear fancy costumes and pretend to kill each other with swords.

"I do not have a costume," Lou said, looking down at his old leather jacket with the cut-off sleeves.

"We can find you something," Tom said. Lou would probably fit into one of his costumes well enough. He had more than he needed, more than most seventeeth-century men had owned. "Lucia could help us out."

"I am not sure," Lou said.

"Well, let me know next week if you want to try it. We'll need to get your entry money in. If not, there's another one later on."

"I will think about it," Lou said.

"Good. And about this other—I may know a lawyer who could help you. I'll check with her. And what about the Center—have you talked to them?"

"No. Mr. Aldrin phoned me, but no one has said anything official and I think I should not say anything until they do."

"It wouldn't hurt to find out what legal rights you have ahead of time," Tom said. "I don't know for sure—I know the laws have changed back and forth, but nothing I do involves research with human subjects, so I'm not up on the current legal situation. You need an expert."

"It would cost a lot," Lou said.

"Maybe," Tom said. "That is something else to find out. Surely the Center can get you that information."

"Thank you," Lou said.

Tom watched him walk away, quiet, contained, a little frightening sometimes in his own harmless way. The very thought of someone experimenting on Lou made him feel sick. Lou was Lou, and fine the way he was.

Inside, Tom found Don sprawled on the floor under the ceiling fan talking a blue streak as usual while Lucia stitched on her embroidery with that expression that meant "Rescue me!" Don turned to him.

"So . . . you think Lou's ready for open competition, huh?" Don asked.

Tom nodded. "You overheard that? Yes, I do. He's improved a lot. He's fencing with the best we have and holding his own."

"It's a lot of pressure for someone like him," Don said.

" 'Someone like him' . . . you mean autistic?"

"Yeah. They don't do well with crowds and noise and stuff, do they? I read that's why the ones who are so good at music don't become concert performers. Lou's okay, but I think you shouldn't push him into tournaments. He'll fold."

Tom choked back his first thought and said instead, "Do you remember your first tournament, Don?"

"Well, yeah. . . . I was pretty young. . . . It was a disaster."

"Yes. Do you remember what you told me after your first bout?"

"No . . . not really. I know I lost . . . I just fell apart."

"You told me you'd been unable to concentrate because of the people moving around."

"Yeah, well, it'd be worse for someone like Lou."

"Don—how could he lose worse than you did?"

Don's face turned red. "Well, I—he—it would just be worse for him. Losing, I mean. For me—"

"You went and drank a six-pack and threw up behind a tree," Tom said. "Then you cried and told me it was the worst day of your life."

"I was young," Don said. "And I let it all out, and it didn't bother me after that. . . . He'll brood."

"I'm glad you're worried about his feelings," Lucia said. Tom almost winced at the sarcasm in her voice, even though it wasn't directed at him.

Don shrugged, though his eyes had narrowed. "Of course I worry," he said. "He's not like the rest of us—"

"That's right," Lucia said. "He's a better fencer than most of us and a better person than some."

"Jeez, Luci, you're in a bad mood," Don said, in the jokey tone that Tom knew meant he wasn't joking.

"You're not improving it," Lucia said, folding her needlework and standing; she was gone before Tom could say anything. He hated it when she said what he was thinking and then he had to cope with the aftermath, knowing that she had expressed the thoughts he tried to keep hidden. Now, predictably, Don was giving him a complicit man-to-man look that invited a shared view of women that he didn't share.

"Is she getting . . . you know . . . sort of midlife?" Don asked.

"No," Tom said. "She's expressing an opinion." Which he happened to share, but should he say that? Why couldn't Don just grow up and quit causing these problems? "Look—I'm tired, and I have an early class tomorrow."

"Okay, okay, I can take a hint," Don said, clambering up with a dramatic wince and a hand to his back.

The problem was, he couldn't take a hint. It was another fifteen minutes before he finally left; Tom locked the front door and turned off the lights before Don could think of something else to say and come back, the way he often did. Tom felt bad; Don had been a charming and enthusiastic boy, years ago, and surely he should have been able to help him grow into a more mature man than he'd become. What else were older friends for?

"It's not your fault," Lucia said from the hall. Her voice was softer now, and he relaxed a little; he had not been looking forward to soothing a furious Lucia. "He'd be worse if you hadn't worked on him."

"I dunno," Tom said. "I still think—"

"Born teacher that you are, Tom, you still think you should be able to save them all from themselves. Think: there's Marcus at Columbia, and Grayson at Michigan, and Vladianoff in Berlin—all your boys once and all better men for knowing you. Don is not your fault."

"Tonight I'll buy that," Tom said. Lucia, backlit by the light from their bedroom, had an almost magical quality.

"That's not all I'm selling," she said, her voice teasing, and she dropped the robe.

IT DOES NOT MAKE SENSE TO ME THAT TOM WOULD ASK ME again about entering a fencing tournament when I was talking about an experimental treatment for autism. I think about that on the drive home. It is clear that I am improving in my fencing and that I can hold my own with the better fencers in the group. But what does that have to do with the treatment or with legal rights?

People who fence in tournaments are serious about it. They have practiced. They have their own equipment. They want to win. I am not sure I want to win, though I do enjoy understanding the patterns and finding my way through them. Maybe Tom thinks I should want to win? Maybe Tom thinks I need to want to win in fencing so that I will want to win in court?

These two things are not connected. Someone can want to win a game or want to win a case in court without wanting to do both.

What is alike? Both are contests. Someone wins and someone else loses. My parents emphasized that everything in life is not a contest, that people can work together, that everyone can win when they do. Fencing is more fun when people are cooperating, trying to enjoy it with each other. I do not think of making touches on someone as winning but as playing the game well.

Both require preparation? Everything requires preparation. Both require—I swerve to avoid a bicyclist whose taillight is out; I barely saw him.

Forethought. Attention. Understanding. Patterns. The thoughts flick through my head like flash cards, each with its nested concepts topped by a neat word that cannot say everything.

I would like to please Tom. When I helped with the fencing surface and the equipment racks, he was pleased. It was like having my father back again, on his good days. I would like to please Tom again, but I do not know whether entering this tournament will do it. What if I fence badly and lose? Will he be disappointed? What does he expect?

It would be fun to fence with people I've never seen before. People whose patterns I do not know. People who are normal and will not know that I am not normal. Or will Tom tell them? Somehow I do not think he will.

Next Saturday I am going to the planetarium with Eric and Linda. The following Saturday, it is the third of the month, and I always spend extra time cleaning my apartment on the third Saturday of the month. The tournament is the Saturday after. I do not have anything planned for then.

When I get home I pencil in "fencing tournament" on the fourth Saturday of the month. I think about calling Tom, but it is late and, besides, he said to tell him next week. I put a reminder sticky on the calendar: "Tell Tom yes."

CHAPTER FIVE

B Y FRIDAY AFTERNOON MR. CRENSHAW HAS STILL NOT said anything to us about the experimental treatment. Maybe Mr. Aldrin was wrong. Maybe Mr. Aldrin talked him out of it. On-line, there's a flurry of discussion, mostly on the private news groups, but nobody seems to know when or where human trials are scheduled.

I do not say anything on-line about what Mr. Aldrin told us. He did not say not to talk about it, but it does not feel right. If Mr. Crenshaw has changed his mind and everyone gets upset, then he will be angry. He looks angry much of the time anyway when he comes to check on us.

The show at the planetarium is "Exploring the Outer Planets and Their Satellites." It has been on since Labor Day, which means it is not too crowded now, even on Saturday. I go early, to the first showing, which is also less crowded even on days when it is crowded. Only a third of the seats are occupied, so Eric and Linda and I can take up a whole row without being too close to anyone.

The amphitheater smells funny, but it always does. As the lights dim and the artificial sky darkens, I feel the same old excitement. Even though these pinpricks of light that begin to show on the dome are not really stars, it is about stars. The light is not as old; it has not been worn smooth by its passage through billions and billions of miles—it has come from a projector less than a ten-thousandth of a light-second away—but I still enjoy it.

What I don't enjoy is the long introduction that talks about what we knew a hundred years ago, and fifty years ago, and so on. I want to know what we know now, not what my parents might have heard when they were children. What difference does it make if someone in the distant past thought there were canals on Mars?

The plush on my seat has a hard, rough spot. I feel it with my fingers—someone has stuck gum or candy there and the cleaning compound hasn't taken it all. Once I notice it, I can't not notice it. I slide my brochure between me and the rough spot.

Finally the program moves out of history and into the present. The latest space-probe photographs of the outer planets are spectacular; the simulated flybys almost make me feel that I could fall out of my seat into the gravity well of one planet after another. I wish I could be there myself. When I was little and first saw newscasts of people in space I wanted to be an astronaut, but I know that's impossible. Even if I had the new LifeTime treatment so I would live long enough, I would still be autistic. What you can't change don't grieve over, my mother said.

I don't learn anything I don't already know, but I enjoy the show anyway. After the show, I am hungry. It is past my usual lunchtime.

"We could have lunch," Eric says.

"I am going home," I say. I have good jerky at home, and apples that will not be crisp much longer.

Eric nods and turns away.

ON SUNDAY I GO TO CHURCH. THE ORGANIST PLAYS MOZART before the service starts. The music sounds right with the formality of the worship. It all matches, like shirt and tie and jacket should match: not alike but fitting together harmoniously. The choir sings a pleasant anthem by Rutter. I do not like Rutter as much as Mozart, but it doesn't make my head hurt.

Monday is cooler, with a damp chill breeze out of the northeast. It is not cold enough to wear a jacket or sweater, but it is more comfortable. I know that the worst of the summer is over.

On Tuesday it is warm again. Tuesdays I do my grocery shopping. The stores are less crowded on Tuesdays, even when Tuesday falls on the first of the month.

I watch the people in the grocery store. When I was a child, we were told that soon there would be no grocery stores. Everyone would order their food over the Internet, and it would be delivered to their doors. The family next door did that for a while, and my mother thought it was silly. She and Mrs. Taylor used to argue about it. Their faces would get shiny, and their voices sounded like knives scraping together. I thought they hated each other when I was little, before I learned that grownups—people—could disagree and argue without disliking each other.

There are still places where you can have your groceries delivered, but around here the places that tried it went out of business. What you can do now is order groceries to be held in the "Quick Pickup" section, where a conveyor belt delivers a box to the pickup lane. I do that sometimes, but not often. It costs 10 percent more, and it is important for me to have the experience of shopping. That's what my mother said. Mrs. Taylor said maybe I was getting enough stress without that, but my mother said Mrs. Taylor was too sensitive. Sometimes I wished that Mrs. Taylor was my mother instead of my mother, but then I felt bad about that, too.

When people in the grocery store are shopping alone, they often look worried and intent and they ignore others. Mother taught me about the social etiquette of grocery stores, and a lot of it came easily to me, despite the noise and confusion. Because no one expects to stop and chat with strangers, they avoid eye contact, making it easy to watch them covertly without annoying them. They don't mind that I don't make eye contact, though it is polite to look directly at the person who takes your card or money, just for a moment. It is polite to say something about the weather, even if the person in front of you in line said almost the same thing, but you don't have to.

Sometimes I wonder how normal normal people are, and I wonder that most in the grocery store. In our Daily Life Skills classes, we were taught to make a list and go directly from one aisle to another, checking off items on the list. Our teacher advised us to research prices ahead of time, in the newspaper, rather than compare prices while standing in the aisle. I thought—he told us—that he was teaching us how normal people shop.

But the man who is blocking the aisle in front of me has not had that lecture. He seems normal, but he is looking at every single jar of spaghetti sauce, comparing prices, reading labels. Beyond him, a short gray-haired woman with thick glasses is trying to peer past him at the same shelves; I think she wants one of the sauces on my side, but he is in the way and she is not willing to bother him. Neither am I. The muscles of his face are tight, making little bulges on his brow and cheeks and chin. His skin is a little shiny. He is angry. The gray-haired woman and I both know that a well-dressed man who looks angry can explode if he is bothered.

Suddenly he looks up and catches my eye. His face flushes and looks redder and shinier. "You could have *said* something!" he says, yanking his basket to one side, blocking the gray-haired woman even more. I smile at her and nod; she pushes her basket out around him, and then I go through.

"It's so stupid," I hear him mutter. "Why can't they all be the same size?"

I know better than to answer him, though it is tempting. If people talk, they expect someone to listen. I am supposed to pay attention and listen when people talk, and I have trained myself to do that most of the time. In a grocery store sometimes people do not expect an answer and they get angry if you answer them. This man is already angry. I can feel my heart beating.

Ahead of me now are two giggling children, very young, pulling packets of seasoning mix out of racks. A young woman in jeans looks around the end of row and snarls, "Jackson! Misty! Put those back!" I jump. I know she wasn't talking to me, but the tone sets my teeth on edge. One child squeals, right beside me now, and the other says, "Won't!" The woman, her face squeezed into a strange shape by her anger, rushes past me. I hear a child yelp and do not turn around. I want to say, "Quiet, quiet, quiet," but it is not my business; it is not all right to tell other people to be quiet if you are not the parent or the boss. I hear other voices now, women's voices, someone scolding the woman with the children, and turn quickly into the cross-aisle. My heart is running in my chest, faster and stronger than usual.

People choose to come to stores like this, to hear this noise and see other people being rushed and angry and upset. Remote ordering and delivery failed because they would rather come and see other people than sit alone and be alone until the delivery comes. Not everywhere: in some cities, remote ordering has been successful. But here . . . I steer around a center display of wine, realize I've gone past the aisle I wanted, and look carefully all ways before turning back.

I always go down the spice aisle, whether I need spices or not. When it's not crowded—and today it's not—I stop and let myself smell the fragrances. Even over floor wax, cleaning fluid, and the scent of bubble gum from some child nearby I can detect a faint blend of spices and herbs. Cinnamon, cumin, cloves, marjoram, nutmeg . . . even the names are interesting. My mother liked to use spices and herbs in cooking. She let me smell them all. Some I did not like, but most of them felt good inside my head. Today I need chili spice. I do not have to stop and look; I know where it is on the shelf, a red-and-white box.

I AM DRENCHED IN SWEAT SUDDENLY. MARJORY IS AHEAD OF me, not noticing me because she is in grocery store shopping mode. She has opened a spice container—which, I wonder, until the air current brings me the unmistakable fragrance of cloves. My favorite. I turn my head quickly and try to concentrate on the shelf of food colorings, candied fruit, and cake decorations. I do not understand why these are in the same aisle with spices and herbs, but they are.

Will she see me? If she sees me, will she speak? Should I speak to her? My tongue feels as big as a zucchini. I sense motion approaching. Is it her or someone else? If I were really shopping, I would not look. I do not want cake decorations or candied cherries.

"Hi, Lou," she says. "Baking a cake?"

I turn to look at her. I have not seen her except at Tom and Lucia's or in the car to and from the airport. I have never seen her in this store before. This is not her right setting . . . or it may be, but I didn't know it. "I—I'm just looking," I say. It is hard to talk. I hate it that I am sweating.

"They are pretty colors," she says, in a voice that seems to hold nothing but mild interest. At least she is not laughing out loud. "Do you like fruitcake?"

"N-no," I say, swallowing the large lump in my throat. "I think . . . I think the colors are prettier than the taste." That is wrong—tastes are not pretty or ugly—but it is too late to change.

She nods, her expression serious. "I feel the same way," she says. "The first time I had fruitcake, when I was little, I expected it to taste good because it was so pretty. And then . . . I didn't like it."

"Do you . . . do you shop here often?" I ask.

"Not usually," she says. "I'm on my way to a friend's house and she asked me to pick up some things for her." She looks at me, and I am once more conscious of how it is hard to talk. It is even hard to breathe, and I feel slimy with the sweat trickling down my back. "Is this your regular store?"

"Yes," I say.

"Then maybe you can show me where to find rice and aluminum foil," she says.

My mind is blank for a moment before I can remember; then I know again. "The rice is third aisle, halfway along," I say. "And the foil's over on Eighteen—"

"Oh, please," she says, her voice sounding happy. "Just show me. I've already wandered around in here for what feels like an hour."

"Show—take you?" I feel instantly stupid; this is what she meant, of course. "Come on," I say, wheeling my basket and earning a glare from a large woman with a basket piled high with produce. "Sorry," I say to her; she pushes past without answering.

"I'll just follow," Marjory says. "I don't want to annoy people. . . ."

I nod and head first for the rice, since we're on Aisle Seven and that is closer. I know that Marjory is behind me; knowing that makes a warm place on my back, like a ray of sun. I am glad she cannot see my face; I can feel the heat there, too.

While Marjory looks at the shelves of rice—rice in bags, rice in boxes, long-grain and short-grain and brown, and rice in combinations with other things, and she does not know where the kind of rice is that she wants—I look at Marjory. One of her eyelashes is longer than the others and darker brown. Her eyes have more than one color in them, little flecks in the iris that make it more interesting.

Most eyes have more than one color, but usually they're related. Blue eyes may have two shades of blue, or blue and gray, or blue and green, or even a fleck or two of brown. Most people don't notice that. When I first went to get my state ID card, the form asked for eye color. I tried to write in all the colors in my own eyes, but the blank space wasn't big enough. They told me to put "brown." I put "brown," but that is not the only color in my eyes. It is just the color that people see because they do not really look at other people's eyes.

I like the color of Marjory's eyes because they are her eyes and because I like all the colors in them. I like all the colors in her hair, too. She probably puts "brown" on forms that ask her for hair color, but her hair has many different colors, more than her eyes. In the store's light, it looks duller than outside, with none of the orange glints, but I know they are there.

"Here it is," she says. She is holding a box of rice, white, long-grained, quick-cooking. "On to the foil!" she says. Then she grins. "The cooking kind, not the fencing kind, I mean."

I grin back, feeling my cheek muscles tighten. I knew what kind of foil she meant. Did she think I didn't know, or was she just making a joke? I lead her to the middle cross-aisle of the store, all the way across to the aisle that has plastic bags and plastic storage dishes and rolls of plastic film and waxed paper and aluminum foil.

"That was quick," she says. She is quicker to pick out the foil she wants than she was with the rice. "Thanks, Lou," she says. "You were a big help."

I wonder if I should tell her about the express lines at this store. Will she be annoyed? But she said she was in a hurry.

"The express lines," I say. My mind blanks suddenly, and I hear my voice going flat and dull. "At this time, people come in and have more than the express lines sign says—"

"That's so frustrating," she says. "Is there one end or the other that's faster?"

I am not sure what she means at first. The two ends of the checkout go the same speed, one coming as another leaves. It's the middle, where the checker is, that can be slow or fast. Marjory is waiting, not rushing me. Maybe she means which end of the row of checkout stands, if not the express lanes, is faster. I know that; it's the end nearest the customer services desk. I tell her, and she nods.

"Sorry, Lou, but I have to rush," she says. "I'm supposed to meet Pam at six-fifteen." It is 6:07; if Pam lives very far away she will not make it.

"Good luck," I say. I watch her move briskly down the aisle away from me, swerving smoothly around the other shoppers.

"So—that's what she looks like," says someone behind me. I turn around. It is Emmy. As usual, she looks angry. "She's not that pretty."

"I think she is pretty," I say.

"I can tell," Emmy says. "You're blushing."

My face is hot. I may be blushing, but Emmy didn't have to say so. It is not polite to comment on someone else's expression in public. I say nothing.

"I suppose you think she's in love with you," Emmy says. Her voice is hostile. I can tell she thinks this is what I think and that she thinks I am wrong, that Marjory is not in love with me. I am unhappy that Emmy thinks these things but happy that I can understand all that in what she says and how she says it. Years ago I would not have understood.

"I do not know," I say, keeping my voice calm and low. Down the aisle, a woman has paused with her hand on a package of plastic storage containers to look at us. "You do not know what I think," I say to Emmy. "And you do not know what she thinks. You are trying to mind-read; that is an error."

"You think you're so smart," Emmy says. "Just because you work with computers and math. You don't know anything about people."

I know the woman down the aisle is drifting closer and listening to us. I feel scared. We should not be talking like this in public. We should not be noticed. We should blend in; we should look and sound and act normal. If I try to tell Emmy that, she will be even angrier. She might say something loud. "I have to go," I say to Emmy. "I'm late."

"For what, for a date?" she asks. She says the word *date* louder than the other words and with an upward-moving tone that means she is being sarcastic.

"No," I say in a calm voice. If I am calm maybe she will let me alone. "I am going to watch TV. I always watch TV on—" Suddenly I cannot think of the day of the week; my mind is blank. I turn away, as if I had said the whole sentence. Emmy laughs, a harsh sound, but she does not say anything else that I can hear. I hurry back to the spice aisle and pick up my box of chili powder and go to the checkout lanes. They all have lines.

In my line there are five people ahead of me. Three women and two men. One with light hair, four with dark hair. One man has a light-blue pullover shirt almost the same shade as a box in his basket. I try to think only about color, but it is noisy and the lights in the store make the colors different than they really are. As they are in daylight, I mean. The store is also reality. The things I don't like are as much reality as the things I do like.

Even so, it is easier if I think about the things I do like and not about the ones I don't. Thinking about Marjory and Haydn's *Te Deum* makes me very happy; if I let myself think of Emmy, even for a moment, the music goes sour and dark and I want to run away. I fix my mind on Marjory, as if she were an assignment at work, and the music dances, happier and happier.

"Is she your girlfriend?"

I stiffen and half turn. It is the woman who was watching Emmy and me; she has come up behind me in the checkout line. Her eyes glisten in the store's bright light; her lipstick has dried in the corners of her mouth to a garish orange. She smiles at me, but it is not a soft smile. It is a hard smile, of the mouth only. I say nothing, and she speaks again.

"I couldn't help noticing," she says. "Your friend was so upset. She's a little . . . different, isn't she?" She bares more teeth.

I do not know what to say. I have to say something; other people in the line are now watching.

"I don't mean to be rude," the woman says. The muscles around her eyes are tense. "It's just . . . I noticed her way of speaking."

Emmy's life is Emmy's life. It is not this woman's life; she has no right to know what is wrong with Emmy. If anything is wrong.

"It must be hard for people like you," the woman says. She turns her head, glancing at the people in the line who are watching us, and gives a little giggle. I do not know what she thinks is funny. I do not think any of this is funny. "Relationships are hard enough for the rest of us," she says. Now she is not smiling. She has the same expression as Dr. Fornum has when she is explaining something she wants me to do. "It must be worse for you."

The man behind her has an odd expression on his face; I can't tell if he agrees with her or not. I wish someone would tell her to be quiet. If I tell her to be quiet, that is rude.

"I hope I haven't upset you," she says, in a higher voice, and her eyebrows lift. She is waiting for me to give the right answer.

I think there is no right answer. "I don't know you," I say, keeping my voice very low and calm. I mean "I don't know you and I do not want to talk about Emmy or Marjory or anything personal with someone I do not know."

Her face bunches up; I turn away quickly. From behind me I hear a huffed, "Well!" and behind that a man's voice softly muttering, "Serves you right." I think it is the man behind the woman, but I will not turn around and look. Ahead of me the line is down to two people; I look straight ahead without focusing on anything in particular, trying to hear the music again, but I can't. All I can hear is noises.

When I carry my groceries out, the sticky heat seems even worse than when I went in. I can smell everything: candy on discarded candy wrappers, fruit peels, gum, people's deodorant and shampoo, the asphalt of the parking lot, exhaust from the buses. I set my groceries on the back of the car while I unlock it.

"Hey," someone says. I jump and turn. It is Don. I did not expect to see Don here. I did not expect to see Marjory here, either. I wonder if other people in the fencing group shop here. "Hi, fella," he says. He is wearing a striped knit shirt and dark slacks. I have not seen him wear anything like this before; when he comes to fencing he wears either a T-shirt and jeans or a costume.

"Hi, Don," I say. I do not want to talk to Don even though he is a friend. It is too hot, and I need to get my groceries home and put them away. I pick up the first sack and put it in the backseat.

"This where you shop?" he asks. It is a silly question when I am standing here with grocery sacks on my car. Does he think I stole them?

"I come here on Tuesdays," I say.

He looks disapproving. Maybe he thinks Tuesdays are the wrong day for grocery shopping—but then why is he here? "Coming to fencing tomorrow?" he asks.

"Yes," I say. I put the other sack in the car, and close the back door.

"Going to that tournament?" He is staring at me in a way that makes me want to look down or away.

"Yes," I say. "But I have to go home now." Milk should be kept at a temperature of thirty-eight degrees F. or below. It is at least ninety degrees F. here in the parking lot, and the milk I bought will be warming up.

"Have a real routine, don't you?" he says.

I do not know what a false routine would be. I wonder if this is like *real heel*.

"Do the same thing every day?" he asks.

"Not the same thing every day," I say. "The same things on the same days."

"Oh, right," he says. "Well, I'll see you tomorrow, you regular guy, you." He laughs. It is a strange laugh, not as if he were really enjoying it. I open the front door and get into my car; he does not say anything or walk off. When I start the engine, he shrugs, an abrupt twitch of the shoulders as if something had stung him.

"Good-bye," I say, being polite.

"Yeah," he says. "Bye." He is still standing there as I drive off. In the rearview mirror I can see him standing in the same place until I am almost to the street. I turn right onto the street; when I glance back, he is gone.

IT IS QUIETER IN MY APARTMENT THAN OUTSIDE, BUT IT IS NOT really quiet. Beneath me, the policeman Danny Bryce has the TV on, and I know that he is watching a game show with a studio audience. Above me, Mrs. Sanderson is dragging chairs to the table in her kitchenette; she does this every night. I can hear the ticking of my windup alarm and a faint hum from the booster power supply for my computer. It changes tone slightly as the power cycles. Outside noises still come in: the rattle of a commuter train, the whine of traffic, voices in the side yard.

When I am upset it is harder to ignore the sounds. If I turn on my music, it will press down on top of them, but they will still be there, like toys shoved under a thick rug. I put my groceries away, wiping the beads of condensation off the milk carton, then turn on my music. Not too loud; I must not annoy my neighbors. The disk in the player is Mozart, which usually works. I can feel my tension letting go, bit by bit.

I do not know why that woman would speak to me. She should not do that. The grocery store is neutral ground; she should not talk to strangers. I was safe until she noticed me. If Emmy hadn't talked so loud, the woman would not have noticed. She said that. I do not like Emmy much anyway; I feel my neck getting hot when I think about what Emmy said and what that woman said.

My parents said that I should not blame other people when they noticed that I was different. I should not blame Emmy. I should look at myself and think what happened.

I do not want to do that. I did not do anything wrong. I need to go grocery shopping. I was there for the right reason. I was behaving appropriately. I did not talk to strangers or talk out loud to myself. I did not take up more space in the aisle than I should. Marjory is my friend; I was not wrong to talk to her and help her find the rice and aluminum foil.

Emmy was wrong. Emmy talked too loud and that is why the woman noticed. But even so, that woman should have minded her own business. Even if Emmy talked too loud, it was not my fault.

*I* NEED TO KNOW IF WHAT *I* FEEL IS WHAT NORMAL PEOPLE feel when they are in love. We had a few stories about people in love in school, in English classes, but the teachers always said those were unrealistic. I do not know the way they were unrealistic. I did not ask then, because I did not care. I thought it was silly. Mr. Neilson in Health said it was all hormones and not to do anything stupid. The way he described sexual intercourse made me wish I had nothing down there, like a plastic doll. I could not imagine having to put *this* into *that*. And the words for the body parts are ugly. Being pricked hurts; who would want to have a prick? I kept thinking of thorns. The others aren't much better, and the official medical term, *penis*, sounds whiny. Teeny, weeny, meanie . . . penis. The words for the act itself are ugly, pounding words; they made me think of pain. The thought of that closeness, of having to breathe someone else's breath, smelling her body up close . . . disgusting. The locker room was bad enough; I kept wanting to throw up.

It was disgusting then. Now . . . the scent off Marjory's hair, when she has been fencing, makes me want to get closer. Even though she uses a scented soap for her clothes, even though she uses a deodorant with a powdery sort of smell, there's something . . . but the *idea* is still awful. I've seen pictures; I know what a woman's body looks like. When I was in school, boys passed around little video clips of naked women dancing and men and women having sex. They always got hot and sweaty when they did this, and their voices sounded different, more like chimpanzee voices on nature programs. I wanted to see at first, because I didn't know—my parents didn't have things like that in the house—but it was kind of boring, and the women all looked a little angry or frightened. I thought if they were enjoying it, they would look happy.

I never wanted to make anyone look scared or angry. It does not feel good to be scared or angry. Scared people make mistakes. Angry people make mistakes. Mr. Neilson said it was normal to have sexual feelings, but he did not explain what they were, not in a way that I could understand. My body grew the same as other boys' bodies; I remember how surprised I was when I found the first dark hairs growing on my crotch. Our teacher had told us about sperm and eggs and how things grew from seeds. When I saw those hairs I thought someone had planted the seeds for them, and I didn't know how it happened. My mother explained it was puberty and told me not to do anything stupid.

I could never be sure which kind of feeling they meant, a body feeling like hot and cold or a mind feeling like happy and sad. When I saw the pictures of naked girls I had a body feeling sometimes, but the only mind feeling I had was disgust.

I have seen Marjory fencing and I know she enjoys it, but she is not smiling most of the time. They said a smiling face is a happy face. Maybe they were wrong? Maybe she would enjoy it?

When I get to Tom and Lucia's, Lucia tells me to go on out. She is doing something in the kitchen; I can hear the rattle of pans. I smell spices. No one else is here yet.

Tom is sanding the nicks off one of his blades when I get to the backyard. I begin stretching. They are the only couple I know who have been married so long since my parents died, and since my parents are dead I cannot ask them what marriage is like.

"Sometimes you and Lucia sound angry at each other," I say, watching Tom's face to see if he is going to be angry with me.

"Married people argue sometimes," Tom said. "It's not easy to stay this close to someone for years."

"Does—" I cannot think how to say what I want to say. "If Lucia is angry at you . . . if you are angry at her . . . it means you are not loving each other?"

Tom looks startled. Then he laughs, a tense laugh. "No, but it's hard to explain, Lou. We love each other, and we love each other even when we're angry. The love is behind the anger, like a wall behind a curtain or the land as a storm passes over it. The storm goes away, and the land is still there."

"If there is a storm," I say, "sometimes there is a flood or a house gets blown away."

"Yes, and sometimes, if love isn't strong enough or the anger is big enough, people do quit loving each other. But we aren't."

I wonder how he can be so sure. Lucia has been angry so many times in the past three months. How can Tom know that she still loves him?

"People sometimes have a bad time for a while," Tom says, as if he knew what I was thinking. "Lucia's been upset lately about a situation at work. When she found that you were being pressured to take the treatment, that also upset her."

I never thought about normal people having trouble at work. The only normal people I know have had the same jobs as long as I have known them. What kind of trouble do normal people have? They cannot have a Mr. Crenshaw asking them to take medicine they don't want to take. What makes them angry at their work?

"Lucia is angry because of her work and because of me?"

"Partly, yes. A lot of things have hit her at once."

"It is not as comfortable when Lucia is angry," I say.

Tom makes a funny sound that is part laugh and part something else. "You can say that again," he says. I know this does not mean that I should say what I said again, though it still seems like a silly thing to say instead of "I agree with you" or "You're right."

"I thought about the tournament," I say. "I decided—"

Marjory comes out into the yard. She always goes through the house, though many people go through the side yard gate. I wonder what it would feel like if Marjory were angry with me the way Lucia gets angry with Tom or the way Tom and Lucia have been angry with Don. I have always been upset when people were angry with me, even people I didn't like. I think it would be worse to have Marjory mad at me than even my parents.

"You decided . . ." Tom does not quite ask. Then he glances up and sees Marjory. "Ah. Well?"

"I would like to try," I say. "If it is still all right."

"Oh," Marjory says. "You've decided to enter the tournament, Lou? Good for you!"

"It is very much all right," Tom says. "But now you have to hear my standard number-one lecture. Go get your stuff, Marjory; Lou has to pay attention."

I wonder how many number lectures he has and why I need a number lecture to enter a fencing tournament. Marjory goes into the house, and then it is easier to listen to Tom.

"First off, between now and then, you'll practice as much as you can. Every day, if possible, until the last day. If you can't come over here, at least do stretches, legwork, and point control at home."

I do not think I can come to Tom and Lucia's every day. When would I do the laundry or the grocery shopping or clean my car? "How many should I do?"

"Whatever you have time for without getting too sore," Tom says. "Then, a week before, check all your equipment. You keep your equipment in good repair, but it's still good to check it. We'll go over it together. Do you have a spare blade?"

"No . . . should I order one?"

"Yes, if you can afford it. Otherwise, you can have one of mine."

"I can order one." It is not in my budget, but I have enough right now.

"Well, then. You want to have all your equipment checked out, have it clean and ready to pack. The day before, you don't practice—you need to relax. Pack your gear, then go take a walk or something."

"Could I just stay home?"

"You could, but it's a good idea to get some exercise, just not overdo it. Eat a good supper; go to bed at your usual time."

I can understand what this plan will accomplish, but it will be hard to do what Tom wants and go to work and do the other things I must do. I do not have to watch TV or play games on the 'net with my friends, and I do not have to go to the Center on Saturday, even though I usually do.

"It will be . . . you will have . . . fencing practice here other nights than Wednesday?"

"For students entering the tournament, yes," Tom says. "Come any day but Tuesday. That's our special night."

I feel my face getting hot. I wonder what it would be like to have a special night. "I do my grocery shopping on Tuesday," I say.

Marjory, Lucia, and Max come out of the house. "Enough lecture," Lucia says. "You'll scare him off. Don't forget the entry form."

"Entry form!" Tom smacks himself on the forehead. He does this whenever he forgets something. I do not know why. It does not help me remember when I try it. He goes into the house. I am through with my stretches now, but the others are just starting. Susan, Don, and Cindy come through the side gate. Don is carrying Susan's blue bag; Cindy has a green one. Don goes inside to get his gear; Tom comes back out with a paper for me to fill out and sign.

The first part is easy: my name, address, contact number, age, height, and weight. I do not know what to put in the space marked "persona."

"Ignore that," Tom says. "It's for people who like to play a part."

"In a play?" I ask.

"No. All day, they pretend to be someone they've made up, from history. Well, from pretend history."

"It is another game?" I ask.

"Yes, exactly. And people treat them as if they were their pretend person."

When I talked about pretend persons to my teachers, they got upset and made notes in my records. I would like to ask Tom if normal people do this often and if he does it, but I do not want to upset him.

"For instance," Tom says, "when I was younger I had a persona named Pierre Ferret—that's spelled like the animal ferret—who was a spy for the evil cardinal."

"What is evil about a bird?" I ask.

"The other kind of cardinal," Tom says. "Didn't you ever read *The Three Musketeers*?"

"No," I say. I never even heard of *The Three Musketeers*.

"Oh, well, you'd love it," he says. "But it would take too long to tell the story now—it's just that there was a wicked cardinal and a foolish queen and an even more foolish young king and three brave musketeers who were the best swordsmen in the world except for D'Artagnan, so naturally half the group wanted to be the musketeers. I was young and wild, so I decided to be the cardinal's spy."

I cannot imagine Tom as a spy. I cannot imagine Tom pretending to be someone named Pierre Ferret and people calling him that instead of Tom. It seems a lot of trouble if what he really wanted to do was fence.

"And Lucia," he goes on. "Lucia made a most excellent lady-in-waiting."

"Don't even start," Lucia says. She does not say what he is not supposed to start, but she is smiling. "I'm too old for that now," she says.

"So are we both," Tom says. He does not sound like he means it. He sighs. "But you don't need a persona, Lou, unless you want to be someone else for a day."

I do not want to be someone else. It is hard enough to be Lou.

I skip all the blanks that concern the persona I do not have and read the Ritual Disclaimer at the bottom. That is what the bold print says, but I do not know exactly what it means. By signing it I agree that fencing is a dangerous sport and that any injuries I may suffer are not the fault of the tournament organizers and therefore I cannot sue them. I further agree to abide by the rules of the sport and the rulings of all referees, which will be final.

I hand the signed form to Tom, who hands it to Lucia. She sighs and puts it in her needlework basket.

THURSDAY EVENING I USUALLY WATCH TELEVISION, BUT I AM going to the tournament. Tom told me to practice every day I could. I change and drive over to Tom and Lucia's. It feels very strange driving this way on a Thursday. I notice the color of the sky, of the leaves on the trees, more than I usually do. Tom takes me outside and tells me to start doing footwork exercises, then drills of specific parry/riposte combinations.

Soon I am breathing hard. "That's good," he says. "Keep going. I'm having you do things you can do at home, since you probably won't make it over here every night."

No one else comes. In half an hour Tom puts on his mask, and we do slow and fast drills on the same moves, over and over. It is not what I expected, but I can see how it will help me. I leave by 8:30 and am too tired to go on-line and play games when I get home. It is much harder when I am fencing all the time, instead of taking turns and watching the others.

I take a shower, feeling the new bruises gingerly. Even though I am tired and stiff, I feel good. Mr. Crenshaw has not said anything about the new treatment and humans. Marjory said, "Oh. Good for you!" when she found out I was going to be in the tournament. Tom and Lucia are not angry with each other, at least not enough to quit being married.

The next day I do laundry, but on Saturday after cleaning, I go to Tom and Lucia's again for another lesson. I am not as stiff on Sunday as I was on Friday. On Monday I have another extra lesson. I am glad Tom and Lucia's special day is Tuesday because this means I do not have to change the day I do grocery shopping. Marjory is not at the store. Don is not at the store. On Wednesday, I go fencing as usual. Marjory is not there; Lucia says she is out of town. Lucia gives me special clothes for the tournament. Tom tells me not to come on Thursday, that I am ready enough.

Friday morning at 8:53 Mr. Crenshaw calls us together and says he has an announcement to make. My stomach knots.

"You are all very lucky," he says. "In today's tough economic climate I am, frankly, very surprised that this is even remotely possible, but in fact . . . you have the chance to receive a brand-new treatment at no cost to yourselves." His mouth is stretched in a big false grin; his face is shiny with the effort he is making.

He must think we are really stupid. I glance at Cameron, then Dale, then Chuy, the only ones I can see without turning my head. Their eyes are moving, too.

Cameron says, in a flat voice, "You mean the experimental treatment developed in Cambridge and reported in *Nature Neuroscience* a few weeks ago?"

Crenshaw pales and swallows. "Who told you about that?"

"It was on the Internet," Chuy says.

"It—it—" Crenshaw stops, and glares at all of us. Then he twists his mouth into a smile again. "Be that as it may, there is a new treatment, which you have the opportunity to receive at no cost to you."

"I don't want it," Linda says. "I do not need a treatment; I am fine the way I am." I turn and look at her.

Crenshaw turns red. "You are *not* fine," he says, his voice getting louder and harsher. "And you are not normal. You are autistics, you are disabled, you were hired under a special provision—"

" 'Normal' is a dryer setting," Chuy and Linda say together. They grin briefly.

"You have to adapt," Crenshaw says. "You can't expect to get special privileges forever, not when there's a treatment that will make you normal. That gym, and private offices, and all that music, and those ridiculous decorations—you can be normal and there's no need for that. It's uneconomic. It's ridiculous." He turns as if to leave and then whirls back. "It has to stop," he says. Then he does leave.

We all look at one another. Nobody says anything for several minutes. Then Chuy says, "Well, it's happened."

"I won't do it," Linda says. "They can't make me."

"Maybe they can," Chuy says. "We don't know for sure."

In the afternoon, we each get a letter by interoffice mail, a letter on paper. The letter says that due to economic pressure and the need to diversify and remain competitive, each department must reduce staff. Individuals actively taking part in research protocols are exempt from consideration for termination, the letter says. Others will be offered attractive separation allowances for voluntary separation. The letter does not specifically say that we must agree to treatment or lose our jobs, but I think that is what it means.

Mr. Aldrin comes by our building in late afternoon and calls us into the hall.

"I couldn't stop them," he says. "I tried." I think again of my mother's saying: "Trying isn't doing." Trying isn't enough. Only doing counts. I look at Mr. Aldrin, who is a nice man, and it is clear that he is not as strong as Mr. Crenshaw, who is not a nice man. Mr. Aldrin looks sad. "I'm really sorry," he says, "but maybe it's for the best," and then he leaves. That is a silly thing to say. How can it be for the best?

"We should talk," Cameron says. "Whatever I want or you want, we should talk about it. And talk to someone else—a lawyer, maybe."

"The letter says no discussion outside the office," Bailey says.

"The letter is to frighten us," I say.

"We should talk," Cameron says again. "Tonight after work."

"I do my laundry on Friday night," I say.

"Tomorrow, at the Center . . ."

"I am going somewhere tomorrow," I say. They are all looking at me; I look away. "It is a fencing tournament," I say. I am a little surprised when no one asks me about it.

"We will talk and we may ask at the Center," Cameron says. "We will bounce you about it later."

"I do not want to talk," Linda says. "I want to be left alone." She walks away. She is upset. We are all upset.

I go into my office and stare at the monitor. The data are flat and empty, like a blank screen. Somewhere in there are the patterns I am paid to find or generate, but today the only pattern I can see is closing like a trap around me, darkness swirling in from all sides, faster than I can analyze it.

I fix my mind on the schedule for tonight and tomorrow: Tom told me what to do to prepare and I will do it.

TOM PULLED INTO THE PARKING LOT OF LOU'S APARTMENT building, aware that he had never before seen where Lou lived while Lou had been in and out of his house for years. It looked like a perfectly ordinary apartment building, built sometime in the previous century. Predictably, Lou was ready on time, waiting outside with all his gear, other than his blades, neatly stowed in a duffel. He looked rested, if tense; he had all the signs of someone who had followed the advice, who had eaten well and slept adequately. He wore the outfit Lucia had helped him assemble; he looked uncomfortable in it, as most first-timers did in period costume.

"You ready?" Tom asked.

Lou looked around himself as if to check and said, "Yes. Good morning, Tom. Good morning, Lucia."

"Good morning to you," Lucia said. Tom glanced at her. They'd had one argument already about Lou; Lucia was ready to dismember anyone who gave him the least trouble, and Tom felt that Lou could handle minor problems on his own. She had been so tense about Lou lately, he thought. She and Marjory were up to something, but Lucia wouldn't explain. He hoped it wouldn't erupt at the tournament.

Lou was silent in the backseat on the way; it was restful, compared to the chatterers Tom was used to. Suddenly Lou spoke up. "Did you ever wonder," he asked, "about how fast dark is?"

"Mmm?" Tom dragged his mind back from wondering whether the middle section of his latest paper needed tightening.

"The speed of light," Lou said. "They have a value for the speed of light in a vacuum . . . but the speed of dark . . ."

"Dark doesn't have a speed," Lucia said. "It's just what's there when light isn't—it's just a word for absence."

"I think . . . I think maybe it does," Lou said.

Tom glanced in the rearview mirror; Lou's face looked a little sad. "Do you have any idea how fast it might be?" Tom asked. Lucia glanced at him; he ignored her. She always worried when he indulged Lou in his word games, but he couldn't see the harm in it.

"It's where light isn't," Lou said. "Where light hasn't come yet. It could be faster—it's always ahead."

"Or it could have no movement at all, because it's already there, in place," Tom said. "A place, not a motion."

"It isn't a *thing*," Lucia said. "It's just an abstraction, just a word for having no light. It can't have motion. . . ."

"If you're going to go that far," Tom said, "light is an abstraction of sorts. And they used to say it existed only in motion, particle, and wave, until early in this century when they stopped it."

He could see Lucia scowl without even looking at her, from the edge in her voice. "Light is real. Darkness is the absence of light."

"Sometimes dark seems darker than dark," Lou said. "Thicker."

"Do you really think it's real?" Lucia asked, half turning in the seat.

" 'Darkness is a natural phenomenon characterized by the absence of light,' " Lou's singsong delivery made it clear this was a quote. "That's from my high school general science book. But it doesn't really tell you anything. My teacher said that although the night sky looks dark between the stars, there's actually light—stars give off light in all directions, so there's light or you couldn't see them."

"Metaphorically," Tom said, "if you take knowledge as light and ignorance as dark, there does sometimes seem to be a real presence to the dark—to ignorance. Something more tactile and muscley than just lack of knowledge. A sort of will to ignorance. It would explain some politicians."

"Metaphorically," Lucia said, "you can call a whale a symbol of the desert or anything something else."

"Are you feeling all right?" Tom asked. He saw her sudden shift in the seat from the corner of his eye.

"I'm feeling annoyed," Lucia said. "And you know why."

"I'm sorry," Lou said from behind.

"Why are you sorry?" Lucia asked.

"I should not have said anything about the speed of dark," Lou said. "It has upset you."

"You did not upset me," Lucia said. "Tom did."

Tom drove on as uncomfortable silence overfilled the car. When they reached the park where the tournament would be, he hurried through the business of getting Lou signed in, his weapons checked, and then took him on a quick tour of the facilities. Lucia went off to talk to friends of hers; Tom hoped she would get over her annoyance, which upset Lou as well as himself.

After a half hour, Tom felt himself relaxing into the familiar camaraderie. He knew almost everyone; familiar conversations flowed around him.

Who was studying with whom, who had entered this tournament or that, who had won or lost. What the current quarrels were and who was not speaking. Lou seemed to be holding up well, able to greet the people Tom introduced him to. Tom coached him through a little warm-up; then it was time to bring him back to the rings for his first match.

"Now remember," Tom said, "your best chance to score is to attack immediately. Your opponent won't know your attack and you won't know his, but you are fast. Just blow past his guard and nail him, or try to. It'll shake him up anyway—"

"Hi, guys," Don said from behind Tom. "Just got here—has he fought yet?"

Trust Don to break Lou's concentration. "No—he's about to. Be with you in a minute." He turned back to Lou. "You'll do fine, Lou. Just remember—it's best three out of five, so don't worry if he does get a touch on you. You can still win. And listen to the ref. . . ." Then it was time, and Lou turned away to enter the roped-off ring. Tom found himself suddenly stricken by panic. What if he had pushed Lou into something beyond his capacity?

Lou looked as awkward as in his first year. Though his stance was technically correct, it looked stiff and contrived, not the stance of someone who could actually move.

"I told you," Don said, quietly for him. "It's too much for him; he—"

"Shut up," Tom said. "He'll hear you."


*I AM READY BEFORE TOM ARRIVES. I AM WEARING THE COS-* tume Lucia assembled for me, but I feel very peculiar wearing it in public. It does not look like normal clothes. The tall socks hug my legs all the way to the knees. The big sleeves of the shirt blow in the breeze, brushing up and down on my arms. Even though the colors are sad colors, brown and tan and dark green, I do not think Mr. Aldrin or Mr. Crenshaw would approve if they saw me in it.

"Promptness is the courtesy of kings," my fourth-grade teacher wrote on the board. She told us to copy it. She explained it. I did not understand about kings then or why we should care what kings did, but I have always understood that making people wait is rude. I do not like it when I have to wait. Tom is also on time, so I do not have to wait long.

The ride to the tournament makes me feel scared, because Lucia and Tom are arguing again. Even though Tom said it was all right, I do not feel that it is all right, and I feel that somehow it is my fault. I do not know how or why. I do not understand why if Lucia is angry about something at work she does not talk about that, instead of snapping at Tom.

At the tournament site, Tom parks on the grass, in a row with other vehicles. There is no place to plug in the batteries here. Automatically, I look at the cars and count colors and type: eighteen blue, five red, fourteen brown or beige or tan. Twenty-one have solar panels on the roof. Most people are wearing costumes. All the costumes are as odd as mine, or odder. One man wears a big flat hat covered with feathers. It looks like a mistake. Tom says it is not, that people really dressed like that centuries ago. I want to count colors, but most of the costumes have many colors, so it is harder. I like the swirling cloaks that are one color on the outside and another on the inside. It is almost like a spin spiral when they move.

First we go to a table where a woman in a long dress checks our names against a list. She hands us little metal circles with holes in them, and Lucia pulls thin ribbons out of her pocket and gives me a green one. "Put it on this," she says, "and then around your neck." Then Tom leads me over to another table with a man in puffy shorts who checks my name off on another list.

"You're up at ten-fifteen," he says. "The chart's over there"—he points to a green-and-yellow-striped tent.

The chart is made of big pieces of cardboard taped together, with lines for names like a genealogy chart, only mostly blank. Only the left-hand set of lines has been filled in. I find my name and the name of my first opponent.

"It's nine-thirty now," Tom says. "Let's take a look at the field and then find you a place to warm up."

When it is my turn and I step into the marked area, my heart is pounding and my hands are shaking. I do not know what I am doing here. I should not be here: I do not know the pattern. Then my opponent attacks and I parry. It is not a good parry—I was slow—but he did not touch me. I take a deep breath and concentrate on his movement, on his patterns.

My opponent does not seem to notice when I make touches. I am surprised, but Tom told me that some people do not call shots against them. Some of them, he said, may be too excited to feel a light or even medium touch, especially if it is their first match. It could happen to you, too, he said. This is why he has been telling me to make firmer touches. I try again, and this time the other man is rushing forward just as I thrust and I hit him too hard. He is upset and speaks to the referee, but the referee says it is his fault for rushing.

In the end, I win the bout. I am breathless, not just from the fight. It feels so different, and I do not know what the difference is. I feel lighter, as if gravity had changed, but it is not the same lightness I feel when I am near Marjory. Is it from fighting someone I did not know or from winning?

Tom shakes my hand. His face is shiny; his voice is excited. "You did it, Lou. You did a great job—"

"Yeah, you did fine," Don interrupts. "And you were a bit lucky, too. You want to watch your parries in three, Lou; I've noticed before that you don't use that often enough and when you do you really telegraph what you're going to do next—"

"Don . . ." Tom says, but Don goes on talking.

"—and when somebody charges you like that, you shouldn't be caught off-guard—"

"Don, he *won*. He did fine. Let up." Tom's eyebrows have come down.

"Yeah, yeah, I know he won, he got lucky in his first bout, but if he wants to go on winning—"

"Don, go get us something to drink." Tom sounds upset now.

Don blinks, startled. He takes the money Tom hands him. "Oh—all right. Be right back."

I do not feel lighter anymore. I feel heavier. I made too many mistakes.

Tom turns to me; he is smiling. "Lou, that's one of the best first bouts I've seen," Tom says. I think he wants me to forget what Don said, but I cannot. Don is my friend; he is trying to help me.

"I . . . I did not do what you said to do. You said attack first—"

"What you did worked. That's the meterstick here. I realized after you went up that it could have been bad advice." Tom's brow is furrowed. I do not know why.

"Yes, but if I had done what you said to do he might not have gotten the first point."

"Lou—listen to me. You did very, very well. He got the first point, but you did not fall apart. You recovered. And you won. If he had called shots fairly, you would have won sooner."

"But Don said—"

Tom shakes his head hard, as if something hurt. "Forget what Don said," he says. "In Don's first tournament, he fell apart at the first match. Completely. Then he was so upset by losing that he blew off the rest of the tournament, didn't even fight in the losers' round-robin—"

"Well, thank *you*," Don says. He is back, holding three cans of soda; he drops two of them on the ground. "I thought you were so hot on caring about people's feelings—" He stalks off with one of the cans. I can tell he is angry.

Tom sighs. "Well . . . it's true. Don't let it worry you, Lou. You did very well; you probably won't win today—first-timers never do—but you've already shown considerable poise and ability, and I'm proud that you're in our group."

"Don is really upset," I say, looking after him. I think Tom should not have said that about Don's first tournament. Tom picks up the sodas and offers me one. It fizzes over when I open it. His fizzes over, too, and he licks the foam off his fingers. I did not know that was acceptable, but I lick the foam off my fingers.

"Yes, but Don is . . . Don," Tom says. "He does this; you've seen it." I am not sure which *this* he means, Don telling other people what they did wrong or Don getting angry.

"I think he is trying to be my friend and help me," I say. "Even though he likes Marjory and I like Marjory and he probably wants her to like him, but she thinks he is a real heel."

Tom chokes on his soda and then coughs. Then he says, "You like Marjory? *Like* as in *like*, or as in *special like*?"

"I like her a lot," I say. "I wish—" But I cannot say that wish out loud.

"Marjory had a bad experience with a man something like Don," Tom says. "She will think of that other man every time she sees Don act the same way."

"Was he a fencer?" I ask.

"No. Someone she knew at work. But sometimes Don acts the way he did. Marjory doesn't like that. Of course she would like you better."

"Marjory said that Don said something not nice about me."

"Does that make you angry?" Tom asks.

"No . . . sometimes people say things because they do not understand. That's what my parents said. I think Don does not understand." I take a sip of my soda. It is not as cold as I like, but it is better than nothing.

Tom takes a long swallow of his soda. In the ring, another match has started; we edge away from it. "What we should do now," he said, staving off that problem, "is register your win with the scribe and be sure you're ready for your next bout."

At the thought of the next bout, I realize I am tired and can feel the bruises where my opponent hit me. I would like to go home now and think about everything that has happened, but there are more bouts to fight and I know Tom wants me to stay and finish.

CHAPTER SEVEN

*I* AM FACING MY SECOND OPPONENT. *IT FEELS VERY DIFFER-*
ent the second time because it is not all a surprise. This man was
wearing the hat like a pizza with feathers. Now he is wearing a
mask that's transparent in front rather than wire mesh. This kind costs a
lot more. Tom told me he is very good but very fair. He will count my
touches, Tom said. I can see the man's expression clearly; he looks almost
sleepy, his eyelids drooping over blue eyes.

The referee drops his handkerchief; my opponent leaps forward in a
blur and I feel his touch on my shoulder. I raise my hand. His sleepy expression does not mean he is slow. I want to ask Tom what to do. I do
not look around; the bout is still on and the man could make another
touch.

This time I move sideways and the man also circles; his blade leaps
out, so fast it seems to disappear and then reappear touching my chest. I
do not know how he moves so fast; I feel stiff and clumsy. I will lose
with another touch. I rush into attack, though it feels strange. I feel my
blade against his—I have parried successfully this time. Again, again—
and finally, when I lunge, I feel in my hand that I have touched something. Instantly he draws back and raises his hand. "Yes," he says. I look
at his face. He is smiling. He does not mind that I made a touch.

We circle the other way, blades flashing. I begin to see that his pattern, while rapid, is understandable, but he gets a third touch on me before I can use these data.

"Thanks," he says, at the end. "You gave me a fight."

"Good job, Lou," Tom says when I come out of the ring. "He'll probably win the tournament; he usually does."

"I got one touch," I say.

"Yes, and a good one. And you almost got him several more times."

"Is it over?" I ask.

"Not quite," Tom says. "You've lost only one bout; now you go into the pool of other one-rounders, and you'll have at least one more match. Are you doing all right?"

"Yes," I say. I am breathless and tired of the noise and movement, but I am not as ready to go home as I was earlier. I wonder if Don was watching; I do not see him anywhere.

"Want some lunch?" Tom asks.

I shake my head. I want to find a quiet place to sit down.

Tom leads me through the crowd. Several people I do not know grab my hand or slap my shoulder and say, "Good fighting." I wish they would not touch me, but I know they are being friendly.

Lucia and a woman I do not know are sitting under a tree. Lucia pats the ground. I know that means "sit here," and I sit down.

"Gunther won, but Lou got a touch on him," Tom says.

The other woman claps her hands. "That's very good," she says. "Almost nobody gets a touch on Gunther their first bout."

"It was not actually my first bout, but my first bout with Gunther," I say.

"That's what I meant," she says. She is taller than Lucia and heavier; she is wearing a fancy costume with a long skirt. She has a little frame in her hands, and her fingers work back and forth. She is weaving a narrow strip of material, a geometric pattern of brown and white. The pattern is simple, but I have never seen anyone weave before and I watch carefully until I am sure how she does it, how she makes the brown pattern change direction.

"Tom told me about Don," Lucia says, glancing at me. I feel cold suddenly. I do not want to remember how angry he was. "Are you all right?" she asks.

"I am all right," I say.

"Don, the boy wonder?" the other woman asks Lucia.

Lucia makes a face. "Yes. He can be a real jerk sometimes."

"What was it this time?" the other woman asks.

Lucia glances at me. "Oh—just the usual kind of thing. Big mouthitis."

I am glad she does not explain. I do not think he is as bad as Tom must have said. It makes me unhappy to think of Tom not being fair to someone.

Tom comes back and tells me that I have another match at 1:45. "It's another first-timer," he says. "He lost his first bout early this morning. You should eat something." He hands me a bun with meat in it. It smells all right. I am hungry. When I take a bite, it tastes good, and I eat it all.

An old man stops to talk to Tom. Tom stands up; I do not know if I should stand up, too. Something about the man catches my eye. He twitches. He talks very fast, too. I do not know what he is talking about—people I do not know, places I have not been.

In my third match, my opponent is wearing all black with red trimming. He also has one of the transparent plastic masks. He has dark hair and eyes and very pale skin; he has long sideburns trimmed to points. He does not move well, though. He is slow and not very strong. He does not carry through his attacks; he jerks his blade back and forth without coming close. I make a touch that he does not call and then a harder touch that he does. His face shows his feelings; he is both alarmed and angry. Even though I am tired, I know I can win if I want to.

It is not right to make people angry, but I would like to win. I move around him; he turns slowly, stiffly. I make another touch. His lower lip sticks out; his forehead stands up in ridges. It is not right to make people feel stupid. I slow down, but he does not make use of this. His pattern is very simple, as if he knew only two parries and attacks. When I move closer, he moves back. But standing still and exchanging blows is boring. I want him to do something. When he does not, I disengage from one of his weak parries and strike past it. His face contracts in anger, and he says a string of bad words. I know I am supposed to shake his hand and say thank you, but he has already walked off. The referee shrugs.

"Good for you," Tom says. "I saw you slow down and give him a chance for an honorable hit . . . too bad the idiot didn't know what to do with it. Now you know why I don't like my students getting into tournaments too early. He wasn't nearly ready."

He was not nearly ready. Nearly ready would be almost ready. He was not ready at all.

When I go to report my win, I find that I am now in a pool of those who have a 2:1 record. Only eight are undefeated. I am feeling very tired now, but I do not want to disappoint Tom, so I do not withdraw. My next match comes almost at once, with a tall dark woman. She wears a plain costume in dark blue and a conventional wire-front mask. She is not at all like the last man; she attacks instantly and after a few exchanges she gets the first touch. I get the second, she the third, and I the fourth. Her pattern is not easy to see. I hear voices from the margins; people are saying it is a good fight. I am feeling light again, and I am happy. Then I feel her blade on my chest and the bout is over. I do not mind. I am tired and sweaty; I can smell myself.

"Good fight!" she says, and clasps my arm.

"Thank you," I say.

Tom is pleased with me; I can tell by his grin. Lucia is there, too; I did not see her come and watch. They are arm in arm; I feel even happier. "Let's see where this puts you in the rankings," he says.

"Rankings?"

"All the fencers will be ranked by their results," he says. "Novices get a separate rank. I expect you did fairly well. There are still some to go, but I think all the first-timers have finished by now."

I did not know this. When we look at the big chart, my name is number nineteen, but down in the lower right-hand corner, where seven first-time fencers are listed, my name is at the top. "Thought so," Tom says. "Claudia—" One of the women writing names on the board turns around. "Are all the first-timers finished?"

"Yes—is this Lou Arrendale?" She glances at me.

"Yes," I say. "I am Lou Arrendale."

"You did really well for a first-timer," she says.

"Thank you," I say.

"Here's your medal," she says, reaching under the table and pulling out a little leather sack with something in it. "Or you can wait and get it at the award ceremony." I did not know I would get a medal; I thought only the person who won all the fights got a medal.

"We have to get back," Tom says.

"Well, then—here it is." She hands it to me. It feels like real leather. "Good luck next time."

"Thank you," I say.

I do not know if I am supposed to open the sack, but Tom says, "Let's see . . ." and I take out the medal. It is a round piece of metal with a sword design molded into it and a little hole near the edge. I put it back in the bag.

On the way home, I replay each match in my mind. I can remember all of it and can even slow down the way Gunther moved, so that next time—I am surprised to know that there will be a next time, that I want to do this again—I can do better against him.

I begin to understand why Tom thought this would be good for me if I have to fight Mr. Crenshaw. I went where no one knew me and competed as a normal person would. I did not need to win the tournament to know that I had accomplished something.

When I get home, I take off the sweaty clothes Lucia loaned me. She said not to wash them, because they are special; she said to hang them up and bring them over to their house on Wednesday, when I come to fencing class. I do not like the way they smell; I would like to take them back tonight or tomorrow, but she said Wednesday. I hang them over the back of the couch in the living room while I shower.

The hot water feels very good; I can see little blue marks showing from some of the touches against me. I take a long shower, until I feel completely clean, and then put on the softest sweatshirt and sweatpants I have. I feel very sleepy, but I need to see what the others e-mailed me about their talk.

I have e-mails from Cameron and Bailey both. Cameron says they talked but didn't decide anything. Bailey says who came—everyone but me and Linda—and that they asked a counselor at the Center what the rules were on human experimentation. He says Cameron made it sound like we had heard about this treatment and we wanted to try it. The counselor is supposed to find out more about the laws involved.

I go to bed early.


ON MONDAY AND TUESDAY, WE HEAR NOTHING MORE FROM Mr. Crenshaw or the company. Maybe the people who would do the treatment are not ready to try it on humans. Maybe Mr. Crenshaw has to argue them into it. I wish we knew more. I feel the way I felt standing in the ring before that first match. Not-knowing definitely seems faster than knowing.

I look again at the abstract of the journal article on-line, but I still do not understand most of the words. Even when I look them up, I still do not understand what the treatment actually does and how it does it. I am not supposed to understand it. It is not my field.

But it is my brain and my life. I want to understand it. When I first began to fence, I did not understand that, either. I did not know why I had to hold the foil a certain way or why my feet had to be pointed out from each other at an angle. I did not know any of the terms or any of the moves. I did not expect to be good at fencing; I thought my autism would get in the way, and at first it did. Now I have been in a tournament with normal people. I didn't win, but I did better than other first-timers.

Maybe I can learn more about the brain than I know now. I do not know if there will be time, but I can try.

On Wednesday, I take the costume clothes back to Tom and Lucia's. They are dry now and do not smell so bad, but I can still smell the sourness of my sweat. Lucia takes the clothes, and I go through the house to the equipment room. Tom is already in the backyard; I pick up my equipment and go out. It is chilly but still, no breeze. He is stretching, and I start stretching, too. I was stiff on Sunday and Monday, but now I am not stiff and only one bruise is still sore.

Marjory comes out into the yard.

"I was telling Marjory how well you did at the tournament," Lucia says, from behind her. Marjory is grinning at me.

"I didn't win," I say. "I made mistakes."

"You won two matches," Lucia says, "and the novice medal. You didn't make that many mistakes."

I do not know how many mistakes "that many" would be. If she means "too many," why does she say "that many"?

Here, in this backyard, I'm remembering Don and how angry he was at what Tom said about him rather than the light feeling I had when I won those two matches. Will he come tonight? Will he be angry with me? I think I should mention him, and then I think I shouldn't.

"Simon was impressed," Tom says. He is sitting up now, rubbing his blade with sandpaper to smooth out the nicks. I feel my blade and do not find any new nicks. "The referee, I mean; we've known each other for years. He really liked the way you handled yourself when that fellow didn't call hits."

"You said that was what to do," I say.

"Yeah, well, not everybody follows my advice," Tom says. "Tell me now—several days later—was it more fun or more bother?"

I had not thought of the tournament as fun, but I had not thought of it as bother, either.

"Or something else entirely?" Marjory says.

"Something else entirely," I say. "I did not think it was bother; you told me what to do to prepare, Tom, and I did that. I did not think of it as fun, but a test, a challenge."

"Did you enjoy it at all?" Tom asked.

"Yes. Parts of it very much." I do not know how to describe the mixture of feelings. "I enjoy doing new things sometimes," I say.

Someone is opening the gate. Don. I feel a sudden tension in the yard.

"Hi," he says. His voice is tight.

I smile at him, but he does not smile back.

"Hi, Don," Tom says.

Lucia says nothing. Marjory nods to him.

"I'll just get my stuff," he says, and goes into the house.

Lucia looks at Tom; he shrugs. Marjory comes up to me.

"Want a bout?" she asks. "I can't stay late tonight. Work."

"Sure," I say. I feel light again.

Now that I have fenced in the tournament, I feel very relaxed fencing here. I do not think about Don; I think only about Marjory's blade. Again I have the feeling that touching her blade is almost like touching her—that I can feel, through the steel, her every movement, even her mood. I want this to last; I slow a little, prolonging the contact, not making touches I could make so that we can keep this going. It is a very different feeling from the tournament, but *light* is the only word I can think of to describe it.

Finally she backs up; she is breathing hard. "That was fun, Lou, but you've worn me out. I'll have to take a breather."

"Thank you," I say.

We sit down side by side, both breathing hard. I time my breaths to hers. It feels good to do that.

Suddenly Don comes out of the equipment room, carrying his blades in one hand, his mask in the other. He glares at me and walks around the corner of the house, stiff-legged. Tom follows him out and shrugs, spreading his hands.

"I tried to talk him out of it," he says to Lucia. "He still thinks I insulted him on purpose at the tournament. And he only placed twentieth, behind Lou. Right now it's all my fault, and he's going to study with Gunther."

"That won't last long," Lucia says. She stretches out her legs. "He won't put up with the discipline."

"It is because of me?" I ask.

"It is because the world does not arrange itself to suit him," Tom says. "I give him a couple of weeks before he's back, pretending nothing has happened."

"And you'll let him back?" Lucia says with an edge to her voice.

Tom shrugs again. "If he behaves, sure. People do grow, Lucia."

"Crookedly, some of them," she says.

Then Max and Susan and Cindy and the others arrive in a bunch and they all speak to me. I did not see them at the tournament, but they all saw me. I feel embarrassed that I didn't notice, but Max explains.

"We were trying to stay out of your way, so you could concentrate. You only want one or two people talking to you at a time like that," he says. That would make sense if other people also had trouble concentrating. I did not know they thought that way; I thought they wanted lots of people around all the time.

Maybe if the things I was told about myself were not all correct, the things I was told about normal people were also not all correct.

I fence with Max and then Cindy and sit down next to Marjory until she says she has to go. I carry her bag out to her car for her. I would like to spend more time with her, but I am not sure how to do it. If I met someone like Marjory—someone I liked—at a tournament, and she did not know I was autistic, would it be easier to ask that person out to dinner? What would that person say? What would Marjory say if I asked her? I stand beside the car after she gets in and wish I had already said the words and was waiting for her answer. Emmy's angry voice rings in my head. I do not believe she is right; I do not believe that Marjory sees me only as my diagnosis, as a possible research subject. But I do not *not* believe it enough to ask her out to dinner. I open my mouth and no words come out: silence is there before sound, faster than I can form the thought.

Marjory is looking at me; I am suddenly cold and stiff with shyness. "Good night," I say.

"Good-bye," she says. "See you next week." She turns on the engine; I back away.

When I get back to the yard, I sit beside Lucia. "If a person asks a person to dinner," I say, "then if the person who is asked does not want to go, is there any way to tell before the person who is asking asks?"

She does not answer for a time I think is over forty seconds. Then she says, "If a person is acting friendly toward a person, that person will not mind being asked but still might not want to go. Or might have something else to do that night." She pauses again. "Have you ever asked someone out to dinner, Lou?"

"No," I say. "Not except people I work with. They are like me. That is different."

"Indeed it is," she says. "Are you thinking of asking someone to dinner?"

My throat closes. I cannot say anything, but Lucia does not keep asking. She waits.

"I am thinking of asking Marjory," I say at last, in a soft voice. "But I do not want to bother her."

"I don't think she'd be bothered, Lou," Lucia says. "I don't know if she'd come, but I don't think she would be upset at all by your asking."

At home and that night in bed I think of Marjory sitting across a table from me, eating. I have seen things like this in videos. I do not feel ready to do it yet.

*THURSDAY MORNING I COME OUT THE DOOR OF MY APART-* ment and look across the lot to my car. It looks strange. All four tires are splayed out on the pavement. I do not understand. I bought those tires only a few months ago. I always check the air pressure when I buy gas, and I bought gas three days ago. I do not know why they are flat. I have only one spare, and even though I have a foot pump in the car, I know that I cannot pump up three tires fast enough. I will be late for work. Mr. Crenshaw will be angry. Sweat is trickling down my ribs already.

"What happened, buddy?" It is Danny Bryce, the policeman who lives here.

"My tires are flat," I say. "I don't know why. I checked the air yesterday."

He comes closer. He is in uniform; he smells like mint and lemon, and his uniform smells like a laundry. His shoes are very shiny. He has a name tag on his uniform shirt that says DANNY BRYCE in little black letters on silver.

"Somebody slashed 'em," he says. He sounds serious but not angry.

"Slashed them?" I have read about this, but it has never happened to me. "Why?"

"Mischief," he says, leaning over to look. "Yup. Definitely a vandal."

He looks at the other cars. I look, too. None of them have flat tires, except for one tire of the old flatbed trailer that belongs to the apartment building owner, and it has been flat for a long time. It looks gray, not black. "And yours is the only one. Who's mad at you?"

"Nobody is mad at me yet. I haven't seen anyone today yet. Mr. Crenshaw is going to be mad at me," I say. "I am going to be late for work."

"Just tell him what happened," he says.

Mr. Crenshaw will be angry anyway, I think, but I do not say that. Do not argue with a policeman.

"I'll call this in for you," he says. "They'll send someone out—"

"I have to go to work," I say. I can feel myself sweating more and more. I can't think what to do first. I don't know the transit schedule, though I do know where the stop is. I need to find a schedule. I should call the office, but I don't know if anyone will be there yet.

"You really should report this," he says. His face has sagged down, a serious expression. "Surely you can call your boss and let him know. . . ."

I do not know Mr. Crenshaw's extension at work. I think if I call him he will just yell at me. "I will call him afterward," I say.

It takes only sixteen minutes before a police car arrives. Danny Bryce stays with me instead of going to work. He does not say much, but I feel better with him there. When the police car arrives, a man wearing tan slacks and a brown sports coat gets out of the car. He does not have a name tag. Mr. Bryce walks over to the car, and I hear the other man call him Dan.

Mr. Bryce and the officer who came are talking; their eyes glance toward me and then away. What is Mr. Bryce saying about me? I feel cold; it is hard to focus my vision. When they start walking toward me, they seem to move in little jumps, as if the light were hopping.

"Lou, this is Officer Stacy," Mr. Bryce says, smiling at me. I look at the other man. He is shorter than Mr. Bryce and thinner; he has sleek black hair that smells of something oily and sweet.

"My name is Lou Arrendale," I say. My voice sounds odd, the way it sounds when I am scared.

"When did you last see your car before this morning?" he asks.

"Nine forty-seven last night," I tell him. "I am sure because I looked at my watch."

He glances at me, then enters something on his handcomp.

"Do you park in the same spot every time?"

"Usually," I say. "The parking places aren't numbered, and sometimes someone else is there when I get home from work."

"You got home from work at nine"—he glances down at his handcomp—"forty-seven last night?"

"No, sir," I say. "I got home from work at five fifty-two, and then I went—" I don't want to say "to my fencing class." What if he thinks there is something wrong with fencing? With me fencing? "To a friend's house," I say instead.

"Is this someone you visit often?"

"Yes. Every week."

"Were there other people there?"

Of course there were other people there. Why would I go visit someone if nobody but me was there? "My friends who live in that house were there," I say. "And some people who do not live in that house."

He blinks and looks briefly at Mr. Bryce. I do not know what that look means. "Ah . . . do you know these other people? Who didn't live in the house? Was it a party?"

Too many questions. I do not know which to answer first. *These other people?* Does he meant the people at Tom and Lucia's who were not Tom and Lucia? *Who didn't live in the house?* Most people did not live in that house . . . do not live in that house. Out of the billions of people in the world, only two people live in that house and that is . . . less than one-millionth of one percent.

"It was not a party," I say, because that is the easiest question to answer.

"I know you go out every Wednesday night," Mr. Bryce says. "Sometimes you're carrying a duffel bag—I thought maybe you went to a gym."

If they talk to Tom or Lucia, they will find out about the fencing. I will have to tell them now. "It is . . . it is a fencing . . . fencing class," I say. I hate it when I stutter or maze.

"Fencing? I've never seen you with blades," Mr. Bryce says. He sounds surprised and also interested.

"I—I keep my things at their house," I say. "They are my instructors. I do not want to have things like that in my car or in my apartment."

"So—you went to a friend's house for a fencing class," the other policeman says. "And you've been doing it—how long?"

"Five years," I say.

"So anyone who wanted to mess with your car would know that? Would know where you were on Wednesday nights?"

"Maybe. . . ." I don't think that, really. I think someone who wanted to damage my car would know where I lived, not where I went when I went out.

"You get along with these people okay?" the officer asks.

"Yes." I think it is a silly question; I would not keep going for five years if they weren't nice people.

"We'll need a name and contact number."

I give him Tom's and Lucia's names and their primary contact number. I do not understand why he needs that, because the car was not damaged at Tom and Lucia's house, but here.

"Probably just vandals," the officer says. "This neighborhood's been quiet for a while, but over across Broadway there've been a lot of tire slashings and broken windshields. Some kid decided it was getting hot over there and came over here. Something could've scared him before he did more than yours." He turned to Mr. Bryce. "Let me know if anything else happens, okay?"

"Sure."

The officer's handcomp buzzes and extrudes a slip of paper. "Here you are—report, case number, investigating officer, everything you need for your insurance claim." He hands me the paper. I feel stupid; I have no idea what to do with it. He turns away.

Mr. Bryce looks at me. "Lou, do you know who to call about the tires?"

"No. . . ." I am more worried about work than about the tires. If I do not have a car, I can ride public transit, but if I lose the job because I am late again, I will have nothing.

"You need to contact your insurance company, and you need to get someone to replace those tires."

Replacing the tires will be expensive. I do not know how I can drive the car to the auto center on four flat tires.

"You want some help?"

I want the day to be some other day, when I am in my car and driving to work on time. I do not know what to say; I want help only because I do not know what to do. I would like to know what to do so that I do not need help.

"If you haven't had to file an insurance claim before, it can be confusing. But I don't want to butt in where you don't want me." Mr. Bryce's expression is one I do not completely understand. Part of his face looks a little sad, but part looks a little angry.

"I have never filed an insurance claim," I say. "I need to learn how to file an insurance claim if I am supposed to file one now."

"Let's go up to your apartment and log on," he says. "I can guide you through it."

For a moment I cannot move or speak. Someone come to my apartment? Into my private space? But I need to know what to do. He knows what I should do. He is trying to help. I did not expect him to do that.

I start toward the apartment building without saying anything else. After a few steps I remember that I should have said something. Mr. Bryce is still standing beside my car. "That is nice," I say. I do not think that is the right thing to say, but Mr. Bryce seems to understand it, for he follows me.

My hands are trembling as I unlock the apartment door. All the serenity that I have created here disappears into the walls, out the windows, and the place is full of tension and fear. I turn on my home system and toggle it quickly to the company 'net. The sound comes up with the Mozart I left on last night, and I turn it down. I need the music, but I do not know what he will think of it.

"Nice place," Mr. Bryce says from behind me. I jump a little, even though I know he is there. He moves to the side, where I can see him. That is a little better. He leans closer. "Now what you need to do is—"

"Tell my supervisor I am late," I say. "I have to do that first."

I have to look up Mr. Aldrin's E-mail on the company Web site. I have not ever e-mailed him from outside before. I do not know how to explain, so I put it very plain:

*I am late because my car's tires were all cut and flat this morning, and the police came. I will come as fast as I can.*

Mr. Bryce does not look at the screen while I'm typing; that is good. I toggle back to the public 'net. "I told him," I say.

"Okay, then, what you need to do now is file with your insurance company. If you have a local agent, start there—either the agent or the company or both will have a site."

I am already searching. I do not have a local agent. The company site comes up, and I quickly navigate through "client services," "auto policies," and "new claims" to find a form on-screen.

"You're good at that," Mr. Bryce says. His voice has the lift that means he is surprised.

"It is very clear," I say. I enter my name and address, pull in my policy number from my personal files, enter the date, and mark the "yes" box for "adverse incident reported to police?"

Other blanks I do not understand. "That's the police incident report number," Mr. Bryce says, pointing to one line on the slip of paper I was given. "And that's the investigating officer's code number, which you enter *there*, and his name *here*." I notice that he does not explain what I have figured out on my own. He seems to understand what I can and cannot follow. I write "in your own words" an account of what happened, which I did not see. I parked my car at night, and in the morning all four tires were flat. Mr. Bryce says that is enough.

After I file the insurance claim, I have to find someone to work on the tires.

"I can't tell you who to call," Mr. Bryce says. "We had a mess about that last year, and people accused the police of getting kickbacks from service outlets." I do not know what "kickback" is. Ms. Tomasz, the apartment manager, stops me on my way back downstairs to say that she knows someone who can do it. She gives me a contact number. I do not know how she knows what happened but Mr. Bryce does not seem surprised that she knows. He acts like this is normal. Could she have heard us talking in the parking lot? That thought makes me feel uncomfortable.

"And I'll give you a ride to the transit station," Mr. Bryce says. "Or I'll be late for work myself."

I did not know that he did not drive to work every day. It is kind of him to give me a ride. He is acting like a friend. "Thank you, Mr. Bryce," I say.

He shakes his head. "I told you before: call me Danny, Lou. We're neighbors."

"Thank you, Danny," I say.

He smiles at me, gives a quick nod, and unlocks the doors of his car. His car is very clean inside, like mine but without the fleece on the seat. He turns on his sound system; it is loud and bumpy and makes my insides quiver. I do not like it, but I like not having to walk to the transit station.

The station and the shuttle are both crowded and noisy. It is hard to stay calm and focus enough to read the signs that tell me what ticket to buy and at which gate to stand in line.

CHAPTER EIGHT

*I*T FEELS VERY STRANGE TO SEE THE CAMPUS FROM THE transit station and not the drive and parking lot. Instead of showing my ID tag to the guard at the car entrance, I show it to a guard at the station exit. Most people on this shift are already at work; the guard glares at me before he jerks his head telling me to go through. Wide sidewalks edged with flower beds lead to the administration building. The flowers are orange and yellow with puffy-looking blossoms; the color seems to shimmer in the sunlight. At the administration building, I have to show my ID to another guard.

"Why didn't you park where you're supposed to?" he asks. He sounds angry.

"Someone slashed my tires," I say.

"Bummer," he says. His face sags; his eyes go back to his desk. I think maybe he is disappointed that he has nothing to be angry about.

"What is the shortest way from here to Building Twenty-one?" I ask.

"Through this building, angle right around the end of Fifteen, then past the fountain with the naked woman on a horse. You can see your parking lot from there." He does not even look up.

I go through Administration, with its ugly green marble floor and its unpleasantly strong lemon smell, and out again into the bright sun. It is already much hotter than it was earlier. Sunlight glares off the walks. Here there are no flower beds; grass comes right up to the pavement.

I am sweating by the time I get to our building and put my ID in the door lock. I can smell myself. It is not a good smell. Inside the building, it is cool and dim and I can relax. The soft color of the walls, the steady glow of old-fashioned lighting, the nonscent of the cool air— all this soothes me. I go directly to my office and turn the AC fan up to high.

My office machine is on, as usual, with a blinking message icon. I turn on one of the whirlies, and my music—Bach, an orchestral version of "Sheep May Safely Graze"—before bringing up the message:

Call as soon as you arrive. [Signed] Mr. Crenshaw, Extension 2313.

I reach for the office phone, but it buzzes before I can pick it up.

"I told you to call as soon as you got to the office," Mr. Crenshaw's voice says.

"I just got here," I say.

"You checked through the main gate twenty minutes ago," he says. He sounds very angry. "It shouldn't take even you twenty minutes to walk that far."

I should say I am sorry, but I am not sorry. I do not know how long it took me to walk from the gate, and I do not know how fast I could have walked if I had tried to walk faster. It was too hot to hurry. I do not know how much more I could do than what I have done. I feel my neck getting tight and hot.

"I did not stop," I say.

"And what's this about a flat tire? Can't you change a tire? You're over two hours late."

"Four tires," I say. "Someone slashed all four tires."

"Four! I suppose you reported it to the police," he says.

"Yes," I say.

"You could have waited until after work," he says. "Or called from work."

"The policeman was there," I say.

"There? Someone saw your car being vandalized?"

"No—" Against the impatience and anger in his voice I am struggling to interpret his words; they sound farther and farther away, less like meaningful speech. It is hard to think what the right answer is. "The policeman who lives with—in my apartment house. He saw the flat tires. He called in the other policeman. He told me what to do."

"He should have told you to go to work," Crenshaw says. "There was no reason for you to hang around. You'll have to make the time up, you know."

"I know." I wonder if he has to make the time up when something delays him. I wonder if he has ever had a flat tire, or four flat tires, on the way to work.

"Be sure you don't put it down as overtime," he says, and clicks off. He did not say he was sorry I had four flat tires. That is the conventional thing to say, "too bad" or "how awful," but although he is normal, he did not say either of those things. Maybe he is not sorry; maybe he has no sympathy to express. I had to learn to say conventional things even when I did not feel them, because that is part of *fitting in* and *learning to get along*. Has anyone ever asked Mr. Crenshaw to fit in, to get along?

It would be my lunch hour, though I am behind, needing to make up time. I feel hollow inside; I start for the office kitchenette and realize that I do not have anything for lunch. I must have left it on the counter when I went back to my apartment to file the insurance claim. There is nothing in the refrigerator box with my initials on it. I had emptied it the day before.

We have no food vending machine in our building. Nobody would eat the food and it spoiled, so they took the machine away. The company has a dining hall across the campus, and there is a vending machine in the next building over. The food in those machines is awful. If it is a sandwich, all the parts of the sandwich are mushed together and slimy with mayonnaise or salad dressing. Green stuff, red stuff, meat chopped up with other flavors. Even if I take one apart and scrape the bread clean of mayonnaise, the smell and taste linger and are on whatever meat it is. The sweet things—the doughnuts and rolls—are sticky, leaving disgusting smears on the plastic containers when you take them out. My stomach twists, imagining this.

I would drive out and buy something, even though we don't usually leave at lunch, but my car is still at the apartment, forlorn on its flat tires. I do not want to walk across the campus and eat in that big, noisy room with people I do not know, people who think of us as weird and dangerous. I do not know if the food there would be any better.

"Forget your lunch?" Eric asks. I jump. I have not talked to any of the others yet.

"Someone cut the tires on my car," I say. "I was late. Mr. Crenshaw is angry with me. I left my lunch at home by accident. My car is at home."

"You are hungry?"

"Yes. I do not want to go to the dining hall."

"Chuy is going to run errands at lunch," Eric says.

"Chuy does not like anyone to ride with him," Linda says.

"I can talk to Chuy," I say.

Chuy agrees to pick up some lunch for me. He is not going to a grocery store, so I will have to eat something he can pick up easily. He comes back with apples and a sausage in a bun. I like apples but not sausage. I do not like the little mixed-up bits in it. It is not as bad as some things, though, and I am hungry, so I eat it and do not think about it much.

It is 4:16 when I remember that I have not called anyone to replace the tires on my car. I call up the local directory listings and print the list of numbers. The on-line listings show the locations, so I begin with the ones closest to my apartment. When I contact them, one after another tells me it is too late to do anything today.

"Quickest thing to do," one of them says, "is buy four mounted tires and put them on yourself, one at a time." It would cost a lot of money to buy four tires and wheels, and I do not know how I would get them home. I do not want to ask Chuy for another favor so soon.

It is like those puzzle problems with a man, a hen, a cat, and a bag of feed on one side of a river and a boat that will hold only two, which he must use to transfer them all to the other side, without leaving alone the cat and the hen or the hen and the bag of feed. I have four slashed tires and one spare tire. If I put on the spare tire and roll the tire from that wheel to the tire store, they can put on a new tire and I can roll it back, put it on, then take the next slashed tire. Three of those, and I will have four whole tires on the car and can drive the car, with the last bad tire, to the store.

The nearest tire store is a mile away. I do not know how long it will take me to roll the flat tire—longer than it would one with air in it, I guess. But this is the only thing I can think of. They would not let me on the transit with a tire, even if it went the right direction.

The tire store stays open until nine. If I work my two extra hours tonight and can get home by eight, then surely I can get that tire to the store before they close. Tomorrow if I leave work on time, I might be able to do two more.

I am home by 7:43. I unlock the trunk of my car and wrestle out the spare. I learned to change a tire in my driving class, but I have not changed a tire since. It is simple in theory, but it takes longer than I want. The jack is hard to position, and the car doesn't go up very fast. The front end sags down onto the wheels; the flat tires make a dull squnch as the tread rubs on itself. I am breathless and sweating a lot when I finally get the wheel off and the spare positioned on it. There is something about the order in which you are supposed to tighten the lug nuts, but I do not remember it exactly. Ms. Melton said it was important to do it right. It is after eight now and dark around the edges of the lights.

"Hey—!"

I jerk upright. I do not recognize the voice at first or the dark bulky figure rushing at me. It slows.

"Oh—it's you, Lou. I thought maybe it was the vandal, come to do more mischief. What'd you do, buy a new set of wheels?"

It's Danny. I feel my knees sag with relief. "No. It is the spare. I will put the spare on, then take the tire to the tire store and have them put on another, and then when I come back I can change that for a bad one. Tomorrow I can do another."

"You—but you could have called someone to come do all four for you. Why are you doing it the hard way?"

"They could not do it until tomorrow or the next day, they said. One place told me to buy a set of tires on rims and change them myself if I wanted it done faster. So I thought about it. I remembered my spare.

I thought how to do it myself and save money and time and decided to start when I got home—"

"You just got home?"

"I was late to work this morning. I worked late today to make up for it. Mr. Crenshaw was very angry."

"Yes, but—it's still going to take you several days. Anyway, the store closes in less than an hour. Were you going to take a cab or something?"

"I will roll it," I say. The wheel with its saggy flat tire mocks me; it was hard enough to roll to one side. When we changed a tire in driving class, the tire had air in it.

"On foot?" Danny shakes his head. "You'll never make it, buddy. Better put it in my car and I'll run you over. Too bad we can't take two of them. . . . Or, actually, we can."

"I do not have two spares," I say.

"You can use mine," he says. "We have the same wheel size." I did not know this. We do not have the same make and model of car, and not all have the same size. How would he know? "You do remember to tighten the ones across from each other—partway—then the others, then tighten the rest of the way in opposites, right? You keep your car so carefully, you may've never needed to know that."

I bend to tighten the lug nuts. With his words, I remember exactly what Ms. Melton said. It is a pattern, an easy pattern. I like patterns with symmetry. By the time I have finished, Danny is back with his spare, glancing at his watch.

"We're going to have to hurry," he says. "Do you mind if I do the next one? I'm used to it—"

"I do not mind," I say. I am not telling the whole truth. If he is right that I can take two tires in tonight, then that is a big help, but he is pushing into my life, rushing me, making me feel slow and stupid. I do mind that. Yet he is acting like a friend, being helpful. It is important to be grateful for help.

At 8:21, both spares are on the back of my car; it looks funny with flat tires in front and full tires behind. Both slashed tires we took off the back of my car are in the trunk of Danny's car, and I am sitting beside him. Again he turns on the sound system and rattling booms shake my body. I want to jump out of there; it is too much sound and the wrong sound. He talks over the sound, but I cannot understand him; the sound and his voice clash.

When we get to the tire store, I help him lug the flat tires on their wheels into the store. The clerk looks at me with almost no expression. Before I can even explain what I want, he is shaking his head.

"It's too late," he says. "We can't change out tires now."

"You are open until nine," I say.

"The desk, yes. But we don't put tires on this late." He glances at the door to the shop, where a lanky man in dark-blue pants and a tan shirt with a patch on it is leaning on the frame, wiping his hands on a red rag.

"But I could not get here earlier," I say. "And you are open until nine."

"Look, mister," the clerk says. One side of his mouth has lifted, but it is not a smile or even half a smile. "I told you—you're too late. Even if we would put tires on now, it'd keep us after nine. I'll bet *you* don't stay late just to finish a job some idiot dumped on you at the last minute."

I open my mouth to say that I do stay late, I stayed late today, and that is why I'm late here, but Danny has moved forward. The man at the desk suddenly stands taller and looks alarmed. But Danny is looking at the man by the door.

"Hello, Fred," he says, in a happy voice, as if he had just met a friend. But under that is another voice. "How's it going these days?"

"Ah . . . fine, Mr. Bryce. Staying clean."

He does not look clean. He has black marks on his hands and dirty fingernails. His pants and shirt have black marks, too.

"That's good, Fred. Look—my friend here had his car vandalized last night. Had to work late because he was late to work this morning. I was really hoping you could help him out."

The man by the door looks at the man behind the desk. Their eyebrows go up and down at each other. The man behind the desk shrugs. "You'll have to close," he said. Then to me, "I suppose you know what kind of tire you want?"

I do know. I bought tires here only a few months ago, so I know what to say. He writes down the numbers and type and hands it to the other man—Fred—who nods and comes forward to take the wheels from me.

It is 9:07 when Danny and I leave with the two whole tires. Fred rolls them out to Danny's car and slings them into the trunk. I am very tired. I do not know why Danny is helping me. I do not like the thought of his spare on my car; it feels wrong, like a lump of fish in a beef stew. When we get back to the apartment house parking lot, he helps me put the two good new tires on the front wheels of my car and the slashed tires from the front into my trunk. It is only then that I realize this means I can drive to work in the morning and at noon I can replace both slashed tires.

"Thank you," I say. "I can drive now."

"That you can," Danny says. He smiles, and it is a real smile. "And I have a suggestion: move your car tonight. Just in case that vandal comes back. Put it over there, toward the back. I'll put an alarm call on it; if anyone touches it I'll hear the alarm."

"That is a good idea," I say. I am so tired it is very hard to say this.

"Por nada," Danny says. He waves and goes into the building.

I get into my car. It smells a little musty, but the seat feels right. I am shaking. I turn on the engine and then the music—the *real* music—and slowly back out, turn the wheel, and edge past the other cars to the slot Danny suggested. It is next to his car.

IT IS HARD TO GO TO SLEEP EVEN THOUGH—OR MAYBE because—I am so tired. My back and legs ache. I keep thinking I hear things and jerk awake. I turn on my music, Bach again, and finally drift to sleep on that gentle tide.

Morning comes too soon, but I jump up and take another shower. I hurry downstairs and do not see my car. I feel cold inside until I remember that it is not in the usual place and walk around the side of the building to find it. It looks fine. I go back inside to eat breakfast and fix my lunch and meet Danny on the stairs.

"I will get the tires replaced at noon," I tell him. "I will return your spare this evening."

"No hurry," he says. "I'm not driving today anyway."

I wonder if he means that. He meant it when he helped me. I will do it anyway, because I do not like his spare; it does not match because it is not mine.


WHEN I GET TO WORK, FIVE MINUTES EARLY, MR. CRENSHAW and Mr. Aldrin are standing in the hall, talking. Mr. Crenshaw looks at me. His eyes look shiny and hard; it does not feel good to look at them, but I try to keep eye contact.

"No flat tires today, Arrendale?"

"No, Mr. Crenshaw," I say.

"Did the police find that vandal?"

"I don't know." I want to get to my office, but he is standing there and I would have to push past him. It is not polite to do that.

"Who's the investigating officer?" Mr. Crenshaw asks.

"I do not remember his name, but I have his card," I say, and pull out my wallet.

Mr. Crenshaw makes a twitch with his shoulders and shakes his head. The little muscles near his eyes have tightened. "Never mind," he says. Then, to Mr. Aldrin, "Come on, let's get over to my office and hash this out." He turns away, his shoulders hunched a little, and Mr. Aldrin follows. Now I can get to my office.

I do not know why Mr. Crenshaw asked the policeman's name but then did not look at his card. I would like to ask Mr. Aldrin to explain, but he has gone away, too. I do not know why Mr. Aldrin, who is normal, follows Mr. Crenshaw around that way. Is he afraid of Mr. Crenshaw? Are normal people afraid of other people like that? And if so, what is the benefit of being normal? Mr. Crenshaw said if we took the treatment and become normal, we could get along with other people more easily, but I wonder what he means by "get along with." Perhaps he wants everyone to be like Mr. Aldrin, following him around. We would not get our work done if we did that.

I put this out of my mind when I start again on my project.

At noon, I take the tires to another tire store, near the campus, and leave them to be replaced. I have the size and kind of tire I want written down and hand that to the desk clerk. She is about my age, with short dark hair; she is wearing a tan shirt with a patch embroidered in red that says: *Customer Service*.

"Thanks," she says. She smiles at me. "You would not believe how many people come in here with no idea what size tire they need and start waving their hands."

"It is easy to write it down," I say.

"Yes, but they don't think of that. Are you going to wait or come back later?"

"Come back later," I say. "How late are you open?"

"Until nine. Or you could come tomorrow."

"I will come before nine," I say. She runs my bankcard through the machine and marks the order slip "Paid in Advance."

"Here's your copy," she says. "Don't lose it—though someone smart enough to write down the tire size is probably smart enough not to lose his order slip."

I walk back out to the car breathing easier. It is easy to fool people into thinking I am like everyone else in encounters like this. If the other person likes to talk, as this woman did, it is easier. All I have to say are a few conventional things and smile and it is done.

Mr. Crenshaw is in our hall again when I get back, three minutes before the end of our official lunchtime. His face twitches when he sees me. I do not know why. He turns around almost at once and walks away. He does not speak to me. Sometimes when people do not speak, they are angry, but I do not know what I have done to make him angry. I have been late twice lately, but neither time was my fault. I did not cause the traffic accident, and I did not cut my own tires.

It is hard to settle down to work.

I am home by 7:00, with my own tires on all four wheels and Danny's spare in the trunk along with mine. I decide to park next to Danny's car although I do not know if he is home. It will be easier to move his spare from one car to another if they are close together.

I knock on his door. "Yes?" His voice.

"It is Lou Arrendale," I say. "I have your spare in my trunk."

I hear his footsteps coming to the door. "Lou, I told you—you didn't have to rush. But thanks." He opens the door. He has the same multi-toned brown/beige/rust carpet on the floor that I have, though I covered mine with something that didn't make my eyes hurt. He has a large dark-gray video screen; the speakers are blue and do not match as a set. His couch is brown with little dark squares on the brown; the pattern is regular, but it clashes with the carpet. A young woman is sitting on the couch; she has on a yellow, green, and white patterned shirt that clashes with both the carpet and the couch. He glances back at her. "Lyn, I'm going to go move my spare from Lou's car to mine."

"Okay." She doesn't sound interested; she looks down at the table. I wonder if she is Danny's girlfriend. I did not know he had a girlfriend. I wonder, not for the first time, why a woman friend is called a girlfriend and not a womanfriend.

Danny says, "Come on in, Lou, while I get my keys." I do not want to come in, but I do not want to seem unfriendly, either. The clashing colors and patterns make my eyes tired. I step in. Danny says, "Lyn, this is Lou from upstairs—he borrowed my spare yesterday."

"Hi," she says, glancing up and then down.

"Hi," I say. I watch Danny as he walks over to a desk and picks up his keys. The desk is very neat on top, a blotter and a telephone.

We go downstairs and out to the parking lot. I unlock my trunk and Danny swings the spare tire out. He opens his trunk and puts it in, then slams his trunk. It makes a different sound than mine does.

"Thank you for your help," I say.

"No problemo," Danny says. "Glad to be of service. And thanks for getting my spare back to me so quickly."

"You're welcome," I say. It does not feel right to say "you're welcome" when he did more to help me, but I do not know what else to say.

He stands there, looking at me. He does not say anything for a moment; then he says, "Well, be seeing you," and turns away. Of course he will be seeing me; we live in the same building. I think this means he does not want to walk back inside with me. I do not know why he could not just say that, if that is what he means. I turn to my car and wait until I hear the front door open and close.

If I took the treatment, would I understand this? Is it because of the woman in his apartment? If I had Marjory visiting me, would I not want Danny to walk back inside with me? I do not know. Sometimes it seems obvious why normal people do things and other times I cannot understand it at all.

Finally I go inside and up to my apartment. I put on quieting music, Chopin preludes. I put two cups of water in the small saucepan and open a packet of noodles and vegetables. As the water boils, I watch the bubbles rise. I can see the pattern of the burner below by the location of the first bubbles, but when the water really boils, it forms several cells of fast-bubbling water. I keep thinking there is something important about that, something more than just a rolling boil, but I haven't figured the whole pattern out yet. I drop the noodles and vegetables in and stir, as the directions say to do. I like to watch the vegetables churn in the boiling water.

And sometimes I am bored by the silly dancing vegetables.

ON FRIDAYS I DO MY LAUNDRY, SO THAT I HAVE THE weekend free. I have two laundry baskets, one for light and one for dark. I take the sheets off the bed and the pillowcase off the pillow and put them in the light basket. The towels go in the dark basket. My mother used two pale-blue plastic baskets for sorted clothes; she called one dark and one light, and that bothered me. I found a dark-green wicker basket and use it for dark clothes; my basket for light clothes is plain wicker, a sort of honey color. I like the woven pattern of the wicker, and I like the word *wicker.* The strands go out around the uprights like the *wih* sound of *wicker* and then comes the sharp *k,* like the stick the strands bend around, and the soft *er* sound as they bend back into the shadow.

I take the exact right change out of my change box, plus one extra coin in case one of them won't work in the machines. It used to make me angry when a perfectly round coin would not make the machine go. My mother taught me to take an extra coin. She said it is not good to stay angry. Sometimes a coin will work in the soft drink machine when it does not work in the washing machine or dryer, and sometimes one that will not work in the soft drink machine will work in the washing machine. This does not make sense, but it is how the world is.

I put the coins in my pocket, tuck the packet of detergent in the light basket, and set the light basket on top of the dark one. Light should go on top of dark. That balances.

I can just see over them to walk down the hall. I fix the Chopin prelude in my mind and head for the laundry room. As usual on Friday nights, only Miss Kimberly is there. She is old, with fuzzy gray hair, but not as old as Miss Watson. I wonder if she thinks about the life extension treatments or if she is too old. Miss Kimberly is wearing light-green knit slacks and a flowered top. She usually wears this on Fridays when it is warm. I think about what she wears instead of the smell in the laundry room. It is a harsh, sharp smell that I do not like.

"Good evening, Lou," she says now. She has already done her wash and is putting her things into the left-hand dryer. She always uses the left-hand dryer.

"Good evening, Miss Kimberly," I say. I do not look at her washing; it is rude to look at women's washing because it may have underwear in it. Some women do not want men looking at their underwear. Some do and that makes it confusing, but Miss Kimberly is old and I do not think she wants me to see the pink puckery things in among the sheets and towels. I do not want to see them anyway.

"Did you have a good week?" she asks. She always asks this. I do not think she really cares whether I had a good week or not.

"My tires were slashed," I say.

She stops putting things in the dryer and looks at me. "Someone slashed your tires? Here? Or at work?"

I do not know why that makes a difference. "Here," I say. "I came out Thursday morning and they were all flat."

She looks upset. "Right here in this parking lot? I thought it was safe here!"

"It was very inconvenient," I say. "I was late to work."

"But . . . vandals! Here!" Her face makes a shape I have never seen on it before. It is something like fear and something like disgust. Then she looks angry, staring right at me as if I had done something wrong. I look away. "I'll have to move," she says.

I do not understand: why does she have to move because my tires were slashed? No one could slash her tires, because she has no tires. She does not have a car.

"Did you see who did it?" she asks. She has left part of her wash hanging over the edge of the machine; it looks very messy and unpleasant, like food hanging over the edge of a plate.

"No," I say. I take the light things out of the light basket and put them in the right-hand washing machine. I add the detergent, measuring carefully because it is wasteful to use too much and things will not be clean if I do not use enough. I put the coins in the slot, close the door, set the machine for warm wash, cool rinse, regular cycle, and push the START button. Inside the machine, something goes *thunk* and water hisses through the valves.

"It's terrible," Miss Kimberly says. She is scooping the rest of her wash into the dryer, the movements of her hands jerky. Something puckery and pink falls to the floor; I turn away and lift clothes out of the dark basket. I put them into the middle washer. "It's all right for people like you," she says.

"What is all right for people like me?" I ask. She has never talked this way before.

"You're young," she says. "And a man. You don't have to worry."

I do not understand. I am not young, according to Mr. Crenshaw. I am old enough to know better. I am a man, but I do not see why this means it is all right for my tires to be slashed.

"I did not want my tires slashed," I say, speaking slowly because I do not know what she will do.

"Well, of course you didn't," she says, all in a rush. Usually her skin looks pale and yellowish in the lights of the laundry room, but now peach-colored patches glow on her cheeks. "But you don't have to worry about people jumping on you. Men."

I look at Miss Kimberly and cannot imagine anyone jumping on her. Her hair is gray and her pink scalp shows through it on top; her skin is wrinkled and she has brown spots on her arms. I want to ask if she is serious, but I know she is serious. She does not laugh, even at me when I drop something.

"I am sorry you are worried," I say, shaking detergent into the washer full of dark things. I put the coins into the slot. The dryer door bangs shut; I had forgotten about the dryer, trying to understand Miss

Kimberly, and my hand jerks. One of the coins misses the slot and falls into the wash. I will have to take everything out to find it, and the detergent will spill off the clothes onto the washer. I feel a buzzing in my head.

"Thank you, Lou," Miss Kimberly says. Her voice is calmer, warmer. I am surprised. I did not expect to say the right thing. "What's wrong?" she asks as I start lifting out the clothes, shaking them so most of the detergent falls back into the washing machine.

"I dropped a coin in," I say.

She is coming closer. I do not want her to come closer. She wears a strong perfume, very sweet-smelling.

"Just use another. That one'll be really clean when you take the clothes out," she says.

I stand still a moment, the clothes in my hand. Can I leave that coin in? I have the spare in my pocket. I drop the clothes and reach for the coin in my pocket. It is the right size. I put it in the slot, close the door, set the machine, and push START. Again the *thunk*, the hiss of water. I feel strange inside. I thought I understood Miss Kimberly before, when she was the predictable old lady who washed her clothes on Friday night, as I do. I thought I understood her a few minutes ago, at least to understand that she was upset about something. But she thought of a solution so fast, while I was thinking she was still upset. How did she do that? Is that something normal people can do all the time?

"It's easier than taking the clothes out," she says. "This way you don't get stuff on the machine and have to clean it up. I always bring some extra coins just in case." She laughs, a little dry laugh. "As I get older, my hands shake sometimes." She pauses, looking at me. I am still wondering how she did that, but I realize she is waiting for something from me. It is always appropriate to say thank you, even when you aren't sure why.

"Thank you," I say.

It was the right thing to say again; she smiles.

"You're a nice man, Lou; I'm sorry about your tires," she says. She looks at her watch. "I need to go make some phone calls; are you going to be here? To watch the dryer?"

"I will be downstairs," I say. "Not in this room; it is too noisy." I have said this before when she has asked me to keep an eye on her clothes. I always think of taking out an eye and putting it on the clothes, but I do not tell her that is what I think. I know what the expression means socially, but it is a silly meaning. She nods and smiles and goes out. I check again that the setting on both washers is correct and then go out into the hall.

The floor in the laundry room is ugly gray concrete, sloping down slightly to a big drain under the washing machines. I know the drain is there because two years ago I brought my washing down and workmen were there. They had moved the machines out and had the cover off the drain. It smelled very bad, sour and sick.

The floor in the hall is tile, each tile streaked with two shades of green on beige. The tiles are twelve-inch squares; the hall is five squares wide and forty-five and a half squares long. The person who laid the tiles laid them so that the streaks are crosswise to each other—each tile is laid so that the streaks are facing ninety degrees to the tile next to it. Most of the tiles are laid in one of two ways, but eight of them are laid upside down to the other tiles in the same orientation.

I like to look at this hall and think about those eight tiles. What pattern could be completed by having those eight tiles laid in reverse? So far I have come up with three possible patterns. I tried to tell Tom about it once, but he was not able to see the patterns in his head the way I can. I drew them all out on a sheet of paper, but soon I could tell that he was bored. It is not polite to bore people. I never tried to talk to him about it again.

But I find it endlessly interesting. When I get tired of the floor—but I never do get tired of the floor—I can look at the walls. All the walls in the hall are painted, but on one wall there was tile-patterned wallboard before. Those pretend tiles were four inches on a side, but unlike the floor tiles, the pretend wall tiles had a space for pretend grout. So the real pattern size is four and a half inches. If it were four inches, then three wall tiles would make one floor tile.

I look for the places where the line between the tiles can go up the wall and over the ceiling and back around without stopping. There is one place in this hall where the line almost makes it, but not quite. I used to think if the hall were twice as long there would be two places, but that's not how it works. When I really look at it, I can tell that the hall would have to be five and a third times as long for all the lines to match exactly twice.

Hearing one washing machine whine down from spin, I go back into the laundry room. I know that it takes me exactly that long to arrive at the machine just as the drum stops turning. It is a kind of game, to take that last step when the machine takes its last turn. The left-hand dryer is still mumbling and bumbling; I take my wet clothes and put them in the empty right-hand dryer. By the time I have them all in and have checked to be sure nothing is left in the washer, the second washer comes spinning down. Once last year I worked out the relationship between the frictional force slowing the rotation and the frequency of the sound it makes. I did it by myself, without a computer, which made it more fun.

I take my clothes from the second machine, and there at the bottom is the missing coin, shiny and clean and smooth in my fingers. I put it in my pocket, put the clothes into the dryer, insert the coins, and start it up. Long ago, I used to watch the tumbling clothes and try to figure out what the pattern was—why this time the arm of a red sweatshirt was in front of the blue robe, falling down and around, and next time the same red arm was between the yellow sweatpants and the pillowcase instead. My mother didn't like it when I mumbled while watching the clothes rise and fall, so I learned to do it all in my head.

Miss Kimberly comes back just as the dryer with her clothes in it stops. She smiles at me. She has a plate with some cookies on it. "Thanks, Lou," she says. She holds out the plate. "Have a cookie. I know boys—I mean young men—like cookies."

She brings cookies almost every week. I do not always like the kind of cookie she brings, but it is not polite to say so. This week it is lemon crisps. I like them a lot. I take three. She puts the plate on the folding table and takes her things out of the dryer. She puts them in her basket; she does not fold her clothes down here. "Just bring the plate up when you're done, Lou," she says. This is the same as last week.

"Thank you, Miss Kimberly," I say.

"You're quite welcome," she says, as she always does.

I finish the cookies, dust the crumbs into the trash basket, and fold my laundry before going upstairs. I hand her the plate and go on to my apartment.

ON SATURDAY MORNINGS, I GO TO THE CENTER. ONE OF THE counselors is available from 8:30 to 12:00, and once a month there's a special program. Today there is no program, but Maxine, one of the counselors, is walking toward the conference room when I arrive. Bailey did not say if she was the counselor they talked to last week. Maxine wears orange lipstick and purple eye shadow; I never ask her anything. I think about asking her anyway, but someone else goes in before I make up my mind.

The counselors know how to find us legal assistance or an apartment, but I do not know if they will understand the problem we face now. They always encourage us to do everything to become more normal. I think they will say we should want this treatment even if they think it is too dangerous to try while it is still experimental. Eventually I will have to talk to someone here, but I am glad someone is ahead of me. I do not have to do it right now.

I am looking at the bulletin board with its notices of AA meetings and other support group meetings (single parents, parents of teens, job seekers) and interest group meetings (funkdance, bowling, technology assistance) when Emmy comes up to me. "Well, how's your girlfriend?"

"I do not have a girlfriend," I say.

"I saw her," Emmy says. "You know I did. Don't lie about it."

"You saw my friend," I say. "Not my girlfriend. A girlfriend is someone who agrees to be your girlfriend and she has not agreed." I am not being honest and that is wrong, but I still do not want to talk to Emmy, or listen to Emmy, about Marjory.

"You asked her?" Emmy says.

"I do not want to talk to you about her," I say, and turn away.

"Because you know I'm right," Emmy says. She moves around me quickly, standing in front of me again. "She is one of those—call themselves normal—using us like lab rats. You're always hanging around with that kind, Lou, and it's not right."

"I do not know what you mean," I say. I see Marjory only once a week—twice the week of the grocery store—so how can that be "hanging around" with her? If I come to the Center every week and Emmy is there, does this mean I am hanging around with Emmy? I do not like that thought.

"You haven't come to any of the special events in months," she says. "You're spending time with your *normal* friends." She makes *normal* into a curse word by her tone.

I have not come to the special events because they do not interest me. A lecture on parenting skills? I have no children. A dance? The music they were going to have is not the kind I like. A pottery demo and class? I do not want to make things out of clay. Thinking about it, I realize that very little in the Center now interests me. It is an easy way to run into other autistics, but they are not all like me and I can find more people who share my interests on-line or at the office. Cameron, Bailey, Eric, Linda . . . we all go to the Center to meet one another before going somewhere else, but it is just a habit. We do not really need the Center, except maybe to talk to the counselors now and then.

"If you're going to look for girlfriends, you should start with your own kind," Emmy says.

I look at her face, with the physical signs of anger all over it—the flushed skin, the bright eyes between tense lids, the square-shaped mouth, the teeth almost together. I do not know why she is angry with me this time. I do not know why it matters to her how much time I spend at the Center. I do not think she is my kind anyway. Emmy is not autistic. I do not know her diagnosis; I do not care about her diagnosis.

"I am not looking for girlfriends," I say.

"So, she came looking for you?"

"I said I do not want to talk about this to you," I say. I look around. I do not see anyone else I know. I thought Bailey might be in this morning, but maybe he has figured out what I just realized. Maybe he isn't coming because he knows he does not need the Center. I do not want to stand here and wait for Maxine to be free.

I turn to go, aware of Emmy behind me, radiating dark feelings faster than I can get away. Linda and Eric come in. Before I can say anything, Emmy blurts out, "Lou's been seeing that girl again, that researcher."

Linda looks down and away; she does not want to hear. She does not like to get involved in arguments anyway. Eric's gaze brushes across my face and finds the pattern on the floor tiles. He is listening but not asking.

"I told him she was a researcher, just out to use him, but he won't listen," Emmy says. "I saw her myself and she's not even pretty."

I feel my neck getting hot. It is not fair of Emmy to say that about Marjory. She does not even know Marjory. I think Marjory is prettier than Emmy, but pretty is not the reason I like her.

"Is she trying to get you to take the treatment, Lou?" Eric asks.

"No," I say. "We do not talk about that."

"I do not know her," Eric says, and turns away. Linda is already out of sight.

"You don't want to know her," Emmy says.

Eric turns back. "If she is Lou's friend, you should not say bad things about her," he says. Then he walks on, after Linda.

I think about following them, but I do not want to stay here. Emmy might follow me. She might talk more. She *would* talk more. It would upset Linda and Eric.

I turn to leave, and Emmy does say more. "Where are you going?" she asks. "You just got here. Don't think you can run away from your problems, Lou!"

I can run away from her, I think. I cannot run away from work or Dr. Fornum, but I can run from Emmy. I smile, thinking that, and she turns even redder.

"What are you smiling about?"

"I am thinking about music," I say. That is always safe. I do not want to look at her; her face is red and shiny and angry. She circles me, trying to make me face her. I look at the floor instead. "I think about music when people are angry with me," I say. That is sometimes true.

"Oh, you're impossible!" she says, and storms off down the hall. I wonder if she has any friends at all. I never see her with other people. That is sad, but it is not something I can fix.

Outside it feels much quieter, even though the Center is on a busy street. I do not have plans now. If I am not spending Saturday morning at the Center, I am not sure what to do. I did my laundry. My apartment is clean. The books say that we do not cope well with uncertainty or changes in schedule. Usually it does not bother me, but this morning I feel shaky inside. I do not want to think of Marjory being what Emmy says she is. What if Emmy is right? What if Marjory is lying to me? It does not feel right, but my feelings can be wrong.

I wish I could see Marjory now. I wish we were going to do something together, something where I could look at her. Just look and listen to her talk to someone else. Would I know if she liked me? I think she does like me. I do not know if she likes me a lot or a little, though. I do not know if she likes me the way she likes other men or as a grownup likes a child. I do not know how to tell. If I were normal I would know. Normal people must know, or they could not ever get married.

Last week at this time I was at the tournament. I did enjoy it. I would rather be there than here. Even with the noise, with all the people, with all the smells. That is a place I belong; I do not belong here anymore. I am changing, or rather I have changed.

I decide to walk back to the apartment, even though it is a long way. It is cooler than it has been, and fall flowers show in some of the yards I walk past. The rhythm of walking eases my tension and makes it easier to hear the music I've chosen to walk with. I see other people with earphones on. They are listening to broadcast or recorded music; I wonder if the ones without earphones are listening to their own music or walking without music.

The smell of fresh bread stops me partway home. I turn aside into a small bakery and buy a loaf of warm bread. Next to the bakery is a flower shop with ranked masses of purples, yellows, blues, bronzes, deep reds. The colors carry more than wavelengths of light; they project joy, pride, sadness, comfort. It is almost too much to bear.

I store the colors and textures in my memory and take the bread home, breathing in that fragrance and combining it with the colors I pass. One house I pass has a late-blooming rose trained up a wall; even across the yard I can catch a hint of its sweetness.


*IT HAS BEEN OVER A WEEK, AND MR. ALDRIN AND MR. CREN-*shaw have not said anything more about the treatment. We have had no more letters. I would like to think this means something has gone wrong with the process and they will forget about it, but I think they will not forget. Mr. Crenshaw always looks and sounds so angry. Angry people do not forget injuries; forgiveness dissolves anger. That is what the sermon this week was about. My mind should not wander during the sermon, but sometimes it is boring and I think of other things. Anger and Mr. Crenshaw seem connected.

On Monday, we all get a notice that we are to meet on Saturday. I do not want to give up my Saturday, but the notice does not include any reason for staying away. Now I wish I had waited to talk to Maxine at the Center, but it is too late.

"Do you think we have to go?" Chuy asks. "Will they fire us if we don't?"

"I don't know," Bailey says. "I want to find out what they're doing, so I would go anyway."

"I will go," Cameron says. I nod, and so do the others. Linda looks most unhappy, but she usually looks most unhappy.


*"LOOK . . . ER . . . PETE. . . ." CRENSHAW'S VOICE OOZED FALSE* friendliness; Aldrin noticed his difficulty in remembering the name. "I know you think I'm a hard-hearted bastard, but the fact is the company's struggling. The space-based production is necessary, but it's eating up profits like you wouldn't believe."

Oh, wouldn't I? Aldrin thought. It was stupid, in his opinion: the advantages to low- and zero-G facilities were far outweighed by their expense and the drawbacks. There were riches enough to be made down here, on the earth, and he would not have voted for the commitment to space if anyone had given him a vote.

"Your guys are fossils, Pete. Face it. The auties older than them were throwaways, nine out of ten. And don't recite that woman, whatever her name was, that designed slaughterhouses or something—"

"Grandin," Aldrin murmured, but Crenshaw ignored him.

"One in a million, and I have the highest respect for someone who pulls themselves up by their bootstraps the way she did. But she was the exception. Most of those poor bastards were hopeless. Not their fault, all right? But still, no good to themselves or anyone else, no matter how much money was spent on them. And if the damned shrinks had kept hold of the category, your guys would be just as bad. Lucky for them the neurologists and behaviorists got some influence. But still . . . they're not normal, whatever you say."

Aldrin said nothing. Crenshaw in full flow wouldn't listen anyway. Crenshaw took that silence for consent and went on.

"And then they figured out what it was that went wrong and started fixing it in babies . . . so your guys are fossils, Pete. Marooned between the bad old days and the bright new ones. Stuck. It's not fair to them."

Very little in life was fair, and Aldrin could not believe that Crenshaw had a clue about fairness.

"Now you say they have this unique talent and deserve the expensive extras we shower on them because they produce. That may've been true five years ago, Pete—maybe even two years ago—but the machines have caught up, as they always do." He held out a printout. "I'll bet you don't keep up with the literature in artificial intelligence, do you?"

Aldrin took the printout without looking at it. "Machines have never been able to do what they do," he said.

"Once upon a time, machines couldn't add two and two," Crenshaw said. "But you wouldn't hire someone now to add up columns of figures with pencil and paper, would you?"

Only during a power outage: small businesses found it expedient to be sure the people who worked checkout registers could, in fact, add two and two with paper and pencil. But mentioning that would not work, he knew.

"You're saying machines could replace them?" he asked.

"Easy as pie," Crenshaw said. "Well . . . maybe not that easy. It'd take new computers and some pretty high-powered software . . . but then all it takes is the electricity. None of that silly stuff they've got."

Electricity that had to be paid for constantly, whereas the supports for his people had been paid off long ago. Another thing Crenshaw wouldn't listen to.

"Suppose they all took the treatment and it worked: would you still want to replace them with machines?"

"Bottom line, Pete, bottom line. Whatever comes out best for the company is what I want. If they can do the work as well and not cost as much as new machines, I'm not out to put anyone on unemployment. But we have to cut costs—have to. In this market, the only way to get investment income is to show efficiency. And that plush private lab and those offices—that's not what any stockholder would call efficiency."

The executive gym and dining room, Aldrin knew, were considered inefficiency by some stockholders, but this had never resulted in loss of executive privileges. Executives, it had been explained repeatedly, needed these perks to help them maintain peak performance. They had earned the privileges they used, and the privileges boosted their efficiency. It was said, but Aldrin didn't believe it. He also didn't say it.

"So, bottom line, Gene—" It was daring to use Crenshaw's first name, but he was in the mood to be daring. "Either they agree to treatment, in which case you might consider letting them stay on, or you'll find a way to force them out. Law or no law."

"The law does not require a company to bankrupt itself," Crenshaw said. "That notion went overboard early this century. We'd lose the tax break, but that's such a tiny part of our budget that it's worthless, really. Now if they'd agree to dispense with their so-called support measures and act like regular employees, I wouldn't push the treatment—though why they wouldn't want it I can't fathom."

"So you want me to do what?" Aldrin asked.

Crenshaw smiled. "Glad to see you're coming onboard with this, Pete. I want you to make it clear to your people what the options are. One way or another, they have to quit being a drag on the company: give up their luxuries now, or take the treatment and give them up if it's really the autism that makes them need that stuff, or . . ." He ran a finger across his throat. "They can't hold the company hostage. There's not a law in this land we can't find a way around or get changed." He sat back and folded his hands behind his head. "We have the resources."

Aldrin felt sick. He had known this all his adult life, but he had never been at a level where anyone said it out loud. He had been able to hide it from himself.

"I'll try to explain," he said, his tongue stiff in his mouth.

"Pete, you've got to quit *trying* and start *doing*," Crenshaw said. "You're not stupid or lazy; I can tell that. But you just don't have the . . . the push."

Aldrin nodded and escaped from Crenshaw's office. He went into the washroom and scrubbed his hands. . . . He still felt soiled. He thought of quitting, of turning in his resignation. Mia had a good job, and they had chosen not to have children yet. They could coast a while on her salary if they had to.

But who would look after his people? Not Crenshaw. Aldrin shook his head at himself in the mirror. He was only fooling himself if he thought he could help. He had to try, but . . . who else in the family could pay his brother's bills for residential treatment? What if he lost his job?

He tried to think of his contacts: Betty in Human Resources. Shirley in Accounting. He didn't know anyone in Legal; he'd never needed to. HR took care of the interface with laws concerning special-needs employees; they talked to Legal if it was necessary.

MR. ALDRIN HAS INVITED THE WHOLE SECTION OUT TO DIN-ner. We are at the pizza place, and because the group is too large for one table, we are at two tables pushed together, in the wrong part of the room.

I am not comfortable with Mr. Aldrin sitting at the table with us, but I do not know what to do about it. He is smiling a lot and talking a lot. Now he thinks the treatment is a good idea, he says. He does not want to pressure us, but he thinks it would benefit us. I try to think about the taste of the pizza and not listen, but it is harder.

After a while he slows down. He has had another beer, and his voice is softening at the edges, like toast in hot chocolate. He sounds more like the Mr. Aldrin I am used to, more tentative. "I still don't understand why they're in such a hurry," he says. "The expense of the gym and things is minimal, really. We don't need the space. It's a drop in the bucket, compared to the profitability of the section. And there aren't enough autistics like you in the world to make this a profitable treatment even if it does work perfectly for all of you."

"Current estimates are that there are millions of autistic persons in the United States alone," Eric says.

"Yes, but—"

"The cost of social services for that population, including residential facilities for the most impaired, is estimated at billions a year. If the treatment works, that money would be available—"

"The workforce can't handle that many new workers," Mr. Aldrin says. "And some of them are too old. Jeremy—" He stops suddenly and his skin turns red and shiny. Is he angry or embarrassed? I am not sure. He takes a long breath. "My brother," he says. "He is too old to get a job now."

"You have a brother who is autistic?" Linda asks. She looks at his face for the first time. "You never told us." I feel cold suddenly, exposed. I thought Mr. Aldrin could not see into our heads, but if he has an autistic brother, then he may know more than I thought.

"I . . . didn't think it was important." His face is still red and shiny, and I think he is not telling the truth. "Jeremy is older than any of you. He's in a residential facility—"

I am trying to put this new idea about Mr. Aldrin, that he has an autistic brother, together with his attitudes toward us, so I say nothing.

"You lied to us," Cameron says. His eyelids have pulled down; his voice sounds angry. Mr. Aldrin's head jerks back, as if someone had pulled a string.

"I did not—"

"There are two kinds of lie," Cameron says. I can tell he is quoting something he was told. "The lie of commission, which states an untruth known to the speaker to be untrue, and the lie of omission, which omits to state a truth known to the speaker to be true. You lied when you did not tell us your brother was autistic."

"I'm your boss, not your friend," Mr. Aldrin blurts out. He turns even redder. He said earlier he was our friend. Was he lying then, or is he lying now? "I mean . . . it had nothing to do with work."

"It is the reason you wanted to be our supervisor," Cameron says.

"It's not. I didn't want to be your supervisor at first."

"At first." Linda is still staring at his face. "Something changed. It was your brother?"

"No. You are not much like my brother. He is . . . very impaired."

"You want the treatment for your brother?" Cameron asks.

"I . . . don't know."

That does not sound like the truth, either. I try to imagine Mr. Aldrin's brother, this unknown autistic person. If Mr. Aldrin thinks his brother is very impaired, what does he think of us, really? What was his childhood like?

"I'll bet you do," Cameron says. "If you think it's a good idea for us, you must think it could help him. Maybe you think if you can get us to do it, they'll reward you with his treatment? Good boy: here's a candy?"

"That's not fair," Mr. Aldrin says. His voice is louder, too. People are turning to look. I wish we were not here. "He's my brother, naturally I want to help him any way I can, but—"

"Did Mr. Crenshaw tell you that if you talked us into it, your brother could get treatment?"

"I . . . it's not that—" His eyes slide from side to side; his face changes color. I see the effort on his face, the effort to fool us convincingly. The book said autistic persons are gullible and easily fooled because they do not understand the nuances of communication. I do not think lying is a nuance. I think lying is wrong. I am sorry Mr. Aldrin is lying to us but glad that he is not doing it very well.

"If there is not enough market for this treatment to autistic persons, what else is it good for?" Linda asks. I wish she had not changed the subject back to before, but it is too late. Mr. Aldrin's face relaxes a little.

I have an idea, but it is not clear yet. "Mr. Crenshaw said he would be willing to keep us on without the treatment if we gave up the support services, isn't that right?"

"Yes, why?"

"So . . . he would like to have what we—what autistic persons—are good at without the things we are not good at."

Mr. Aldrin's brow wrinkles. It is the movement that shows confusion. "I suppose," he says slowly. "But I'm not sure what that has to do with the treatment."

"Somewhere in the original article is the profit," I say to Mr. Aldrin. "Not changing autistic persons—there are no more kids born like we were born, not in this country. There are not enough of us. But something we do is valuable enough that if normal people could do it, that would be profitable." I think of that time in my office when for a few moments the meaning of the symbols, the beautiful intricacy of the patterns of data, went away and left me confused and distracted. "You have watched us work for years now; you must know what it is—"

"Your ability in pattern analysis and math, you know that."

"No—you said Mr. Crenshaw said the new software could do that as well. It is something else."

"I still want to know about your brother," Linda says.

Aldrin closes his eyes, refusing contact. I was scolded for doing just that. He opens them again. "You're . . . relentless," he says. "You just don't quit."

The pattern forming in my mind, the light and dark shifting and circling, begins to cohere. But it is not enough; I need more data.

"Explain the money," I say to Aldrin.

"Explain . . . what?"

"The money. How does the company make money to pay us?"

"It's . . . very complicated, Lou. I don't think you could understand."

"Please try. Mr. Crenshaw claims we cost too much, that the profits suffer. Where do the profits really come from?"

CHAPTER TEN

M R. ALDRIN JUST STARES AT ME. FINALLY HE SAYS, "I don't know how to say it, Lou, because I don't know what the process is, exactly, or what it could do if applied to someone who isn't autistic."

"Can't you even—"

"And . . . and I don't think I should be talking about this. Helping you is one thing. . . ." He has not helped us yet. Lying to us is not helping us. "But speculating about something that doesn't exist, speculating that the company is contemplating some broader action that may be . . . that could be construed as . . ." He stops and shakes his head without finishing the sentence. We are all looking at him. His eyes are very shiny, as if he were about to cry.

"I shouldn't have come," he says after a moment. "This was a big mistake. I'll pay for the meal, but I have to go now."

He pushes back his chair and gets up; I see him at the cash register with his back to us. None of us says anything until he has gone out the front door.

"He's crazy," Chuy says.

"He's scared," Bailey says.

"He hasn't helped us, not really," Linda says. "I don't know why he bothered—"

"His brother," Cameron says.

"Something we said bothered him even more than Mr. Crenshaw or his brother," I say.

"He knows something he doesn't want us to know." Linda brushes the hair off her forehead with an abrupt gesture.

"He doesn't want to know it himself," I say. I am not sure why I think that, but I do. It is something we said. I need to know what it was.

"There was something, back around the turn of the century," Bailey says. "In one of the science journals, something about making people sort of autistic so they would work harder."

"Science journal or science fiction?" I ask.

"It was—wait; I'll look it up. I know somebody who will know." Bailey makes a note on his handcomp.

"Don't send it from the office," Chuy says.

"Why—? Oh. Yes." Bailey nods.

"Pizza tomorrow," Linda says. "Coming here is normal."

I open my mouth to say that Tuesday is my day to shop for groceries and shut it again. This is more important. I can go a week without groceries, or I can shop a little later.

"Everybody look up what you can find," Cameron says.

At home, I log on and e-mail Lars. It is very late where he is, but he is awake. I find out that the original research was done in Denmark, but the entire lab, equipment and all, was bought up and the research base shifted to Cambridge. The paper I first heard about weeks ago was based on research done more than a year ago. Mr. Aldrin was right about that. Lars thinks much of the work to make the treatments human-compatible has been done; he speculates on secret military experiments. I do not believe this; Lars thinks everything is a secret military experiment. He is a very good game player, but I do not believe everything he says.

Wind rattles my windows. I get up and lay a hand on the glass. Much colder. A spatter of rain and then I hear thunder. It is late anyway; I shut down my system and go to bed.

Tuesday we do not speak to one another at work, other than "good morning" and "good afternoon." I spend fifteen minutes in the gym when I finish another section of my project, but then I go back to work. Mr. Aldrin and Mr. Crenshaw both come by, not quite arm in arm, but as if they were friendly. They do not stay long, and they do not talk to me.

After work, we go back to the pizza place. "Two nights in a row!" says Hi-I'm-Sylvia. I cannot tell if she is happy or unhappy about that. We take our usual table but pull over another one so there is room for everybody.

"So?" Cameron says, after we've ordered. "What have we found out?"

I tell the group what Lars said. Bailey has found the text of the old article, which is clearly fiction and not nonfiction. I did not know that science journals ever published science fiction on purpose, and apparently it only happened for one year.

"It was supposed to make people really concentrate on an assigned project and not waste time on other things," Bailey said.

"Like Mr. Crenshaw thinks we waste time?" I say.

Bailey nods.

"We don't waste as much time as he wastes walking around looking angry," Chuy says.

We all laugh, but quietly. Eric is drawing curlicues with his colored pens; they look like laughing sounds.

"Does it say how it was going to work?" Linda asks.

"Sort of," Bailey says. "But I'm not sure the science is good. And that was decades ago. What they thought would work might not be what really works."

"They don't want autistic people like us," Eric says. "They wanted— or the story said they wanted—savant talents and concentration without the other side effects. Compared to a savant we waste a lot of time, though not as much as Mr. Crenshaw thinks."

"Normal people waste a lot of time on nonproductive things," Cameron says. "At least as much as we do, maybe more."

"It would take what to turn a normal person into a savant without the other problems?" Linda asks.

"I don't know," Cameron says. "They would have to be smart to start with. Good at something. Then they would have to want to do that instead of anything else."

"It wouldn't do any good if they wanted to do something they were bad at," Chuy says. I imagine a person determined to be a musician who has no rhythm and no pitch sense; it is ridiculous. We all see the funny side of this and laugh.

"Do people ever want to do what they aren't good at?" Linda asks. "Normal people, that is?" For once she does not make the word *normal* sound like a bad word.

We sit and think a moment; then Chuy says, "I had an uncle who wanted to be a writer. My sister—she reads a lot—she said he was really bad. Really, really bad. He was good at doing things with his hands, but he wanted to write."

"Here y'are, then," Hi-I'm-Sylvia says, putting down the pizzas. I look at her. She is smiling, but she looks tired and it is not even seven yet.

"Thank you," I say. She waves a hand and hurries away.

"Something to keep people from paying attention to distraction," Bailey says. "Something to make them like the right things."

"'Distractibility is determined by the sensory sensitivity at every level of processing and by the strength of sensory integration,'" Eric recites. "I read that. Part of it's inborn. That's been known for forty or fifty years; late in the twentieth century that knowledge had worked its way down to the popular level, in books on parenting. Attention control circuitry is developed early in fetal life; it can be compromised by later injury. . . ."

I feel almost sick for a moment, as if something were attacking my brain right now, but push that feeling aside. Whatever caused my autism is in the past, where I cannot undo it. Now it is important not to think about me but about the problem.

All my life I've been told how lucky I was to be born when I was— lucky to benefit from the improvements in early intervention, lucky to be born in the right country, with parents who had the education and resources to be sure I got that good early intervention. Even lucky to be born too soon for definitive treatment, because—my parents said—having to struggle gave me the chance to demonstrate strength of character.

What would they have said if this treatment had been available for me when I was a child? Would they have wanted me to be stronger or be normal? Would accepting treatment mean I had no strength of character? Or would I find other struggles?

*I AM STILL THINKING ABOUT THIS THE NEXT EVENING AS I* change clothes and drive to Tom and Lucia's for fencing. What behaviors do we have that someone could profit from, other than the occasional savant talents? Most of the autistic behaviors have been presented to us as deficits, not strengths. Unsocial, lacking social skills, problems with attention control . . . I keep coming back to that. It is hard to think from their perspective, but I have the feeling that this attention control issue is at the middle of the pattern, like a black hole at the center of a space-time whirlpool. That is something else we are supposed to be deficient in, the famous Theory of Mind.

I am a little early. No one else is parked outside yet. I pull up carefully so that there is the most room possible behind me. Sometimes the others are not so careful, and then fewer people can park without inconveniencing others. I could be early every week, but that would not be fair to others.

Inside, Tom and Lucia are laughing about something. When I go in, they grin at me, very relaxed. I wonder what it would be like to have someone in the house all the time, someone to laugh with. They do not always laugh, but they seem happy more often than not.

"How are you, Lou?" Tom asks. He always asks that. It is one of the things normal people do, even if they know that you are all right.

"Fine," I say. I want to ask Lucia about medical things, but I do not know how to start or if it is polite. I start with something else. "The tires on my car were slashed last week."

"Oh, no!" Lucia says. "How awful!" Her face changes shape; I think she means to express sympathy.

"It was in the parking lot at the apartment," I say. "In the same place as usual. All four tires."

Tom whistles. "That's expensive," he says. "Has there been a lot of vandalism in the area? Did you report it to the police?"

I cannot answer one of those questions at all. "I did report it," I say. "There is a policeman who lives in our apartment building. He told me how to report it."

"That's good," Tom says. I am not sure if he means it is good that a policeman lives in our building or that I reported it, but I do not think it is important to know which.

"Mr. Crenshaw was angry that I was late to work," I say.

"Didn't you tell me he's new?" Tom asks.

"Yes. He does not like our section. He does not like autistic people."

"Oh, he's probably . . ." Lucia begins, but Tom looks at her and she stops.

"I don't know why you think he doesn't like autistic people," Tom says.

I relax. It is so much easier to talk to Tom when he says things this way. The question is less threatening. I wish I knew why.

"He says we should not need the supportive environment," I say. "He says it is too expensive and we should not have the gym and . . . and the other things." I have never actually talked about the special things that make our workplace so much better. Maybe Tom and Lucia will think the same way as Mr. Crenshaw when they find out about them.

"That's . . ." Lucia pauses, looks at Tom, and then goes on. "That's ridiculous. It doesn't matter what he thinks; the law says they have to provide a supportive work environment."

"As long as we're as productive as other employees," I say. It is hard to talk about this; it is too scary. I can feel my throat tightening and hear my own voice sounding strained and mechanical. "As long as we fit the diagnostic categories under the law . . ."

"Which autism clearly does," Lucia says. "And I'm sure you're productive, or they wouldn't have kept you this long."

"Lou, is Mr. Crenshaw threatening to fire you?" Tom asks.

"No . . . not exactly. I told you about that experimental treatment. They didn't say anything more about it for a while, but now they—Mr. Crenshaw, the company—they want us to take that experimental treatment. They sent a letter. It said people who were part of a research protocol were protected from cutbacks. Mr. Aldrin talked to our group; we are having a special meeting on Saturday. I thought they could not make us take it, but Mr. Aldrin says that Mr. Crenshaw says they can shut down our section and refuse to rehire us for something else because we are not trained in something else. He says if we do not take the treatment they will do this and it is not firing because companies can change with the times."

Tom and Lucia both look angry, their faces knotted with tight muscle and the shiny look coming out on their skin. I should not have said this now; this was the wrong time, if anything was the right time.

"Those *bastards*," Lucia says. She looks at me and her face changes from the tight knots of anger, smoothing out around the eyes. "Lou— Lou, listen: I am not angry with you. I am angry with people who hurt you or do not treat you well . . . not with you."

"I should not have said this to you," I say, still uncertain.

"Yes, you should," Lucia says. "We are your friends; we should know if something goes wrong in your life, so that we can help."

"Lucia's right," Tom says. "Friends help friends—just as you've helped us, like when you built the mask rack."

"That is something we both use," I say. "My work is just about me."

"Yes and no," Tom says. "Yes in that we are not working with you and cannot help you directly. But no when it is a big problem that has general application, like this one. This isn't just about you. It could affect every disabled person who's employed anywhere. What if they decided that a person in a wheelchair didn't need ramps? You definitely need a lawyer, all of you. Didn't you say that the Center could find one for you?"

"Before the others get here, Lou," Lucia says, "why don't you tell us more about this Mr. Crenshaw and his plans?"

I sit down on the sofa, but even though they have said they want to listen it is hard to talk. I look at the rug on their floor, with its wide border of blue-and-cream geometric patterns—there are four patterns within a frame of plain blue stripes—and try to make the story clear.

"There is a treatment they—someone—used on adult apes," I say. "I did not know apes could be autistic, but what they said was that autistic apes became more normal when they had this treatment. Now Mr. Crenshaw wants us to have it."

"And you don't want it?" Tom asks.

"I do not understand how it works or how it will make things better," I say.

"Very sensible," Lucia says. "Do you know who did the research, Lou?"

"I do not remember the name," I say. "Lars—he's a member of an international group of autistic adults—e-mailed me about it several weeks ago. He sent me the journal Web site and I went there, but I did not understand much of it. I did not study neuroscience."

"Do you still have that citation?" Lucia asks. "I can look it up, see what I can find out."

"You could?"

"Sure. And I can ask around in the department, find out if the researchers are considered any good or not."

"We had an idea," I say.

"We who?" Tom asks.

"We . . . the people I work with," I say.

"The other autistic people?" Tom asks.

"Yes." I close my eyes briefly to calm down. "Mr. Aldrin bought us pizza. He drank beer. He said that he did not think there was enough profit in treating adult autistic persons—because they now treat preborns and infants and we are the last cohort who will be like us. At least in this country. So we wondered why they wanted to develop this treatment and what else it could do. It is like some pattern analysis I have done. There is one pattern, but it is not the only pattern. Someone can think they are generating one pattern and actually generate several more, and one of those may be useful or not useful, depending on what the problem is." I look up at Tom and he is looking at me with a strange expression. His mouth is a little open.

He shakes his head, a quick jerk. "So—you are thinking maybe they have something else in mind, something that you people are just part of?"

"It might be," I say cautiously.

He looks at Lucia, and she nods. "It certainly could be," he says. "Trying whatever it is on you would give them additional data, and then . . . Let me think. . . ."

"I think it is something to do with attention control," I say. "We all have a different way of perceiving sensory input and . . . and setting attention priorities." I am not sure I have the words right, but Lucia nods vigorously.

"Attention control—of course. If they could control that in the architecture, not chemically, it'd be a lot easier to develop a dedicated workforce."

"Space," Tom says.

I am confused, but Lucia only blinks and then nods.

"Yes. The big limitation in space-based employment is getting people to concentrate, not be distracted. The sensory inputs up there are not what we're used to, what worked in natural selection." I do not know how she knows what he is thinking. I would like to be able to read minds like that. She grins at me. "Lou, I think you're onto something big, here. Get me that citation, and I'll run with it."

I feel uneasy. "I am not supposed to talk about work outside the campus," I say.

"You're not talking about work," she says. "You're talking about your work *environment*. That's different."

I wonder if Mr. Aldrin would see it that way.

Someone knocks on the door, and we quit talking. I am sweaty even though I have not been fencing. The first to arrive are Dave and Susan. We go through the house, collect our gear, and start stretching in the backyard.

Marjory is next to arrive, and she grins at me. I feel lighter than air again. I remember what Emmy said, but I cannot believe it when I see Marjory. Maybe tonight I will ask her to go to dinner with me. Don has not come. I suppose he is still angry with Tom and Lucia for not acting like friends. It makes me sad that they are not all still friends; I hope they do not get angry with me and quit being friends with me.

I am fencing with Dave when I hear a noise from the street and then a squeal of tires moving fast. I ignore it and do not change my attack, but Dave stops and I hit him too hard in the chest.

"I'm sorry," I say.

"It's okay," he says. "That sounded close; did you hear it?"

"I heard something," I say. I am trying to replay the sounds, *thump-crash-tinkle-tinkle-squeal-roar*, and think what it could be. Someone dropped a bowl out of their car?

"Maybe we'd better check," Dave says.

Several of the others have gotten up to look. I follow the group to the front yard. In the light from the streetlight on the corner I can see a glitter on the pavement.

"It's your car, Lou," Susan says. "The windshield."

I feel cold.

"Your tires last week . . . what day was that, Lou?"

"Thursday," I say. My voice shakes a little and sounds harsh.

"Thursday. And now this. . . ." Tom looks at the others, and they look back. I can tell that they are thinking something together, but I do not know what it is. Tom shakes his head. "I guess we'll have to call the police. I hate to break up the practice, but—"

"I'll drive you home, Lou," Marjory says. She has come up behind me; I jump when I hear her voice.

Tom calls the police because, he says, it happened in front of his house. He hands the phone to me after a few minutes, and a bored voice asks my name, my address, my phone number, the license number of the car. I can hear noise in the background on the other end, and people are talking in the living room; it is hard to understand what the voice is saying. I am glad it is just routine questions; I can figure those out.

Then the voice asks something else, and the words tangle together and I cannot figure it out. "I'm sorry . . ." I say.

The voice is louder, the words more separated. Tom shushes the people in the living room. This time I understand.

"Do you have any idea who might have done this?" the voice asks.

"No," I say. "But someone slashed my tires last week."

"Oh?" Now it sounds interested. "Did you report that?"

"Yes," I say.

"Do you remember who the investigating officer was?"

"I have a card; just a minute—" I put the phone down and get out my wallet. The card is still there. I read off the name, Malcolm Stacy, and the case number.

"He's not in now; I'll put this report on his desk. Now . . . are there any witnesses?"

"I heard it," I say, "but I didn't see it. We were in the backyard."

"Too bad. Well, we'll send someone out, but it'll be a while. Just stay there."

By the time the patrol car arrives, it is almost 10:00 P.M.; everyone is sitting around the living room tired of waiting. I feel guilty, even though it is not my fault. I did not break my own windshield or tell the police to tell people to stay. The police officer is a woman named Isaka, short and dark and very brisk. I think she thinks this is too small a reason to call the police.

She looks at my car and the other cars and street and sighs. "Well, someone broke your windshield, and someone slashed your tires a few days ago, so I'd say it's your problem, Mr. Arrendale. You must've really pissed someone off, and you probably know who it is, if you'll just think. How are you getting along at work?"

"Fine," I say, without really thinking. Tom shifts his weight. "I have a new boss, but I do not think Mr. Crenshaw would break a windshield or cut tires." I cannot imagine that he would, even though he gets angry.

"Oh?" she says, making a note.

"He was angry when I was late for work after my tires were slashed," I say. "I do not think he would break my windshield. He might fire me."

She looks at me but says nothing more to me. She is looking now at Tom. "You were having a party?"

"A fencing club practice night," he says.

I see the police officer's neck tense. "Fencing? Like with weapons?"

"It's a sport," Tom says. I can hear the tension in his voice, too. "We had a tournament week before last; there's another coming up in a few weeks."

"Anyone ever get hurt?"

"Not here. We have strict safety rules."

"Are the same people here every week?"

"Usually. People do miss a practice now and then."

"And this week?"

"Well, Larry's not here—he's in Chicago on business. And I guess Don."

"Any problems with the neighbors? Complaints about noise or anything of that sort?"

"No." Tom runs his hand through his hair. "We get along with the neighbors; it's a nice neighborhood. Not usually any vandalism, either."

"But Mr. Arrendale has had two episodes of vandalism against his car in less than a week. . . . That's pretty significant." She waits; no one says anything. Finally she shrugs and goes on.

"It's like this. If the car was headed east, on the right-hand side of the road, the driver would have had to stop, get out, break the glass, run around his own car, get in, and drive off. There's no way to break the glass while in the driver's seat of a car going the same way your car was parked, not without a projectile weapon—and even then the angles are bad. If the car was headed west, though, the driver could reach across with something—a bat, say—or lob a rock through the windshield while still in motion. And then be gone before anyone got out to the front yard."

"I see," I say. Now that she has said it, I can visualize the approach, the attack, the escape. But why?

"You have to have *some* idea who's upset with you," the police officer says. She sounds angry with me.

"It does not matter how angry you are with someone; it is not all right to break things," I say. I am thinking, but the only person I know who has been angry with me about going fencing is Emmy. Emmy does not have a car; I do not think she knows where Tom and Lucia live. I do not think Emmy would break windshields anyway. She might come inside and talk too loud and say something rude to Marjory, but she would not break anything.

"That's true," the officer says. "It's not all right, but people do it anyway. Who is angry with you?"

If I tell her about Emmy, she will make trouble for Emmy and Emmy will make trouble for me. I am sure it is not Emmy. "I don't know," I say. I feel a stirring behind, me, almost a pressure. I think it is Tom, but I am not sure.

"Would it be all right, Officer, if the others left now?" Tom asks.

"Oh, sure. Nobody saw anything; nobody heard anything; well, you heard something, but you didn't see anything—did anyone?"

A murmur of "no" and "not me" and "if I had only moved faster," and the others trickle away to their cars. Marjory and Tom and Lucia stay.

"If you're the target, and it appears you are, then whoever it is knew you would be here tonight. How many people know you come here on Wednesdays?"

Emmy does not know what night I go fencing. Mr. Crenshaw does not know I do fencing at all.

"Everyone who fences here," Tom answers for me. "Maybe some of those from the last tournament—it was Lou's first. Do people at your job know, Lou?"

"I don't talk about it much," I say. I do not explain why. "I've mentioned it, but I don't remember telling anyone where the class is. I might have."

"Well, we're going to have to find out, Mr. Arrendale," the officer says. "This kind of thing can escalate to physical harm. You be careful now." She hands me a card with her name and number on it. "Call me, or Stacy, if you think of anything."

When the police car moves away, Marjory says again, "I'll be glad to drive you home, Lou, if you'd like."

"I will take my car," I say. "I will need to get it fixed. I will need to contact the insurance company again. They will not be happy with me."

"Let's see if there's glass on the seat," Tom says. He opens the car door. Light glitters on the tiny bits of glass on the dashboard, the floor, in the sheepskin pad of the seat. I feel sick. The pad should be soft and warm; now it will have sharp things in it. I untie the pad and shake it out onto the street. The bits of glass make a tiny high-pitched noise as they hit the pavement. It is an ugly sound, like some modern music. I am not sure that all the glass is gone; little bits may be in the fleece like tiny hidden knives.

"You can't drive it like that, Lou," Marjory says.

"He'll have to drive it far enough to get a new windshield," Tom says. "The headlights are all right; he could drive it, if he took it slow."

"I can drive it home," I say. "I will go carefully." I put the sheepskin pad in the backseat and sit very gingerly on the front seat.

At home, later, I think about things Tom and Lucia said, playing the tape of it in my head.

"The way I look at it," Tom said, "your Mr. Crenshaw has chosen to look at the limitations and not the possibilities. He could have considered you and the rest of your section as assets to be nurtured."

"I am not an asset," I said. "I am a person."

"You're right, Lou, but we're talking here of a corporation. As with armies, they look at people who work for them as assets or liabilities. An employee who needs anything different from other employees can be seen as a liability—requiring more resources for the same output. That's the easy way to look at it, and that's why a lot of managers do look at it that way."

"They see what is wrong," I said.

"Yes. They may also see your worth—as an asset—but they want to get the asset without the liability."

"What good managers do," Lucia said, "is help people grow. If they're good at part of their job and not so good at the rest of it, good managers help them identify and grow in those areas where they're not as strong—but only to the point where it doesn't impair their strengths, the reason they were hired."

"But if a newer computer system can do it better—"

"That doesn't matter. There's always something. Lou, no matter if a computer or another machine or another person can do any particular task you do . . . do it faster or more accurately or whatever . . . one thing nobody can do better than you is be *you*."

"But what good is that if I do not have a job?" I asked. "If I cannot get a job . . ."

"Lou, you're a person—an individual like no one else. That's what's good, whether you have a job or not."

"I'm an autistic person," I said. "That is what I am. I have to have some way . . . If they fire me, what else can I do?"

"Lots of people lose their jobs and then get other jobs. You can do that, if you have to. If you want to. You can choose to make the change; you don't have to let it hit you over the head. It's like fencing—you can be the one who sets the pattern or the one who follows it."

I play this tape several times, trying to match tones to words to expressions as I remember them. They told me several times to get a lawyer, but I am not ready to talk to anyone I do not know. It is hard to explain what I am thinking and what has happened. I want to think it out for myself.

If I had not been what I am, what would I have been? I have thought about that at times. If I had found it easy to understand what people were saying, would I have wanted to listen more? Would I have learned to talk more easily? And from that, would I have had more friends, even been popular? I try to imagine myself as a child, a normal child, chattering away with family and teachers and classmates. If I had been that child, instead of myself, would I have learned math so easily? Would the great complicated constructions of classical music have been so obvious to me at first hearing? I remember the first time I heard Bach's *Toccata and Fugue in D Minor* . . . the intensity of joy I felt. Would I have been able to do the work I do? And what other work might I have been able to do?

It is harder to imagine a different self now that I am an adult. As a child, I did imagine myself into other roles. I thought I would become normal, that someday I would be able to do what everyone else did so easily. In time, that fantasy faded. My limitations were real, immutable, thick black lines around the outline of my life. The only role I play is normal.

The one thing all the books agreed on was the permanence of the deficit, as they called it. Early intervention could ameliorate the symptoms, but the central problem remained. I felt that central problem daily, as if I had a big round stone in the middle of myself, a heavy, awkward presence that affected everything I did or tried to do.

What if it weren't there?

I had given up reading about my own disability when I finished school. I had no training as a chemist or biochemist or geneticist. . . . Though I work for a pharmaceutical company, I know little of drugs. I know only the patterns that flow through my computer, the ones I find and analyze, and the ones they want me to create.

I do not know how other people learn new things, but the way I learn them works for me. My parents bought me a bicycle when I was seven and tried to tell me how to start riding. They wanted me to sit and pedal first, while they steadied the bike, and then begin to steer on my own. I ignored them. It was clear that steering was the important thing and the hardest thing, so I would learn that first.

I walked the bicycle around the yard, feeling how the handlebars jiggled and twitched and jerked as the front wheel went over the grass and rocks. Then I straddled it and walked it around that way, steering it, making it fall, bringing it back up again. Finally I coasted down the slope of our driveway, steering from side to side, my feet off the ground but ready to stop. And then I pedaled and never fell again.

It is all knowing what to start with. If you start in the right place and follow all the steps, you will get to the right end.

If I want to understand what this treatment can do that will make Mr. Crenshaw rich, then I need to know how the brain works. Not the vague terms people use, but how it really works as a machine. It is like the handlebars on the bicycle—it is the way of steering the whole person. And I need to know what drugs really are and how they work.

All I remember about the brain from school is that it is gray and uses a lot of glucose and oxygen. I did not like the word *glucose* when I was in school. It made me think of glue, and I did not like to think of my brain using glue. I wanted my brain to be like a computer, something that worked well by itself and did not make mistakes.

The books said that the problem with autism was in the brain, and that made me feel like a faulty computer, something that should be sent back or scrapped. All the interventions, all the training, were like software designed to make a bad computer work right. It never does, and neither did I.

CHAPTER ELEVEN

*TOO MANY THINGS ARE HAPPENING TOO FAST. IT FEELS* like the speed of events is faster than light, but I know that is not objectively true. Objectively true is a phrase I found in one of the texts I've been trying to read on-line. Subjectively true, that book said, is what things feel like to the individual. It feels to me that too many things are happening so fast that they cannot be seen. They are happening ahead of awareness, in the dark that is always faster than light because it gets there first.

I sit by the computer, trying to find a pattern in this. Finding patterns is my skill. Believing in patterns—in the existence of patterns—is apparently my creed. It is part of who I am. The book's author writes that who a person is depends on the person's genetics, background, and surroundings.

When I was a child, I found a book in the library that was all about scales, from the tiniest to the largest. I thought that was the best book in the building; I did not understand why other children preferred books with no structure, mere stories of messy human feelings and desires. Why was reading about an imaginary boy getting on a fictional softball team more important than knowing how starfish and stars fitted into the same pattern?

Who I was thought abstract patterns of numbers were more important than abstract patterns of relationship. Grains of sand are real. Stars are real. Knowing how they fit together gave me a warm, comfortable feeling. People around me were hard enough to figure out, impossible to figure out. People in books made even less sense.

Who I am now thinks that if people were more like numbers, they would be easier to understand. But who I am now knows that they are not like numbers. Four is not always the square root of sixteen, in human fours and sixteens. People are people, messy and mutable, combining differently with one another from day to day—even hour to hour. I am not a number, either. I am Mr. Arrendale to the police officer investigating the damage to my car and Lou to Danny, even though Danny is also a police officer. I am Lou-the-fencer to Tom and Lucia but Lou-the-employee to Mr. Aldrin and Lou-the-autistic to Emmy at the Center.

It makes me feel dizzy to think about that, because on the inside I feel like one person, not three or four or a dozen. The same Lou, bouncing on the trampoline or sitting in my office or listening to Emmy or fencing with Tom or looking at Marjory and feeling that warm feeling. The feelings move over me like light and shadow over a landscape on a windy day. The hills are the same, whether they are in the shadow of a cloud or in the sunlight.

In the time-lapse pictures of clouds blowing across the sky, I have seen patterns . . . clouds growing on one side and dissolving into clear air on the other, where the hills make a ridge.

I am thinking about patterns in the fencing group. It makes sense to me that whoever broke my windshield tonight knew where to find that particular windshield he wanted to break. He knew I would be there, and he knew which car was mine. He was the cloud, forming on the ridge and blowing away into the clear air. Where I am, there he is.

When I think of the people who know my car by sight and then the people who know where I go on Wednesday nights, the possibilities contract. The evidence sucks in to a point, dragging along a name. It is an impossible name. It is a friend's name. Friends do not break windshields of friends. And he has no reason to be angry with me, even if he is angry with Tom and Lucia.

It must be someone else. Even though I am good at patterns, even though I have thought about this carefully, I cannot trust my reasoning when it comes to how people act. I do not understand normal people;

they do not always fit reasonable patterns. There must be someone else, someone who is not a friend, someone who dislikes me and is angry with me. I need to find that other pattern, not the obvious one, which is impossible.

PETE ALDRIN LOOKED THROUGH THE LATEST COMPANY DIREC-tory. So far the firings were still a mere trickle, not enough to raise media awareness, but at least half the names he knew weren't on the list anymore. Soon word would begin to spread. Betty in Human Resources . . . took early retirement. Shirley in Accounting . . .

The thing was, he had to make it look like he was helping Crenshaw, whatever he did. As long as he thought about opposing him, the knot of icy fear in Aldrin's stomach kept him from doing anything. He didn't dare go over Crenshaw's head. He didn't know if Crenshaw's boss knew about the plan, too, or if it had all been Crenshaw's idea. He didn't dare confide in any of the autists; who knew if they could understand the importance of keeping a secret?

He was sure Crenshaw hadn't really checked this out with upstairs. Crenshaw wanted to be seen as a problem solver, a forward-thinking future executive, someone managing his own empire efficiently. He wouldn't ask questions; he wouldn't ask permission. This could be a nightmare of adverse publicity if it got out; someone higher up would have noticed that. But how far up? Crenshaw was counting on no publicity, no leaks, no gossip. That wasn't reasonable, even if he did have a choke hold on everyone in his division.

And if Crenshaw went down and Aldrin was perceived as his helper, he'd lose his job then, too.

What would it take to convert Section A into a group of research subjects? They would have to have time off work: how much? Would they be expected to fold their vacation and sick leave time into it, or would the company provide leave? If extra leave was needed, what about pay? What about seniority? What about the accounting through his section—would they be paid out of this section's operating funds or out of Research?

Had Crenshaw already made deals with someone in HR, in Accounting, in Legal, in Research? What kind of deals? He didn't want to use Crenshaw's name at first; he wanted to see what reaction he got without it.

Shirley was still in Accounting; Aldrin called her. "Remind me what kind of paperwork I need if someone's being transferred to another section," he said to start with. "Do I take it off my budget right away or what?"

"Transfers are frozen," Shirley said. "This new management—" He could hear her take a breath. "You didn't get the memo?"

"Don't think so," Aldrin said. "So—if we have an employee who wants to take part in a research protocol, we can't just transfer their pay source to Research?"

"Good grief, no!" Shirley said. "Tim McDonough—you know, head of Research—would have your hide tacked to the wall in no time." After a moment, she said, "What research protocol?"

"Some new drug thing," he said.

"Oh. Well, anyway, if you have an employee who wants to get on it, they'll have to do it as a volunteer—stipend's fifty dollars per day for protocols that require overnight clinic residence, twenty-five dollars per day for others, with a minimum of two hundred and fifty dollars. Of course, with clinic residence they also get bed and board and all necessary medical support. You wouldn't get me to test drugs for that, but the ethics committee says there shouldn't be a financial incentive."

"Well . . . would they still get paid their salary?"

"Only if they're working or it's paid vacation time," Shirley said. She chuckled. "It would save the company money if we could make everyone into a research subject and just pay the stipends, wouldn't it? Lot simpler accounting—no FICA or FUCA or state withholding. Thank God they can't."

"I guess so," Aldrin said. So, he wondered, what was Crenshaw planning to do about pay and about research stipends? Who was funding this? And why hadn't he thought of this before? "Thanks, Shirley," he said belatedly.

"Good luck," she said.

So, supposing the treatment would take, he realized he had no idea how long it might take. Was that in the stuff Crenshaw had given him? He looked it up and read it carefully, lips pursed. If Crenshaw hadn't made some arrangement to have Research fund Section A's salary, then he was converting technical staff with seniority to low-paid lab rats . . . and even if they were out of rehab in a month (the most optimistic estimate in the proposal) that would save . . . a lot of money. He ran the figures. It looked like a lot of money, but it wasn't, compared to the legal risks the company would run.

He didn't know anybody high on the tree in Research, just Marcus over in Data Support. Back to Human Resources . . . with Betty gone, he tried to remember other names. Paul. Debra. Paul was on the list; Debra wasn't.

"Make it snappy," Paul said. "I'm leaving tomorrow."

"Leaving?"

"One of the famous ten percent," Paul said. Aldrin could hear the anger in his voice. "No, the company's not losing money, no, the company's not cutting personnel; they just happen to be no longer in need of my services."

Icy fingers ran down his back. This could be himself next month. No, today, if Crenshaw realized what he was doing.

"Buy you coffee," Aldrin said.

"Yeah, like I need something to keep me awake nights," Paul said.

"Paul, listen. I need to talk to you, and not on the phone."

A long silence, then, "Oh. You, too?"

"Not yet. Coffee?"

"Sure. Ten-thirty, snack bar?"

"No, early lunch. Eleven-thirty," Aldrin said, and hung up. His palms were sweaty.


"SO, WHAT'S THE BIG SECRET?" PAUL ASKED. HIS FACE SHOWED nothing; he sat hunched over a table near the middle of the snack bar.

Aldrin would have chosen a table in the corner, but now—seeing Paul out in the middle—he remembered a spy thriller he'd seen. Corner tables might be monitored. For all he knew, Paul was wearing a . . . a wire, they called it. He felt sick.

"C'mon, I'm not recording anything," Paul said. He sipped his coffee. "It will be more conspicuous if you stand there gaping at me or pat me down. You must have one helluva secret."

Aldrin sat, his coffee slopping over the edge of his mug. "You know my new division head is one of the new brooms—"

"Join the club," Paul said, with an intonation of *get on with it*.

"Crenshaw," Aldrin said.

"Lucky bastard," Paul said. "He's got quite a reputation, our Mr. Crenshaw."

"Yeah, well, remember Section A?"

"The autistics, sure." Paul's expression sharpened. "Is he taking after *them*?"

Aldrin nodded.

"That's stupid," Paul said. "Not that he's not, but—that's really stupid. Our Section Six-fourteen-point-eleven tax break depends on 'em. Your division is marginal anyway for Six-fourteen-point-eleven employees, and they're worth one-point-five credits each. Besides, the publicity . . ."

"I know," Aldrin said. "But he's not listening. He says they're too expensive."

"He thinks everyone but himself is too expensive," Paul said. "He thinks he's underpaid, if you can believe it." He sipped his coffee again. Aldrin noticed he didn't say what Crenshaw was paid, even now. "We had a time with him when he came through our office—he knows every benefit and tax trick in the book."

"I'm sure," Aldrin said.

"So what's he want to do, fire them? Dock their pay?"

"Threaten them into volunteering for a human-trials research protocol," Aldrin said.

Paul's eyes widened. "You're kidding! He can't do that!"

"He is." Aldrin paused, then went on. "He says there's not a law the company can't get around."

"Well, that may be true, but—we can't just ignore the laws. We have to subvert them. And human trials—what is it, a drug?"

"A treatment for adult autistics," Aldrin said. "Supposed to make them normal. It supposedly worked on an ape."

"You can't be serious." Paul stared at him. "You *are* serious. Crenshaw's trying to bully Category Six-fourteen-point-eleven employees into stage-one human trials on something like that? It's asking for a publicity nightmare; it could cost the company billions—"

"You know that and I know that, but Crenshaw . . . has his own way of looking at things."

"So—who signed off on it upstairs?"

"Nobody that I know of," Aldrin said, crossing mental fingers. That was the literal truth, because he hadn't asked.

Paul no longer looked sour and sulky. "That power-mad idiot," he said. "He thinks he can pull this off and gain ground on Samuelson."

"Samuelson?"

"Another one of the new brooms. Don't you keep up with what's going on?"

"No," Aldrin said. "I'm not any good at that sort of thing."

Paul nodded. "I used to think I was, but this pink slip proves I'm not. But anyway, Samuelson and Crenshaw came in as rivals. Samuelson's cut manufacturing costs without raising a ripple in the press—though that's going to change soon, I think. Anyway, Crenshaw must think he can pull a triple play—get some volunteers who'll be too scared for their jobs to complain about it if something goes wrong, push it through all on his own without letting anyone else know, and then take the credit. And you'll go down with him, Pete, if you don't do something."

"He'll fire me in a second if I do," Aldrin said.

"There's always the ombudsman. They haven't cut that position yet, though Laurie's feeling pretty shaky."

"I can't trust it," Aldrin said, but he filed it away. Meanwhile he had other questions. "Look—I don't know how he's going to account for their time, if they do this. I was hoping to find out more about the law—can he make them put their sick leave and vacation time into it? What's the rule for special employees?"

"Well, basically, what he's proposing is illegal as hell. First off, if

Research gets a whiff that they're not genuine volunteers, they'll stomp all over it. They have to report to NIH, and they don't want the feds down on them for half a dozen breaches of medical ethics and the fair employment laws. Then, if it'll put 'em out of the office more than thirty days—will it?" Aldrin nodded and Paul went on. "Then it can't be classed as vacation time, and there are special rules for leave and sabbatical, especially regarding special-category employees. They can't be made to lose seniority. Or salary for that matter." He ran his finger around the rim of his mug. "Which is not going to make Accounting happy. Except for senior scientists on sabbatical in other institutions, we have no accounting category for employees not actually on the job who are receiving full salary. Oh, and it'll shoot your productivity to hell and gone, too."

"I thought of that," Aldrin murmured.

Paul's mouth quirked. "You can really nail this guy," he said. "I know I can't get my job back, not the way things are, but . . . I'll enjoy knowing what's going on."

"I'd like to do it subtly," Aldrin said. "I mean—of course I'm worried about my job, but that's not all of it. He thinks I'm stupid and cowardly and lazy, except when I lick his boots, and then he only thinks I'm a natural-born bootlicker. I thought of sort of blundering along, trying to help in a way that exposes him—"

Paul shrugged. "Not my style. I'd stand up and yell, myself. But you're you, and if that's what rocks your boat . . ."

"So—who can I talk to in Human Resources to arrange leave time for them? And what about Legal?"

"That's awfully roundabout. It'll take longer. Why not talk to the ombudsman while we have one or, if you're feeling heroic, go make an appointment with the top guns? Bring all your little retards or whatever they are along; make it really dramatic."

"They aren't retards," Aldrin said automatically. "They're autists. And I don't know what would happen if they had a clue how illegal this all was. They should know, by rights, but what if they called a reporter or something? Then the shit really would be in the fire."

"So go by yourself. You might even like the rarefied heights of the managerial pyramid." Paul laughed a little too loudly, and Aldrin wondered if Paul had put something in his coffee.

"I dunno," he said. "I don't think they'll let me get far enough up. Crenshaw would find out I was making an appointment, and you remember that memo about chain of command."

" 'Swhat we get for hiring a retired general as CEO," Paul said.

But now the lunch crowd was thinning out, and Aldrin knew he had to go.

HE WASN'T SURE WHAT TO DO NEXT, WHICH APPROACH WOULD be most fruitful. He still wished that maybe Research would put the lid back on the box and he wouldn't have to do anything.

Crenshaw disposed of that idea in late afternoon. "Okay, here's the research protocol," he said, slamming a data cube and some printouts on Aldrin's desk. "I do not understand why they need all these preliminary tests—PET scans, for God's sake, and MRIs and all the rest of it—but they say they do, and I don't run Research." The *yet* of Crenshaw's ambition did not have to be spoken to be heard.

"Get your people scheduled in for the meetings, and liaise with Bart in Research about the test schedules."

"Test schedules?" Aldrin asked. "What about when tests conflict with normal working hours?"

Crenshaw scowled, then shrugged. "Hell, we'll be generous—they don't have to make up the time."

"And what about the accounting end? Whose budget—?"

"Oh, for God's sake, Pete, just take care of it!" Crenshaw had turned an ugly puce. "Get your thumb out and start solving problems, not finding them. Run it past me; I'll sign off on it; in the meantime use the authorization code on those." He nodded at the pile of paper.

"Right, sir," Aldrin said. He couldn't back away—he was standing behind his desk—but after a moment Crenshaw turned and went back to his own office.

Solve problems. He would solve problems, but they wouldn't be Crenshaw's problems.

*I DO NOT KNOW WHAT I CAN UNDERSTAND AND WHAT I MIS-*
understand while thinking I understand it. I look up the lowest-level text in neurobiology that I can find on the 'net, looking first at the glossary. I do not like to waste time linking to definitions if I can learn them first. The glossary is full of words I never saw before, hundreds of them. I do not understand the definitions, either.

I need to start further back, find light from a star further away, deeper in the past.

A text on biology for high school students: that might be at my level. I glance at the glossary: I know these words, though I have not seen some of them in years. Only perhaps a tenth are new to me.

When I start the first chapter, it makes sense, though some of it is different than I remember. I expect that. It does not bother me. I finish the book before midnight.

The next night, I do not watch my usual show. I look up a college text. It is too simple; it must have been written for college students who had not studied biology in high school. I move on to the next level, guessing at what I need. The biochemistry text confuses me; I need to know organic chemistry. I look up organic chemistry on the Internet and download the first chapters of a text. I read late into the night again and before and after work on Friday and while I am doing my laundry.

On Saturday we have the meeting at the campus; I want to stay home and read, but I must not. The book fizzes in my head as I drive; little jumbled molecules wriggle in patterns I can't quite grasp yet. I have never been to the campus on a weekend; I did not know that it would be almost as busy as on a weekday.

Cameron's and Bailey's cars are there when I arrive; the others haven't come yet. I find my way to the designated meeting room. It has walls paneled in fake wood, with a green carpet. There are two rows of chairs with metal legs and padded seats and backs covered with rose-colored fabric with little flecks of green in it facing one end of the room. Someone I don't know, a young woman, stands by the door. She is holding a pasteboard box with name tags in it. She has a list with little photographs, and she looks at me, then says my name. "Here's yours," she says, handing me a name tag. It has a little metal clip on it. I hold it in my hand. "Put it on," she says. I do not like this kind of clip; it makes my shirt pull. I clip it on anyway and go in.

The others are sitting in chairs; each empty chair has a folder with a name on it, one for each of us. I find my seat. I do not like it; I am in the front row on the right-hand side. It might not be polite to move. I glance along the row and see that we have been put in alphabetical order, from the point of view of a speaker facing us.

I am seven minutes early. If I had brought a printout of the text I have been reading, I could read now. Instead, I think about what I have read. So far everything makes sense.

When all of us are in the room, we sit in silence, waiting, for two minutes and forty seconds. Then I hear Mr. Aldrin's voice. "Are they all here?" he asks the woman at the door. She says yes.

He comes in. He looks tired but otherwise normal. He is wearing a knit shirt and tan slacks and loafers. He smiles at us, but it is not a whole smile.

"I'm glad to see you all here," he says. "In just a few minutes, Dr. Ransome will explain to prospective volunteers what this project is about. In your folders are questionnaires about your general health history; please fill those out while you're waiting. And sign the nondisclosure agreement."

The questionnaires are simple, multiple-choice rather than fill-in-the-blank. I am almost finished with mine (it takes little time to check the "no" box for heart disease, chest pain, shortness of breath, kidney disease, difficulty in urination . . .) when the door opens and a man in a white coat comes in. His coat has *Dr. Ransome* embroidered on the pocket. He has curly gray hair and bright blue eyes; his face looks too young to have gray hair. He, too, smiles at us, with eyes and mouth both.

"Welcome," he says. "I'm glad to meet you. I understand you're all interested in this clinical trial?" He does not wait for the answer we do not give. "This will be brief," he says. "Today, anyway, is just a chance for you to hear what this is about, the projected schedule of preliminary tests and so on. First, let me give a little history."

He talks very fast, reading from a notebook, rattling off a history of the research on autism, starting around the turn of the century with the discovery of two genes associated with autistic spectrum disorders. By the time he turns on a projector and shows us a picture of the brain, my mind is numb, overloaded. He points to different areas with a light pen, still talking fast. Finally he gets to the current project, again starting at the beginning, with the original researcher's early work on primate social organization and communication, leading—in the end—to this possible treatment.

"That's just some background," he says. "It's probably too much for you, but you'll have to excuse my enthusiasm. There's a simplified version in your folders, including diagrams. Essentially what we're going to do is normalize the autistic brain, and then train it in an enhanced and faster version of infant sensory integration, so the new architecture works properly." He pauses, sips from a glass of water, and goes on. "Now that's about it for this meeting; you'll be scheduled for tests—it's all in your folders—and there will be more meetings with the medical teams, of course. Just hand in your questionnaires and other paperwork to the girl at the door, and you'll be notified if you are accepted onto the protocol." He turns away and is gone before I can think of anything to say. Neither does anyone else.

Mr. Aldrin stands up and turns to us. "Just hand me your finished questionnaires and the signed nondisclosure—and don't worry; you will all be accepted onto the protocol."

That is not what worries me. I finish my questionnaire, sign the statement, hand both to Mr. Aldrin, and leave without talking to the others. It has wasted almost my whole Saturday morning, and I want to go back to my reading.

I drive home as quickly as the speed limit allows and start reading as soon as I am back in my apartment. I do not stop to clean my apartment or my car. I do not go to church on Sunday. I take printouts of the chapter I am on, and the next, with me to work on Monday and Tuesday and read during my lunch break as well as late into the night. The information flows in, clear and organized, its patterns stacked neatly in paragraphs and chapters and sections. My mind has room for them all.

By the following Wednesday, I feel ready to ask Lucia what I should read to understand the way the brain works. I have taken the on-line assessment tests in biology level one, biology level two, biochemistry levels one and two, organic chemistry theory one. I glance at the neurology book, which now makes much more sense, but I am not sure it is the right one. I do not know how much time I have; I do not want to waste it on the wrong book.

I am surprised that I have not done this before. When I started fencing, I read all the books that Tom recommended and watched the videos he said would be helpful. When I play computer games, I read all about them.

Yet I have never before set out to learn all about the way my own brain works. I do not know why. I know that it felt very strange at first and I was almost sure I would not be able to figure out what the books said. But it is actually easy. I think I could have completed a college degree in this if I had tried. All my advisers and counselors told me to go into applied mathematics, so I did. They told me what I was capable of, and I believed them. They did not think I had the kind of brain that could do real scientific work. Maybe they were wrong.

I show Lucia the list I have printed out, of all the things I have read, and the scores I got on the assessment tests. "I need to know what to read next," I say.

"Lou—I'm ashamed to say I'm amazed." Lucia shakes her head. "Tom, come see this. Lou's just about done the work for an undergraduate biology degree in one week."

"Not really," I say. "This is all aimed at one thing, and the undergraduate requirements would include a course in population biology, a course in botany—"

"I was thinking more of the depth and not the breadth," Lucia says. "You've gone from lower-level to challenging upper-division courses. . . . Lou, do you really understand organic synthesis?"

"I do not know," I say. "I have not done any of the lab work. But the patterns of it are obvious, the way the chemicals fit together—"

"Lou, can you tell me why some groups attach to a carbon ring adjacent to one another and some have to skip a carbon or two?"

It is a silly question, I think. It is obvious that the place groups join is the result of their shape or the charge they carry. I can see them easily in my mind, the lumpy shapes with the positive or negative charge clouds around them. I do not want to tell Tom I think it is a silly question. I remember the paragraphs in the text that explain, but I think he wants it in my words, not parroted. So I say it as clearly as I can, not using any of the same phrases.

"And you got that just from reading the book—how many times?"

"Once," I say. "Some paragraphs twice."

"Holy shit," Tom says. Lucia clucks at him. She does not like strong language. "Lou—do you have any idea how hard most college students work to learn that?"

Learning is not hard. Not learning is hard. I wonder why they are not learning it for long enough to feel like work. "It is easy to see in my head," I say instead of asking that. "And the books have pictures."

"Strong visual imagination," Lucia murmurs.

"Even with the pictures, even with the video animations," Tom says, "most college students have trouble with organic chemistry. And you got that much of it with just one run through the book—Lou, you've been holding out on us. You're a genius."

"It may be a splinter skill," I say. Tom's expression scares me; if he thinks I am a genius maybe he will not want to let me fence with them.

"Splinter skill, hooey," Lucia says. She sounds angry; I feel my stomach clenching. "Not you," she says quickly. "But the whole concept of splinter skills is so . . . antiquated. Everybody has strengths and weaknesses; everybody fails to generalize many of the skills they have. Physics students who make top grades in mechanics mess up driving vehicles on slick roads: they know the theory, but they can't generalize to real driving. And I've known you for years now—your skills are *skills*, not splinter skills."

"But I think it's mostly memorizing," I say, still worried. "I can memorize really rapidly. And I am good at most standardized tests."

"Explaining it in your own words isn't memorizing," Tom says. "I know the on-line text. . . . You know, Lou, you haven't ever asked what I do for a living."

It is a shock, like touching a doorknob in cold weather. He is right. I did not ask what his job was; it does not occur to me to ask people what their jobs are. I met Lucia at the clinic so I knew she was a doctor, but Tom?

"What is your job?" I ask now.

"I'm on the university faculty," he says. "Chemical engineering."

"You teach classes?" I ask.

"Yes. Two undergraduate classes and one graduate-level class. Chem-E majors have to take organic chemistry, so I know what they think of it. And how kids who understand it describe it, as opposed to those who don't."

"So—you really think I do?"

"Lou, it's *your* mind. Do you think you understand it?"

"I think so . . . but I am not sure I would know."

"I think so, too. And I have never known anyone who picked it up cold in less than a week. Did you ever have an IQ test, Lou?"

"Yes." I do not want to talk about that. I had tests every year, not always the same ones. I do not like tests. The ones where I was supposed to guess which meaning of the word the person who made the test meant from the pictures, for instance. I remember the time the word was *track* and the pictures included the mark of a tire on a wet street and some cupolas on top of a long, tall building that looked—to me, anyway—like the grandstand at a racetrack. I picked that for the word *track*, but it was wrong.

"And did they tell you the result or just your parents?"

"They didn't tell my parents, either," I say. "It made my mother upset. They said they did not want to affect her expectations for me. But they said I should be able to graduate from high school."

"Umm. I wish we had some idea . . . Would you take the tests again?"

"Why?" I ask.

"I guess . . . I just want to know . . . but if you can do this stuff without, what difference does it really make?"

"Lou, who has your records?" Lucia asks.

"I don't know," I say. "I suppose—the schools back home? The doctors? I haven't been back since my parents died."

"They're your records: you should be able to get them now. If you want to."

This is something else I never thought of before. Do people get their school records and medical records after they grow up and move away? I do not know if I want to know exactly what people put in those records. What if they say worse things about me than I remember?

"Anyway," Lucia goes on. "I think I know a good book for you to try next. It's kind of old, but nothing in it is actually wrong, though a lot more's been learned. Cego and Clinton's *Brain Functionality*. I have a copy . . . I think. . . ." She goes out of the room, and I try to think about everything she and Tom said. It is too much; my head is buzzing with thoughts like swift photons bouncing off the inside of my skull.

"Here, Lou," Lucia says, handing me a book. It is heavy, a thick volume of paper with cloth cover. The title and authors are printed in gold on a black rectangle on the spine. It has been a long time since I saw a paper book. "It may be on-line somewhere by now, but I don't know where. I bought it back when I was just starting med school. Take a look."

I open the book. The first page has nothing on it. The next one has the title, the authors' names—Betsy R. Cego and Malcolm R. Clinton. I wonder if the *R.* stands for the same middle name in both and if that is why they wrote the book together. Then blank space, and at the bottom a company name and date. I guess that is the book company. R. Scott Landsdown & Co. Publishers. Another *R.* On the back of that page is some information in small print. Then another page with the title and authors. The next page says "Preface." I start reading.

"You can skip that and the introduction," Lucia says. "I want to see if you're okay with the level of instruction in the chapters."

Why would the authors put in something that people weren't going to read? What is the preface for? The introduction? I do not want to argue with Lucia, but it seems to me that I should read that part first because it is first. If I am supposed to skip over it for now, why is it first? For now, though, I page through until I find chapter 1.

It is not hard to read, and I understand it. When I look up, after ten pages or so, Tom and Lucia are both watching me. I feel my face getting hot. I forgot about them while I was reading. It is not polite to forget about people.

"Is it okay, Lou?" Lucia asks.

"I like it," I say.

"Good. Take it home and keep it as long as you like. I'll e-mail you some other references that I know are on-line. How's that?"

"Fine," I say. I want to go on reading, but I hear a car door slam outside and know it is time to do fencing instead.

*T*HE OTHERS ARRIVE IN A BUNCH, WITHIN JUST A COUPLE
of minutes. We move to the backyard, then stretch and put on
our gear and start fencing. Marjory sits with me between bouts.
I am happy when she sits next to me. I would like to touch her hair, but
I do not.

We do not talk much. I do not know what to say. She asks if I got
the windshield fixed, and I say yes. I watch her fence with Lucia; she is
taller than Lucia, but Lucia is the better fencer. Marjory's brown hair
bounces when she moves; Lucia wears her light hair in a ponytail. They
both wear white fencing jackets tonight; soon Marjory's has little brown
smudges where Lucia has scored hits.

I am still thinking about Marjory when I fence with Tom. I am seeing Marjory's pattern, and not Tom's, and he kills me quickly twice.

"You're not paying attention," he says to me.

"I'm sorry," I say. My eyes slide to Marjory.

Tom sighs. "I know you've got a lot on your mind, Lou, but one reason to do this is to get a break from it."

"Yes . . . I'm sorry." I drag my eyes back and focus on Tom and his
blade. When I concentrate, I can see his pattern—a long and complicated one—and now I can parry his attacks. Low, high, high, low, reverse, low, high, low, low, reverse . . . he's throwing a reverse shot every
fifth and varying the setup to it. Now I can prepare for the reverse, piv-
oting and then making a quick diagonal step: attack obliquely, one of
the old masters says, never directly. It is like chess in that way, with the

knight and bishop attacking at an angle. At last I set up the series I like best and get a solid hit.

"Wow!" Tom says. "I thought I'd managed real randomness—"

"Every fifth is a reverse," I say.

"Damn," Tom said. "Let's try that again—"

This time he doesn't reverse for nine shots, the next time seven—I notice he's always using a reverse attack on the odd numbers. I test that through longer series, just waiting. Sure enough . . . nine, seven, five, then back to seven. That's when I step past on the diagonal and get him again.

"That wasn't five," he says. He sounds breathless.

"No . . . but it was an odd number," I say.

"I can't think fast enough," Tom says. "I can't fence *and* think. How do you do it?"

"You move, but the pattern doesn't," I say. "The pattern—when I see it—is still. So it is easier to hold in mind because it doesn't wiggle around."

"I never thought of it that way," Tom says. "So—how do you plan your own attacks? So they aren't patterned?"

"They are," I say. "But I can shift from one pattern to another. . . ." I can tell this is not getting across to him and try to think of another way of saying it. "When you drive somewhere, there are many possible routes . . . many patterns you might choose. If you start off on one and a road you would use for that pattern is blocked, you take another and get onto one of your other patterns, don't you?"

"You see routes as patterns?" Lucia says. "I see them as strings—and I have real trouble shifting from one to another unless the connection is within a block."

"I get completely lost," Susan says. "Mass transit's a real boon to me—I just read the sign and get on. In the old days, if I'd had to drive everywhere, I'd have been late all the time."

"So, you can hold different fencing patterns in your head and just . . . jump or something . . . from one to another?"

"But mostly I'm reacting to the opponent's attacks while I analyze the pattern," I say.

"That would explain a lot about your learning style when you started fencing," Lucia says. She looks happy. I do not understand why that would make her happy. "Those first bouts, you did not have time to learn the pattern—and you were not skilled enough to think and fence both, right?"

"I . . . it's hard to remember," I say. I am uncomfortable with this, with other people picking apart how my brain works. Or doesn't work.

"It doesn't matter—you're a good fencer now—but people do learn differently."

The rest of the evening goes by quickly. I fence with several of the others; in between I sit beside Marjory if she is not fencing. I listen for noise from the street but hear nothing. Sometimes cars drive by, but they sound normal, at least from the backyard. When I go out to my car, the windshield is not broken and the tires are not flat. The absence of damage was there before the damage occurred—if someone came to damage my car, the damage would be subsequent . . . very much like dark and light. The dark is there first, and then comes light.

"Did the police ever get back to you about the windshield?" Tom asks. We are all out in the front yard together.

"No," I say. I do not want to think about the police tonight. Marjory is next to me and I can smell her hair.

"Did you think who might have done it?" he asks.

"No," I say. I do not want to think about that, either, not with Marjory beside me.

"Lou—" He scratches his head. "You *need* to think about it. How likely is it that your car was vandalized twice in a row, on fencing night, by strangers?"

"It was not anyone in our group," I say. "You are my friends."

Tom looks down, then back at my face. "Lou, I think you need to consider—" My ears do not want to hear what he will say next.

"Here you are," Lucia says, interrupting. Interrupting is rude, but I am glad she interrupts. She has brought the book with her. She hands it to me when I have put my duffel back in the trunk. "Let me know how you get on with it."

In the light from the street lamp on the corner the book's cover is a dull gray. It feels pebbly under my fingers.

"What are you reading, Lou?" Marjory asks. My stomach tightens. I do not want to talk about the research with Marjory. I do not want to find out that she already knows about it.

"Cego and Clinton," Lucia says, as if that is a title.

"Wow," Marjory says. "Good for you, Lou."

I do not understand. Does she know the book just from its authors? Did they write only one book? And why does she say the book is good for me? Or did she mean "good for you" as praise? I do not understand that meaning, either. I feel trapped in this whirlpool of questions, not-knowing swirling around me, drowning me.

Light speeds toward me from the distant specks, the oldest light taking longest to arrive.

I drive home carefully, even more aware than usual of the pools and streams of light washing over me from street lamps and lighted signs. In and out of the fast dark—and it does feel faster in the dark.

TOM SHOOK HIS HEAD AS LOU DROVE AWAY. "I DON'T KNOW— " he said, and paused.

"Are you thinking what I'm thinking?" Lucia asked.

"It's the only real possibility," Tom said. "I don't like to think it, it's hard to believe Don could be capable of anything this serious, but . . . who else could it be? He would know Lou's name; he could find out his address; he certainly knows when fencing practice is and what Lou's car looks like."

"You didn't tell the police," Lucia said.

"No. I thought Lou would figure it out, and it's his car, after all. I felt I shouldn't horn in. But now . . . I wish I'd gone on and told Lou flat out to beware of Don. He still thinks of him as a friend."

"I know." Lucia shook her head. "He's so—well, I don't know if it's really loyalty or just habit. Once a friend, always a friend? Besides—"

"It might not be Don. I know. He's been a nuisance and a jerk at times, but he's never done anything violent before. And nothing happened tonight."

"The night's not over," Lucia said. "If we hear about anything else, we have to tell the police. For Lou's sake."

"You're right, of course." Tom yawned. "Let's just hope nothing happens and it's random coincidence."

AT THE APARTMENT, I CARRY THE BOOK AND MY DUFFEL UP-stairs. I hear no sound from Danny's apartment as I go past it. I put my fencing jacket in the dirty-clothes basket and take the book to my desk. In the light of the desk lamp, the cover is light blue, not gray.

I open it. Without Lucia to prompt me to skip them, I read all the pages carefully. On the page headed "Dedications," Betsy R. Cego has put: "For Jerry and Bob, with thanks," and Malcolm R. Clinton has put: "To my beloved wife, Celia, and in memory of my father, George." The foreword, written by Peter J. Bartleman, M.D., Ph.D., Professor Emeritus, Johns Hopkins University School of Medicine, includes the information that Betsy R. Cego's *R.* stands for *Rodham* and Malcom R. Clinton's *R.* stands for *Richard*, so the *R.* probably has nothing to do with their coauthorship. Peter J. Bartleman says the book is the most important compilation of the current state of knowledge on brain function. I do not know why he wrote the foreword.

The preface answers that question. Peter J. Bartleman taught Betsy R. Cego when she was in medical school and awakened a lifelong interest in and commitment to the study of brain function. The phrasing seems awkward to me. The preface explains what the book is about, why the authors wrote it, and then thanks a lot of people and companies for their help. I am surprised to find the name of the company I work for in that list. They provided assistance with computational methods.

Computational methods are what our division develops. I look again at the copyright date. When this book was written I was not yet working there.

I wonder if any of those old programs are still around.

I turn to the glossary in back and read quickly through the definitions. I know about half of them now. When I turn to the first chapter, a review of brain structure, it makes sense. The cerebellum, amygdala, hippocampus, cerebrum . . . diagrammed in several ways, sectioned top to bottom and front to back and side to side. I have never seen a diagram that showed the functions of the different areas, though, and I look at it closely. I wonder why the main language center is in the left brain when there is a perfectly good auditory processing area in the right brain. Why specialize like that? I wonder if sounds coming into one ear are heard more as language than sounds coming in the other ear. The tiers of visual processing are just as hard to understand.

It is on the last page of that chapter that I find a sentence so overwhelming that I have to stop and stare at it: "Essentially, physiological functions aside, the human brain exists to analyze and generate patterns."

My breath catches in my chest; I feel cold, then hot. That is what I do. If that is the essential function of the human brain, then I am not a freak, but normal.

This cannot be. Everything I know tells me that I am the different one, the deficient one. I read the sentence again and again, trying to make it fit with what I know.

Finally, I read past it to the rest of the paragraph: "The pattern-analysis or pattern-making may be flawed, as with some mental diseases, resulting in mistaken analysis or patterns generated on the basis of erroneous 'data,' but even in the most severe cognitive failure, these two activities are characteristic of the human brain—and indeed, of brains much less sophisticated than human ones. Readers interested in these functions in nonhumans should consult references below."

So perhaps I am normal *and* freakish . . . normal in seeing and making patterns, but perhaps I make the wrong patterns?

I read on, and when I finally stop, feeling shaky and exhausted, it is almost three in the morning. I have reached chapter 6, "Computational Assessments of Visual Processing."

I AM CHANGING ALREADY. A FEW MONTHS AGO, I DID NOT know that I loved Marjory. I did not know I could fence in a tournament with strangers. I did not know I could learn biology and chemistry the way I have been. I did not know I could change this much.

One of the people at the rehab center where I spent so many hours as a child used to say that disabilities were God's way of giving people a chance to show their faith. My mother would pinch her lips together, but she did not argue. Some government program at that time funneled money through churches to provide rehab services, and that was what my parents could afford. My mother was afraid that if she argued, they might kick me out of the program. Or at least she'd have to listen to more of the sermonizing.

I do not understand God that way. I do not think God makes bad things happen just so that people can grow spiritually. Bad parents do that, my mother said. Bad parents make things hard and painful for their children and then say it was to help them grow. Growing and living are hard enough already; children do not need things to be harder. I think this is true even for normal children. I have watched little children learning to walk; they all struggle and fall down many times. Their faces show that it is not easy. It would be stupid to tie bricks on them to make it harder. If that is true for learning to walk, then I think it is true for other growing and learning as well.

God is supposed to be the good parent, the Father. So I think God would not make things harder than they are. I do not think I am autistic because God thought my parents needed a challenge or I needed a challenge. I think it is like if I were a baby and a rock fell on me and broke my leg. Whatever caused it was an accident. God did not prevent the accident, but He did not cause it, either.

Accidents happen to people; my mother's friend Celia said most accidents weren't really accidents, they were caused by someone doing something stupid, but the person who gets hurt isn't always the one who did something stupid. I think my autism was an accident, but what I do with it is me. That is what my mother said.

That is what I think most of the time. Sometimes I am not sure.

IT IS A GRAY MORNING, WITH LOW CLOUDS. THE SLOW LIGHT has not yet chased all the darkness away. I pack my lunch. I pick up Cego and Clinton and go downstairs. I can read during my lunch break.

My tires are all still full. My new windshield is unbroken. Perhaps the person who is not my friend is tired of hurting my car. I unlock the car, put my lunch and the book on the passenger seat, and get in. The morning music I like for driving is playing in my head.

When I turn the key, nothing happens. The car will not start. There is no sound but the little click of the turning key. I know what that means. My battery is dead.

The music in my head falters. My battery was not dead last night. The charge level indicator was normal last night.

I get out and unlatch the hood of the car. When I lift the hood, something jumps out at me; I stagger back and almost fall over the curb.

It is a child's toy, a jack-in-the-box. It is sitting where the battery should be. The battery is gone.

I will be late for work. Mr. Crenshaw will be angry. I close the hood over the engine without touching the toy. I did not like jack-in-the-box toys when I was a child. I must call the police, the insurance company, the whole dreary list. I look at my watch. If I hurry to the transit stop, I can catch a commuter train to work and I will not be late.

I take the lunch sack and the book from the passenger seat, relock the car, and walk quickly to the transit stop. I have the cards of the police officers in my wallet. I can call them from work.

On the crowded train, people stare past one another without making eye contact. They are not all autistic; they know somehow that it is appropriate not to make eye contact on the train. Some read news faxes. Some stare at the monitor at the end of the car. I open the book and read what Cego and Clinton said about how the brain processes visual signals. At the time they wrote, industrial robots could use only simple visible input to guide movement. Binocular vision in robots hadn't been developed yet except for the laser targeting of large weapons.

I am fascinated by the feedback loops between the layers of visual processing; I had not realized that something this interesting went on inside normal people's heads. I thought they just looked at things and recognized them automatically. I thought my visual processing was faulty when—if I understand this correctly—it is only slow.

When I get to the campus stop, I now know which way to go, and it takes less time to walk to our building. I am three minutes and twenty seconds early. Mr. Crenshaw is in the hall again, but he does not speak to me; he moves aside without speaking, so that I can get to my office. I say, "Good morning, Mr. Crenshaw," because that is appropriate, and he grunts something that might have been, "Morning." If he had had my speech therapist, he would enunciate more clearly.

I put the book on my desk and go out in the hall to take my lunch to the kitchenette. Mr. Crenshaw is now by the door, looking out at the parking lot. He turns around and sees me. "Where's your car, Arrendale?" he asks.

"Home," I say. "I took the transit."

"So you *can* take the transit," he says. His face is a little shiny. "You don't really need a special parking lot."

"It is very noisy," I say. "Someone stole my battery last night."

"A car's only a constant problem for someone like you," he says, coming closer. "People who don't live in secure areas, with secure parking, really shouldn't flaunt having a car."

"Nothing happened until a few weeks ago," I say. I do not understand why I want to argue with him. I do not like to argue.

"You were lucky. But it looks like someone has found you out now, doesn't it? Three episodes of vandalism. At least this time you weren't late."

"I was only late once because of that," I say.

"That's not the point," he says. I wonder what the point is, besides his dislike of me and the others. He glances at my office door. "You'll want to get back to work," he says. "Or start—" Now he looks at the clock in the hall. It is two minutes, eighteen seconds past starting time. What I want to say is, *You made me late,* but I do not say that. I go in my office and shut the door. I am not going to make up the two minutes, eighteen seconds. It is not my fault. I feel a little excited about that.

I call up yesterday's work, and the beautiful patterns form again in my mind. One parameter after another flows in, shifting the pattern from one structure to another, seamlessly. I vary the parameters across the permitted range, checking to see that there is no unwanted shift. When I look up again, it is an hour and eleven minutes later. Mr. Crenshaw will not be in our building now. He never stays this long. I go out in the hall for some water. The hall is empty, but I see the sign on the gym door. Someone is in there. I do not care.

I write down the words I will need to say, then call the police and ask for the investigating officer from the first incident, Mr. Stacy. When he comes onto the line, I can hear noises in the background. Other people are talking, and there is a kind of rumbling noise.

"This is Lou Arrendale," I say. "You came when my car had its tires slashed. You said to call—"

"Yes, yes," he says. He sounds impatient and as if he is not really listening. "Officer Isaka told me about the windshield the following week. We haven't had time to follow that up—"

"Last night my battery was stolen," I say. "And someone put a toy where the battery should be."

"What?"

"When I went out this morning, my car would not start. I looked under the hood and something jumped at me. It was a jack-in-the-box someone had put where the battery should have been."

"Just stay there and I'll send someone over—" he says.

"I am not at home," I say. "I am at work. My boss would be angry if I did not come on time. The car is at home."

"I see. Where is the toy?"

"In the car," I say. "I did not touch it. I do not like jack-in-the-box toys. I just shut the lid." I meant "hood," but the wrong word came in my mouth.

"I'm not happy about this," he says. "Someone really does not like you, Mr. Arrendale. Once is mischief, but—do you have any idea who might have done it?"

"The only person I know who has been angry with me is my boss, Mr. Crenshaw," I say. "When I came in late, that time. He does not like autistic people. He wants us to try an experimental treatment—"

"Us? Are there other autistic people where you work?"

I realize he does not know; he did not ask about this before. "Our section is all autistic people," I say. "But I do not think Mr. Crenshaw would do this sort of thing. Although . . . he does not like it that we have special permits to drive and a separate parking lot. He thinks we should all ride the train like everyone else."

"Hmmm. And all the attacks have been on your car."

"Yes. But he does not know about my fencing class." I cannot imagine Mr. Crenshaw driving around the city to find my car and then smashing the windshield.

"Anything else? Anything at all?"

I do not want to make false accusations. Making false accusations is very wrong. But I do not want my car to be damaged again. It takes my time away from other things; it messes up my schedule. And it costs money.

"There is someone at the Center, Emmy Sanderson, who thinks I should not have normal friends," I say. "But she does not know where the fencing group is." I do not really think it is Emmy, but she is the one person, besides Mr. Crenshaw, who has been angry with me in the last month or so. The pattern does not really fit for her or for Mr. Crenshaw, but the pattern must be wrong, because a possible name has not come out.

"Emmy Sanderson," he says, repeating the name. "And you don't think she knows where the house is?"

"No." Emmy is not my friend, but I do not believe she has done these things. Don is my friend, and I do not want to believe he has done these things.

"Isn't it more likely someone connected to your fencing group? Is there someone you don't get along with?"

I am sweating suddenly. "They are my friends," I say. "Emmy says they can't really be friends, but they are. Friends do not hurt friends."

He grunts. I do not know what that grunt means. "There are friends and friends," he says. "Tell me about the people in that group."

I tell him about Tom and Lucia first and then the others; he takes down the names, asking me how to spell some of them.

"And were they all there, these last few weeks?"

"Not all every week," I say. I tell him what I can remember, who was on a business trip and who was there. "And Don switched to a different instructor; he got upset with Tom."

"With Tom. Not with you?"

"No." I do not know how to say this without criticizing friends, and criticizing friends is wrong. "Don teases sometimes, but he is my friend," I say. "He got upset with Tom because Tom told me about something Don did a long time ago and Don wanted him not to have told me."

"Something bad?" Stacy asks.

"It was at a tournament," I say. "Don came to me after the match and told me what I did wrong, and Tom—my instructor—told him to let me alone. Don was trying to help me, but Tom thought he wasn't helping me. Tom said I had done better than Don had at his first tournament, and Don heard him, and then he was angry with Tom. After that he quit coming to our group."

"Huh. Sounds more like a reason to slash your instructor's tires. I suppose we'd better check him out, though. If you think of anything else, let me know. I'll send someone over to retrieve that toy; we'll see if we can get some fingerprints or something off of it."

When I have put the phone down, I sit thinking of Don, but that is not pleasant. I think of Marjory instead, and then Marjory and Don. It makes me feel a little sick in my stomach to think of Don and Marjory as . . . friends. In love. I know Marjory does not like Don. Does he like her? I remember how he sat beside her, how he stood between me and her, how Lucia shooed him away.

Has Marjory told Lucia she likes me? This is another thing that normal people do, I think. They know when someone likes someone and how much. They do not have to wonder. It is like their other mind reading, knowing when someone is joking and when someone is serious, knowing when a word is used correctly and when it is used in a joking way. I wish I could know for sure if Marjory likes me. She smiles at me. She talks to me in a pleasant voice. But she might do that anyway, as long as she did not dislike me. She is pleasant to people; I saw that in the grocery store.

Emmy's accusations come back to me. If Marjory does see me as an interesting case, a research subject even though not in her field, she might still smile and talk to me. It would not mean she liked me. It would mean she is a nicer person than Dr. Fornum, and even Dr. Fornum smiles an appropriate smile when she says hello and good-bye, though it never reaches her eyes as Marjory's smile does. I have seen Marjory smile at other people and her smile is always whole. Still, if Marjory is my friend, she is telling me the truth when she tells me about her research, and if I am her friend, I should believe her.

I shake my head to drive these thoughts back into the darkness where they belong. I turn on the fan to make my spin spirals whirl. I need that now; I am breathing too fast and I can feel sweat on my neck. It is because of the car, because of Mr. Crenshaw, because of having to call the police. It is not because of Marjory.

After a few minutes, my brain's functionality returns to pattern analysis and pattern generation. I do not let my mind drift to Cego and Clinton. I will work through part of my lunch hour to make up the time I spent talking to the police, but not the two minutes and eighteen seconds Mr. Crenshaw cost me.

Immersed in the complexity and beauty of the patterns, I do not emerge for lunch break until 1:28:17.

THE MUSIC IN MY HEAD IS BRUCH'S VIOLIN CONCERTO NO. 2. I have four recordings of it at home. A very old one with a twentieth century soloist named Perlman, my favorite. Three newer, two fairly competent but not very interesting and one with last year's Tchaikovsky Competition winner, Idris Vai-Kassadelikos, who is still very young. Vai-Kassadelikos may be as good as Perlman when she is older. I do not know how good he was when he was her age, but she plays with passion, pulling out the long notes in smooth, heartbreaking phrases.

This is music that makes it easier to see some kinds of patterns than others. Bach enhances most of them, but not the ones that are . . . elliptical is the best way I can say it. The long sweep of this music, which obscures the rosetted patterns Bach brings out, helps me find and build the long, asymmetrical components that find rest in fluidity.

It is dark music. I hear it as long, undulating streaks of darkness, like blue-black ribbons blowing in the wind at night, obscuring and revealing the stars. Now soft, now louder, now the single violin, with the orchestra just breathing behind it, and now louder, the violin riding up over the orchestra like the ribbons on a current of air.

I think it will be good music to have in mind while I am reading Cego and Clinton. I eat my lunch quickly and set a timer on my fan. That way the moving twinkles of light will let me know when it is time to go back to work.

Cego and Clinton talk about the way the brain processes edges, angles, textures, colors, and how the information flows back and forth between the layers of visual processing. I did not know there was a separate area for facial recognition, though the reference they cite goes back to the twentieth century. I did not know that the ability to recognize an object in different orientations is impaired in those born blind who gain sight later.

Again and again they talk about things I have had trouble with in the context of being born blind or having brain trauma from a head injury or stroke or aneurysm. When my face does not turn strange like other people's do when they feel strong emotion, is it just that my brain doesn't process the change of shape?

A tiny hum: my fan coming on. I shut my eyes, wait three seconds, and open them. The room is awash in color and movement, the spin spirals and whirligigs all moving, reflecting light as they move. I put the book down and go back to work. The steady oscillation of the twinkles soothes me; I have heard normal people call it chaotic, but it is not. It is a pattern, regular and predictable, and it took me weeks to get it right. I think there must be some easier way to do it, but I had to adjust each of the moving parts until it moved at the right speed in relation to the others.

My phone rings. I do not like it when the phone rings; it jerks me out of what I am doing, and there will be someone on the other end who expects me to be able to talk right away. I take a deep breath. When I answer, "This is Lou Arrendale," at first I hear only noise.

"Ah—this is Detective Stacy," the voice says. "Listen—we sent someone over to your apartment. Tell me again what your license number is."

I recite it for him.

"Um. Well, I'm going to need to talk to you in person." He stops and I think he expects me to say something, but I do not know what to say. Finally he goes on. "I think you may be in danger, Mr. Arrendale. Whoever's doing this is not a nice guy. When our guys tried to get that toy out, there was a small explosion."

"Explosion!"

"Yes. Luckily, our guys were careful. They didn't like the setup, so they called the bomb squad. But if you'd picked up that toy, you might've lost a finger or two. Or the thing might've hit you in the face."

"I see." I could in fact see it, imagine it visually. I had almost reached out and grabbed the toy . . . and if I had . . . I feel cold suddenly; my hand starts to tremble.

"We really need to find this person. Nobody's home at your fencing instructor's—"

"Tom teaches at the university," I say. "Chemical engineering."

"That'll help. Or his wife?"

"Lucia's a doctor," I say. "She works at the medical center. Do you really think this person wants to hurt me?"

"He sure wants to cause you trouble," the officer said. "And the vandalism seems more violent each time. Can you come down to the station?"

"I cannot leave here until after work," I say. "Mr. Crenshaw would be angry with me." If someone is trying to hurt me, I do not want anyone else angry.

"We're sending someone out," Mr. Stacy says. "Which building are you in?" I tell him that and which gate to enter and which turns to take to arrive in our parking area, and he continues, "Should be there within a half hour. We have fingerprints; we'll need to take yours to compare with the others. Your fingerprints should be all over that car—and you've had it in for repairs lately, too, so there'll be others. But if we find a set that doesn't match yours or any of the repair people . . . we'll have something solid to go on."

I wonder if I should tell Mr. Aldrin or Mr. Crenshaw that the police are coming here to talk to me. I do not know which would make Mr. Crenshaw more angry. Mr. Aldrin does not seem to get angry as often. I call his office.

"The police are coming to talk to me," I say. "I will make up the time."

"Lou! What's wrong? What have you done?"

"It is my car," I say.

Before I can say more, he is talking fast. "Lou, don't say anything to them. We'll get you a lawyer. Was anyone hurt?"

"Nobody was hurt," I say. I hear his breath gush out.

"Well, that's a mercy," he says.

"When I opened the hood, I did not touch the device."

"Device? What are you talking about?"

"The . . . the thing that someone put in my car. It looked like a toy, a jack-in-the-box."

"Wait—wait. Are you telling me that the police are coming because of something that happened to you, that someone else did? Not something you did?"

"I did not touch it," I say. The words he has just said filter through slowly, one by one; the excitement in his voice made it hard to hear them clearly. He thought at first that I had done something wrong, something to bring the police here. This man I have known since I started working here—he thinks I could do something so bad. I feel heavier.

"I'm sorry," he says before I can say anything. "It sounds like—it must sound like—I jumped to the conclusion that you had done something wrong. I'm sorry. I know you would not. But I still think you need one of the company's lawyers with you when you talk to the police."

"No," I say. I feel chilly and bitter; I do not want to be treated like a child. I thought Mr. Aldrin liked me. If he does not like me, then Mr. Crenshaw, who is so much worse, must really hate me. "I do not want a lawyer. I do not need a lawyer. I have not done anything wrong. Someone has been vandalizing my car."

"More than once?" he asks.

"Yes," I say. "Two weeks ago, when all my tires were flat. Someone had slashed them. That is the time I was late. Then, the following Wednesday, while I was at a friend's house, someone smashed my windshield. I called the police then, too."

"But you didn't tell me, Lou," Mr. Aldrin says.

"No . . . I thought Mr. Crenshaw would be angry. And this morning, my car wouldn't start. The battery was gone, and a toy was there instead. I came to work and called the police. When they went to look, the toy had an explosive under it."

"My God, Lou—that's . . . you could have been hurt. That's horrible. Do you have any idea—no, of course you don't. Listen, I'm coming right over."

He has hung up before I can ask him not to come right over. I am too excited to work now. I do not care what Mr. Crenshaw thinks. I need my time in the gym. No one else is there. I put on bouncing music and begin bouncing on the trampoline, big, swooping bounces. At first I am out of rhythm with the music, but then I stabilize my movement. The music lifts me, swings me down; I can feel the beat in the compression of my joints as I meet the stretchy fabric and spring upward again.

By the time Mr. Aldrin arrives, I am feeling better. I am sweaty and I can smell myself, but the music is moving strongly inside me. I am not shaky or scared. It is a good feeling.

Mr. Arrendale looks worried, and he wants to come closer than I want him to come. I do not want him to smell me and be offended. I do not want him to touch me, either. "Are you all right, Lou?" he asks. His hand keeps reaching out, as if to pat me.

"I am doing okay," I say.

"Are you sure? I really think we should have a lawyer here, and maybe you should go by the clinic—"

"I was not hurt," I say. "I am all right. I do not need to see a doctor, and I do not want the lawyer."

"I left word at the gate for the police," Mr. Aldrin says. "I had to tell

Mr. Crenshaw." His brow lowers. "He was in a meeting. He will get the message when he gets out."

The door buzzer sounds. Employees authorized to be in this building have their own key cards. Only visitors have to ring the buzzer. "I'll go," Mr. Aldrin says. I do not know whether to go in my office or stand in the hall. I stand in the hall and watch Mr. Aldrin go to the door. He opens it and says something to the man who is standing there. I cannot see if it is the same man I talked to before until he is much closer, and then I can tell that it is.

CHAPTER THIRTEEN

"HI, MR. ARRENDALE," HE SAYS, AND PUTS OUT HIS HAND. I put out mine, though I do not like to shake hands. I know it is appropriate. "Is there somewhere we could talk?" he asks.

"My office," I say. I lead the way in. I do not have visitors, so there is no extra chair. I see Mr. Stacy looking at all the twinklies, the spin spirals and pinwheels and other decorations. I do not know what he thinks about it. Mr. Aldrin speaks softly to Mr. Stacy and leaves. I do not sit down because it is not polite to sit when other people have to stand, unless you are their boss. Mr. Aldrin comes in with a chair that I recognize from the kitchenette. He puts it down in the space between my desk and the files. Then he stands by the door.

"And you are?" Mr. Stacy asks, turning to him.

"Pete Aldrin; I'm Lou's immediate supervisor. I don't know if you understand—" Mr. Aldrin gives me a look that I am not sure of, and Mr. Stacy nods.

"I've interviewed Mr. Arrendale before," he says. Once more I am astonished at how they do it, the way they pass information from one to another without words. "Don't let me keep you."

"But . . . but I think he needs—"

"Mr. Aldrin, Mr. Arrendale here isn't in trouble. We're trying to help him, keep this nutcase from hurting him. Now if you've got a safe place for him to stay for a few days, while we try to track this person down, that would be a help, but otherwise—I don't think he needs baby-sitting while I chat with him. Though it's up to him . . ." The policeman looks at me. I see something in his face that I think may be laughter, but I am not sure. It is very subtle.

"Lou is very capable," Mr. Aldrin says. "We value him highly. I just wanted—"

"To be sure he would get fair treatment. I understand. But it's up to him."

They are both looking at me; I feel impaled on their gaze like one of those exhibits at the museums. I know Mr. Aldrin wants me to say he should stay, but he wants it for the wrong reason and I do not want him to stay. "I will be all right," I say. "I will call you if anything happens."

"Be sure you do," he says. He gives Mr. Stacy a long look and then leaves. I can hear his footsteps going down the hall and then the scrape of the other chair in the kitchenette and the *plink* and *clunk* of money going into the drink machine and a can of something landing down below. I wonder what he chose. I wonder if he will stay there in case I want him.

The policeman closes the door to my office, then sits in the chair Mr. Aldrin placed for him. I sit down behind my desk. He is looking around the room.

"You like things that turn around, don't you?" he says.

"Yes," I say. I wonder how long he will stay. I will have to make up the time.

"Let me explain about vandals," he says. "There's several kinds. The person—usually a kid—who just likes to make a little trouble. They may spike a tire or break a windshield or steal a stop sign—they do it for the excitement, as much as anything, and they don't know, or care, who they're doing it to. Then there's what we call spillover. There's a fight in a bar, and it continues outside, and there's breaking windshields in the parking lot. There's a crowd in the street, someone gets rowdy, and the next thing you know they're breaking windows and stealing stuff. Now some of these people are the kind that aren't usually violent—they shock themselves with how they act in a crowd." He pauses, looking at me, and I nod. I know he wants some response.

"You're saying that some vandals aren't doing it to hurt particular people."

"Exactly. There's the individual who likes making messes but doesn't know the victim. There's the individual who doesn't usually make messes but is involved in something else where the violence spills over. Now when we first get an example of vandalism—as with your tires—that clearly isn't spillover, we first think of the random individual. That's the commonest form. If another couple cars got their tires slashed in the same neighborhood—or on the same transit route—in the next few weeks, we'd just assume we had a bad boy thumbing his nose at the cops. Annoying, but not dangerous."

"Expensive," I say. "To the people with the cars, anyway."

"True, which is why it's a crime. But there's a third kind of vandal, and that's the dangerous kind. The one who is targeting a particular person. Typically, this person starts off with something annoying but not dangerous—like slashing tires. Some of these people are satisfied with one act of revenge for whatever it was. If they are, they're not that dangerous. But some aren't, and these are the ones we worry about. What we see in your case is the relatively nonviolent tire slashing, followed by the more violent windshield smashing and the still more violent placement of a small explosive device where it could do you harm. Every incident has escalated. That's why we're concerned for your safety."

I feel as if I am floating in a crystal sphere, unconnected to anything outside. I do not feel endangered.

"You may feel safe," Mr. Stacy says, reading my mind again. "But that doesn't mean you *are* safe. The only way for you to be safe is for that nutcase who's stalking you to be behind bars."

He says "nutcase" so easily; I wonder if that is what he thinks of me as well.

Again, he reads my thoughts. "I'm sorry—I shouldn't have said 'nutcase.' . . . You probably hear enough of that sort of thing. It just makes me mad: here you are, hardworking and decent, and this—this *person* is after you. What's his problem?"

"Not autism," I want to say, but I do not. I do not think any autistic would be a stalker, but I do not know all of them and I could be wrong.

"I just want you to know that we take this threat seriously," he says. "Even if we didn't move fast at first. So, let's get serious. It has to be aimed at you—you know the phrase about three times enemy action?"

"No," I say.

"Once is accident, twice is coincidence, and third time is enemy action. So if something that only might be aimed at you happens three times, then it's time to consider someone's after you."

I puzzle over this a moment. "But . . . if it is enemy action, then it was enemy action the first time, too, wasn't it? Not an accident at all?"

He looks surprised, eyebrows up and mouth rounded. "Actually—yeah—you're right, but the thing is you don't know about that first one until the others happen and then you can put it in the same category."

"If three real accidents happen, you could think they were enemy action and still be wrong," I say.

He stares at me, shakes his head, and says, "How many ways are there to be wrong and how few to be right?"

The calculations run through my head in an instant, patterning the decision carpet with the colors of accident (orange), coincidence (green), and enemy action (red). Three incidents, each of which can have one of three values, three theories of truth, each of which is either true or false by the values assigned each action. And there must be some filter on the choice of incidents, rejecting for inclusion those that cannot be manipulated by the person who may be the enemy of the one whose incidents are used as a test.

It is just such problems I deal with daily, only in far greater complexity.

"There are twenty-seven possibilities," I say. "Only one is correct if you define correctness by all parts of the statement being true—that the first incident is in fact accident, the second is in fact coincidence, and the third is in fact enemy action. Only one—but a different one—is true if you define correctness as all three incidents being in fact enemy action. If you define correctness as the third incident being enemy action in all cases, regardless of the reality of the first two cases, then the statement will correctly alert you to enemy action in nine cases. If, however, the first two cases are not enemy action, but the third is, then the choice of related incidents becomes even more critical."

He is staring at me now with his mouth a little open. "You . . . calculated that? In your head?"

"It is not hard," I say. "It is simply a permutation problem, and the formula for permutations is taught in high school."

"So there's only one chance in twenty-seven that it is actually true?" he asks. "That's nuts. It wouldn't be an old saw if it wasn't truer than that . . . that's what? About four percent? Something's wrong."

The flaw in his mathematical knowledge and his logic is painfully clear. "Actually true depends on what your underlying purpose is," I say. "There is only one chance in twenty-seven that all parts of the statement are true: that the first incident is an accident, the second incident is a coincidence, and the third incident is enemy action. That is three-point-seven percent, giving an error rate of ninety-six-point-three for the truth value of the entire statement. But there are nine cases—one-third of the total—in which the *last* case is enemy action, which drops the error rate with respect to the final incident to sixty-seven percent. And there are nineteen cases in which enemy action can occur—as first, second, or last incident or a combination of them. Nineteen out of twenty-seven is seventy-point-thirty-seven percent: that is the probability that enemy action occurred in at least one of the three incidents. Your presumption of enemy action will still be wrong twenty-nine-point-sixty-three percent of the time, but that's less than a third of the time. Thus if it is important to be alert to enemy action—if it is worth more to you to detect enemy action than to avoid suspecting it when it does not exist—it will be profitable to guess that enemy action has occurred when you observe three reasonably related incidents."

"Good God," he says. "You're serious." He shakes his head abruptly. "Sorry. I hadn't—I didn't know you were a math genius."

"I am not a math genius," I say. I start to say again that these calculations are simple, within the ability of schoolchildren, but that might be inappropriate. If he cannot do them, it could make him feel bad.

"But . . . what you're saying is . . . following that saying means I'm going to be wrong a lot of the time anyway?"

"Mathematically, the saying cannot be right more often than that. It is just a saying, not a mathematical formula, and only formulae get it right in mathematics. In real life, it will depend on your choice of incidents to connect." I try to think how to explain. "Suppose on the way to work on the train, I put my hand on something that has just been painted. I did not see the WET PAINT sign, or it got knocked off by accident. If I connect the accident of paint on my hand to the accident of dropping an egg on the floor and then to tripping on a crack in the sidewalk and call that enemy action—"

"When it's your own carelessness. I see. Tell me, does the percentage of error go down as the number of related incidents goes up?"

"Of course, if you pick the right incidents."

He shakes his head again. "Let's get back to you and make sure we pick the right incidents. Someone slashed the tires on your car sometime Wednesday night two weeks ago. Now on Wednesdays, you go over to a friend's house for . . . fencing practice? Is that sword fighting or something?"

"They're not real swords," I say. "Just sport blades."

"Okay. Do you keep them in your car?"

"No," I say. "I store my things at Tom's house. Several people do."

"So the motive couldn't have been theft, in the first place. And the following week, your windshield was broken while you were at fencing, a drive-by. Again, the attack's on your car, and this time the location of your car makes it clear the attacker knew where you went on Wednesdays. And this third attack was accomplished on Wednesday night, between the time you got home from your fencing group and when you got up in the morning. The timing suggests to me that this is connected to your fencing group."

"Unless it is someone who has only Wednesday night to do things," I say.

He looks at me a long moment. "It sounds like you don't want to face the possibility that someone in your fencing group—or someone who was in your fencing group—has a grudge against you."

He is right. I do not want to think that people I have been meeting every week for years do not like me. That even one of them does not like me. I felt safe there. They are my friends. I can see the pattern Mr. Stacy wants me to see—it is obvious, a simple temporal association, and I have already seen it—but it is impossible. Friends are people who want good things for you and not bad ones.

"I do not . . ." My throat closes. I feel the pressure in my head that means I will not be able to talk easily for a while. "It is not . . . right . . . to . . . to . . . say . . . what . . . you are . . . not sure . . . is true." I wish I had not said anything about Don before. I feel wrong about it.

"You don't want to make a false accusation," he says.

I nod, mute.

He sighs. "Mr. Arrendale, everyone has people that don't like them. You don't have to be a bad person to have people not like you. And it doesn't make you a bad person to take reasonable precautions not to let other people hurt you. If there's someone in that group who has a grudge against you, fair or unfair, that person still may not be the one who did this. I know that. I'm not going to throw someone into criminal rehab just because they don't like you. But I don't want you to get killed because we didn't take this seriously."

I still cannot imagine someone—Don—trying to kill me. I have not done anyone harm that I know of. People do not kill for trivial reasons.

"My point is," Mr. Stacy says, "that people kill for all sorts of stupid reasons. Trivial reasons."

"No," I mutter. Normal people have reasons for what they do, big reasons for big things and little reasons for little things.

"Yes," he says. His voice is firm; he believes what he is saying. "Not everyone, of course. But someone who would put that stupid toy in your car, with the explosive—that is not a normally sane person, Mr. Arrendale, in my opinion. And I am professionally familiar with the kind of people who kill. Fathers who knock a child into the wall for taking a piece of bread without permission. Wives and husbands who grab for a weapon in the midst of an argument about who forgot what at the grocery store. I do not think you are the sort of man who makes idle accusations. Trust us to investigate carefully whatever you tell us and give us something to work on. This person who is stalking you might stalk someone else another time."

I do not want to talk; my throat is so tight it hurts. But if it could happen to someone else . . .

As I am thinking what to say and how, he says, "Tell me more about this fencing group. When did you start going there?"

This is something I can answer, and I do. He asks me to tell him how the practice works, when people come, what they do, what time they leave.

I describe the house, the yard, the equipment storage. "My things are always in the same place," I say.

"How many people store their gear at Tom's, instead of taking it back and forth?" he asks.

"Besides me? Two," I say. "Some of the others do, if they're going to a tournament. But three of us regularly. Don and Sheraton are the others." There. I have mentioned Don without choking.

"Why?" he asks quietly.

"Sheraton travels a lot for work," I say. "He doesn't make it every week, and he once lost a complete set of blades when his apartment was broken into while he was overseas on business. Don—" My throat threatens to close again, but I push on. "Don was always forgetting his stuff and borrowing from people, and finally Tom told him to leave it there, where he couldn't forget it."

"Don. This is the same Don you told me about over the phone?"

"Yes," I say. All my muscles are tight. It is so much harder when he is here in my office, looking at me.

"Was he in the group when you joined it?"

"Yes."

"Who are some of your friends in the group?"

I thought they were all my friends. Emmy said it was impossible for them to be my friends; they are normal and I am not. But I thought they were. "Tom," I say. "Lucia. Brian. M-Marjory . . ."

"Lucia is Tom's wife, right? Who is this Marjory?"

I can feel my face getting hot. "She . . . she is a person who . . . who is my friend."

"A girlfriend? Lover?"

Words fly out of my head faster than light. I can only shake my head, mute again.

"Someone you wish was a girlfriend?"

I am seized into rigidity. Do I wish? Of course I wish. Dare I hope? No. I cannot shake my head or nod it; I cannot speak. I do not want to see the look on Mr. Stacy's face; I do not want to know what he thinks. I want to escape to some quiet place where no one knows me and no one will ask questions.

"Let me suggest something here, Mr. Arrendale," Mr. Stacy says. His voice sounds staccato, chopped into sharp little bits of sound that cut at my ears, at my understanding. "Suppose you really like this woman, this Marjory—"

*This Marjory* as if she were a specimen, not a person. The very thought of her face, her hair, her voice, floods me with warmth.

"And you're kinda shy—okay, that's normal in a guy who hasn't had that many relationships, which I'm guessing you haven't. And maybe she likes you, and maybe she just enjoys being admired from afar. And this other person—maybe Don, maybe not—is pissed that she seems to like you. Maybe he likes her. Maybe he just doesn't like you. Whatever, he sees something he doesn't like between the two of you. Jealousy is a pretty common cause of violent behavior."

"I . . . do not . . . want . . . him . . . to be the one . . ." I say, gasping it out.

"You like him?"

"I . . . know . . . think . . . thought . . . I know . . . knew . . . him . . ."
A sick blackness inside swirls around and through the warm feeling about Marjory. I remember the times he joked, laughed, smiled.

"Betrayal is never fun," Mr. Stacy says, like a priest reciting the Ten Commandments. He has his pocket set out and is entering commands.

I can sense something dark hovering over Don, like a great thundercloud over a sunny landscape. I want to make it go away, but I do not know how.

"When do you get off work?" Mr. Stacy asks.

"I would usually leave at five-thirty," I say. "But I have lost time today because of what happened to my car. I have to make that time up."

His eyebrows go up again. "You have to make up time that you lost because of talking to me?"

"Of course," I say.

"Your boss didn't seem that picky," Mr. Stacy says.

"It is not Mr. Aldrin," I say. "I would make up the time anyway, but it is Mr. Crenshaw who gets angry if he thinks we are not working hard enough."

"Ah, I see," he says. His face flushes; he is very shiny now. "I suspect I might not like your Mr. Crenshaw."

"I do not like Mr. Crenshaw," I say. "But I must do my best anyway. I would make up the time even if he did not get angry."

"I'm sure you would," he says. "What time do you think you will leave work today, Mr. Arrendale?"

I look at the clock and calculate how much time I have to make up. "If I start back to work now, I can leave at six fifty-three," I say. "There is a train leaving from the campus station at seven-oh-four, and if I hurry I can make it."

"You aren't riding on the train," he says. "We'll see that you have transport. Didn't you hear me say we're worried about your safety? Do you have someone you can stay with for a few days? It's safer if you're not in your own apartment."

I shake my head. "I do not know anyone," I say. I have not stayed at anyone's house since I left home; I have always stayed in my own apartment or a hotel room. I do not want to go to a hotel now.

"We're looking for this Don fellow right now, but he's not easy to find. His employer says he hasn't been in for several days, and he's not at his apartment. You'll be all right here for a few hours, I guess, but don't leave without letting us know, okay?"

I nod. It is easier than arguing. I have the feeling that this is happening in a movie or show, not in real life. It is not like anything anyone ever told me about.

The door opens suddenly; I am startled and jump. It is Mr. Crenshaw. He looks angry again.

"Lou! What's this I hear about you being in trouble with the police?" He glances around the office and stiffens when he sees Mr. Stacy.

"I'm Lieutenant Stacy," the policeman says. "Mr. Arrendale isn't in trouble. I'm investigating a case in which he is the victim. He told you about the slashed tires, didn't he?"

"Yes—" Mr. Crenshaw's color fades and flushes again. "He did. But is that any reason to send a policeman out here?"

"No, it's not," Mr. Stacy says. "The two subsequent attacks, including the explosive device placed in his automobile, are."

"Explosive device?" Mr. Crenshaw pales again. "Someone is trying to hurt Lou?"

"We think so, yes," Mr. Stacy says. "We are concerned about Mr. Arrendale's safety."

"Who do you think it is?" Mr. Crenshaw asks. He does not wait for an answer but goes on talking. "He's working on some sensitive projects for us; it could be a competitor wants to sabotage them—"

"I don't think so," Mr. Stacy says. "There is evidence to suggest something completely unrelated to his workplace. I'm sure you're concerned, though, to protect a valuable employee—does your company have a guest hostel or someplace Mr. Arrendale could stay for a few days?"

"No . . . I mean, you really think this is a serious threat?"

The policeman's eyelids droop a little. "Mr. Crenshaw is it? I thought I recognized you from Mr. Arrendale's description. If someone took the battery out of your car and replaced it with a device intended to explode when you opened the hood of the car, would you consider that a serious threat?"

"My God," Mr. Crenshaw says. I know he is not calling Mr. Stacy his god. It is his way of expressing surprise. He glances at me, and his expression sharpens. "What have you been up to, Lou, that someone's trying to kill you? You know company policy; if I find out you've been involved with criminal elements—"

"You're jumping the gun, Mr. Crenshaw," Mr. Stacy says. "There's no indication whatever that Mr. Arrendale has done anything wrong. We suspect that the perpetrator may be someone who is jealous of Mr. Arrendale's accomplishments—who would rather he be less able."

"Resentful of his privileges?" Mr. Crenshaw says. "That would make sense. I always said special treatment for these people would rouse a backlash from those who suffer as a consequence. We have workers who see no reason why this section should have its own parking lot, gym, music system, and dining facility."

I look at Mr. Stacy, whose face has stiffened. Something Mr. Crenshaw said has made him angry, but what? His voice comes out in a drawl that has an edge to it, a tone that I have been taught means some kind of disapproval.

"Ah, yes . . . Mr. Arrendale told me that you disapproved of supportive measures to retain the disabled in the workforce," he says.

"I wouldn't put it that way," Mr. Crenshaw says. "It depends on whether they're really necessary or not. Wheelchair ramps, that sort of thing, but some so-called support is nothing but indulgence—"

"And you, being so expert, know which is which, do you?" Mr. Stacy asks. Mr. Crenshaw flushes again. I look at Mr. Stacy. He does not look scared at all.

"I know what the balance sheet is," Mr. Crenshaw says. "There's no law that can compel us to go broke to coddle a few people who think they need foofaraws like . . . like that—" He points at the spin spirals hanging over my desk.

"Cost a whole dollar thirty-eight," Mr. Stacy says. "Unless you bought 'em from a defense contractor." That is nonsense. Defense contractors do not sell spin spirals; they sell missiles and mines and aircraft. Mr. Crenshaw says something I do not hear as I try to figure out why Mr. Stacy, who seemed generally knowledgeable except about permutations, would suggest buying spin spirals from a defense contractor. It is just silly. Could it be some kind of joke?

". . . But it *is* the point," Mr. Stacy is saying when I catch up to the conversation again. "This gym, now: it's already installed, right? It probably costs diddly to maintain it. Now say you kick out this whole section—sixteen, twenty people maybe?—and convert it to . . . there's nothing I can think of to do in the space taken up by even a large gym that will make you as much money as paying employer's share of unemployment for that many people will. Not to mention losing your certification as a provider-employer for this disability class, and I'm sure you're getting a tax break that way."

"What do you know about that?" Mr. Crenshaw asks.

"Our department has disabled employees, too," Mr. Stacy says. "Some disabled on the job and some hired that way. We had one flaming scuzzbucket of a city councilman, a few years ago, wanted to cut costs by getting rid of what he called freeloaders. I spent way too many off-duty hours working on the stats to show that we'd lose money by dumping 'em."

"You're tax-supported," Mr. Crenshaw said. I could see his pulse pounding in one of the blood vessels on his red, shiny forehead. "You don't have to worry about profit. We have to make the money to pay your damned salary."

"Which I'm sure curdles your beer," Mr. Stacy says. His pulse is pounding, too. "Now if you'll excuse us, I need to talk to Mr. Arrendale—"

"Lou, you'll make up this wasted time," Mr. Crenshaw said, and went out, slamming the door behind him.

I look at Mr. Stacy, who shakes his head. "Now that's a real piece of work. I had a sergeant like that once, years ago when I was just a patrolman, but he transferred to Chicago, thank God. You might want to look for another job, Mr. Arrendale. That one's out to get rid of you."

"I do not understand it," I say. "I work—we all work—very hard here. Why does he want to get rid of us?" Or make us into someone else. . . . I wonder whether to tell Mr. Stacy about the experimental protocol or not.

"He's a power-hungry SOB," Mr. Stacy says. "That kind are always out to make themselves look good and someone else look bad. You're sitting there doing a good job quietly, no fuss. You look like someone he can kick around safely. Unluckily for him, this other thing's happened to you."

"It does not feel lucky," I say. "It feels worse."

"Probably does," Mr. Stacy says. "But it's not. This way, see, your Mr. Crenshaw has to deal with me—and he'll find his arrogance doesn't go far with the police."

I am not sure I believe this. Mr. Crenshaw is not just Mr. Crenshaw;

he is also the company, and the company has a lot of influence on city policy.

"Tell you what," Mr. Stacy says. "Let's get back to those incidents, so I can get out of your hair and you don't have to stay later. Have you had any other interactions with Don, however trivial, that indicated he was upset with you?"

It seems silly, but I tell him about the time Don stood between Marjory and me at practice and about Marjory calling him a real heel even though he cannot be literally a heel.

"So what I'm hearing is a pattern here of your other friends protecting you from Don, making it clear that they don't like how he treats you, is that right?"

I had not thought of it that way. When he says it, I can see the pattern as clearly as any on my computer or in fencing, and I wonder why I did not see it before. "He would be unhappy," I say. "He would see that I am treated differently than he is, and—" I stop, struck suddenly by another pattern I have not seen before. "It's like Mr. Crenshaw," I say. My voice goes up; I can hear the tension in it, but it is too exciting. "He does not like it for the same reason." I stop again, trying to think it through. I reach out and flip on my fan; the spin spirals help me think when I am excited.

"It is the pattern of people who do not really believe we need supports and resent the supports. If I—if we—did worse, they would understand more. It is the combination of doing well and having the supports that upsets them. I am too normal—" I look back at Mr. Stacy; he is smiling and nodding. "That is silly," I say. "I am not normal. Not now. Not ever."

"It may not seem that way to you," he says. "And when you do something like you did with that old catchphrase about coincidence and enemy action, you are clearly not average . . . but most of the time you look normal and act normal. You know, I even thought—what we were told back in the psych classes we had to take was that autistic people were mostly nonverbal, reclusive, rigid." He grins. I do not know what the grin means when he has just said so many bad things about us. "And here I find you driving a car, holding down a job, falling in love, going to fencing meets—"

"Only one so far," I say.

"All right, only one so far. But I see a lot of people, Mr. Arrendale, who function less well than you and some who look to function at the same level. Doing it without supports. Now I see the reason for supports and the economy of them. It's like putting a wedge under the short leg of a table—why not have a solid, foursquare table? Why endure a tippy unstable surface when such a little thing will make it stable? But people aren't furniture, and if other people see that wedge as a threat to them . . . they won't like it."

"I do not see how I am a threat to Don or to Mr. Crenshaw," I say.

"You personally may not be. I don't even think your supports are, to anyone. But some people don't think too well, and it's easy for them to blame someone else for anything that's wrong in their own lives. Don probably thinks if you weren't getting preferential treatment he'd be successful with that woman."

I wish he would use her name, Marjory. "That woman" sounds as if she had done something wrong.

"She probably wouldn't like him anyway, but he doesn't want to face that—he'd rather blame you. That is, if he's the one doing all this." He glances down at his pocket set. "From the information we have on him, he's had a series of low-level jobs, sometimes quitting and sometimes being fired . . . his credit rating's low . . . he could see himself as a failure and be looking for someone to blame for everything."

I never thought of normal people as needing to explain their failures. I never thought of them as having failures.

"We'll send someone to pick you up, Mr. Arrendale," he says. "Call this number when you're ready to leave for home." He hands me a card. "We aren't going to post a guard here, your corporate security's good enough, but do believe me—you need to be careful."

It is hard to go back to work when he is gone, but I focus on my project and accomplish something before it is time to leave and call for a ride.

PETE ALDRIN TOOK A DEEP BREATH AFTER CRENSHAW LEFT HIS office, in a rage about the "stuck-up cop" who had come to interview Lou Arrendale, and picked up the phone to call Human Resources. "Bart—" That was the name Paul had suggested in Human Resources, a young and inexperienced employee who would certainly ask around for directions and help. "Bart, I need to arrange some time off for my entire Section A; they're going to be involved in a research project."

"Whose?" Bart asked.

"Ours—first human trial of a new product aimed at autistic adults. Mr. Crenshaw considers this a top priority in our division, so I'd really appreciate it if you'd expedite setting up indefinite leave. I think that'd be best; we don't know how long it will take—"

"For all of them? At once?"

"They may go through the protocol staggered; I'm not sure yet. I'll let you know when the consent forms are signed. But it'll be at least thirty days—"

"I don't see how—"

"Here's the authorization code. If you need Mr. Crenshaw's signature—"

"It's just not—"

"Thanks," Aldrin said, and hung up. He could imagine Bart looking puzzled and alarmed both, then running off to his supervisor to ask what to do. Aldrin took a deep breath, then called Shirley in Accounting.

"I need to arrange for direct deposit of Section A's salaries into their banks while they're on indefinite leave—"

"Pete, I told you: that's not how it works. You have to have clearance—"

"Mr. Crenshaw considers it a top priority. I have the project authorization code and I can get his signature—"

"But how am I supposed to—"

"Can't you just say they're working at a secondary location? That wouldn't require any changes to the existing departmental budgets."

He could hear her sucking her teeth over the phone. "I could, I guess, if you told me where the secondary location was."

"Building Forty-two, Main Campus."

A moment's silence, then, "But that's the clinic, Pete. What are you trying to pull? Double-dipping for company employees as research subjects?"

"I'm not trying to pull anything," Aldrin said as huffily as he could. "I'm trying to expedite a project Mr. Crenshaw feels strongly about. They won't be double-dipping if they get the salary and not the honoraria."

"I have my doubts," Shirley said. "I'll see what I can do."

"Thanks," Aldrin said, and hung up again. He was sweating; he could feel it running down his ribs. Shirley was no novice; she knew perfectly well that this was an outrageous request, and she would sound off about it.

Human Resources, Accounting . . . Legal and Research had to come next. He rummaged through the papers Crenshaw had left until he found the chief scientist's name on the protocol. Liselle Hendricks . . . not, he noticed, the man who had been sent to talk to the volunteers. Dr. Ransome was listed as "physician liaison, recruitment" in the list of associated technical staff.

"Dr. Hendricks," Aldrin said a few minutes later. "I'm Pete Aldrin, over in Analysis. I'm in charge of Section A, where your volunteers are coming from. Do you have the consent forms ready yet?"

"What are you talking about?" Dr. Hendricks asked. "If you want volunteer recruitment, you need Extension three-thirty-seven. I don't have anything to do with it."

"You are the chief scientist, aren't you?"

"Yes. . . ." Aldrin could imagine the woman's puzzled face.

"Well, I'm just wondering when you'll send over the consent forms for the volunteers."

"Why should I send them to you?" Hendricks asked. "Dr. Ransome is supposed to take care of that."

"Well, they all work here," Aldrin said. "Might be simpler."

"All in one section?" Hendricks sounded more surprised than Aldrin expected. "I didn't know that. Isn't that going to give you some problems?"

"I'll manage," Aldrin said, forcing a chuckle. "After all, I'm a manager." She did not respond to the joke, and he went on. "Now the thing is, they haven't all made up their minds. I'm sure they will, what with . . . one thing and another, but anyway—"

Hendricks's voice sharpened. "What do you mean, with one thing and another? You're not putting pressure on them, are you? It would not be ethical—"

"Oh, I wouldn't worry about that," Aldrin said. "Of course no one can be forced to cooperate, we're not talking about any kind of coercion, of course, but these are difficult times, economically speaking, Mr. Crenshaw says—"

"But . . . but—" It was almost a splutter.

"So if you could get those forms to me promptly, I'd really appreciate it," Aldrin said, and hung up. Then he quickly dialed Bart, the man Crenshaw had told him to contact.

"When are you going to have those consent forms?" he said. "And what kind of schedule are we talking about? Have you talked to Accounting about the payroll issues? Have you talked to Human Resources?"

"Er . . . no." Bart sounded too young to be important, but he was probably a Crenshaw appointee. "I just thought, I think Mr. Crenshaw said he—his section—would be taking care of the details. All I was supposed to do was make sure they qualified for the protocol over here. Consent forms, I'm not sure we have them drafted yet—"

Aldrin smiled to himself. Bart's confusion was a bonus; any manager might easily go over the head of such a disorganized little twit. He had his excuse now for calling Hendricks; if he was lucky—and he felt lucky—no one would realize which one he'd called first.

Now the question was when to go higher. He would prefer to carry the whole tale just when rumors were beginning to rise that high, but he had no idea how long that took. How long would Shirley or Hendricks sit on the new data he'd given them before doing anything? What would they do first? If they went straight upstairs, top management would know in a few hours, but if they waited a day or so, it might be as long as a week.

His stomach churned; he ate two antacid tablets.

CHAPTER FOURTEEN

O N FRIDAY, THE POLICE ARRANGED TO HAVE ME PICKED up and taken to work. My car was towed to the police station for examination; they say they will bring it back by Friday night. Mr. Crenshaw does not come to our section. I make a lot of progress on my project.

The police send a car to take me home, but first we go by a store to buy a replacement battery for my car and then to the place where the police keep cars. It is not the regular police station but a place called an impoundment. That is a new word to me. I have to sign papers stating that my car is my car and that I am taking custody of it. A mechanic puts the new battery I just bought into my car. One of the policemen offers to drive home with me, but I do not think I need help. He says that they have put my apartment on a watch list.

The inside of my car is dirty, with pale dust on the surfaces. I want to clean it, but first I need to drive home. It is a longer drive than coming straight home from work, but I do not get lost. I park my car next to Danny's and go up to my apartment.

I am not supposed to leave my apartment, for my own safety, but it is Friday night and I need to do my laundry. The laundry room is in the building. I think Mr. Stacy meant I should not leave the building. It will be safe in the building, because Danny lives here and he is a policeman. I will not leave the building, but I will do my laundry.

I put the dark things into the dark basket and the light things into the light basket, balance the detergent on top, and carefully look through the peephole before opening the door. No one, of course. I open the door, carry my laundry through, relock the door. It is important to lock the door every time.

As usual on Friday evening, the apartment building is quiet. I can hear the television in someone's apartment as I go down the stairs. The hall outside the laundry room looks the same as usual. I do not see anyone looking in from outside. I am early this week, and no one else is in the laundry room. I put the dark clothes in the right-hand washing machine and the light clothes in the one next to them. When no one is here to watch me, I can put the money in both boxes and start both machines at the same time. I have to stretch my arms to do it, but it sounds better that way.

I have brought Cego and Clinton, and I sit in one of the plastic chairs by the folding table. I would like to take it out into the hall, but there is a sign that says: RESIDENTS ARE STRICTLY FORBIDDEN TO TAKE CHAIRS OUT OF LAUNDRY AREA. I do not like this chair—it is a strange ugly shade of blue-green—but when I am sitting in it I do not have to see it. It still feels bad, but it is better than no chair.

I have read eight pages when old Miss Kimberly comes in with her laundry. I do not look up. I do not want to talk. I will say hello if she speaks to me.

"Hello, Lou," she says. "Reading?"

"Hello," I say. I do not answer the question, because she can see that I am reading.

"What's that?" she says, coming closer. I close the book with my finger in my place, so that she can see the cover.

"My, my," she says. "That's a thick book. I didn't know you liked to read, Lou."

I do not understand the rules about interrupting. It is always impolite for me to interrupt other people, but other people do not seem to think it is impolite for them to interrupt me in circumstances when I should not interrupt them.

"Yes, sometimes," I say. I do not look up from the book because I hope she will understand that I want to read.

"Are you upset with me about something?" she asks.

I am upset now because she will not let me read in peace, but she is an older woman and it would not be polite to say so.

"Usually you're friendly, but you brought in that big fat book; you can't really be reading it—"

"I am," I say, stung. "I borrowed it from a friend Wednesday night."

"But it's—it looks like a very difficult book," she says. "Are you really understanding it?"

She is like Dr. Fornum; she does not think I can really do much.

"Yes," I say. "I do understand it. I am reading about how the visual processing parts of the brain integrate intermittent input, as on a TV monitor, to create a stable image."

"Intermittent input?" she says. "You mean when it flickers?"

"In a way," I say. "Researchers have identified the area of the brain where the flickering images are made smooth."

"Well, I don't see the practical use of it," she says. She takes her clothes out of the basket and begins stuffing them into a machine. "I'm quite happy to let my insides work without watching them while they do it." She measures out detergent, pours it in, inserts the money, and pauses before pushing START. "Lou, I don't think it's healthy, too much concern with how the brain works. People can go crazy that way, you know."

I did not know. It never occurred to me that knowing too much about the way my brain worked could make me insane. I do not think that is a true statement. She pushes the button and the water whooshes into that machine. She comes over to the folding table.

"Everybody knows psychiatrists' and psychologists' children are crazier than average," she says. "Back in the twentieth century, there was a famous psychiatrist who put his own child in a box and kept it there and it went crazy."

I know that is not true. I do not think she will believe me if I tell her it is not true. I do not want to explain anything, so I open the book again. She makes a sharp blowing sound and I hear her shoes click on the floor as she walks away.

When I was in school, they taught us that the brain is like a computer but not so efficient. Computers do not make mistakes if they are correctly built and programmed, but brains do. From this I got the idea that any brain—even a normal brain, let alone mine—was an inferior sort of computer.

This book makes it clear that brains are a lot more complex than any computer and that my brain *is* normal—that it does function exactly like the normal human brain—in many ways. My color vision is normal. My visual acuity is normal. What is not normal? Only the slightest things . . . I think.

I wish I had my medical records from childhood. I do not know if they did all the tests on me that this book discusses. I do not know if they tested the transmission speed of my sensory neurons, for instance. I remember that my mother had a big accordion file, green on the outside and blue on the inside, stuffed with papers. I don't remember seeing it after my parents died, when I packed up things from their house. Maybe my mother threw it away when I was grown up and living on my own. I know the name of the medical center my parents took me to, but I do not know if they would help me, if they even keep records of children who are now grown.

The book talks about a variation in the ability to capture brief transitory stimuli. I think back to the computer games that helped me hear and then learn to say consonants like *p* and *t* and *d*, especially at the ends of words. There were eye exercises, too, but I was so little that I don't remember much of them.

I look at the paired faces in the illustration, which test discrimination of facial features by either placement or type. All the faces look much the same to me; I can just tell—with the prompting of the text labels—that these two have the same eyes, nose, and mouth, but one has them stretched out, farther from the other features. If they were moving, as on a real person's face, I would never notice. Supposedly this means something wrong with a specific part of the brain involved in facial recognition.

Do normal people really perform all these tasks? If so, it's no wonder they can recognize one another so easily, at such distances, in different clothes.

*WE DO NOT HAVE A COMPANY MEETING THIS SATURDAY. I GO* to the Center, but the assigned counselor is out sick. I look at the number for Legal Aid posted on the bulletin board and memorize it. I do not want to call it by myself. I do not know what the others think. After a few minutes, I go home again and continue reading the book, but I do take the time to clean my apartment and my car to make up for last week. I decide to throw away the old fleece seat cover, because I can still feel occasional pricks from glass fragments, and buy a new one. The new one has a strong leathery smell and feels softer than the old one. On Sunday I go to the early service at church, so that I have more time to read.

Monday a memo arrives for all of us, giving the dates and times of preliminary tests. PET scan. MRI scan. Complete physical. Psychological interview. Psychological testing. The memo says we can take time off from work for these tests without penalty. I am relieved; I would not want to make up all the hours these tests will take up. The first test is Monday afternoon, a physical exam. We all go over to the clinic. I do not like it when strangers touch me, but I know how to behave in a clinic. The needle to draw blood doesn't really hurt, but I do not understand what my blood and urine have to do with how my brain functions. No one even tries to explain.

On Tuesday, I have a baseline CT scan. The technician keeps telling me it won't hurt and not to be frightened when the machine moves me into the narrow chamber. I am not frightened. I am not claustrophobic.

After work, I need to go grocery shopping because last Tuesday I met with the others in our group instead. I am supposed to be careful about Don, but I do not think he is really going to hurt me, anyway. He is my friend. By now he is probably sorry for what he did . . . if he is the one who did those things. Besides, it is my day for shopping. I look around the parking lot when I leave and do not see anyone I should not see. The guards at the campus gates would keep out intruders.

At the store, I park as near to one of the lights as I can, in case it is dark when I come out. It is a lucky space, a prime: eleven out from the end of the row. The store is not too busy tonight, so I have time to get everything on my list. Even though I do not have a written list, I know what I need, and I do not have to double back anywhere to find something I forgot. I have too much for one of the express lanes, almost a full basket, so I pick the shortest regular lane.

When I come out it is darker already but not really dark. The air is cool, even above the parking lot pavement. I push the basket along, listening to the rattling rhythm made by the one wheel that only touches the pavement now and then. It is almost like jazz, but less predictable. When I get to the car, I unlock the door and start putting the grocery sacks in carefully. Heavy things like laundry detergent and juice cans on the floor where they cannot fall off and crush something. Bread and eggs on the backseat.

Behind me, the cart suddenly rattles; I turn and do not recognize the face of the man in the dark jacket. Not at first, anyway, and then I realize it is Don.

"It's all your fault. It's your fault Tom kicked me out," he says. His face is all bunched up, the muscles sticking out in knots. His eyes look scary; because I do not want to see them I look at other parts of his face. "It's your fault Marjory told me to go away. It's sick, the way women fall for that disability stuff. You probably have dozens of 'em, perfectly normal women all falling for that helpless act you do." His voice goes high and squeaky and I can tell he is quoting someone or pretending to. "'Poor Lou, he can't help it,' and, 'Poor Lou, he needs me.'" Now his voice is lower again. "Your kind doesn't need normal women," he says. "Freaks should mate with freaks, if they have to mate at all. The very thought of you taking out your—being that way—with a normal woman just makes me puke. It's disgusting."

I cannot say anything. I think I should be frightened, but what I feel is not fear but sadness, sadness so great it is like a heavy weight all over me, dark and formless. Don is normal. He could have been—could have done—so much, so easily. Why did he give it up to be this way?

"I wrote it all down," he says. "I can't take care of all your sort, but they'll know why I did this when they read it."

"It is not my fault," I say.

"The hell it's not," he says. He moves closer. His sweat has an odd smell. I do not know what it is, but I think he ate or drank something that gave it that smell. The collar on his shirt is crooked. I glance down. His shoes are scuffed; the lace of one is loose. Good grooming is important. It makes a good impression. Right now Don is not making a good impression, but no one seems to be noticing. From the corner of my eye I see other people walking to their cars, walking to the store, ignoring us. "You're a *freak*, Lou—you understand what I'm saying? You're a freak and you belong in a zoo."

I know that Don is not making sense and that what he says is objectively not fact, but I feel bruised anyway by the force of his dislike of me. I feel stupid, too, that I did not recognize this in him earlier. He was my friend; he smiled at me; he tried to help me. How could I know?

He takes his right hand out of his pocket, and I see the black circle of a weapon pointing at me. The outside of the barrel gleams a little in the light, but the inside is dark as space. The dark rushes toward me.

"All that social-support crap—hell, if it weren't for you and your kind, the rest of the world wouldn't be sliding into another depression. I'd have the career I should have, not this lousy dead-end job I'm stuck in."

I do not know what kind of work Don does. I should know. I do not think what is happening with money is my fault. I do not think he would have the career he wants if I were dead. Employers choose people who have good grooming and good manners, people who work hard and get along with others. Don is dirty and messy; he is rude and he does not work hard.

He moves suddenly, his arm with the weapon jerking toward me. "Get in the car," he says, but I am already moving. His pattern is simple, easy to recognize, and he is not as fast or as strong as he thinks. My hand catches his wrist as it moves forward, parries it to the side. The noise it makes is not much like the noise of weapons on television. It is louder and uglier; it echoes off the front of the store. I do not have a blade, but my other hand strikes in the middle of his body. He folds around the blow; bad-smelling breath gusts out of him.

"Hey!" someone yells. "Police!" someone else yells. I hear screams. People appear from nowhere in a lump and land on Don. I stagger and almost fall as people bump into me; someone grabs my arms and whirls me around, pushing me against the side of the car.

"Let him go," another voice says. "He's the victim." It is Mr. Stacy. I do not know what he is doing here. He scowls at me. "Mr. Arrendale, didn't we tell you to be careful? Why didn't you go straight home from work? If Dan hadn't told us we should keep an eye on you—"

"I . . . thought . . . I was careful," I say. It is hard to talk with all the noise around me. "But I needed groceries; it is my day to get groceries." Only then do I remember that Don knew it was my day to get groceries, that I had seen him here before on a Tuesday.

"You're damned lucky," Mr. Stacy says.

Don is facedown on the ground, with two men kneeling on him; they have pulled his arms back and are putting on restraints. It takes longer and looks messier than it does on the news. Don is making a strange noise; it sounds like crying. When they pull him up, he is crying. Tears are running down his face, making streaks in the dirt. I am sorry. It would feel very bad to be crying in front of people like that.

"You bastard!" he says to me when he sees me. "You set me up."

"I did not set you up," I say. I want to explain that I did not know the policemen were here, that they are upset with me for leaving the apartment, but they are taking him away.

"When I say it's people like you who make our job harder," Mr. Stacy says, "I do not mean autistic people. I mean people who won't take ordinary precautions." He still sounds angry.

"I needed groceries," I say again.

"Like you needed to do your laundry last Friday?"

"Yes," I say. "And it is daylight."

"You could have let someone get them for you."

"I do not know who to ask," I say.

He looks at me strangely and then shakes his head.

I do not know the music that is pounding in my head now. I do not understand the feeling. I want to bounce, to steady myself, but there is nowhere here to do it—the asphalt, the rows of cars, the transit stop. I do not want to get in the car and drive home.

People keep asking me how I feel. Some of them have bright lights they shine in my face. They keep suggesting things like "devastated" and "scared." I do not feel devastated. *Devastated* means "made desolate or ravaged." I felt desolate when my parents died, abandoned, but I do not feel that way now. At the time Don was threatening me, I felt scared, but more than that I felt stupid and sad and angry.

Now what I feel is very alive and very confused. No one has guessed that I might feel very happy and excited. Someone tried to kill me and did not succeed. I am still alive. I feel very alive, very aware of the texture of my clothes on my skin, of the color of the light, of the feel of the air going in and out of my lungs. It would be overwhelming sensory input except that tonight it is not: it is a good feeling. I want to run and jump and shout, but I know that is not appropriate. I would like to grab Marjory, if she were here, and kiss her, but that is very inappropriate.

I wonder if normal people react to not dying by being devastated and sad and upset. It is hard to imagine anyone not being happy and relieved instead, but I am not sure. Maybe they think my reactions would be different because I am autistic; I am not sure, so I do not want to tell them how I really feel.

"I don't think you should drive home," Mr. Stacy says. "Let one of our guys drive you, why don't you?"

"I can drive," I say. "I am not that upset." I want to be alone in the car, with my own music. And there is no more danger; Don can't hurt me now.

"Mr. Arrendale," the lieutenant says, putting his head close to mine, "you may not think you're upset, but anyone who's been through an experience like this is upset. You will not drive as safely as usual. You should let someone else drive."

I know I will be safe to drive, so I shake my head. He jerks his shoulders and says, "Someone will come by to take your statement later, Mr. Arrendale. Maybe me, maybe someone else." Then he walks off. Gradually the crowd scatters.

The grocery cart is on its side; sacks are split, the food scattered and battered on the ground. It looks ugly and my stomach turns for a moment. I cannot leave this mess here. I still need groceries; these are spoiled. I cannot remember which are in the car, and safe, and which I will need to replace. The thought of going back into the noisy store again is too much.

I should pick up the mess. I reach down; it is disgusting, the bread smashed and trodden into the dirty pavement, the splattered juice, the dented cans. I do not have to like it; I only have to do it. I reach, lift, carry, trying to touch things as little as possible. It is a waste of food and wasting food is wrong, but I cannot eat dirty bread or spilled juice.

"Are you all right?" someone asks. I jump, and he says, "Sorry . . . you just didn't look well."

The police cars are gone. I do not know when they left, but it is dark now. I do not know how to explain what happened.

"I am all right," I say. "The groceries aren't."

"Want some help?" he asks. He is a big man, going bald, with curly hair around the bald spot. He has on gray slacks and a black T-shirt. I do not know if I should let him help or not. I do not know what is appropriate in this situation. It is not something we were taught in school. He has already picked up two dented cans, one of tomato sauce and one of baked beans. "These are okay," he says. "Just dented." He reaches out to me, holding them.

"Thank you," I say. It is always appropriate to say thank you when someone hands you something. I do not want the dented cans, but it does not matter if you want the present; you must say thank you.

He picks up the flattened box that should have had rice in it and drops it in the waste container. When everything we can pick up easily is in the waste container or my car, he waves and walks off. I do not know his name.

WHEN I GET HOME, IT IS NOT EVEN 7:00 P.M. YET. I DO NOT know when a policeman will come. I call Tom to tell him what happened because he knows Don and I do not know any other person to call. He says he will come to my apartment. I do not need him to come, but he wants to come.

When he arrives, he looks upset. His eyebrows are pulled together and there are wrinkles on his forehead. "Lou, are you all right?"

"I am fine," I say.

"Don really attacked you?" He does not wait for me to answer; he rushes on. "I can't believe—we told that policeman about him—"

"You told Mr. Stacy about Don?"

"After the bomb thing. It was obvious, Lou, that it had to be someone from our group. I tried to tell you—"

I remember the time Lucia interrupted us.

"We could see it," Tom went on. "He was jealous of you with Marjory."

"He blames me about his job, too," I say. "He said I was a freak, that it was my fault he didn't have the job he wanted, that people like me should not have normal women like Marjory for friends."

"Jealousy is one thing; breaking things and hurting people is something else," Tom says. "I'm sorry you had to go through this. I thought he was angry with me."

"I am fine," I say again. "He did not hurt me. I knew he did not like me, so it was not as bad as it could have been."

"Lou, you're . . . amazing. I still think it was partly my fault."

I do not understand this. Don did it. Tom did not tell Don to do it. How could it be Tom's fault, even a little bit?

"If I had seen it coming, if I had handled Don better—"

"Don is a person, not a thing," I say. "No one can completely control someone else and it is wrong to try."

His face relaxes. "Lou, sometimes I think you are the wisest of all of us. All right. It wasn't my fault. I'm still sorry you had to go through all that. And the trial, too—that's not going to be easy for you. It's hard on anyone involved in a trial."

"Trial? Why do I need to be on trial?"

"You don't, but you'll have to be a witness at Don's trial, I'm sure. Didn't they tell you?"

"No." I do not know what a witness at a trial does. I have never wanted to watch shows about trials on TV.

"Well, it won't happen anytime soon, and we can talk about it. Right now—is there anything Lucia and I can do for you?"

"No. I am fine. I will come to fencing tomorrow."

"I'm glad of that. I wouldn't want you to stay away because you were afraid someone else in the group would start acting like Don."

"I did not think that," I say. It seems a silly thought, but then I wonder if the group needed a Don and someone else would have to step into that role. Still, if someone who is normal like Don can hide that kind of anger and violence, maybe all normal people have that potential. I do not think I have it.

"Good. If you have the slightest concern about it, though—about anyone—please let me know right away. Groups are funny. I've been in groups where when someone that everybody disliked left we immediately found someone else to dislike and they became the outcast."

"So that is a pattern in groups?"

"It's one pattern." He sighs. "I hope it's not in this group, and I'll be watching for it. Somehow we missed the problem with Don."

The buzzer goes off. Tom looks around, then at me. "I think it will be a policeman," I say. "Mr. Stacy said someone would come to take my statement."

"I'll go on, then," Tom says.


THE POLICEMAN, MR. STACY, SITS ON MY COUCH. HE IS WEAR-ing tan slacks and a checked shirt with short sleeves. His shoes are brown, with a pebbly surface. When he came in he looked around and I could tell that he was seeing everything. Danny looks at things the same way, assessing.

"I have the reports on the earlier vandalism, Mr. Arrendale," he says. "So if you'll just tell me about what happened this evening . . ." This is silly. He was there. He asked me at the time and I told him then, and he put things in his pocket set. I do not understand why he is here again.

"It is my day to go grocery shopping," I say. "I always go grocery shopping at the same store because it is easier to find things in a store when someone has been there every week."

"Do you go at the same time every week?" he asks.

"Yes. I go after work and before fixing supper."

"And do you make a list?"

"Yes." I think, Of course, but maybe Mr. Stacy doesn't think everyone makes a list. "I threw the list away when I got home, though." I wonder if he wants me to get it from the trash.

"That's all right. I just wondered how predictable your movements were."

"Predictable is good," I say. I am beginning to sweat. "It is important to have routines."

"Yes, of course," he says. "But having routines makes it easier for someone who wants to hurt you to find you. Remember I warned you about that last week."

I had not thought of it like that.

"But go on—I didn't mean to interrupt you. Tell me everything."

It feels strange to have someone listening so intently to such unimportant things as the order in which I buy groceries. But he said to tell him everything. I do not know what this has to do with the attack, but I tell him anyway, how I organized my shopping and did not have to retrace my steps.

"Then I walked outside," I say. "It was dusk, not completely dark, but the lights in the parking lot were bright. I had parked in the left-hand row, eleven spaces out." I like it when I can park in prime numbers, but I did not tell him that. "I had the keys in my hand and unlocked the car. I took the sacks of groceries out of the basket and put them in the car." I do not think he wants to hear about putting heavy things on the floor and light things on the seat. "I heard the basket move behind me and turned around. That is when Don spoke to me."

I pause, trying to remember the exact words he used and the order. "He sounded very angry," I say. "His voice was hoarse. He said, 'It's all your fault. It's your fault Tom kicked me out.'" I pause again. He said a lot of words very fast, and I am not sure I remember all of them in the right order. It would not be right to say it wrong.

Mr. Stacy waits, looking at me.

"I am not sure I remember everything exactly right," I say.

"That's okay," he says. "Just tell me what you do remember."

"He said, 'It's your fault Marjory told me to go away.' Tom is the person who organized the fencing group. Marjory is . . . I told you about Marjory last week. She was never Don's girlfriend." I am uncomfortable talking about Marjory. She should speak for herself. "Marjory likes me, in a way, but—" I cannot say this. I do not know how Marjory likes me, whether it is as acquaintance or friend or . . . or more. If I say "not as a lover" will that make it true? I do not want that to be true.

"He said, 'Freaks should mate with freaks, if they have to mate at all.' He was very angry. He said it is my fault there is a depression and he does not have a good job."

"Um." Mr. Stacy just makes that faint sound and sits there.

"He told me to get in the car. He moved the weapon toward me. It is not good to get in the car with an attacker; that was on a news program last year."

"It's on the news every year," Mr. Stacy says. "But some people do it anyway. I'm glad you didn't."

"I could see his pattern," I say. "So I moved—parried his weapon hand and hit him in the stomach. I know it is wrong to hit someone, but he wanted to hurt me."

"Saw his pattern?" Mr. Stacy says. "What is that?"

"We have been in the same fencing group for years," I say. "When he swings his right arm forward to thrust, he always moves his right foot with it, and then his left to the side, and then he swings his elbow out and his next thrust is around far to the right. That is how I knew that if I parried wide and then thrust in the middle, I would have a chance to hit him before he hurt me."

"If he's been fencing you for years, how come he didn't see that coming?" Mr. Stacy asks.

"I don't know," I say. "But I am good at seeing patterns in how other people move. It is how I fence. He is not as good at that. I think maybe because I did not have a blade, he did not think I would use the same countermove as in fencing."

"Huh. I'd like to see you fence," Mr. Stacy says. "I always thought of it as a sissy excuse for a sport, all that white suit and wires stuff, but you make it sound interesting. So—he threatened you with the weapon, you knocked it aside and hit him in the stomach, and then what?"

"Then lots of people started yelling and people jumped on him. I guess it was policemen, but I had not seen them before." I stop. Anything else he can find out from the police who were there, I think.

"Okay. Let's just go back over a few things. . . ." He leads me through it again and again, and each time I remember another detail. I worry about that—am I really remembering all this, or am I filling in the blanks to make him happy? I read about this in the book. It feels real to me, but sometimes that is a lie. Lying is wrong. I do not want to lie.

He asks me again and again about the fencing group: who liked me and who didn't. Which ones I liked and didn't. I thought I liked everyone; I thought they liked me, or at least tolerated me, until Don. Mr. Stacy seems to want Marjory to be my girlfriend or lover; he keeps asking if we're seeing each other. I am getting very sweaty talking about Marjory. I keep telling the truth, which is that I like her a lot and think about her, but we are not going out.

Finally he stands up. "Thank you, Mr. Arrendale; that's all for now. I'll have it written up; you'll need to come down to the station and sign it, and then we'll be in touch when this comes up for trial."

"Trial?" I ask.

"Yes. As the victim of this assault, you'll be a witness for the prosecution. Any problem with that?"

"Mr. Crenshaw will be angry if I take too much time off work," I say. That is true if I still have a job by then. What if I do not?

"I'm sure he'll understand," Mr. Stacy says.

I am sure he will not, because he will not want to understand.

"There's a chance that Poiteau's lawyer will deal with the DA," Mr. Stacy says. "Take a reduced sentence in return for not risking worse in a trial. We'll let you know." He walks to the door. "Take care, Mr. Arrendale. I'm glad we caught this guy and that you weren't hurt."

"Thank you for your help," I say.

When he has gone, I smooth the couch where he sat and put the pillow back where it was. I feel unsettled. I do not want to think about Don and the attack anymore. I want to forget it. I want it not to have happened at all.

I fix my supper quickly, boiled noodles and vegetables, and eat it, then wash the bowl and pot. It is already 8:00 P.M. I pick up the book and start chapter 17, "Integrating Memory and Attention Control: The Lessons of PTSD and ADHD."

By now I am finding the long sentences and complicated syntax much easier to understand. They are not linear but stacked or radial. I wish someone had taught me that in the first place.

The information the authors want to convey is organized logically. It reads like something I might have written. It is strange to think that someone like me might write a chapter in a book on brain functionality. Do I sound like a textbook when I talk? Is that what Dr. Fornum means by "stilted language"? I always imagined performers in gaudy costumes on stilts dancing above the crowd when she said that. It did not seem reasonable; I am not tall and gaudy. If she meant I sounded like a textbook, she could have said so.

By now I know that PTSD is "Post-Traumatic Stress Disorder" and that it produces strange alterations in memory function. It is a matter of complex control and feedback mechanisms, inhibition and disinhibition of signal transmission.

It occurs to me that I am now post-traumatic myself, that being attacked by someone who wants to kill me is what they mean by trauma, though I do not feel very stressed or excited. Maybe normal people do not sit down to read a textbook a few hours after nearly being killed, but I find it comforting. The facts are still there, still arranged in logical order, set down by someone who took care to make them clear. Just as my parents told me the stars shone on, undiminished and undamaged by anything that happened to us on this planet. I like it that order exists somewhere even if it shatters near me.

What would a normal person feel? I remember a science experiment from middle school, when we planted seeds in pots set at angles. The plants grew upward to the light, no matter which way their stems had to turn. I remember wondering if someone had planted me in a sideways pot, but my teacher said it wasn't the same thing at all.

It still feels the same. I am sideways to the world, feeling happy when other people think I should feel devastated. My brain is trying to grow toward the light, but it can't straighten back up when its pot is tipped.

If I understand the textbook, I remember things like what percentage of cars in the parking lot are blue because I pay attention to color and number more than most people. They don't notice, so they don't care. I wonder what they do notice when they look at a parking lot. What else is there to see besides the rows of vehicles, so many blue and so many tan and so many red? What am I missing, as they miss seeing the beautiful numeric relationships?

I remember color and number and pattern and ascending and descending series: that is what came most easily through the filter my sensory processing put between me and the world. These then became the parameters of my brain's growth, so that I saw everything—from the manufacturing processes for pharmaceuticals to the moves of an opposing fencer—in the same way, as expressions of one kind of reality.

I glance around my apartment and think of my own reactions, my need for regularity, my fascination with repeating phenomena, with series and patterns. Everyone needs some regularity; everyone enjoys series and patterns to some degree. I have known that for years, but now I understand it better. We autistics are on one end of an arc of human behavior and preference, but we are connected. My feeling for Marjory is a normal feeling, not a weird feeling. Maybe I am more aware of the different colors in her hair or her eyes than someone else would be, but the desire to be close to her is a normal desire.

It is almost time for bed. When I step in the shower, I look at my perfectly ordinary body—normal skin, normal hair, normal fingernails and toenails, normal genitals. Surely there are other people who prefer unscented soap, who like the same water temperature, the same texture of washcloth.

I finish the shower, brush my teeth, and rinse out the basin. My face in the mirror looks like my face—it is the face I know best. The light rushes into the pupil of my eye, carrying with it the information that is within range of my vision, carrying with it the world, but what I see when I look at where the light goes in is blackness, deep and velvety. Light goes in and darkness looks back at me. The image is in my eye and in my brain, as well as in the mirror.

I turn off the light in the bathroom and go to bed, turning off the light beside the bed after I am sitting down. The afterimage of light burns in the darkness. I close my eyes and see the opposites balanced in space, floating across from each other. First the words, and then the images replacing the words.

Light is the opposite of dark. Heavy is the opposite of light. Memory is the opposite of forgetting. Attending is the opposite of absence. They are not quite the same: the word for the kind of light that is opposite of heavy seems lighter than the shiny balloon that comes as an image. Light gleams on the shiny sphere as it rises, recedes, vanishes . . .

I asked my mother once how I could have light in my dreams when my eyes were closed in sleep. Why were dreams not all dark, I asked. She did not know. The book told me a lot about visual processing in the brain, but it did not tell me that.

I wonder why. Surely someone else has asked why dreams can be full of light even in the dark. The brain generates images, yes, but where does it come from, the *light* in them? In deep blindness people no longer see light—or it is not thought they do, and the brain scans indicate different patterns. So is the light in dreams a memory of light or something else?

I remember someone saying, of another child, "He likes baseball so much that if you opened his head there'd be a ball field inside. . . ." That was before I knew that much of what people said did not mean what the words meant. I wondered what would be inside my head if someone opened it. I asked my mother and she said, "Your brain, dear," and showed me a picture of a gray wrinkled thing. I cried because I knew I did not like it enough for it to fill my head. I was sure no one else had something that ugly inside their head. They would have baseball fields or ice cream or picnics.

I know now that everybody does have a gray wrinkled brain inside their head, not ball fields or swimming pools or the people they love. Whatever is in the mind does not show in the brain. But at the time it seemed proof that I was made wrong.

What I have in my head is light and dark and gravity and space and swords and groceries and colors and numbers and people and patterns so beautiful I get shivers all over. I still do not know why I have those patterns and not others.

The book answers questions other people have thought of. I have thought of questions they have not answered. I always thought my questions were wrong questions because no one else asked them. Maybe no one thought of them. Maybe darkness got there first. Maybe I am the first light touching a gulf of ignorance.

Maybe my questions matter.

CHAPTER FIFTEEN

*L*IGHT. *MORNING LIGHT. I REMEMBER STRANGE DREAMS,* but not what they were about, only that they were strange. It is a bright, crisp day; when I touch the window glass it feels cold.

In the cooler air, I feel wide-awake, almost bouncy. The cereal flakes in the bowl have a crisp, ruffled texture; I feel them in my mouth, crunchy and then smooth.

When I come outside, the bright sun glints off pebbles in the parking lot pavement. It is a day for bright, brisk music. Possibilities surge through my mind; I settle on Bizet. I touch my car gingerly, noticing that even though Don is in jail my body is remembering that it might be dangerous. Nothing happens. The four new tires still smell new. The car starts. On the way to work, the music plays in my head, bright as the sunlight. I think of going out to the country to look at stars tonight; I should be able to see the space stations, too. Then I remember that it is Wednesday and I will go to fencing. I have not forgotten that in a long time. Did I mark the calendar this morning? I am not sure.

At work, I pull into my usual parking space. Mr. Aldrin is there standing just inside the door as if he were waiting for me.

"Lou, I saw it on the news—are you all right?"

"Yes," I say. I think it should be obvious just from looking at me.

"If you don't feel well, you can take the day off," he says.

"I am fine," I say. "I can work."

"Well . . . if you're sure." He pauses, as if he expects me to say something, but I cannot think of anything to say. "The newscast said you disarmed the attacker, Lou—I didn't know you knew how to do that."

"I just did what I do in fencing," I say. "Even though I didn't have a blade."

"Fencing!" His eyes widen; his brows lift up. "You do fencing? Like . . . with swords and things?"

"Yes. I go to fencing class once a week," I say. I do not know how much to tell him.

"I never knew that," he says. "I don't know anything about fencing, except they wear those white suits and have those wires trailing behind them."

We do not wear the white suits or use electric scoring, but I do not feel like explaining it to Mr. Aldrin. I want to get back to my project, and this afternoon we have another meeting with the medical team. Then I remember what Mr. Stacy said.

"I may have to go to the police station and sign a statement," I say.

"That's fine," Mr. Aldrin says. "Whatever you need. I'm sure this must have been a terrible shock."

My phone rings. I think it is going to be Mr. Crenshaw, so I do not hurry to answer it, but I do answer it.

"Mr. Arrendale? . . . This is Detective Stacy. Look, can you come down to the station this morning?"

I do not think this is a real question. I think it is like when my father said, "You pick up that end, okay?" when he meant "Pick up that end." It may be more polite to give commands by asking questions, but it is also more confusing, because sometimes they are questions. "I will have to ask my boss," I say.

"Police business," Mr. Stacy says. "We need you to sign your statement, some other paperwork. Just tell them that."

"I will call Mr. Aldrin," I say. "I should call you back?"

"No—just come on down when you can. I'll be here all morning." In other words, he expects me to come down no matter what Mr. Aldrin says. It was not a real question.

I call Mr. Aldrin's office.

"Yes, Lou," he says. "How are you?" It is silly; he has already asked me that this morning.

"The police want me to go to the station and sign my statement and some other paperwork," I say. "They said come now."

"But are you all right? Do you need someone to go with you?"

"I am fine," I say. "But I need to go to the police station."

"Of course. Take the whole day."

Outside, I wonder what the guard thinks as I drive out past the checkpoint after driving in just a short time ago. I cannot tell anything from his face.

IT IS NOISY IN THE POLICE STATION. AT A LONG, HIGH COUN-ter, rows of people stand in line. I stand in line, but then Mr. Stacy comes out and sees me. "Come on," he says. He leads me to another noisy room with five desks all covered with stuff. His desk—I think it is his desk—has a docking station for his handcomp and a large display.

"Home sweet home," he says, waving me to a chair beside the desk.

The chair is gray metal with a thin green plastic cushion on the seat. I can feel the frame through the cushion. I smell stale coffee, cheap candy bars, chips, paper, the fried-ink smell of printers and copiers.

"Here's the hard copy of your statement last night," he says. "Read through it, see if there are any errors, and, if not, sign it."

The stacked ifs slow me down, but I work through them. I read the statement quickly, though it takes me a while to grasp that "complainant" is me and "assailant" is Don. Also, I do not know why Don and I are re-ferred to as "males" and not "men" and Marjory as a "female" and not a "woman." I think it is rude to, say, call her "a female known to both males in a social context." There are no actual errors, so I sign it.

Then Mr. Stacy tells me I must sign a complaint against Don. I do not know why. It is against the law to do the things Don did, and there is evidence he did them. It should not matter whether I sign or not. If that is what the law requires, though, then I will do it.

"What will happen to Don if he is found guilty?" I ask.

"Serial escalating vandalism ending in a violent assault? He's not getting out without custodial rehab," Mr. Stacy says. "A PPD—a programmable personality determinant brain chip. That's when they put in a control chip—"

"I know," I say. It makes me feel squirmy inside; at least I do not have to contemplate having a chip inserted in my brain.

"It's not like it is on the shows," Mr. Stacy says. "No sparks, no lightning flashes—he just won't be able to do certain things."

What I heard—what we heard at the Center—is that the PPD overrides the original personality and prevents the rehabilitant, the term they like, from doing anything but what he is told.

"Couldn't he just pay for my tires and windshield?" I ask.

"Recidivism," Mr. Stacy says, pawing through a pile of hard copies. "They do it again. It's been proved. Just like you can't stop being you, the person who is autistic, he can't stop being him, the person who is jealous and violent. If it'd been found when he was an infant, well, then . . . here we are." He pulls out one particular sheet. "This is the form. Read it carefully, sign on the bottom where the *X* is, and date it."

I read the form, which has the city's seal at the top. It says that I, Lou Arrendale, make a complaint of a lot of things I never even thought of. I thought it would be simple: Don tried to scare me and then tried to hurt me. Instead the form says I am complaining of malicious destruction of property, theft of property valued at more than $250, manufacturing an explosive device, placing an explosive device, assault with intent to murder with an explosive device— "That could have killed me?" I ask. "It says here 'assault with a deadly weapon.' "

"Explosives are a deadly weapon. It's true that the way he had it wired up, it didn't go off when it was supposed to, and the amount is marginal: you might have lost only part of your hands and your face. But it counts under the law."

"I did not know that one act, like taking out the battery and putting in the jack-in-the-box, could break more than one law," I say.

"Neither do a lot of criminals," Mr. Stacy says. "But it's quite common. Say a perp breaks into a house while the owners are gone and steals stuff. There's a law about unlawful entry and another law about theft."

I did not really complain about Don manufacturing an explosive device because I did not know he was doing it. I look at Mr. Stacy; it is clear he has an answer for everything and it will not do any good to argue. It does not seem fair that so many complaints could come out of one act, but I have heard people talk about other things like this, too.

The form goes on to list what Don did in less formal language: the tires, the windshield, the theft of a vehicle battery worth $262.37, the placing of the explosive device under the hood, and the assault in the parking lot. With it all laid out in order, it looks obvious that Don did it all, that he seriously intended to hurt me, that the very first incident was a clear warning sign.

It is still hard to grasp. I know what he said, the words he used, but they do not make much sense. He is a normal man. He could talk to Marjory easily; he did talk to Marjory. Nothing stopped him from becoming friends with her, nothing but himself. It is not my fault that she liked me. It is not my fault that she met me at the fencing group; I was there first and did not know her until she came.

"I do not know why," I say.

"What?" Mr. Stacy says.

"I do not know why he got so angry with me," I say.

He tips his head to one side. "He told you," he says. "And you told me what he said."

"Yes, but it does not make sense," I say. "I like Marjory a lot, but she is not my girlfriend. I have never taken her out. She has never taken me out. I have never done anything to hurt Don." I do not tell Mr. Stacy that I would like to take Marjory out, because he might ask why I haven't and I do not want to answer.

"Maybe it doesn't make sense to you," he says, "but it makes sense to me. We see lots of this kind of thing, jealousy souring into rage. You didn't have to do anything; it was all about him, all about his insides."

"He is normal inside," I say.

"He's not formally disabled, Lou, but he is not normal. Normal people do not wire explosive devices into someone's car."

"Do you mean he is insane?"

"That's for a court to decide," Mr. Stacy says. He shakes his head. "Lou, why are you trying to excuse him?"

"I'm not . . . I agree what he did is wrong, but having a chip put in his brain to make him someone else—"

He rolls his eyes. "Lou, I wish you people—I mean people who aren't in criminal justice—would understand about the PPD. It is not making him into someone else. It is making him Don without the compulsion to harm people who annoy him in any way. That way we don't have to keep him locked up for years because he's likely to do it again— he just won't do it again. To anyone. It's a lot more humane than what we used to do, lock people like this up for years with other vicious men in an environment that only made them worse. This doesn't hurt; it doesn't make him into a robot; he can live a normal life. . . . He just can't commit violent crimes. It's the only thing we've found that works, other than the death penalty, which I will agree is a bit extreme for what he did to you."

"I still don't like it," I say. "I would not want anyone putting a chip in my brain."

"There are legitimate medical uses," he says. I know that; I know about people with intractable seizures or Parkinsonism or spinal cord injuries: specific chips and bypasses have been developed for them, and that is a good thing. But this I am not sure of.

Still, it is the law. There is nothing in the form that is untrue. Don did these things. I called the police about them, except the last one, which they witnessed. There is a line at the bottom of the form, between the body of the text and the line for my signature, and there is a line of text that says that I swear everything in the statement is true. It is true as far as I know, and that will have to be enough. I sign on the line, date it, and hand it to the police officer.

"Thanks, Lou," he says. "Now the DA wants to meet you and she will explain what happens next."

The district attorney is a middle-aged woman with frizzy black hair mixed with gray. The nameplate on her desk says: ASS'T DA BEATRICE HUNSTON. She has skin the color of gingerbread. Her office is bigger than mine at work and has shelves all around it with books. They are old, tan with black and red squares on the spines. They do not look as if anyone ever read them, and I wonder if they are real. There is a data plate on her desktop, and the light from it makes the underside of her chin a funny color, even though from my side the desktop looks plain black.

"I'm glad you're alive, Mr. Arrendale," she says. "You were quite lucky. I understand you've signed the complaint against Mr. Donald Poiteau, is that right?"

"Yes," I say.

"Well, let me explain what happens next. The law says that Mr. Poiteau is entitled to a jury trial if he wants one. We have ample evidence that he is the person involved in all the incidents, and we are sure that evidence will stand up in court. But most likely his legal adviser will tell him to accept a plea. Do you know what that means?"

"No," I say. I know she wants to tell me.

"If he does not use up state resources by demanding a trial, it will reduce the amount of time he must serve, down to that required for implantation and adaptation of the PPD, the chip. Otherwise, if convicted, he would face a minimum of five years in detention. In the meantime, he'll be finding out what detention is like, and I suspect he'll agree to the plea."

"But he might not be convicted," I say.

The DA smiles at me. "That doesn't happen anymore," she says. "Not with the kind of evidence we've got. You don't have to worry; he's not going to be able to hurt you anymore."

I am not worried. Or I was not worried until she said that. Once Don was in custody, I did not worry more about him. If he escapes, I will worry again. I am not worried now.

"If it does not come to trial, if his attorney accepts a plea bargain, then we will not need to call you in again," she says. "We will know that in a few days. If he does demand a trial, then you will appear as a witness for the prosecution. This will mean spending time with me or someone in my office preparing your testimony and then time in court. Do you understand that?"

I understand what she is saying. What she is not saying and maybe does not know is that Mr. Crenshaw will be very angry if I miss time from work. I hope that Don and his lawyer do not insist on a trial. "Yes," I say.

"Good. The whole procedure's changed in the past ten years, with the availability of the PPD chip; it's a lot more straightforward. Fewer cases going to trial. Not so much time lost by the victims and the witnesses. We'll be in touch, Mr. Arrendale."

The morning is almost over when I finally leave the Justice Center. Mr. Aldrin said I did not have to come in at all today, but I do not want Mr. Crenshaw to have any reason to be angry with me, so I go back to the office for the afternoon. We have another test, one of those where we are supposed to match patterns on a computer screen. We are all very fast at this and finish quickly. The other tests are easy, too, but boring. I do not work the time I missed this morning, because that was not my fault.

BEFORE I LEAVE FOR FENCING, I WATCH THE SCIENCE NEWS ON TV because it is a program on space. A consortium of companies is building another space station. I see a logo I recognize; I did not know that the company I work for had an interest in space-based operations. The announcer is talking about the billions it will cost and the commitment of the various partners.

Maybe this is one reason Mr. Crenshaw insists he needs to cut costs. I think it is good that the company wants to invest in space, and I wish I had a chance to go out there. Maybe if I were not autistic, I could have been an astronaut or space scientist. But even if I change now, with the treatment, it would be too late to retrain for that career.

Maybe this is why some people want the LifeTime treatment to extend their lives, so they can train for a career they could not have before. It is very expensive, though. Not many people can afford it yet.

THREE OTHER CARS ARE PARKED IN FRONT OF TOM AND LUCIA'S when I arrive. Marjory's car is there. My heart is thumping faster. I feel out of breath, but I have not been running.

A chill wind blows down the street. When it is cool, it is easier to fence, but it is harder to sit out in the back and talk.

Inside, Lucia, Susan, and Marjory are talking. They stop when I come in.

"How are you doing, Lou?" Lucia asks.

"I am fine," I say. My tongue feels too big.

"I'm so sorry about what Don did," Marjory says.

"You did not tell him to do it," I say. "It is not your fault." She should know this.

"I didn't mean that," she says. "I just—it's too bad for you."

"I am fine," I say again. "I am here and not—" It is hard to say. "Not in detention," I say, avoiding *not dead*. "It is hard—they say they will put a chip in his brain."

"I should hope so," Lucia says. Her face is twisted into a scowl. Susan nods and mutters something I can't quite hear.

"Lou, you look like you don't want that to happen to him," Marjory says.

"I think it is very scary," I say. "He did something wrong, but it is scary that they will turn him into someone else."

"It's not like that," Lucia says. She is staring at me now. She should understand if anyone can; she knows about the experimental treatment; she knows why it would bother me that Don will be compelled to be someone else. "He did something wrong—something very bad. He could have killed you, Lou. Would have, if he hadn't been stopped. If they turned him into a bowl of pudding it would be fair, but all the chip does is make him unable to do anyone harm."

It is not that simple. Just as a word can mean one thing in one sentence and something else in another or change meaning with a tone, so an act can be helpful or harmful depending on the circumstance. The PPD chip doesn't give people better judgment about what is harmful and what is not; it removes the volition, the initiative, to perform acts that are more often harmful than not. That means it also prevents Don from doing good things sometimes. Even I know that and I am sure Lucia knows it, too, but she is ignoring it for some reason.

"To think I trusted him in the group so long!" she says. "I never thought he would do anything like this. That scum-sucking viper: I could rip his face off myself."

In one of those inside flashes, I know that Lucia is thinking more about her feelings than mine right now. She is hurt because Don fooled her; she feels he made her seem stupid and she does not want to be stupid. She is proud of being intelligent. She wants him punished because he damaged her—at least her feelings about herself.

It is not a very nice way to be, and I did not know Lucia could be like this. Should I have known about her, the way she thinks she should have known about Don? If normal people expect to know all about one another, all the hidden things, how can they stand it? Doesn't it make them dizzy?

"You can't read minds, Lucia," Marjory says.

"I know that!" Lucia moves in little jerky movements, tossing her hair, flicking her fingers. "It's just—damn, I hate to be made a fool of, and that's what I feel he did." She looks up at me. "Sorry, Lou, I'm being selfish here. What really matters is you and how you're doing."

It is like watching a crystal forming in a supersaturated solution to see her normal personality—her usual personality—return from the angry person she was a moment ago. I feel better that she has understood what she was doing and is not going to do it again. It is slower than the way she analyzes other people. I wonder if it takes normal people longer to look inside themselves and see what is really happening than it does autistic people or if our brains work at the same speed there. I wonder if she needed what Marjory said to make her capable of that self-analysis.

I wonder what Marjory really thinks of me. She is looking at Lucia now, with quick glances back at me. Her hair is so beautiful . . . I find myself analyzing the color, the ratio of the different colors of hairs, and then the way the light shifts along them as she moves.

I sit on the floor and begin my stretches. After a moment, the women also start stretching out. I am a little stiff; it takes me several tries before I can touch my forehead to my knees. Marjory still can't do it; her hair falls forward, brushing her knees, but her forehead doesn't come within four inches.

When I have stretched, I get up and go to the equipment room for my gear. Tom is outside with Max and Simon, the referee from the tournament. The ring of lights makes a bright area in the middle of the dark yard, with strong shadows everywhere else.

"Hey, buddy," Max says. He calls all the men buddy when they first arrive. It is a silly thing to do, but it is how he is. "How are you?"

"I am fine," I say.

"I hear you used a fencing move on him," Max says. "Wish I'd seen it."

I think Max would not have wanted to be there in real life, whatever he thinks now.

"Lou, Simon was wondering if he could fence with you," Tom says. I am glad that he does not ask how I am.

"Yes," I say. "I will put my mask on."

Simon is not quite as tall as Tom and thinner. He is wearing an old padded fencing jacket, just like the white jackets that are used in formal competition fencing, but it is a streaky green instead. "Thanks," he says. And then, as if he knew that I was looking at the color of his jacket, he says, "My sister wanted a green one for a costume once—and she knew more about fencing than dyeing clothes. It looked worse when it had just been done; it's faded out now."

"I never saw a green one," I say.

"Neither had anyone else," he says. His mask is an ordinary white one that has yellowed with age and use. His gloves are brown. I put on my mask.

"What weapons?" I ask.

"What's your favorite?" he asks.

I do not have a favorite; each weapon and combination has its own patterns of skill.

"Try épée and dagger," Tom says. "That'll be fun to watch."

I pick up my épée and dagger and shift them in my hands until they are comfortable—I can hardly feel them, which is right. Simon's épée has a big bell guard, but his dagger has a simple ring. If he is not very good with his parries, I may be able to get a hit on his hand. I wonder if he will call hits or not. He is a referee: surely he will be honest.

He stands relaxed, knees bent, someone who has fenced enough to be comfortable with it. We salute; his blade whines through the air on the downstroke of the salute. I feel my stomach tighten. I do not know what he will do next. Before I can imagine anything, he lunges toward me, something we almost never do in this yard, his arm fully extended and his back leg straight. I twist away, flicking my dagger down and out for the parry and aiming a thrust over his dagger—but he is fast, as fast as Tom, and he has that arm up, ready to parry. He recovers from the lunge so quickly I cannot take advantage of that momentary lack of mobility and gives me a nod as he returns to the neutral guard position. "Good parry," he says.

My stomach tightens even more, and I realize it is not fear but excitement. He may be better than Tom. He will win, but I will learn. He moves sideways, and I follow. He makes several more attacks, all fast, and I manage to parry them all, though I do not attack. I want to see his pattern, and it is very different. Again, again. Low high high low low high low low low high high: anticipating the next, I launch my own attack as his comes low again, and this time he does not quite parry mine and I get a light glancing touch on his shoulder.

"Good," he says, stepping back. "Excellent." I glance at Tom, who nods and grins. Max clenches his hands together over his head; he is grinning, too. I feel a little sick. In the moment of contact, I saw Don's face and felt the blow I gave and saw him fold over when I hit him. I shake my head.

"Are you all right?" Tom asks. I do not want to say anything. I do not know if I want to go on.

"I could use a break," Simon says, though we have only fenced a couple of minutes. I feel stupid; I know he is doing it for me, and I should not be upset, but I am upset. Now it comes again and again, the feel in my hand, the smell of Don's breath whooshing out, the sound and sight and feel all together. Part of my mind remembers the book, the discussion of memory and stress and trauma, but most of it is simply misery, a tight spiral of sadness and fear and anger all tied together.

I struggle, blinking, and a phrase of music ripples through my mind; the spiral opens out again and lifts away. "I . . . am . . . all . . . right . . ." I say. It is still hard to talk, but already I feel better. I lift my blade; Simon steps back and lifts his.

We salute again. This time his attack is just as fast but different; I cannot read his pattern at all and decide to attack anyway. His blade gets past my parry and hits low on the left abdomen. "Good," I say.

"You are making me work entirely too hard," Simon says. I can hear that he is breathing hard; I know I am. "You almost got me four times."

"I missed that parry," I say. "It wasn't strong enough—"

"Let's see if you make that mistake again," he says. He salutes, and this time I am the one to attack first. I do not get a touch, and his attacks seem to be faster than mine; I must parry two or three times before I can see an opening. Before I get a touch, he has made one on my right shoulder.

"Definitely too hard," he says. "Lou, you are quite a fencer. I thought so at the tournament; first-timers never win and you had some first-timer problems, but it was clear you knew what you were doing. Did you ever consider taking up classical fencing?"

"No," I say. "I just know Tom and Lucia—"

"You should think about it. Tom and Lucia are better trainers than most backyard fencers—" Simon grins at Tom, who makes a face back at him. "But some classical technique would improve your footwork. What got you that last time wasn't speed but the extra reach that came from my knowing exactly how to place my foot for the best extension with the least exposure." Simon takes off his mask, hangs his épée on the outdoor rack, and holds out his hand to me. "Thanks, Lou, for a good round. When I catch my breath, maybe we can fight again."

"Thank you," I say, and shake his hand. Simon's grasp is firmer than Tom's. I am out of breath; I hang up my blade and put my mask under an empty chair and sit down. I wonder if Simon really likes me or if he will be like Don and hate me later. I wonder if Tom has told him I am autistic.

I'M SORRY," LUCIA SAYS; SHE HAS COME OUTSIDE WITH HER gear and sits beside me on my right. "I should not have blown up like that."

"I am not upset," I say. I am not, now that I know she knows what was wrong and is not doing it.

"Good. Look . . . I know that you like Marjory and she likes you. Don't let this mess with Don ruin it for you, okay?"

"I do not know if Marjory likes me in a special way," I say. "Don said she does, but she has not said she does."

"I know. It's difficult. Grownups are not as direct as preschoolers and make a lot of trouble for themselves that way."

Marjory comes out of the house, zipping up her fencing jacket. She grins at me or at Lucia—I am not sure of the direction of her grin—as the zipper jams. "I have been eating too many doughnuts," she says. "Or not walking enough or something."

"Here—" Lucia holds out her hand, and Marjory comes over so that Lucia can unjam the zipper and help her. I did not know that holding out a hand was a signal for offering help. I thought holding out a hand was a signal for asking help. Maybe it only goes with "here."

"Do you want to fence, Lou?" Marjory asks me.

"Yes," I say. I can feel my face getting hot. I put my mask on and pick up my épée. "Do you want to use épée and dagger?"

"Sure," Marjory says. She puts her mask on and I cannot see her face, only the gleam of her eyes and her teeth when she speaks. I can see the shape of her under the fencing jacket, though. I would like to touch that shape, but that is not appropriate. Only boyfriends with their girlfriends.

Marjory salutes. She has a simpler pattern than Tom's and I could make a touch, but then it would be over. I parry, thrust short, parry again. When our blades touch, I can feel her hand through the connection; we are touching without touching. She circles, reverses, moves back and forth, and I move with her. It is like some kinds of dance, a pattern of movement, except for not having music. I sort through the music I remember, trying to find the right music for this dance. It gives me a strange feeling to match my pattern to hers, not to defeat her but just to feel that connection, that touch-and-touch of blades to hands and back.

Paganini. *The First Violin Concerto* in D Major, Opus 6, the third movement. It is not exactly right, but it is closer than anything else I can think of. Stately but quick, with the little breaks where Marjory does not keep an exact rhythm changing directions. In my mind, I speed up or slow the music to stay with our movements.

I wonder what Marjory hears. I wonder if she can hear the music I hear. If we were both thinking of the same music, would we hear it the same way? Would we be in phase or out? I hear the sounds as color on dark; she might hear the sounds as dark lines on light, as music is printed.

If we put the two together, would they cancel out sight, dark on light and light on dark? Or . . .

Marjory's touch breaks the chain of thought. "Good," I say, and step back. She nods, and we salute again.

I read something once where thinking was described as light and not thinking as dark. I am thinking about other things while we fence, and Marjory was faster to make a touch than I was. So if she is not thinking about other things, did this not-thinking make her faster, and is that dark faster than the light of my not-thinking?

I do not know what the speed of thought is. I do not know if the speed of thought is the same for everyone. Is it thinking faster or thinking further that makes different thinking different?

The violin rises up in a spiraling pattern and Marjory's pattern falls apart and I sweep forward in the dance that is now a solo dance and make my touch on her.

"Good," she says, and steps back. Her body is moving with the deep breaths she's taking. "You wore me out, Lou; that was a long one."

"How about me?" Simon says. I would like to be with Marjory more, but I liked fencing Simon before and want to do that, too.

This time the music starts when we do, different music. Sarasate's *Carmen Fantasy* . . . perfect for the feline prowl that is Simon circling me, looking for an opening, and for my intense concentration. I never thought I could dance before—it was a social thing, and I always got stiff and clumsy. Now—with a blade in hand—it feels right to move to the internal music.

Simon is better than I am, but it does not bother me. I am eager to see what he can do, what I can do. He gets a touch, another one, but then I get another one on him. "Best of five?" he asks. I nod, breathless. This time neither of us gets a touch right away; this time we fight on and on, until I finally make another touch, more by luck than skill. We are even now. The others are quiet, watching. I can feel their interest, a warm space on my back as I circle. Forward, sideways, around, back. Simon knows and counters every move I make; I am just able to counter his. Finally he does something I do not even see—his blade reappears just where I thought I had parried it away, and he gets the final touch of the match.

I am dripping with sweat even though it is a cool night. I am sure I smell bad, and I am surprised when Marjory comes up to me and touches my arm.

"That was gorgeous, Lou," she says. I take off my mask. Her eyes are gleaming; the smile on her face goes all the way to her hair.

"I am sweaty," I say.

"So you should be, after that," she says. "Wow again. I didn't know you could fence like that."

"Neither did I," I say.

"Now that we know," Tom said, "we've got to get you to more tournaments. What do you think, Simon?"

"He's more than ready. The top fencers in the state can take him, but once he gets over tournament nerves, they'll have to work at it."

"So, would you like to come with us to another tournament, Lou?" Tom asks.

I feel cold all the way through. I think they mean to do something nice for me, but Don got mad at me because of the tournament. What if someone gets mad at me every tournament and because of me one after another have to have a PDD chip?

"It is all day Saturday," I say.

"Yes, and sometimes all day Sunday as well," Lucia says. "Is that a problem?"

"It—I go to church on Sunday," I say.

Marjory looks at me. "I didn't know you went to church, Lou," she says. "Well, you could just go on Saturday. . . . What's the problem with Saturdays, Lou?"

I have no answer ready. I do not think they will understand if I tell them about Don. They are all looking at me, and I feel myself folding together inside. I do not want them to be angry.

"The next tournament nearby is after Thanksgiving," Simon says. "No need to decide tonight." He is looking at me curiously. "Are you worried about someone not counting hits again, Lou?"

"No. . . ." I feel my throat closing up. I close my eyes to steady myself. "It is Don," I say. "He was angry at the tournament. I think that is why he . . . got so upset. I do not want that to happen to anyone else."

"It is not your fault," Lucia says. But she sounds angry. This is what happens, I think. People get angry about me even when they are not angry with me. It does not have to be my fault for me to cause it.

"I see your point," Marjory says. "You don't want to make trouble, is that it?"

"Yes."

"And you cannot be sure that no one will be angry with you."

"Yes."

"But—Lou—people get mad at other people for no reason, too. Don was angry with Tom. Other people may have been angry with Simon; I know people have been angry with me. That just happens. As long as people aren't doing anything wrong, they can't stop and think all the time if it is making someone else angry."

"Maybe it does not bother you as much," I say.

She gives me a look that I can tell is supposed to mean something, but I cannot tell what. Would I know if I were normal? How *do* normal people learn what these looks mean?

"Maybe it doesn't," she says. "I used to think it was always my fault. I used to worry about it more. But that is—" She pauses and I can tell she is searching for a polite word. I know that because so often I am slow speaking when I am searching for a polite word. "It is hard to know how much to worry about it," she says finally.

"Yes," I say.

"People who want you to think everything is your fault are the problem," Lucia says. "They always blame other people for their feelings, especially anger."

"But some anger is justified," Marjory says. "I don't mean with Lou and Don; Lou didn't do anything wrong. That was all Don's jealousy getting the better of him. But I see what Lou means, that he doesn't want to be the cause of someone else's getting in trouble."

"He won't," Lucia says. "He's not the type." She gives me a look, a different look than Marjory gave me. I am not sure what this look means, either.

"Lucia, why don't you fight Simon," Tom says. Everyone stops and looks at him.

Lucia's mouth is a little open. Then she closes it with a little snap. "Fine," she says. "It's been a long time. Simon?"

"My pleasure," he says, smiling.

I watch Lucia and Simon. He is better than she is, but he is not making as many points as he could. I can tell that he is fighting at the edge of her level, not using everything he could. That is very polite. I am aware of Marjory beside me, of the smell of the dry leaves that have drifted against the stone edging, of the chilly breeze on the back of my neck. It feels good.

*BY NINE IT IS MORE THAN CHILLY; IT IS COLD. WE ALL GO IN-*side, and Lucia fixes a kettle of hot chocolate. It is the first time this year. The others are all talking; I sit with my back against the green leather hassock and try to listen while I watch Marjory. She uses her hands a lot when she talks. A couple of times, she flaps them in the way that I was told was a sign of autism. I have seen other people do that, too, and always wondered if they were autistic or partly autistic.

They are talking about tournaments now—ones they remember from the past, who won and who lost and who was the referee and how people behaved. Nobody mentions Don. I lose track of the names; I do not know the people. I cannot understand why "Bart is such a toad" from what they say about Bart, and I am sure they do not mean that Bart is actually an amphibian with warty skin, any more than Don was an actual heel. My gaze shifts from Marjory to Simon to Tom to Lucia to Max to Susan and back, trying to keep up with who is speaking when, but I cannot anticipate when one is going to stop and another is going to start, or which. Sometimes there is a break of two or three seconds between speakers, and sometimes one starts while another is still talking.

It is fascinating, in its way. It is like watching almost-patterns in a chaotic system. Like watching molecules break apart and re-form as a solution's balance shifts this way and that. I keep feeling that I almost understand it, and then something happens I did not anticipate. I do not know how they can participate and keep track of it at the same time.

Gradually I am able to notice that everyone pauses if Simon speaks and lets him into the conversation. He does not interrupt often, but no one interrupts him. One of my teachers said that the person who is speaking indicates who he expects to speak next by glancing at them. At that time I usually could not tell where someone was looking unless they looked there a long time. Now I can follow most glances. Simon glances at different people. Max and Susan always glance first at Simon, giving him priority. Tom glances at Simon about half the time. Lucia glances at Simon about a third of the time. Simon does not always speak again when someone glances at him; that person then glances at some-one else.

But it is so fast: how can they see it all? And why does Tom glance at Simon some of the time and not the rest of the time? What tells him when to glance at Simon?

I realize that Marjory is watching me and feel my face and neck go hot. The voices of the others blur; my vision clouds. I want to hide in the shadows, but there are no shadows. I look down. I listen for her voice, but she is not talking much.

Then they start on equipment: steel blades versus composites, old steel versus new steel. Everyone seems to prefer steel, but Simon talks about a recent formal match he saw in which composite blades had a chip in the grip to emit a steel-like sound when the blades touched. It was weird, he says.

Then he says he has to go and stands up. Tom stands up, too, and Max. I stand up. Simon shakes Tom's hand and says, "It was fun—thanks for the invitation."

Tom says, "Anytime."

Max puts out his hand and says, "Thanks for coming; it was an honor."

Simon shakes his hand and says, "Anytime."

I do not know whether to put out my hand or not, but Simon quickly offers his so I shake it even though I do not like to shake hands—it seems so pointless—and then he says, "Thanks, Lou; I enjoyed it."

"Anytime," I say. There is a moment's tension in the room, and I am worried that I said something inappropriate—even though I was copying Tom and Max—and then Simon taps my arm with his finger.

"I hope you change your mind about tournaments," he says. "It was a pleasure."

"Thank you," I say.

While Simon goes out the door, Max says, "I have to leave, too," and Susan uncoils from the floor. It is time to leave. I look around; all the faces look friendly, but I thought Don's face looked friendly. If one of them is angry with me, how would I know?

On Thursday we have the first of the medical briefings where we have been able to ask the doctors questions. There are two doctors, Dr. Ransome, with the curly gray hair, and Dr. Handsel, who has straight dark hair that looks as if it had been glued onto his head.

"It is reversible?" Linda asks.

"Well . . . no. Whatever it does, it does."

"So if we don't like it, we can't go back to being our normal selves?"

Our selves are not normal to start with, but I do not say that aloud. Linda knows it as well as I do. She is making a joke.

"Er . . . no, you can't. Probably. But I don't see why—"

"I'd want to?" Cameron says. His face is tense. "I like who I am now. I do not know if I will like who I become."

"It shouldn't be that different," Dr. Ransome says.

But every difference is a difference. I am not the same person as before Don began to stalk me. Not only what he did but meeting those police officers has changed me. I know about something I didn't know before, and knowledge changes people. I raise my hand.

"Yes, Lou," Dr. Ransome says.

"I do not understand how it can *not* change us," I say. "If it normalizes our sensory processing, that will change the rate and kind of data input, and that will change our perceptions, and our processing—"

"Yes, but you—your personality—will be the same, or much the same. You will like the same things; you will react the same—"

"Then what's the change *for*?" Linda asks. She sounds angry; I know she is more worried than angry. "They tell us they want us to change, to not need the supports we need—but if we do not need them, then that means our likes and dislikes have changed . . . doesn't it?"

"I've spent so much time learning to tolerate overload," Dale says. "What if that means I suddenly don't pick up on things I should?" His left eye flickers, ticcing wildly.

"We don't think any of that will happen," the doctor says again. "The primatologists found only positive changes in social interaction—"

"I'm not a fucking chimp!" Dale slams his hand down on the table. For a moment his left eye stays open; then it starts ticcing again.

The doctor looks shocked. Why should he be surprised that Dale is upset? Would he like to have his behavior presumed on the basis of a primatologist's studies of chimpanzees? Or is this something normals do? Do they see themselves as just like other primates? I can't believe that.

"No one's suggesting you are," the doctor says, in a slightly disapproving voice. "It's just that . . . they're the best model we have. And they had recognizable personalities after treatment, with only the social deficits changed. . . ."

All the chimps in the world now live in protected environments, zoos, or research establishments. Once they lived wild, in the forests of Africa. I wonder if the autistic-like chimpanzees would have been that way in the wild or if the stress of living as prisoners has changed them.

A slide lights up the screen. "This is the normal brain's activity pattern when picking a known face from a photograph of several faces," he says. There is a gray outline of a brain, with little glowing green spots. Thanks to my reading, I recognize some of the locations . . . no, I recognize the slide. It is illustration 16-43.d, from chapter 16 of *Brain Functionality*. "And here—" The slide changes. "This is the autistic brain's activity pattern during the same task." Another gray outline with little glowing green spots. Illustration 16-43.c from the same chapter.

I try to remember the captions in the book. I do not think that the text said the first was normal brain activity when picking a known face from a photographed group. I think it was normal brain activity when viewing a familiar face. A composite of . . . yes, I remember. Nine healthy male volunteers recruited from college students according to a protocol approved by the human ethics research committee . . .

Another slide is already showing. Another gray outline, another set of colored splotches, these blue. The doctor's voice drones on. This is another slide I recognize. I struggle to remember what the book said and hear what he is saying, but I cannot. The words are tangling.

I raise my hand. He stops and says, "Yes, Lou?"

"Can we have a copy of this, to look at later? It is hard to take in all at once."

He frowns. "I don't think that's a good idea, Lou. This is still proprietary—very confidential. If you want to know more, you can ask me or your counselor questions and you can look at the slides again, though"—he chuckles—"I don't think they'll mean much since you're not a neurologist."

"I've read some," I say.

"Really. . . ." His voice softens to a drawl. "What have you read, Lou?"

"Some books," I say. Suddenly I do not want to tell him what book I have been reading, and I do not know why.

"About the brain?" he asks.

"Yes—I wanted to understand how it worked before you did anything with the treatment."

"And . . . did you understand it?"

"It's very complicated," I say. "Like a parallel-processing computer, only more so."

"You're right; it's very complicated," he says. He sounds satisfied. I think he is glad I did not say I understood it. I wonder what he would say if I told him that I recognize those illustrations.

Cameron and Dale are looking at me. Even Bailey gives me a quick glance and looks away. They want to know what I know. I do not know if I should tell them, partly because I do not yet know what I know—what it means in this context.

I put aside thoughts of the book and just listen, meanwhile memorizing the slides as they come and go. I do not take in information as well this way—none of us do—but I think I can retain enough to compare it to the book later.

Eventually the slides change from gray outlines of brains with colored spots to molecules. I do not recognize them; they are not anything in the organic chemistry book. But I do recognize a hydroxy group here, an amino group there.

"This enzyme regulates gene expression of neural growth factor eleven," the doctor says. "In normal brains, this is part of a feedback loop that interacts with attention control mechanisms to build in preferential processing of socially important signals—that's one of the things you people have a problem with."

He has given up any pretense that we are anything but cases.

"It's also part of the treatment package for autistic newborns, those who weren't identified and treated in utero, or for the children who suffer certain childhood infections that interfere with normal brain development. What our new treatment does is modify it—because it functions like this only in the first three years of development—so that it can affect the neural growth of the adult brain."

"So—it makes us pay attention to other people?" Linda asks.

"No, no—we know you already do that. We're not like those idiots back in the mid–twentieth century who thought autistics were just ignoring people. What it does is help you attend to social *signals*—facial expression, vocal tone, gesture, that kind of thing."

Dale makes a rude gesture; the doctor does not attend to it. I wonder if he really did not see or he chose to ignore it.

"But don't people have to be trained—like blind people were—to interpret new data?"

"Of course. That's why there's a training phase built into the treatment. Simulated social encounters, using computer-generated faces—" Another slide, this one of a chimpanzee with its upper lip curled and its lower lip pouted out. We all break into roars of laughter, uncontrollable. The doctor flushes angrily. "Sorry—that's the wrong slide. Of course it's the wrong slide. Human faces, I mean, and practice in human social interactions. We'll do a baseline assessment and then you'll have two to four months of post-treatment training—"

"Looking at monkey faces!" Linda says, laughing so hard she's almost crying. We are all giggling.

"I said it was a mistake," the doctor says. "We have trained psychotherapists to lead the intervention. . . . It's a serious matter."

The chimpanzee's face has been replaced by a picture of a group of people sitting in a circle; one is talking and the others are listening intently. Another slide, this time of someone in a clothing store talking to a salesperson. Another, of a busy office with someone on a phone. It all looks very normal and very boring. He does not show a picture of someone in a fencing tournament or someone talking to the police after a mugging in a parking lot. The only picture with a policeman in it could be titled *Asking Directions*. The policeman, with a stiff smile on his face, has one arm outstretched, pointing; the other person has a funny hat, a little backpack, and a book that says *Tourist Guidebook* on the cover.

It looks posed. All the pictures look posed, and the people may not even be real people. They could be—probably are—computer composites. We are supposed to become normal, real people, but they expect us to learn from these unreal, imaginary people in contrived, posed situations. The doctor and his associates assume they know the situations we deal with or will need to deal with and they will teach us how to deal with those. It reminds me of those therapists in the last century who thought they knew what words someone needed to know and taught an "essential" vocabulary. Some of them even told parents not to let children learn other words, lest it impede their learning of the essential vocabulary.

Such people do not know what they do not know. My mother used to recite a little verse that I did not understand until I was almost twelve, and one line of it went: "Those who know not, and know not they know not, are fools. . . ." The doctor does not know that I needed to be able to deal with the man at the tournament who would not call hits and the jealous would-be lover in the fencing group and the various police officers who took reports on vandalism and threats.

Now the doctor is talking about the generalization of social skills. He says that after the treatment and training our social skills should generalize to all situations in everyday life. I wonder what he would have thought of Don's social skills.

I glance at the clock. The seconds flick over, one after another; the two hours are nearly done. The doctor asks if there are any questions. I look down. The questions I want to ask are not appropriate in a meeting like this, and I do not think he will answer them anyway.

"When do you think you would start?" Cameron asks.

"We would like to start with the first subject—uh, patient—as soon as possible. We could have everything in place by next week."

"How many at once?" asks Bailey.

"Two. We would like to do two at a time, three days apart—this ensures that the primary medical team can concentrate on those during the first few critical days."

"What about waiting after the first two until they complete treatment to see if it works?" Bailey asks.

The doctor shakes his head. "No, it's better to have the whole cohort close in time."

"Makes it faster to publication," I hear myself say.

"What?" the doctor asks.

The others are looking at me. I look at my lap.

"If we all do it fairly quickly and together, then you can write it up and get it published faster. Otherwise it would be a year or more." I glance quickly at his face; his cheeks are red and shiny again.

"That's not the reason," he says, a little loudly. "It's just that the data are more comparable if the subjects—if you—are all close in time. I mean, suppose something happened that changed things between the time the first two started and finished . . . something that affected the rest of you—"

"Like what, a bolt from the blue that makes us normal?" Dale asks. "You're afraid we'll get galloping normality and be unsuitable subjects?"

"No, no," the doctor says. "More like something political that changes attitudes. . . ."

I wonder what the government is thinking. Do governments think? The chapter in *Brain Functionality* on the politics of research protocols comes to mind. Is something about to happen, some regulation or change in policy, which would make this research impossible in a few months?

That is something I can find out when I get home. If I ask this man, I do not think he will give me an honest answer.

When we leave, we walk at angles, all out of rhythm with one another. We used to have a way of merging, accommodating one another's peculiarities, so that we moved as a group. Now we move without harmony. I can sense the confusion, the anger. No one talks. I do not talk. I do not want to talk with them, who have been my closest associates for so long.

When we are back in our own building, we go quickly into our individual offices. I sit down and start to reach for the fan. I stop myself, and then I wonder why I stopped myself.

I do not want to work. I want to think about what it is they want to do to my brain and think about what it means. It means more than they say; everything they say means more than it says. Beyond the words is the tone; beyond the tone is the context; beyond the context is the unexplored territory of normal socialization, vast and dark as night, lit by the few pinpricks of similar experience, like stars.

Starlight, one writer said, perfuses the entire universe: the whole thing glows. The dark is an illusion, that writer said. If that is so, then Lucia was right and there is no speed of dark.

But there is simple ignorance, not knowing, and willful ignorance that refuses to know, that covers the light of knowledge with the dark blanket of bias. So I think there may be positive darkness, and I think dark can have a speed.

The books tell me that my brain works very well, even as it is, and that it is much easier to derange the functions of the brain than to repair them. If normal people really can do all the things that are claimed for them, it would be helpful to have that ability . . . but I am not sure they do.

They do not always understand why other people act as they do. That is obvious when they argue about their reasons, their motives. I have heard someone tell a child, "You are only doing that to annoy me," when it is clear to me that the child was doing it because the child enjoyed the act itself . . . was oblivious to its effect on the adult. I have been oblivious like that, so I recognize it in others.

My phone buzzes. I pick it up. "Lou it is Cameron. Do you want to go to supper and have pizza?" His voice runs the words together, mechanically.

"It is Thursday," I say. "Hi-I'm-Jean is there."

"Chuy and Bailey and I are going anyway, so we can talk. And you, if you come. Linda is not coming. Dale is not coming."

"I do not know if I want to come," I say. "I will think about it. You will go when?"

"As soon as it is five," he says.

"There are places it is not a good idea to talk about this," I say.

"The pizza place is not one of those places," Cameron says.

"Many people know we go there," I say.

"Surveillance?" Cameron says.

"Yes. But it is a good thing to go there, because we go there. Then meet somewhere else."

"The Center."

"No," I say, thinking of Emmy. "I do not want to go to the Center."

"Emmy likes you," Cameron says. "She is not very intelligent, but she likes you."

"We are not talking about Emmy," I say.

"We are talking about the treatment, after pizza," Cameron says. "I do not know where to go except the Center."

I think of places, but they are all public places. We should not talk about this in public places. Finally I say, "You could come to my apartment." I have never invited Cameron to my apartment. I have never invited anyone to my apartment.

He is silent a long moment. He has never invited me to his home, either. Finally he says, "I will come. I do not know about the others."

"I will come to eat supper with you," I say.

I cannot get to work. I turn on the fan and the spin spirals and pinwheels turn, but the dancing colored reflections do not soothe me. All I can think about is the project looming over us. It is like the picture of an ocean wave towering over someone on a surfboard. The skillful surfer can survive, but the one who is less skilled will be smashed. How can we ride this wave?

I write and print out my address and the directions from the pizza place to my apartment. I have to stop and look at the city map to be sure the directions are right. I am not used to giving directions to other drivers.

At five, I turn off the fan, get up, and leave my office. I have done nothing useful for hours. I feel dull and thick, the internal music like Mahler's First Symphony, ponderous and heavy. Outside, it is cool, and I shiver. I get into my car, comforted by all four whole tires, a whole windshield, and an engine that starts when I turn the key. I have sent my insurance company a copy of the police report, as the police suggested.

At the pizza place, our usual table is empty; I am earlier than usual. I sit down. Hi-I'm-Jean glances at me and looks away. A moment later

Cameron comes in, then Chuy and Bailey and Eric. The table feels unbalanced with only five of us. Chuy moves his chair to the end, and the rest of us shift a little: now it is symmetrical.

I can see the beer sign easily, with its blinking pattern. Tonight it annoys me; I turn a little away. Everyone is twitchy; I am having to bounce my fingers on my legs, and Chuy is twisting his neck back and forth, back and forth. Cameron's arm moves; he is bouncing his plastic dice in his pocket. As soon as we have ordered, Eric takes out his multicolored pen and starts drawing his patterns.

I wish Dale and Linda were here, too. It feels odd to be without them. When our food comes we eat, almost in silence. Chuy is making a little rhythmic "hunh" between bites, and Bailey is clicking his tongue. When most of the food is gone, I clear my throat. Everyone looks at me quickly, then away.

"Sometimes people need a place to talk," I say. "Sometimes it can be at someone's place."

"It could be at your place?" Chuy asks.

"It could," I say.

"Not everyone knows where you live," Cameron says. I know he does not know, either. It is strange how we have to talk about something.

"Here are directions," I say. I take out the papers and put them on the table. One at a time, the others take the sheets. They do not look at them right away.

"Some people have to get up early," Bailey says.

"It is not late now," I say.

"Some people will have to leave before others if others are staying late."

"I know that," I say.

CHAPTER SEVENTEEN

*T*HERE ARE ONLY TWO VISITOR SLOTS IN THE PARKING LOT, but I know there is room for my visitors' cars; most of the residents do not keep cars. This apartment building was built back when everyone had at least one car.

I wait in the parking lot until the others have arrived. Then I lead them upstairs. All those feet sound loud on the stairs. I did not know it would be this loud. Danny opens his door.

"Oh—hi, Lou. I wondered what was happening."

"It is my friends," I say.

"Good, good," Danny says. He does not close his door. I do not know what he wants. The others follow me to my door, and I unlock it and let them in.

It feels very strange to have other people in the apartment. Cameron walks around and finally disappears into the bathroom. I can hear him in there. It is like when I lived in a group residence. I did not like that much. Some things should be private; it is not nice to hear someone else in the bathroom. Cameron flushes the toilet, and I hear the water running in the basin, and then he comes out. Chuy looks at me, and I nod. He goes into the bathroom, too. Bailey is looking at my computer.

"I do not have a desk model at home," he says. "I use my handheld to work through the computer at work."

"I like having this one," I say.

Chuy comes back to the living room. "So—what now?"

Cameron looks at me. "Lou, you have been reading about this, haven't you?"

"Yes." I get *Brain Functionality* off the shelf where I put it. "My—a friend loaned me this book. She said it was the best place to start."

"Is it the woman Emmy talks about?"

"No, someone else. She is a doctor; she is married to a man I know."

"Is she a brain doctor?"

"I don't think so."

"Why did she give you the book? Did you ask her about the project?"

"I asked her for a book on brain function. I want to know what they are going to do to our brains."

"People who have not studied do not know anything about how the brain works," Bailey says.

"I did not know until I started reading," I say. "Only what they taught us in school, and that was not a lot. I wanted to learn because of this."

"Did you?" Cameron asks.

"It takes a long time to learn everything that is known about brains," I say. "I know more than I did, but I do not know if I know enough. I want to know what they think it will do and what can go wrong."

"It is complicated," Chuy says.

"You know about brain function?" I ask.

"Not much. My older sister was a doctor, before she died. I tried to read some of her books when she was in medical school. That is when I lived at home with my family. I was only fifteen, though."

"I want to know if you think they can do what they say they can do," Cameron says.

"I do not know," I say. "I wanted to see what the doctor was saying today. I am not sure he is right. Those pictures they showed are like ones in this book—" I pat the book. "He said they meant something different. This is not a new book, and things change. I need to find new pictures."

"Show us the pictures," Bailey says.

I turn to the page with the pictures of brain activitation and lay the book on the low table. They all look. "It says here this shows brain activation when someone sees a human face," I say. "I think it looks exactly like the picture the doctor said showed looking at a familiar face in a crowd."

"It is the same," Bailey says, after a moment. "The ratio of line width to overall size is exactly the same. The colored spots are in the same place. If it is not the same illustration, it is a copy."

"Maybe for normal brains the activation pattern is the same," Chuy says.

I had not thought of that.

"He said the second picture was of an autistic brain looking at a familiar face," Cameron says. "But the book says it is the activation pattern for looking at a composite unknown face."

"I do not understand composite unknown," Eric says.

"It is a computer-generated face using features of several real faces," I say.

"If it is true that the activation pattern for autistic brains looking at a familiar face is the same as normal brains looking at an unfamiliar face, then what is the autistic pattern for looking at an unfamiliar face?" Bailey asks.

"I always had trouble recognizing people I was supposed to know," Chuy says. "It still takes me longer to learn people's faces."

"Yes, but you do," Bailey says. "You recognize all of us, don't you?"

"Yes," Chuy says. "But it took a long time, and I knew you first by your voices and size and things."

"The thing is, you do now, and that's what matters. If your brain is doing it a different way, at least it's doing it."

"They told me that the brain can make different pathways to do the same thing," Cameron says. "Like if someone is injured, they give them that drug—I don't remember what it is—and some training, and they can relearn how to do things but use a different part of the brain."

"They told me that, too," I say. "I asked them why they didn't give me the drug and they said it wouldn't work for me. They did not say why."

"Does this book?" Cameron asks.

"I don't know. I haven't read that far," I say.

"Is it hard?" Bailey asks.

"In some places, but not as hard as I thought it would be," I say. "I started reading some other stuff first. That helped."

"What other?" Eric asks.

"I read through some of the courses on the Internet," I say. "Biology, anatomy, organic chemistry, biochemistry." He is staring at me; I look down. "It is not as hard as it sounds."

No one says anything for several minutes. I can hear them breathe; they can hear me breathe. We can all hear all the noises, smell all the smells. It is not like being with my friends at fencing, where I have to be careful what I notice.

"I'm going to do it," Cameron says suddenly. "I want to."

"Why?" Bailey asks.

"I want to be normal," Cameron says. "I always did. I hate being different. It is too hard, and it is too hard to pretend to be like everyone else when I am not. I am tired of that."

" 'But aren't you proud of who you are?' " Bailey's tone makes it clear he is quoting the slogan from the Center: We are proud of who we are.

"No," Cameron says. "I pretended to be. But really—what is there to be proud of? I know what you're going to say, Lou—" He looks at me. He is wrong. I was not going to say anything. "You'll say that normal people do what we do, only in smaller amounts. Lots of people self-stim, but they don't even realize it. They tap their feet or twirl their hair or touch their faces. Yes, but they're normal and no one makes them stop. Other people don't make good eye contact, but they're normal and no one nags them to make eye contact. They have something else to make up for the tiny bit of themselves that acts autistic. That's what I want. I want—I want not to have to try so hard to look normal. I just want to *be* normal."

" 'Normal' is a dryer setting," Bailey says.

"Normal is other people." Cameron's arm twitches and he shrugs violently; sometimes that stops it. "This—this stupid arm . . . I'm tired of trying to hide what's wrong. I want it to be *right*." His voice has gotten loud, and I do not know if he will be angrier if I ask him to be quieter. I wish I had not brought them here. "Anyway," Cameron says, slightly softer, "I'm going to do it, and you can't stop me."

"I am not trying to stop you," I say.

"Are you going to?" he asks. He looks at each of us in turn.

"I do not know. I am not ready to say."

"Linda won't," Bailey says. "She says she will quit her job."

"I do not know why the patterns would be the same," Eric says. He is looking at the book. "It does not make sense."

"A familiar face is a familiar face?"

"The task is finding familiar in different. The activation pattern should be more similar to finding a familiar nonface in different unfaces. Do they have that picture in this book?"

"It is on the next page," I say. "It says the activation pattern is the same except that the face task activates the facial recognition area."

"They care more about facial recognition," Eric says.

"Normal people care about normal people," Cameron says. "That is why I want to be normal."

"Autistic people care about autistic people," Eric says.

"Not the same," Cameron says. He looks around the group. "Look at us. Eric is making patterns with his finger. Bailey is chewing on his lip, Lou is trying so hard to sit still that he looks like a piece of wood, and I'm bouncing whether I want to or not. You accept it that I bounce, you accept it that I have dice in my pocket, but you do not care about me. When I had flu last spring, you did not call or bring food."

I do not say anything. There is nothing to say. I did not call or bring food because I did not know Cameron wanted me to do that. I think it is unfair of him to complain now. I am not sure that normal people always call and bring food when someone is sick. I glance at the others. They are all looking away from Cameron, as I am. I like Cameron; I am used to Cameron. What is the difference between liking and being used to? I am not sure. I do not like not being sure.

"You don't, either," Eric says finally. "You have not been to any meetings of the society in over a year."

"I guess not," Cameron's voice is soft now. "I kept seeing—I can't say it—the older ones, worse than we are. No young ones; they're all cured at birth or before. When I was twenty it was a lot of help. But now . . . we are the only ones like us. The older autistics, the ones who didn't get the good early training—I do not like to be around them. They make me afraid that I could go back to that, being like them. And there is no one for us to help, because there are no young ones."

"Tony," Bailey says, looking at his knees.

"Tony is the youngest and he is . . . what, twenty-seven? He's the only one under thirty. All the rest of the younger people at the Center are . . . different."

"Emmy likes Lou," Eric says. I look at him; I do not know what he means by that.

"If I'm normal, I will never have to go to a psychiatrist again," Cameron says. I think of Dr. Fornum and think that not seeing her is almost enough reason to risk the treatment. "I can marry without a certificate of stability. Have children."

"You want to get married," Bailey says.

"Yes," Cameron says. His voice is louder again, but only a little louder, and his face is red. "I want to get married. I want to have children. I want to live in an ordinary house in an ordinary neighborhood and take the ordinary public transportation and live the rest of my life as a normal person."

"Even if you aren't the same person?" Eric asks.

"Of course I'll be the same person," Cameron says. "Just normal."

I am not sure this is possible. When I think of the ways in which I am not normal, I cannot imagine being normal and being the same person. The whole point of this is to change us, make us something else, and surely that involves the personality, the self, as well.

"I will do it by myself if no one else will," Cameron says.

"It is your decision," Chuy says, in his quoting voice.

"Yes." Cameron's voice drops. "Yes."

"I will miss you," Bailey says.

"You could come, too," Cameron says.

"No. Not yet, anyway. I want to know more."

"I am going home," Cameron says. "I will tell them tomorrow." He stands up, and I can see his hand in his pocket, jiggling the dice, up and down, up and down.

We do not say good-bye. We do not need to do that with each other. Cameron walks out and shuts the door quietly behind him. The others look at me and then away.

"Some people do not like who they are," Bailey says.

"Some people are different than other people think," Chuy says.

"Cameron was in love with a woman who did not love him," Eric says. "She said it would never work. It was when he was in college." I wonder how Eric knows that.

"Emmy says Lou is in love with a normal woman who is going to ruin his life," Chuy says.

"Emmy does not know what she is talking about," I say. "Emmy should mind her own business."

"Does Cameron think this woman will love him if he is normal?" Bailey asks.

"She married someone else," Eric says. "He thinks he might love someone who would love him back. I think that is why he wants the treatment."

"I would not do it for a woman," Bailey says. "If I do it, I need a reason for me." I wonder what he would say if he knew Marjory. If I knew it would make Marjory love me, would I do it? It is an uncomfortable thought; I put it aside.

"I do not know what normal would feel like. Normal people do not all look happy. Maybe it feels bad to be normal, as bad as being autistic." Chuy's head is twisting up and around, back and down.

"I would like to try it," Eric says. "But I would like to be able to get back to this self if it didn't work."

"It doesn't work like that," I say. "Remember what Dr. Ransome said to Linda? Once the connections are formed between neurons, they stay formed unless an accident or something breaks the connection."

"Is that what they will do, make new connections?"

"What about the old ones? Won't there be"—Bailey waves his arms—"like when things collide? Confusion? Static? Chaos?"

"I do not know," I say. All at once I feel swallowed by my ignorance, so vast an unknowing. Out of that vastness so many bad things might come. Then an image of a photograph taken by one of the space-based telescopes comes to mind: that vast darkness lit by stars. Beauty, too, may be in that unknown.

"I would think they would have to turn off the circuits that are working now, build new circuits, and then turn on the new ones. That way only the good connections would be working."

"That is not what they told us," Chuy says.

"No one would agree to having their brain destroyed to build a new one," Eric says.

"Cameron—" Chuy says.

"He does not think that is what will happen," Eric says. "If he knew . . ." He pauses, his eyes closed, and we wait. "He might do it anyway if he is unhappy enough. It is no worse than suicide. Better, if he comes back the person he wants to be."

"What about memories?" Chuy asks. "Would they remove the memories?"

"How?" Bailey asks.

"Memories are stored in the brain. If they turn everything off, the memories will go away."

"Maybe not. I have not read the chapters on memory yet," I say. "I will read them; they are next." Some parts of memory have already been discussed in the book, but I do not understand all of it yet and I do not want to talk about it. "Besides," I say, "when you turn off a computer not all the memory is lost."

"People are not conscious in surgery, but they do not lose all their memories," Eric says.

"But they do not remember the surgery, and there are those drugs that interfere with memory formation," Chuy says. "If they can interfere with memory formation, maybe they can remove old memories."

"That is something we can look up on-line," Eric says. "I will do that."

"Moving connections and making new ones is like hardware," Bailey says. "Learning to use the new connections is like software. It was hard enough to learn language the first time; I do not want to go through that again."

"Normal kids learn it faster," Eric says.

"It still takes years," Bailey says. "They're talking about six to eight weeks of rehab. Maybe that's enough for a chimpanzee, but chimps don't talk."

"It is not like they never made mistakes before," Chuy says. "They used to think all sorts of wrong things about us. This could be wrong, too."

"More is known about brain functions," I say. "But not everything."

"I do not like doing something without knowing what will happen," Bailey says.

Chuy and Eric say nothing: they agree. I agree, too. It is important to know the consequences before acting. Sometimes the consequences are not obvious.

The consequences of not acting are also not obvious. If I do not take the treatment, things will still not stay the same. Don proved that, in his attacks on my car and then on me. No matter what I do, no matter how predictable I try to make my life, it will not be any more predictable than the rest of the world. Which is chaotic.

"I am thirsty," Eric says suddenly. He stands up. I stand up, too, and go to the kitchen. I get out a glass and fill it with water. He makes a face when he tastes the water; I remember then that he drinks bottled water. I do not have the brand he likes.

"I am thirsty, too," Chuy says. Bailey says nothing.

"Do you want water?" I ask. "It is all I have except one bottle of fruit drink." I hope he will not ask for the fruit drink. It is what I like for breakfast.

"I want water," he says. Bailey puts his hand up. I fill two more glasses with water and bring them into the living room. At Tom and Lucia's house, they ask if I want something to drink even when I don't. It makes more sense to wait until people say they want something, but probably normal people ask first.

It feels very strange to have people here in my apartment. The space seems smaller. The air seems thicker. The colors change a little because of the colors they are wearing and the colors they are. They take up space and breathe.

I wonder suddenly how it would be if Marjory and I lived together—how it would be to have her taking up space here in the living room, in the bathroom, in the bedroom. I did not like the group home I used to live in, when I first left home. The bathroom smelled of other people, even though we cleaned it every day. Five different toothpastes. Five different preferences in shampoo and soap and deodorant.

"Lou! Are you all right?" Bailey looks concerned.

"I was thinking about . . . something," I say. I do not want to think about not liking Marjory in my apartment, that it might not be good, that it might feel crowded or noisy or smelly.

CAMERON IS NOT AT WORK. CAMERON IS WHEREVER THEY TOLD him to go to start the procedure. Linda is not at work. I do not know where she is. I would rather wonder where Linda is than think about what is happening to Cameron. I know Cameron the way he is now—the way he was two days ago. Will I know the person with Cameron's face who comes out of this?

The more I think about it, the more it seems like those science fiction films where someone's brain is transplanted into another person or another personality is inserted in the same brain. The same face, but not the same person. It is scary. Who would live behind my face? Would he like fencing? Would he like good music? Would he like Marjory? Would she like him?

Today they're telling us more about the procedure.

"The baseline PET scans let us map your individual brain function," the doctor says. "We'll have tasks for you to do during the scans that identify how your brain processes information. When we compare that to the normal brain, then we'll know how to modify yours—"

"Not all normal brains are exactly alike," I say.

"Close enough," he says. "The differences between yours and the average of several normal brains are what we want to modify."

"What effect will this have on my basic intelligence?" I ask.

"Shouldn't have any, really. That whole notion of a central IQ was pretty much exploded last century with the discovery of the modularity of processing—it's what makes generalization so difficult—and it's you people, autistic people, who sort of proved that it's possible to be very intelligent in math, say, and way below the curve in expressive language."

Shouldn't have any is not the same thing as won't have any. I do not really know what my intelligence is—they would not give us our own IQ scores, and I've never bothered to take any of the publicly available ones—but I know I am not stupid, and I do not want to be.

"If you're concerned about your pattern-analysis skills," he says, "that's not the part of the brain that the treatment will affect. It's more like giving that part of your brain access to new data—socially important data—without your having to struggle for it."

"Like facial expressions," I say.

"Yes, that sort of thing. Facial recognition, facial expressions, tonal nuance in language—a little tweak to the attention control area so it's easier for you to notice them and it's pleasurable to do so."

"Pleasure—you're tying this to the intrinsic endorphin releasers?"

He turns red suddenly. "If you mean are you going to get high on being around people, certainly not. But autistics do not find social interaction rewarding, and this will make it at least less threatening." I am not good at interpreting tonal nuances, but I know he is not telling the whole truth.

If they can control the amount of pleasure we get from social interaction, then they could control the amount normal people get from it. I think of teachers in school, being able to control the pleasure students get from other students . . . making them all autistic to the extent that they would rather study than talk. I think of Mr. Crenshaw, with a section full of workers who ignore everything but work.

My stomach is knotted; a sour taste comes into my mouth. If I say that I see these possibilities, what will happen to me? Two months ago, I would have blurted out what I saw, what I worried about; now I am more cautious. Mr. Crenshaw and Don have given me that wisdom.

"You mustn't get paranoid, Lou," the doctor says. "It's a constant temptation to anyone outside the social mainstream to think people are plotting something dire, but it's not a healthy way to think."

I say nothing. I am thinking about Dr. Fornum and Mr. Crenshaw and Don. These people do not like me or people like me. Sometimes people who do not like me or people like me may try to do me real harm. Would it have been paranoia if I had suspected from the first that Don slashed my tires? I do not think so. I would have correctly identified a danger. Correctly identifying danger is not paranoia.

"You must trust us, Lou, for this to work. I can give you something to calm you—"

"I am not upset," I say. I am not upset. I am pleased with myself for thinking through what he is saying and finding the hidden meaning, but I am not upset, even though that hidden meaning is that he is manipulating me. If I know it, then it is not really manipulation. "I am trying to understand, but I am not upset."

He relaxes. The muscles in his face release a little, especially around his eyes and in his forehead. "You know, Lou, this is a very complicated subject. You're an intelligent man, but it's not really your field. It takes years of study to really understand it all. Just a short lecture and maybe looking at a few sites on the 'net aren't enough to bring you up to speed. You'll only confuse and worry yourself if you try. Just as I wouldn't be able to do what you do. Why not just let us do our work and you do yours?"

Because it is my brain and my self that you are changing. Because you have not told the whole truth and I am not sure you have my best interest—or even my interest at all—in mind.

"Who I am is important to me," I say.

"You mean you like being autistic?" Scorn edges his voice; he cannot imagine anyone wanting to be like me.

"I like being me," I say. "Autism is part of who I am; it is not the whole thing." I hope that is true, that I am more than my diagnosis.

"So—if we get rid of the autism, you'll be the same person, only not autistic."

He hopes this is true; he may think he thinks it is true; he does not believe absolutely that it is true. His fear that it is not true wafts from him like the sour stink of physical fear. His face crinkles into an expression that is supposed to convince me he believes it, but false sincerity is an expression I know from childhood. Every therapist, every teacher, every counselor has had that expression in their repertoire, the worried/caring look.

What frightens me most is that they may—surely they will—tinker with memory, not just current connections. They must know as well as I do that my entire past experience is from this autistic perspective. Changing the connections will not change that, and that has made me who I am. Yet if I lose the memory of what this is like, who I am, then I will have lost everything I've worked on for thirty-five years. I do not want to lose that. I do not want to remember things only the way I remember what I read in books; I do not want Marjory to be like someone seen on a video screen. I want to keep the feelings that go with the memories.

CHAPTER EIGHTEEN

*O*N SUNDAYS, THE PUBLIC TRANSPORTATION DOES NOT run on the usual workday schedule, even though Sunday is a holy day for only a minority of people. If I do not drive to church, then I get there either very early or a little late. It is rude to be late, and being rude to God is ruder than other kinds of rude.

It is very quiet when I arrive. The church I go to has a very early service, with no music, and a 10:30 service, with music. I like to come early and sit in the dim quiet, watching the light move through the colored glass of the windows. Now once more I sit in the dim quiet of the church and think about Don and Marjory.

I am not supposed to think about Don and Marjory but about God. Fix your mind on God, said a priest who used to be here, and you will not go far wrong. It is hard to fix your mind on God when the image in my mind is that of the open end of the barrel of Don's gun. Round and dark like a black hole. I could feel the attraction of it, the pull as if the hole, the opening, had mass that wanted to pull me into itself, into permanent blackness. Death. Nothingness.

I do not know what comes after death. Scripture tells me one thing here and another there. Some people emphasize that all the virtuous will be saved and go to heaven, and others say that you have to be Elect. I do not imagine it is anything we can describe. When I try to think of it, up to now, it always looks like a pattern of light, intricate and beautiful, like the pictures astronomers take or create from space-telescope images, each color for a different wavelength.

But now, in the aftermath of Don's attack, I see dark, faster than light, racing out of the barrel of the gun to draw me into it, beyond the speed of light, forever.

Yet I am here, in this seat, in this church, still alive. Light pours in through the old stained-glass window over the altar, rich glowing color that stains the altar linens, the wood itself, the carpet. This early, the light reaches farther into the church than during the service, angling to the left because of the season.

I take a breath, smelling candle wax and the faintest hint of smoke from the early service, the smell of books—our church still uses paper prayer books and hymnals—and the cleaning compounds used on wood and fabric and floor.

I am alive. I am in the light. The darkness was not, this time, faster than the light. But I feel unsettled, as if it were chasing me, coming nearer and nearer behind me, where I can't see.

I am sitting at the back of the church, but behind me is an open space, more unknown. Usually it does not bother me, but today I wish there were a wall there.

I try to focus on the light, on the slow movement of the colored bars down and across as the sun rises higher. In an hour, the light moves a distance that anyone could see, but it is not the light moving: it is the planet moving. I forget that and use the common phrasing just like everyone else and get that shock of joy each time I remember, again, that the earth does move.

We are always spinning into the light and out of it again. It is our speed, not the light's speed or the dark's speed, that makes our days and nights. Was it my speed, and not Don's speed, that brought us into the dark space where he wanted to hurt me? Was it my speed that saved me?

I try again to concentrate on God, and the light recedes enough to pick out the brass cross on its wooden stand. The glint of yellow metal against the purple shadows behind it is so striking that my breath catches for a moment.

In this place, light is always faster than dark; the speed of dark does not matter.

"Here you are, Lou!"

The voice startles me. I flinch but manage not to say anything, and even smile at the gray-haired woman holding out a service leaflet. Usually I am more aware of the time passing, people arriving, so that I am not surprised. She is smiling.

"I didn't mean to startle you," she says.

"It's all right," I say. "I was just thinking."

She nods and goes back to greet other arrivals without saying anything more. She has a name tag on, *Cynthia Kressman*. I see her every third week handing out service leaflets, and on other Sundays she usually sits across the center aisle and four rows ahead of me.

I am alert now and notice people coming in. The old man with two canes, who totters down the aisle to the very front. He used to come with his wife, but she died four years ago. The three old women who always come in together except when one is sick and sit in the third row on the left. One and two and three, four and two and one and one, people trickle in. I see the organist's head lift over the top of the organ console and drop back down. Then a soft "mmph" and the music begins.

My mother said it was wrong to go to church just for the music. That is not the only reason I go to church. I go to church to learn how to be a better person. But the music is one reason I go to this church. Today it is Bach again—our organist likes Bach—and my mind effortlessly picks up the many strands of the pattern and follows them as she plays them.

Hearing music like this, all around in real life, is different from hearing a recording. It makes me more aware of the space I am in; I can hear the sound bouncing off the walls, forming harmonies unique to this place. I have heard Bach in other churches, and somehow it always makes harmonies, not disharmonies. This is a great mystery.

The music stops. I can hear a soft murmur behind me as the choir and clergy line up. I pick up the hymnal and find the number for the processional hymn. The organ starts again, playing the melody once, and then behind me the loud voices ring out. Someone is a little flat and slides up to each pitch a moment behind the others. It is easy to pick out who it is, but it would be rude to say anything about it. I bow my head as the crucifer leads the procession, and then the choir comes past me. They walk by, in their dark-red robes with the white cottas over them, the women first and then the men, and I hear each individual voice. I read the words and sing as best I can. I like it best when the last two men come by; they both have very deep voices, and the sound they make trembles in my chest.

After the hymn, there is a prayer, which we all say together. I know the words by heart. I have known the words by heart since I was a boy. Another reason besides the music that I go to this church is the predictable order of service. I can say the familiar words without stumbling over them. I can be ready to sit or stand or kneel, speak or sing or listen, and do not feel clumsy and slow. When I visit other churches I am more worried about whether I am doing the right thing at the right time than about God. Here the routines make it easier to listen to what God wants me to do.

Today, Cynthia Kressman is one of the readers. She reads the Old Testament lesson. I read along in the service leaflet. It is hard to understand everything just listening or just reading; both together work better. At home I read the lessons ahead of time, from the calendar the church hands out every year. That also helps me know what is coming. I enjoy it when we read the Psalm responsively; it makes a pattern like a conversation.

When I look past the lessons and the Psalm to the Gospel reading, it is not what I expect. Instead of a reading from Matthew, it is a reading from John. I read intently as the priest reads aloud. It is the story of the man lying by the pool of Siloam, who wanted healing but had no one to lower him into the pool. Jesus asked him if he really wanted to be healed.

It always seemed a silly question to me. Why would the man be by the healing pool if he did not want to be healed? Why would he complain about not having someone to lower him into the water if he did not want to be healed?

God does not ask silly questions. It must not be a silly question, but if it is not silly, what does it mean? It would be silly if I said it or if a doctor said it when I went to get medicine for an illness, but what does it mean here?

Our priest begins the sermon. I am still trying to puzzle out how a seemingly silly question could be meaningful when his voice echoes my thought.

"Why does Jesus ask the man if he wants to be healed? Isn't that kind of silly? He's lying there waiting for his chance at healing. . . . Surely he wants to be healed."

Exactly, I think.

"If God isn't playing games with us, being silly, what then does this question mean, *Do you want to be healed?* Look at where we find this man: by the pool known for its healing powers, where 'an angel comes and stirs the water at intervals . . .' and the sick have to get into the water while it's seething. Where, in other words, the sick are patient patients, waiting for the cure to appear. They know—they've been told—that the way to be cured is to get in the water while it seethes. They aren't looking for anything else. . . . They are in that place, at that time, looking for not just healing, but healing by that particular method.

"In today's world, we might say they are like the person who believes that one particular doctor—one world-famous specialist—can cure him of his cancer. He goes to the hospital where that doctor is, he wants to see that doctor and no one else, because he is sure that only that method will restore him to health.

"So the paralyzed man focuses on the healing pool, sure that the help he needs is someone to carry him into the water at the right time.

"Jesus's question, then, challenges him to consider whether he wants to be well or he wants that particular experience, of being in the pool. If he can be healed without it, will he accept that healing?

"Some preachers have discussed this story as an example of self-inflicted paralysis, hysterical paralysis—if the man wants to stay paralyzed, he will. It's about mental illness, not physical illness. But I think the question Jesus asks has to do with a cognitive problem, not an emotional problem. Can the man see outside the box? Can he accept healing that is not what he's used to? That will go beyond fixing his legs and back and start working on him from the inside out, from the spirit to the mind to the body?"

I wonder what the man would say if he were not paralyzed but autistic. Would he even go to the pool for healing? Cameron would. I close my eyes and see Cameron lowering himself into bubbling water, in a shimmer of light. Then he disappears. Linda insists we do not need healing, that there is nothing wrong with us the way we are, just something wrong with others for not accepting us. I can imagine Linda pushing her way through the crowd, headed away from the pool.

I do not think I need to be healed, not of autism. Other people want me to be healed, not me myself. I wonder if the man had a family, a family tired of carrying him around on his litter. I wonder if he had parents who said, "The least you could do is *try* to be healed," or a wife who said, "Go on, try it; it can't hurt," or children teased by other children because their father couldn't work. I wonder if some of the people who came did not come because they wanted to be healed, themselves, but because other people wanted them to do it, to be less of a burden.

Since my parents died, I am not anyone's burden. Mr. Crenshaw thinks I am a burden to the company, but I do not believe this is true. I am not lying beside a pool begging people to carry me into it. I am trying to keep them from throwing me into it. I do not believe it is a healing pool anyway.

". . . so the question for us today is, Do we want the power of the Holy Spirit in our own lives, or are we just pretending?" The priest has said a lot I have not heard. This I hear, and I shiver.

"Are we sitting here beside the pool, waiting for an angel to come trouble the water, waiting patiently but passively, while beside us the living God stands ready to give us life everlasting, abundant life, if only we will open our hands and hearts and take that gift?

"I believe many of us are. I believe all of us are like that at one time or another, but right now, still, many of us sit and wait and lament that there is no one to lower us into the water when the angel comes." He pauses and looks around the church; I see people flinch and others relax when his gaze touches them. "Look around you, every day, in every place, into the eyes of everyone you meet. Important as this church may be in your life, God should be greater—and He is everywhere, everywhen, in everyone and everything. Ask yourself, 'Do I want to be healed?' and—if you can't answer yes—start asking why not. For I am sure that He stands beside each of you, asking that question in the depths of your soul, ready to heal you of all things as soon as you are ready to be healed."

I stare at him and almost forget to stand up and say the words of the Nicene Creed, which is what comes next.

I believe in God the Father, maker of heaven and earth and of all things seen and unseen. I believe God is important and does not make mistakes. My mother used to joke about God making mistakes, but I do not think if He is God He makes mistakes. So it is not a silly question.

Do I want to be healed? And of what?

The only self I know is this self, the person I am now, the autistic bioinformatics specialist fencer lover of Marjory.

And I believe in his only begotten son, Jesus Christ, who actually in the flesh asked that question of the man by the pool. The man who perhaps—the story does not say—had gone there because people were tired of him being sick and disabled, who perhaps had been content to lie down all day, but he got in the way.

What would Jesus have done if the man had said, "No, I don't want to be healed; I am quite content as I am"? If he had said, "There is nothing wrong with me, but my relatives and neighbors insisted I come"?

I say the words automatically, smoothly, while my mind wrestles with the reading, the sermon, the words. I remember another student, back in my hometown, who found out I went to church and asked, "Do you really believe that stuff or is it just a habit?"

If it is just habit, like going to the healing pool when you are sick, does that mean there is no belief? If the man had told Jesus that he didn't really want to be healed, but his relatives insisted, Jesus might still think the man needed to be able to get up and walk.

Maybe God thinks I would be better if I weren't autistic. Maybe God wants me to take the treatment.

I am cold suddenly. Here I have felt accepted—accepted by God, accepted by the priest and the people, or most of them. God does not spurn the blind, the deaf, the paralyzed, the crazy. That is what I have been taught and what I believe. What if I was wrong? What if God wants me to be something other than I am?

I sit through the rest of the service. I do not go up for Communion. One of the ushers asks if I am all right, and I nod. He looks worried but lets me alone. After the recessional, I wait where I am until the others have left, and then I go out the door. The priest is still standing there, chatting with one of the ushers. He smiles at me.

"Hello, Lou. How are you?" He gives my hand one firm, quick shake, because he knows that I do not like long handshakes.

"I do not know if I want to be healed," I say.

His face contracts into a worried look. "Lou, I wasn't talking about you—about people like you. I'm sorry if you think that—I was talking about spiritual healing. You know we accept you as you are—"

"You do," I say, "but God?"

"God loves you as you are and as you will become," the priest says. "I'm sorry if something I said hurt you—"

"I am not hurt," I say. "I just do not know—"

"Do you want to talk about it?" he asks.

"Not now," I say. I do not know what I think yet, so I will not ask until I am sure.

"You did not come up for Communion," he says. I am surprised; I did not expect him to notice. "Please, Lou—don't let anything I said get between you and God."

"It won't," I say. "It is just—I need to think." I turn away and he lets me go. This is another good thing about my church. It is there, but it is not always grabbing. For a while when I was in school I went to a church where everyone wanted to be in everyone's life all the time. If I had a cold and missed a service, someone would call to find out why. They said they were concerned and caring, but I felt smothered. They said I was cold and needed to develop a fiery spirituality; they did not understand about me, and they would not listen.

I turn back to the priest; his eyebrows go up, but he waits for me to speak.

"I do not know why you talked about that Scripture this week," I say. "It is not on the schedule."

"Ah," he says. His face relaxes. "Did you know that the Gospel of John is not ever on the schedule? It's like a kind of secret weapon we priests can pull out when we think a congregation needs it."

I had noticed that, but I had never asked why.

"I chose that Scripture for this particular day because—Lou, how involved are you in parish business?"

When someone starts an answer and then turns it into something else it is hard to understand, but I try. "I go to church," I say. "Almost every Sunday—"

"Do you have other friends in the congregation?" he asks. "I mean, people you spend time with outside of church and maybe talk with about how the church is getting along?"

"No," I say. Ever since that one church, I have not wanted to get too close to the people in church.

"Well, then, you may not be aware that there's been a lot of argument about some things. We've had a lot of new people join—most of them have come from another church where there was a big fight, and they left."

"A fight in church?" I can feel my stomach tighten; it would be very wrong to fight in church.

"These people were angry and upset when they came," the priest says. "I knew it would take time for them to settle down and heal from that injury. I gave them time. But they are still angry and still arguing— with the people at their old church, and here they've started arguments with people who have always gotten along." He is looking at me over the top of his glasses. Most people have surgery when their eyes start to go bad, but he wears old-fashioned glasses.

I puzzle through what he has said. "So . . . you talked about wanting to be healed because they are still angry?"

"Yes. They needed the challenge, I thought. I want them to realize that sticking in the same rut, having the same old arguments, staying angry with the people they left behind, is not the way to let God work in their lives for healing." He shakes his head, looks down for a moment and then back at me. "Lou, you look a little upset still. Are you sure that you can't tell me what it is?"

I do not want to talk to him about the treatment right now, but it is worse not to tell the truth here in church than anywhere else.

"Yes," I say. "You said God loved us, accepted us, as we are. But then you said people should change, should accept healing. Only, if we are accepted as we are, then maybe that is what we should be. And if we should change, then it would be wrong to be accepted as we are."

He nods. I do not know if that means he agrees that I said it correctly or that we should change. "I truly did not aim that arrow at you, Lou, and I'm sorry it hit you. I always thought of you as someone who had adapted very well—who was content within the limits God had put on his life."

"I don't think it was God," I say. "My parents said it was an accident, that some people are just born that way. But if it was God, it would be wrong to change, wouldn't it?"

He looks surprised.

"But everyone has always wanted me to change as much as I could, be as normal as I could, and if that is a correct demand, then they cannot believe that the limits—the autism—come from God. That is what I cannot figure out. I need to know which it is."

"Hmmm. . . ." He rocks back and forth, heel to toe, looking past me for a long moment. "I never thought of it that way, Lou. Indeed, if people think of disabilities as literally God-given, then waiting by the pool is the only reasonable response. You don't throw away something God gives you. But actually—I agree with you. I can't really see God wanting people born with disabilities."

"So I should want to be cured of it, even if there is no cure?"

"I think what we are supposed to want is what God wants, and the tricky thing is that much of the time we don't know what that is," he says.

"You know," I say.

"I know part of it. God wants us to be honest, kind, helpful to one another. But whether God wants us to pursue every hint of a cure of conditions we have or acquire . . . I don't know that. Only if it doesn't interfere with who we are as God's children, I suppose. And some things are beyond human power to cure, so we must do the best we can to cope with them. Good heavens, Lou, you come up with difficult ideas!" He is smiling at me, and it looks like a real smile, eyes and mouth and whole face. "You'd have made a very interesting seminary student."

"I could not go to seminary," I say. "I could not ever learn the languages."

"I'm not so sure," he says. "I'll be thinking more about what you said, Lou. If you ever want to talk . . ."

It is a signal that he does not want to talk more now. I do not know why normal people cannot just say, "I do not want to talk more now," and go. I say, "Good-bye," quickly and turn away. I know some of the signals, but I wish they were more reasonable.

The after-church bus is late, so I have not missed it. I stand on the corner waiting, thinking about the sermon. Few people ride the bus on Sunday, so I find a seat by myself, and look out at the trees, all bronze and coppery in the autumn light. When I was little, the trees still turned red and gold, but those trees all died from the heat, and now the trees that turn color at all are duller.

At the apartment, I start reading. I would like to finish Cego and Clinton by the morning. I am sure that they will summon me to talk about the treatment and make a decision. I am not ready to make a decision.


"PETE," THE VOICE SAID. ALDRIN DIDN'T RECOGNIZE IT. "THIS is John Slazik." Aldrin's mind froze; his heart stumbled and then raced. Gen. John L. Slazik, USAF, Ret. Currently CEO of the company.

Aldrin gulped, then steadied his voice. "Yes, Mr. Slazik." A second later, he thought maybe he should have said, "Yes, General," but it was too late. He didn't know, anyway, if retired generals used their rank in civilian settings.

"Listen, I'm just wondering what you can tell me about this little project of Gene Crenshaw's." Slazik's voice was deep, warm, smooth as good brandy, and about as potent.

Aldrin could feel the fire creeping along his veins. "Yes, sir." He tried to organize his thoughts. He had not expected a call from the CEO himself. He rattled off an explanation that included the research, the autistic unit, the need to cut costs, his concern that Crenshaw's plan would have negative consequences for the company as well as the autistic employees.

"I see," Slazik said. Aldrin held his breath. "You know, Pete," Slazik said, in the same relaxed drawl, "I'm a little concerned that you didn't come to me in the first place. Granted, I'm new around here, but I really like to know what's going on before the hot potato hits me in the face."

"Sorry, sir," Aldrin said. "I didn't know. I was trying to work within the chain of command—"

"Um." A long and obvious indrawn breath. "Well, now, I see your point, but the thing is, there's a time—rare, but it exists—when you've tried going up and got stymied and you need to know how to hop a link. And this was one of the times it sure would've been helpful— to me."

"Sorry, sir," Aldrin said again. His heart was pounding.

"Well, I think we caught it in time," Slazik said. "So far it's not out in the media, at least. I was pleased to hear that you had a concern for your people, as well as the company. I hope you realize, Pete, that I would not condone any illegal or unethical actions taken toward our employees or any research subjects. I am more than a little surprised and disappointed that one of my subordinates tried to screw around that way." For the length of that last sentence the drawl hardened into something more like saw-edged steel; Aldrin shivered involuntarily.

Then the drawl returned. "But that's not your problem. Pete, we've got a situation with those people of yours. They've been promised a treatment and threatened with loss of their jobs, and you're going to have to straighten that out. Legal is going to send someone to explain the situation, but I want you to prepare them."

"What—what is the situation now, sir?" Aldrin asked.

"Obviously their jobs are safe, if they want to keep them," Slazik said. "We don't coerce volunteers; this isn't the military, and I understand that even if . . . someone doesn't. They have rights. They don't have to agree to the treatment. On the other hand, if they want to volunteer, that's fine; they've already been through the preliminary tests. Full pay, no loss of seniority—it's a special case."

Aldrin wanted to ask what would happen to Crenshaw and himself, but he was afraid that asking would make whatever it was worse.

"I'm going to be calling Mr. Crenshaw in for an interview," Slazik said. "Don't talk about this, except to reassure your people that they're not in jeopardy. Can I trust you for that?"

"Yes, sir."

"No gossiping with Shirley in Accounting or Bart in Human Resources or any of your other contacts?"

Aldrin felt faint. How much did Slazik know? "No, sir, I won't talk to anyone."

"Crenshaw may call you—he should be fairly steamed with you—but don't worry about it."

"No, sir."

"I'll have to meet you personally, Pete, when this settles down a bit."

"Yes, sir."

"If you can learn to work a little better with the system, your dedication to both company goals and personnel—and your awareness of the public-relations aspects of such things—could be a real asset to us." Slazik hung up before Aldrin could say anything. Aldrin took a long breath—it felt like the first in a long time—and sat staring at the clock until he realized the numbers on it were still changing.

Then he headed over to Section A, before Crenshaw—who must have heard by now—could blow up at him on the phone. He felt fragile, vulnerable. He hoped his team would make the announcement easy.

*I HAVE NOT SEEN CAMERON SINCE HE LEFT LAST WEEK. I DO* not know when I will see Cameron again. I do not like not having his car to park my car facing into. I do not like not knowing where he is or whether he is all right or not.

The symbols on the screen I watch are shifting in and out of reality, patterns forming and dissolving, and this is not something that had happened before. I turn on my fan. The whirling of the spin spirals, the movements of reflected light, make my eyes hurt. I turn the fan off.

I read another book last night. I wish I had not read it.

What we were taught about ourselves, as autistic children, was only part of what the people who taught us believed to be true. Later I found out some of that, but some I never really wanted to know. I thought it was hard enough coping with the world without knowing everything other people thought was wrong with me. I thought making my outward behavior fit in was enough. That is what I was taught: act normal, and you will be normal enough.

If the chip they will implant in Don's brain makes him act normal, does this mean he is normal enough? Is it normal to have a chip in your brain? To have a brain that needs a chip to make it able to govern normal behavior?

If I can seem normal without a chip and Don needs a chip, does that mean I am normal, more normal than he is?

The book said that autistics tend to ruminate excessively on abstract philosophical questions like these, in much the same way that psychotics sometimes do. It referred to older books that speculated that autistic persons had no real sense of personal identity, of self. It said they do have self-definition, but of a limited and rule-dictated sort.

It makes me feel queasy to think about this, and about Don's custodial rehabilitation, and about what is happening with Cameron.

If my self-definition is limited and rule-dictated, at least it is my self-definition, and not someone else's. I like peppers on pizza and I do not like anchovies on pizza. If someone changes me, will I still like peppers and not anchovies on pizza? What if the someone who changes me wants me to want anchovies . . . can they change that?

The book on brain functionality said that expressed preferences were the result of the interaction of innate sensory processing and social conditioning. If the person who wants me to like anchovies has not been successful with social conditioning and has access to my sensory processing, then that person can make me like anchovies.

Will I even remember that I don't like anchovies—that I didn't like anchovies?

The Lou who does not like anchovies will be gone, and the new Lou who likes anchovies will exist without a past. But who I am is my past as well as whether I like anchovies now or not.

If my wants are supplied, does it matter what they are? Is there any difference between being a person who likes anchovies and being a person who does not like anchovies? If everyone liked anchovies or everyone didn't like anchovies, what difference would it make?

To the anchovies a lot. If everyone liked anchovies, more anchovies would die. To the person selling anchovies a lot. If everyone liked anchovies, that person would make more money selling them. But to me, the me I am now or the me I will be later? Would I be healthier or less healthy, kinder or less kind, smarter or less smart, if I liked anchovies? Other people I have seen who eat or do not eat anchovies seem much the same. For many things I think it does not matter what people like: what colors, what flavors, what music.

Asking if I want to be healed is like asking if I want to like anchovies. I cannot imagine what liking anchovies would feel like, what taste they would have in my mouth. People who like anchovies tell me they taste good; people who are normal tell me being normal feels good. They cannot describe the taste or the feeling in a way that makes sense to me.

Do I need to be healed? Who does it hurt if I am not healed? Myself, but only if I feel bad the way I am, and I do not feel bad except when people say that I am not one of them, not normal. Supposedly autistic persons do not care what others think of them, but this is not true. I do care, and it hurts when people do not like me because I am autistic.

Even refugees who flee with nothing but their clothes are not forbidden their memories. Bewildered and frightened as they may be, they have themselves for a comparison. Maybe they can never taste their favorite food again, but they can remember that they liked it. They may not see the land they knew again, but they can remember that they lived there. They can judge if their life is better or worse by comparing it to their memories.

I want to know if Cameron remembers the Cameron he was, if he thinks the country he has come to is better than the country he left behind.

This afternoon we are to meet with the treatment advisers again. I will ask about this.

I look at the clock. It is 10:37:18, and I have accomplished nothing this morning. I do not want to accomplish anything in my project. It is the anchovy seller's project and not my project.

R. ALDRIN COMES INTO OUR BUILDING. HE KNOCKS on my door and says, "Please come out; I want to talk to you in the gym." My stomach knots up. I hear him knocking on the others' doors. They come out, Linda and Bailey and Chuy and Eric and all, and we file into the gym, all with tight faces. It is big enough to hold all of us. I try not to worry, but I can feel myself starting to sweat. Are they going to start the treatment right away? No matter what we decide?

"This is complicated," Mr. Aldrin says. "Other people are going to explain it to you again, but I want to tell you right away." He looks excited and not as sad as he did a few days ago. "You remember that I said at the beginning I thought it was wrong for them to try to force you to take the treatment? When I called you on the phone?"

I remember that, and I remember that he did not do anything to help us and later told us we should agree for our own good.

"The company has decided that Mr. Crenshaw acted wrongly," Mr. Aldrin says. "They want you to know that your jobs are completely safe, whatever you decide. You can stay just as you are, and you can work here, with the same supports you have now."

I have to close my eyes; it is too much to bear. Against the dark lids dancing shapes form, bright-colored and glowing with joy. I do not have to do this. If they are not going to do the treatment, I do not even have to decide if I want it or not.

"What about Cameron?" Bailey asks.

Mr. Aldrin shakes his head. "I understand that he has already begun the treatment," he says. "I don't think they can stop at this point. But he will be fully compensated—"

I think this is a silly thing to say. How can you compensate someone for changing his brain?

"Now for the rest of you," Mr. Aldrin says, "if you want the treatment, of course it will still be available, as promised."

It was not promised but threatened. I do not say this.

"You will receive full pay for the duration of treatment and rehab, and you will continue to receive any pay raises or promotions that you would have received otherwise; your seniority will not be affected. The company's legal department is in contact with the Legal Aid organization familiar with your Center, and representatives of both will be available to explain the legal aspects to you and help you with any legal paperwork that's necessary. For instance, if you choose to participate you will need to make arrangements to have bills paid directly out of your accounts, and so on."

"So . . . it's completely voluntary? Really voluntary?" Linda asks, looking down.

"Yes. Completely."

"I do not understand the reason Mr. Crenshaw would change his mind," she says.

"It wasn't exactly Mr. Crenshaw," Mr. Aldrin says. "Someone—people—higher up decided Mr. Crenshaw had made a mistake."

"What will happen to Mr. Crenshaw?" Dale asks.

"I don't know," Mr. Aldrin says. "I am not supposed to talk to anyone about what might happen, and they didn't tell me anyway."

I think that if Mr. Crenshaw works for this company he will find a way to cause us trouble. If the company can turn around so far in this direction, it could always turn back the other way, with a different person in charge, just as a car can go any direction depending on the driver.

"Your meeting this afternoon with the medical team will also be attended by representatives of our legal department and Legal Aid," Mr.

Aldrin says. "And probably a few other people as well. You will not have to make a decision right away, though." He smiles suddenly, and it is a complete smile, mouth and eyes and cheeks and forehead, all the lines working the same way to show that he is really happy and more relaxed. "I'm very relieved," he says. "I'm happy for you."

This is another expression that makes no literal sense. I can be happy or sad or angry or scared, but I cannot have a feeling that someone else should have instead of that person having it. Mr. Aldrin cannot really be happy for me; I have to be happy for myself, or it isn't real. Unless he means that he is happy because he thinks we will be happier if we are not feeling forced into treatment and "I'm happy for you" means "I'm happy because of circumstances that benefit you."

Mr. Aldrin's beeper goes off, and he excuses himself. A moment later he puts his head back into the gym and says, "I have to go—see you this afternoon."


THE MEETING HAS BEEN MOVED TO A LARGER ROOM. MR. AL-drin is at the door when we arrive, and other men and women in suits are inside the room, milling around the table. This one also has wood paneling that does not look as fake and a green carpet. The chairs are the same kind, but the fabric on the padding is dull gold with green flecks shaped like little daisies. At the front is a big table, with groups of chairs to either side, and a big viewscreen hanging on the wall. There are two stacks of folders on the table. One has five folders, and the other has enough for each of us to have one.

As before, we take our seats, and the others slowly take theirs. Dr. Ransome I know; Dr. Handsel is not here. There is another doctor, an older woman; she has a name tag with L. HENDRICKS on it. She is the one who stands up first. She tells us her name is Hendricks; she tells us she is heading the research team and that she wants only willing participants. She sits down. A man in a dark suit stands up and tells us his name is Godfrey Arakeen, an attorney from the company's legal division, and we have nothing to worry about.

I am not worried yet.

He talks about the regulations that govern hiring and firing of handicapped employees. I did not know that the company got a tax credit for hiring us, dependent on the percentage of disabled workers by division and specialty. He makes it seem that our value to the company is that we are a tax credit, not the work we do. He says that Mr. Crenshaw should have informed us of our right to talk to a company ombudsman. I do not know what an ombudsman is, but Mr. Arakeen is already explaining the word. He introduces another man in a suit; Mr. Vanagli, it sounds like. I am not sure how to spell his name, and it is not easy to hear all the sounds in it. Mr. Vanagli says if we have any concerns about anything at work we should come talk to him.

His eyes are closer together than Mr. Arakeen's eyes, and the pattern on his tie is distracting, gold and blue in little diamond shapes arranged like steps going up or down. I do not think I could tell him about my concerns. He does not stay, anyway, but leaves after telling us to come to him anytime in office hours.

Then a woman in a dark suit tells us that she is the lawyer from Legal Aid who normally works with our Center and that she is there to protect our rights. Her name is Sharon Beasley. Her name makes me think of weasels, but she has a broad, friendly face that does not look like a weasel at all. Her hair is soft and curly and hangs down to her shoulders. It is not as shiny as Marjory's hair. She has on earrings with four concentric circles; each one has a different-colored piece of glass in it: blue, red, green, purple. She tells us that Mr. Arakeen is there to protect the company and that although she has no doubt of his honesty and sincerity—I see Mr. Arakeen shift in his seat and his mouth tighten, as if he is getting angry—still we need to have someone on our side, and she is that person.

"We need to make clear what the situation is now, regarding you and this research protocol," Mr. Arakeen says, when she sits down again. "One of your group has already begun the procedure; the rest of you have been promised a chance at this experimental treatment." I think again that it was a threat, not a promise, but I do not interrupt. "The company stands by that promise, so that any of you who decide to take part in the experimental protocol can do so. You will receive full pay, but not the stipend for research subjects, if you choose to do so. You will be considered as employed at another site, with the employment being participation in this research. The company is prepared to cover all medical expenses arising from the treatment, even though this would not normally be covered by your health care policy." He pauses and nods to Mr. Aldrin. "Pete, why don't you hand out those folders now."

The folders each have a name on the cover, on a little sticker, and another little sticker that says: PRIVATE AND CONFIDENTIAL: NOT TO BE REMOVED FROM THIS BUILDING.

"As you'll see," Mr. Arakeen says: "these folders describe in detail what the company is prepared to do for you, whether you choose to participate in this research or not." He turns and hands one to Ms. Beasley. She opens hers quickly and starts reading. I open mine.

"Now, if you choose not to participate, you will see—on page seven, paragraph one—that there will be no repercussions whatsoever on your terms of employment here. You will not lose your job; you will not lose seniority; you will not lose your special status. You will simply continue as you are, with the same necessary supportive work environment—"

I wonder about that. What if Mr. Crenshaw was right and there really are computers that can do what we do and do it better and faster? Someday the company could decide to change, even if they do not change now. Other people lose their jobs. Don had lost jobs. I could lose my job. It would not be easy to find another.

"Are you saying that we have a job for life?" Bailey asks.

Mr. Arakeen has a strange expression on his face. "I . . . did not say that," he says.

"So if the company finds out we do not make enough money for them in a few years, we could still lose our jobs."

"The situation could require reevaluation in light of later economic conditions, yes," Mr. Arakeen says. "But we do not anticipate any such situation at this time."

I wonder how long "at this time" will last. My parents lost their jobs in the economic upheavals of the early aughts, and my mother told me once that she had thought, in the late nineties, that they were set for life. Life throws curves, she said, and it's your job to catch them anyway.

Ms. Beasley sits up straight. "I think a minimum period of safe employment might be specified," she says. "In light of our clients' concerns and the previous illegal threats of your manager."

"Threats which higher management had no knowledge of," Mr. Arakeen says. "I don't see that we could be expected to—"

"Ten years," she says.

Ten years is a long time, not a minimum time. Mr. Arakeen's face reddens. "I don't think—"

"So you are planning termination in the long term?" she asks.

"I didn't say that," he says. "But who can foresee what might happen? And ten years is far too long a period. No one could make a promise like that."

"Seven," she says.

"Four," he says.

"Six."

"Five."

"Five with a good severance package," she says.

His hands come up, palms forward. I do not know what this gesture means. "All right," he says. "We can discuss the details later, can't we?"

"Of course," she says. She smiles at him with her lips, but her eyes are not smiling. She touches the hair on the left side of her neck, pats it, and pushes it back a little.

"Well, then," Mr. Arakeen says. He turns his head one way and another, as if to ease his collar. "You are guaranteed employment under the same conditions, for at least five years, whether you choose to participate in the protocol or not." He glances at Ms. Beasley, then looks at us again. "So you see, you do not lose by a decision either way, as far as your job security is concerned. It's entirely up to you. You've all qualified medically for the protocol, however."

He pauses, but no one says anything. I think about it. In five years, I will still be in my forties. It would be hard to find a job when I am over forty, but retirement would not start for a long time. He gives a short nod and goes on. "Now, we'll give you a little time to review the material in your folders. As you can see, these folders are not to be removed from the building for legal reasons. Meanwhile, Ms. Beasley and I will confer on some of the legal details, but we'll be here to answer your questions. After that, Dr. Hendricks and Dr. Ransome will continue with the planned medical briefing for today, though of course no decision will be expected from you today on whether or not to participate."

I read the material in the folder. At the end is a sheet of paper with a space on it for my signature. It says that I have read and understood everything in the folder and that I have agreed not to talk about it to anyone outside the section except the ombudsman and the Center Legal Aid lawyer. I do not sign it yet.

Dr. Ransome gets up and again introduces Dr. Hendricks. She begins to tell us what we have already heard before. It is hard to pay attention because I know that part already. What I want to know comes later, when she starts talking about what will actually happen to our brains.

"Without enlarging your heads, we can't just pack new neurons in," she says. "We have to keep adjusting the number, so there is the right amount of neural tissue making the right connections. The brain does this itself, during normal maturation: you lose a lot of the neurons you started with, when they don't make connections—and it would be chaos if they did."

I raise my hand and she nods at me. "Adjust—does this mean that you take some tissue out, to make room for the new?"

"Not physically take out; it's a biological mechanism, actually, resorption—"

Cego and Clinton described resorption during development: redundant neurons disappear, resorbed by the body, a process controlled by feedback control mechanisms using sensory data in part. As an intellectual model, it is fascinating; I was not upset to learn that so many of my neurons had disappeared when I knew that it happened to everyone. But if she is not quite saying what I think she is not quite saying, they are proposing to resorb some of the neurons I have now, as an adult. That is different. The neurons I have now all do something useful for me. I raise my hand again.

"Yes, Lou?" This time it is Dr. Ransome who speaks. His voice sounds a little tense. I think he thinks I ask too many questions.

"So . . . you are going to destroy some of our neurons to make room for the new growth?"

"Not exactly destroy," he says. "It's quite a complicated thing, Lou; I'm not sure you'll understand." Dr. Hendricks glances at him, then away.

"We aren't stupid," mutters Bailey.

"I know what resorption means," Dale says. "It means that tissue goes away and is replaced by other tissue. My sister had cancer and they programmed her body to resorb the tumor. If you resorb neurons, they're gone."

"I suppose you could look at it that way," Dr. Ransome says, looking more tense. He glares at me; he blames me for starting it, I think.

"But that's right," Dr. Hendricks says. She does not look tense but excited, like someone waiting to ride on a favorite carnival ride. "We resorb the neurons that have made bad connections and grow neurons which will make good connections."

"Gone is gone," Dale says. "That is the truth. Tell the truth." He is getting upset; his eye is flickering very fast. "When some is gone, the right kind may not grow anyway."

"No!" Linda says loudly. "No, no, no! Not my brain. Not taking apart. Not good, not good." She puts her head down, refusing eye contact, refusing to listen.

"It is not taking anyone's brain apart," Dr. Hendricks says. "It is not like that at all. . . . It is just adjustment—the new neural attachments grow, and nothing's changed."

"Except we aren't autistic," I say. "If it works right."

"Exactly." Now Dr. Hendrick smiles as if I had just said exactly the right thing. "You will be just as you are, but not autistic."

"But autistic is who I am," Chuy says. "I do not know how to be someone else, someone who is not. I have to start over, a baby, and grow up again, to be someone else."

"Well, not exactly," the doctor says. "Many of the neurons aren't affected, only a few at a time, so you have that past to draw on. Of course there is some relearning, some rehabilitation, to be done—that's in the consent package; your personal counselor will explain it to you—but it's all covered by the company. You don't have to pay for any of it."

"Lifetime," Dale says.

"I beg your pardon?" the doctor says.

"If I have to start over, I want more time to be that other person. To live." Dale is the oldest of us, ten years older than I am. He does not look old. His hair is still all dark, and thick on top. "I want LifeTime," he says, and I realize that he is not just talking about something lasting a lifetime but about the commercial antiaging treatment LifeTime.

"But . . . but that's absurd," Mr. Arakeen says, before the doctors can say anything. "It would add . . . a lot of money to the expense of the project." He glances at the other company people sitting to one side at the front of the room. None of them look at him.

Dale closes his eyes tightly; I can see the lid of the left eye flickering even so. "If this relearning takes longer than you think. Years even. I want to have time to live as a normal person. As many years as I have lived autistic. More." He pauses, his face squeezing together with effort. "It will be more data," he says. "Longer follow-up." His face relaxes and he opens his eyes. "Add LifeTime and I do it. No LifeTime, I go away."

I glance around. Everyone is staring at Dale, even Linda. Cameron might do something like this, but not Dale. He has already changed. I know I have already changed. We are autistic, but we change. Maybe we do not need the treatment, even to change more, even to be—not just seem—normal.

But as I think about that and how long it might take, paragraphs from the book come back to me. "No," I say. Dale turns and looks at me. His face is immobile. "It is not a good idea," I say. "This treatment does things to the neurons and so does LifeTime. This one is experimental; nobody knows if it will work at all."

"We know it works," Dr. Hendricks puts in. "It's just—"

"You don't know for sure how it works on humans," I say, interrupting her even though interrupting is rude. She interrupted me first.

"That is why you need us, or people like us. It is not a good idea to do both. In science, you change one variable at a time."

Mr. Arakeen looks relieved; Dale says nothing, but his eyelids droop. I do not know what he is thinking. I know how I feel, shaky inside.

"I want to live longer," Linda says. Her hand flings out as if it had a life of its own. "I want to live longer and not change."

"I do not know if I want to live longer or not," I say. The words come slowly but even Dr. Hendricks does not interrupt. "What if I become someone I don't like and am stuck living longer like that? First I want to know who I would be, before I can decide about living longer."

Dale nods slowly.

"I think we should decide on the basis of this treatment alone. They are not trying to force us. We can think about it."

"But—but—" Mr. Arakeen seems caught on the word, jerking it out, then makes a twisting movement with his head and goes on. "You're saying you will think. . . . How long will that take?"

"As long as they want," Ms. Beasley says. "You've already got one subject undergoing treatment; it would be prudent to space them out anyway, see how it goes."

"I don't say I'll do it," Chuy says. "But I would think about it more . . . more in favor . . . if LifeTime is part of it. Maybe not at the same time, but later."

"I will think about it," Linda says. She is pale and her eyes are moving around the way they do before she shuts down, but she says it. "I will think about it, and living longer would make it better, but I do not really want it."

"Me, either," Eric says. "I do not want someone changing my brain. Criminals have their brains changed and I am not a criminal. Autistic is different, not bad. It is not wrong to be different. Sometimes it is hard, but it is not wrong."

I do not say anything. I am not sure what I want to say. It is too fast. How can I decide? How can I choose to be someone else I do not know and cannot predict. Change comes anyway, but it is not my fault if I did not choose it.

"I want it," Bailey says. He squeezes his eyes shut and speaks that way, with his eyes shut and his voice very tense. "It is this to exchange for that—for Mr. Crenshaw threatening us and the risk it has of not working and making things worse. It is this I need to make a balance."

I look at Dr. Hendricks and Dr. Ransome; they are whispering to each other, moving their hands. I think they are already thinking how the two treatments might interact.

"It is too dangerous," Dr. Ransome says, looking up. "We can't possibly do them at the same time." He glances at me. "Lou was right. Even if you get a life extension treatment later, it can't be done at the same time."

Linda shrugs and looks down. Her shoulders are tense; her hands are fisted in her lap. I think she will not take the treatment without the promise of longer life. If I do it and she does not, we may not see each other again. I feel strange about that; she was in this unit before I was. I have seen her every working day for years.

"I will talk to the board about this," Mr. Arakeen says, more calmly. "We'll have to get more legal and medical advice. But if I understand you, some of you are demanding life extension treatment as part of the package, at some time in the future, as a condition of participation, is that right?"

"Yes," Bailey says. Linda nods.

Mr. Arakeen stands there, his body swaying a little as he shifts from foot to foot. The light catches on his name tag, moving with his motion. One button on his coat disappears and reappears behind the podium as he rocks back and forth. Finally he stops and gives a sharp nod.

"All right. I will ask the board. I think they will say no, but I will ask them."

"Keep in mind," Ms. Beasley says, "that these employees have not agreed to the procedure, only to think about it."

"All right." Mr. Arakeen nods and then twists his neck again. "But I expect you all to keep your word. Really think about it."

"I do not lie," Dale says. "Do not lie to me." He gets up, unfolding a bit stiffly as he does. "Come on," he says to the rest of us. "Work to do."

None of them say anything, not the lawyers nor the doctors, nor

Mr. Aldrin. Slowly, we get up; I feel uncertain, almost shaky. Is it all right to just walk away? But when I am moving, walking, I start to feel better. Stronger. I am scared, but I am also happy. I feel lighter, as if gravity were less.

Out in the corridor, we turn left to go to the elevators. When we get to the place where the hall widens out for the elevators, Mr. Crenshaw is standing there, holding a cardboard box in both hands. It is full of things, but I can't see all of them. Balanced on top is a pair of running shoes, an expensive brand I remember seeing in the sporting goods catalog. I wonder how fast Mr. Crenshaw runs. Two men in the light-blue shirts of company security stand beside him, one on each side. His eyes widen when he sees us.

"What are you doing here?" he says to Dale, who is slightly ahead of the rest of us. He turns toward him, taking a step, and the two men in uniform put their hands on his arms. He stops. "You're supposed to be in G-Twenty-eight until four P.M.; this isn't even the right building."

Dale does not slow down; he walks on by without saying a word.

Mr. Crenshaw's head turns like a robot's and then swings back. He glares at me. "Lou! What is going on here?"

I want to know what he is doing with a box in his hands, with a security guard escort, but I am not rude enough to ask. Mr. Aldrin said we did not have to worry about Mr. Crenshaw anymore, so I do not have to answer him when he is rude to me. "I have a lot of work to do, Mr. Crenshaw," I say. His hands jerk, as if he wants to drop the box and reach out to me, but he does not, and I am past him, following Dale.

When we are back in our own building, Dale speaks. "Yes, yes, yes, yes, yes," he says. And louder, "YES, YES, YES!"

"I am not bad," Linda says. "I am not bad person."

"You are not a bad person," I agree.

Her eyes fill with tears. "It is bad to be autistic person. It is bad to be angry to be autistic person. It is bad to want not be—not want be— autistic person. All bad ways. No right way."

"It is stupid," Chuy says. "Tell us to want to be normal, and then tell us to love ourselves as we are. If people want to change it means they do not like something about how they are now. That other—impossible."

Dale is smiling, a wide, tight smile I have not seen him use before. "When someone says something impossible, someone is wrong."

"Yes," I say. "It is a mistake."

"Mistake," Dale says. "And mistake to believe impossible wrong."

"Yes," I say. I can feel myself tensing up, afraid Dale will start talking about religion.

"So if normal people tell us to do something impossible, then we do not have to think everything normal people say is true."

"Not all lies," Linda says.

"Not all lies does not mean all true," Dale says.

That is obvious, but I had not thought before that it was really impossible for people to want to change and at the same time be happy with who they were before the change. I do not think any of us thought that way until Chuy and Dale said it.

"I started thinking at your place," Dale said. "I could not say it all then. But that helped."

"If it goes wrong," Eric said, "it will be even more expensive for them to take care of . . . what happens. If it lasts longer."

"I do not know how Cameron is doing," Linda says.

"He wanted to be first," Chuy says.

"It would be better if we could go one at a time and see what happens to the others," Eric says.

"The speed of dark would be slower," I say. They look at me. I remember that I have not told them about the speed of dark and the speed of light. "The speed of light in a vacuum is one hundred and eighty-six thousand miles per second," I say.

"I know that," Dale says.

"What I wonder," Linda says, "is, since things fall faster as they get nearer the ground and that is gravity, does light go faster near a lot of gravity, like a black hole?"

I never knew Linda was interested in the speed of light at all. "I do not know," I say. "But the books do not say anything about the speed of dark. Some people told me it does not have a speed, that it is just not light, where light is not, but I think it had to get there."

They are all silent a moment. Dale says, "If LifeTime can make time longer for us, maybe something can make light faster."

Chuy says, "Cameron wanted to be first. Cameron will be normal first. That is faster than us."

Eric says, "I am going to the gym." He turns away.

Linda's face has tightened, a ridged furrow on her forehead. "Light has a speed. Dark should have a speed. Opposites share everything but direction."

I do not understand that. I wait.

"Positive and negative numbers are alike except for direction," Linda goes on, slowly. "Large and small are both size, but in different directions. To and from mean the same path, but in different directions. So light and dark are opposite, but alike just in the same direction." She throws her arms out suddenly. "What I like about astronomy," she says. "So much out there, so many stars, so many distances. Everything from nothing to everything, altogether."

I did not know Linda liked astronomy. She has always seemed the most remote of us, the most autistic. I know what she means, though. I also like the series from small to large, from near to far, from the photon of light that enters my eye, closer than close, to where it came from, light-years away across the universe.

"I like stars," she says. "I want—I wanted—to work with stars. They said no. They said, 'Your mind does not work the right way. Only a few people can do that.' I knew it was math. I knew I was good in math, but I had to take adaptive math even though I always made hundreds, and when I finally got into the good classes they said it was too late. At college they said take applied math and study computers. There are jobs in computers. They said astronomy was not practical. If I live longer, it will not be too late anymore."

This is the most I have ever heard Linda talk. Her face is pinker on the cheeks now; her eyes wander less.

"I did not know you liked stars," I say.

"Stars are far apart from each other," she says. "They do not have to touch to know each other. They shine at each other from far away."

I start to say that stars do not know each other, that stars are not alive, but something stops me. I read that in a book, that stars are incandescent gas, and in another book that gas is inanimate matter. Maybe the book was wrong. Maybe they are incandescent gas and alive.

Linda looks at me, actually makes eye contact. "Lou—do you like stars?"

"Yes," I say. "And gravity and light and space and—"

"Betelgeuse," she says. She grins, and it is suddenly lighter in the hall. I did not know it was dark before. The dark was there first, but the light caught up. "Rigel. Antares. Light and all colors. Wavelengths . . ." Her hands ripple in the air, and I know she means the pattern that wavelength and frequency make.

"Binaries," I say. "Brown dwarfs."

Her face twists and relaxes. "Oh, that's *old*," she says. "Chu and Sanderly have reclassified a lot of those—" She stops. "Lou—I thought you spent all your time with normals. Playing normal."

"I go to church," I say. "I go to fencing club."

"Fencing?"

"Swords," I say. Her worried look does not change. "It's . . . a kind of game," I say. "We try to poke each other."

"Why?" She still looks puzzled. "If you like stars—"

"I like fencing, too," I say.

"With normal people," she says.

"Yes, I like them."

"It's hard . . ." she says. "I go to the planetarium. I try to talk to the scientists who come, but . . . the words tangle. I can tell they do not want to talk to me. They act like I am stupid or crazy."

"The people I know, they are not too bad," I say. I feel guilty as I say it, because Marjory is more than "not too bad." Tom and Lucia are better than "not too bad." "Except for the one who tried to kill me."

"Tried to kill you?" Linda says. I am surprised that she did not know but remember that I never told her. Maybe she does not watch the news.

"He was angry with me," I say.

"Because you are autistic?"

"Not exactly . . . well . . . yes." What was the core of Don's anger, after all, but the fact that I, a mere incomplete, a false-person, was succeeding in his world?

"That is sick," Linda says, with emphasis. She gives a great shrug and turns away. "Stars," she says.

I go into my office, thinking of light and dark and stars and the space between them that is full of light they pour out. How can there be any dark in space with all the stars in it? If we can see the stars, that means there is light. And our instruments that see other than visible light, they detect it in a great blur—it is everywhere.

I do not understand why people speak of space as cold and dark, unwelcoming. It is as if they never went out in the night and looked up. Wherever real dark is, it is beyond the range of our instruments, far on the edge of the universe, where dark came first. But the light catches up.

Before I was born, people thought even more wrong things about autistic children. I have read about it. Darker than dark.

I did not know Linda liked stars. I did not know she wanted to work in astronomy. Maybe she even wanted to go into space, the way I did. Do. Do still. If the treatment works, maybe I can—the very thought holds me motionless, frozen in delight, and then I have to move. I stand up and stretch, but it is not enough.

Eric is just getting off the trampoline as I come into the gym. He has been bouncing to Beethoven's *Fifth Symphony*, but it is too strong for what I want to think about. Eric nods at me, and I change the music, scrolling through the possibilities until something feels right. *Carmen.* The orchestral suite. Yes.

I need that excitement. I need that explosive quality. I bounce higher and higher, feeling the wonderful openness of free fall before I feel the equally wonderful compression, joints squeezing, muscles working to push me to a higher bounce. Opposites are the same thing in different directions. Action and reaction. Gravity—I do not know an opposite for gravity, but the elasticity of the trampoline creates one. Numbers and patterns race through my mind, forming, breaking up, re-forming.

I remember being afraid of water, the unstable, unpredictable shifts and wobbles in it as it touched me. I remember the explosive joy of finally swimming, the realization that even though it was unstable, even though I could not predict the changing pressure in the pool, I could still stay afloat and move in the direction I chose to go. I remember being afraid of the bicycle, of its wobbly unpredictability, and the same joy when I figured out how to ride out that unpredictability, how to use my will to overcome its innate chaos. Again I am afraid, more afraid because I understand more—I could lose all the adaptations I have made and have nothing—but if I can ride this wave, this biological bicycle, then I will have incomparably more.

As my legs tire, I bounce lower, lower, lower, and finally stop.

They do not want us stupid and helpless. They do not want to destroy our minds; they want to use them.

I do not want to be used. I want to use my own mind, myself, for what I want to do.

I think I may want to try this treatment. I do not have to. I do not need to: I am all right as I am. But I think I am beginning to want to because maybe, if I change, and if it is my idea and not theirs, then maybe I can learn what I want to learn and do what I want to do. It is not any one thing; it is all the things at once, all the possibilities. "I will not be the same," I say, letting go of the comfortable gravity, flying up out of that certainty into the uncertainty of free fall.

When I walk out, I feel light in both ways, still in less than normal gravity and still full of more light than darkness. But gravity returns when I think of telling my friends what I am doing. I think they will not like it any better than the Center's lawyer.

CHAPTER TWENTY

MR. ALDRIN COMES BY TO TELL US THAT THE COM-pany will not agree to provide LifeTime treatments at this time, though they may—he emphasizes that it is only a possibility—assist those of us who want to have LifeTime treatments after the other treatment, if it is successful. "It is too dangerous to do them together," he says. "It increases the risk, and then if something does go wrong it would last longer."

I think he should say it plainly: if the treatment causes more damage, we would be worse off and the company would have to support us for longer. But I know that normal people do not say things plainly.

We do not talk among ourselves after he leaves. The others all look at me, but they do not say anything. I hope Linda takes the treatment anyway. I want to talk to her more about stars and gravity and the speed of light and dark.

In my own office, I call Ms. Beasley at Legal Aid and tell her that I have decided to agree to the treatment. She asks me if I am sure. I am not sure, but I am sure enough. Then I call Mr. Aldrin and tell him. He also asks if I am sure. "Yes," I say, and then I ask, "Is your brother going to do it?" I have been wondering about his brother.

"Jeremy?" He sounds surprised that I asked. I think it is a reasonable question. "I don't know, Lou. It depends on the size of the group. If they open it up to outsiders, I'll consider asking him. If he could live on his own, if he could be happier . . ."

"He is not happy?" I ask.

Mr. Aldrin sighs. "I . . . don't talk about him much," he says. I wait. Not talking about something much does not mean someone doesn't want to talk about it. Mr. Aldrin clears his throat and then goes on. "No, Lou, he's not happy. He's . . . very impaired. The doctors then . . . my parents . . . he's on a lot of medication, and he never learned to talk very well." I think I understand what he is not saying. His brother was born too early, before the treatments that helped me and the others. Maybe he didn't get the best treatment, even of those available at the time. I think of the descriptions in the books; I imagine Jeremy being stuck where I was as a young child.

"I hope the new treatment works," I say. "I hope it works for him, too."

Mr. Aldrin makes a sound I do not understand; his voice is hoarse when he speaks again. "Thank you, Lou," he says. "You're—you're a good man."

I am not a good man. I am just a man, like he is, but I like it that he thinks I am good.


*TOM AND LUCIA AND MARJORY ARE ALL IN THE LIVING ROOM* when I arrive. They are talking about the next tournament. Tom looks up at me.

"Lou—have you decided?"

"Yes," I say. "I will do it."

"Good. You'll need to fill out this entry form—"

"Not that," I say. I realize that he would not know I meant something else. "I will not fight in this tournament—" Will I ever fight in another tournament? Will the future me want to fence? Can you fence in space? I think it would be very hard in free fall.

"But you said," Lucia says; then her face changes, seems to flatten out with surprise. "Oh—you mean . . . you're going through with the treatment?"

"Yes," I say. I glance at Marjory. She is looking at Lucia, and then at me, and then back. I do not remember if I talked to Marjory about the treatment.

"When?" asks Lucia before I have time to think about how to explain to Marjory.

"It will start Monday," I say. "I have a lot to do. I have to move into the clinic."

"Are you sick?" Marjory says; her face is pale now. "Is something wrong?"

"I am not sick," I say to Marjory. "There is an experimental treatment that may make me normal."

"Normal! But, Lou, you're fine the way you are. I *like* the way you are. You don't have to be like everybody else. Who has been telling you that?" She sounds angry. I do not know if she is angry with me or with someone she thinks told me I needed to change. I do not know if I should tell her the whole story or part of it. I will tell her everything.

"It started because Mr. Crenshaw at work wanted to eliminate our unit," I say. "He knew about this treatment. He said it will save money."

"But that's—that's coercion. It's wrong. It's against the law. He can't do that—"

She is really angry now, the color coming and going on her cheeks. It makes me want to grab her and hug her. That is not appropriate.

"That is how it started," I say. "But you are right; he could not do what he said he would do. Mr. Aldrin, our supervisor, found a way to stop him." I am still surprised by this. I was sure Mr. Aldrin had changed his mind and would not help us. I still do not understand what Mr. Aldrin did that stopped Mr. Crenshaw and caused him to lose his job and be escorted out by security guards with his things in a box. I tell them what Mr. Aldrin said and then what the lawyers said in the meeting. "But now I want to change," I say, at the end.

She takes a deep breath. I like to watch her take deep breaths; the front of her clothes pulls tight. "Why?" she asks in a quieter voice. "It isn't because of . . . because of . . . us, is it? Me?"

"No," I say. "It is not about you. It is about me."

Her shoulders sag. I do not know if it is relief or sadness. "Then was it Don? Did he make you do this, convince you that you weren't all right as you were?"

"It was not Don . . . not only Don. . . ." It is obvious, I think, and I do not know why she cannot see it. She was there when the security man at the airport stopped me and my words stuck and she had to help me. She was there when I needed to talk to the police officer and my words stuck and Tom had to help me. I do not like being the one who always needs help. "It is about me," I say again. "I want not to have problems at the airport and sometimes with other people when it is hard to talk and have people looking at me. I want to go places and learn things I did not know I could learn. . . ."

Her faces changes again, smoothing out, and her voice loses some of its emotional tone. "What is the treatment like, Lou? What will happen?"

I open the packet I have brought. We are not supposed to discuss the treatment since it is proprietary and experimental, but I think this is a bad idea. If things go wrong, someone outside should know. I did not tell anyone I was taking my packet out, and they did not stop me.

I begin to read. Almost at once, Lucia stops me.

"Lou—do you understand this stuff now?"

"Yes. I think so. After Cego and Clinton, I could read the on-line journals pretty easily."

"Why don't you let me read that, then? I can understand it better if I see the words. Then we can talk about it."

There is nothing to talk about, really. I am going to do it. But I hand Lucia the packet, because it is always easier to do what Lucia says. Marjory scoots closer to her and they both begin to read. I look at Tom. He raises his eyebrows and shakes his head.

"You're a brave man, Lou. I knew that, but this—! I don't know if I'd have the guts to let someone mess with my brain."

"You don't need to," I say. "You are normal. You have a job with tenure. You have Lucia and this house." I cannot say the rest that I think, that he is easy in his body, that he sees and hears and tastes and smells and feels what others do, so his reality matches theirs.

"Will you come back to us, do you think?" Tom asks. He looks sad.

"I do not know," I say. "I hope that I will still like to fence, because it is fun, but I do not know."

"Do you have time to stay tonight?" he asks.

"Yes," I say.

"Then let's go on out." He gets up and leads the way to the equipment room. Lucia and Marjory stay behind, reading. When we get to the equipment room, he turns to me. "Lou, are you sure you aren't doing this because you're in love with Marjory? Because you want to be a normal man for her? That would be a noble thing to do, but—"

I feel myself going hot all over. "It is not about her. I like her. I want to touch her and hold her and . . . things that are not appropriate. But this is . . ." I reach out and touch the upright end of the stand that holds the blades, because suddenly I am trembling and afraid I might fall. "Things do not stay the same," I say. "I am not the same. I cannot not change. This is just . . . faster change. But I choose it."

" 'Fear change, and it will destroy you; embrace change, and it will enlarge you,' " Tom says, in the voice he uses for quotes. I do not know what he is quoting from. Then in his normal voice, with a little joking voice added, he says, "Choose your weapon, then: if you aren't going to be here for a while, I want to be sure to get my licks in tonight."

I take my blades and my mask and have put on my leather before I remember that I did not stretch. I sit down on the patio and begin the stretches. It is colder out here; the flagstones are hard and cold under me.

Tom sits across from me. "I've done mine, but more never hurts as I get older," he says. I can see, when he bends to put his face on his knee, that the hair on the top of his head is thinning, and there is gray in it. He puts one arm over his head and pulls on it with the other arm. "What will you do when you're through the treatment?"

"I would like to go into space," I say.

"You—? Lou, you never cease to amaze me." He puts the other arm on top of his head now and pulls on the elbow. "I didn't know you wanted to go into space. When did that start?"

"When I was little," I say. "But I knew I could not do it. I knew it was not appropriate."

"When I think of the waste—!" Tom says, bending his head now to his other knee. "Lou, as much as I worried about this before, I think you're right now. You have too much potential to be locked up in a diagnosis the rest of your life. Though it's going to hurt Marjory when you grow away from her."

"I do not want to hurt Marjory," I say. "I do not think I will grow away from her." It is a strange expression; I am sure it cannot be literal. If two things close to each other both grow, they will get closer together, not apart.

"I know that. You like her a lot—no, you love her. That's clear. But, Lou—she's a nice woman, but as you say, you're about to make a big change. You won't be the same person."

"I will always like—love—her," I say. I had not thought that becoming normal would make that harder or impossible. I do not understand why Tom thinks so. "I do not think she pretended to like me just to do research on me, whatever Emmy says."

"Good heavens, who thought that up? Who's Emmy?"

"Someone at the Center," I say. I do not want to talk about Emmy, so I hurry through it. "Emmy said Marjory was a researcher and just talked to me as a subject, not a friend. Marjory told me that her research was on neuromuscular disorders, so I knew Emmy was wrong."

Tom stands up, and I scramble up, too. "But for you—it's a great opportunity."

"I know," I say. "I wanted—I thought once—I almost asked her out, but I don't know how."

"Do you think the treatment will help?"

"Maybe." I put on my mask. "But if it does not help with that, it will help with other things, I think. And I will always like her."

"I'm sure you will, but it won't be the same. Can't be. It's like any system, Lou. If I lost a foot, I might still fence, but my patterns would be different, right?"

I do not like thinking of Tom losing a foot, but I can understand what he means. I nod.

"So if you make a big change in who you are, then you and Marjory will be in a different pattern. You may be closer, or you may be further apart."

Now I know what I did not know a few minutes ago, that I had had a deep and hidden thought about Marjory and the treatment and me. I did think it would be easier. I did have a hope that if I were normal, we might be normal together, might marry and have children and a normal life.

"It won't be the same, Lou," Tom says again from behind his mask. I can see the glitter of his eyes. "It can't be."

Fencing is the same and it is not the same. Tom's patterns are clearer now each time I fence with him, but my pattern slides in and out of focus. My attention wavers. Will Marjory come outside? Will she fence? What are she and Lucia saying about the consent packet? When I concentrate, I can make touches on him, but then I lose track of where he is in his pattern and he makes touches on me. It is three touches to five when Marjory and Lucia come out, and Tom and I have just stopped for breath. Even though it is a cool night, we are sweaty.

"Well," Lucia says. I wait. She says nothing more.

"It looks dangerous to me," Marjory says. "Mucking about with neural reabsorption and then regeneration. But I haven't read the original research."

"Too many places it can go wrong," Lucia says. "Viral insertion of genetic material, that's old hat, a proven technology. Nanotech cartilage repair, blood vessel maintenance, inflammation management, fine. Programmable chips for spinal cord injuries, okay. But tinkering with gene switches—they haven't got all the bugs out of that yet. That mess with marrow in bone regeneration—of course that's not nerves and it was in children, but still."

I do not know what she is talking about, but I do not want another reason to be scared.

"What bothers me most is that it's all in-house with your employer, an incestuous mess if ever I saw one. Anything goes wrong, you have no patient advocate to speak up for you. Your Legal Aid person doesn't have the medical expertise. . . . But it's your decision."

"Yes," I say. I look at Marjory. I cannot help it.

"Lou . . ." Then she shakes her head, and I know she is not going to say what she was going to say. "Want to fence?" she asks.

I do not want to fence. I want to sit with her. I want to touch her. I want to eat dinner with her and lie in bed with her. But that is something I cannot do, not yet. I stand up and put on my mask.

What I feel when her blade touches mine I cannot describe. It is stronger than before. I feel my body tightening, reacting, in a way that is not appropriate but is wonderful. I want this to go on and I want to stop and grab her. I slow down, so that I do not make a touch too quickly, and so that this will last.

I could still ask her if she will have dinner with me. I could do it before or after treatment. Maybe.

*THURSDAY MORNING. IT IS CHILLY, WINDY, WITH GRAY CLOUDS* scudding across the sky. I am hearing Beethoven's *Mass in C.* The light looks heavy and slow, though the wind is moving fast. Dale, Bailey, and Eric are already here—or their cars are. Linda's car is not in place yet; neither is Chuy's. As I walk from the parking lot to the building, the wind blows my slacks against my legs; I can feel the rippling of the fabric against my skin; it feels like many little fingers. I remember begging my mother to cut the tags out of my T-shirts when I was little, until I was old enough to do it myself. Will I still notice that afterward?

I hear a car behind me and turn. It is Linda's car. She parks in her usual place. She gets out without looking at me.

At the door, I insert my card, put my thumb on the plate, and the door lock clicks and clunks to release. I push the door open and wait for Linda. She has opened her car's trunk and is taking out a box. It is like the box Mr. Crenshaw had, but it has no markings on the side.

I did not think to bring a box to put things in. I wonder if I can find a box during lunch hour. I wonder if Linda bringing a box means she has decided to take the treatment.

She holds the box under one arm. She walks fast, the wind blowing her hair back. She usually has it tied up; I did not know it would ripple like that in the wind. Her face looks different, uncluttered and spare, as if it were a carving without any fear or worry.

She walks past me holding the box and I follow her inside. I remember to touch the screen for two people entering on one card. Bailey is in the hall.

"You have a box," he says to Linda.

"I thought someone might need it," Linda says. "I brought it in case."

"I will bring a box tomorrow," Bailey says. "Lou, are you leaving today or tomorrow?"

"Today," I say. Linda looks at me and holds the box. "I could use the box," I say, and she hands it to me without meeting my eyes.

I go into my office. It looks strange already, like someone else's office. If I left it alone, would it look strange like this when I come back afterward? But since it looks strange now, does that mean that already I am living partly in afterward?

I move the little fan that makes the spin spirals and whirligigs turn, and then I move it back. I sit in my chair and look again. It is the same office. I am not the same person.

I look in the drawers of my desk and see nothing but the same old stack of manuals. Down at the bottom—though I have not looked at it in a long time—is the *Employees' Manual*. On top are the different system upgrade manuals. These are not supposed to be printed out, but it is still easier to read things on paper where the letters are absolutely still. Everyone uses my manuals. I do not want to leave these illicit copies here while I am in treatment. I pull them all out and turn the stack upside down so the *Employees' Manual* is on top. I do not know what to do with them.

In the bottom drawer is an old mobile that I used to have hanging here until the biggest fish got bent. Now the shiny surface of the fishes has little black spots. I pull it out, wincing at the jingly noise it makes, and rub at one of the black spots. It doesn't come off. It looks sick. I put it in the wastebasket, wincing again at the noise.

In the flat drawer above the kneehole I keep colored pens and a little plastic container with some change for the soda machine. I put the container in my pocket and put the pens on top of the desk. I look at the shelving. All that is project information, files, things the company owns. I do not have to clean off the shelves. I take down the spin spirals that are not my favorites first, the yellow and silver and the orange and red.

I hear Mr. Aldrin's voice in the hall, speaking to someone. He opens my door.

"Lou—I forgot to remind everyone not to take any project work off-campus. If you want to store any project-related materials, you can stack them with a label explaining that they must go in secured storage."

"Yes, Mr. Aldrin," I say. I feel uneasy about those system update printouts in the box, but they are not project-related.

"Will you be on-campus at all tomorrow?"

"I do not think so," I say. "I do not want to start something and leave it unfinished, and I will have everything cleared out today."

"Fine. You did get my list of recommended preparations?"

"Yes," I say.

"Good, then. I—" He looks back over his shoulder and then comes into my office and shuts the door. I feel myself tensing; my stomach churns. "Lou—" He hesitates, clears his throat, and looks away. "Lou, I—I want to tell you I'm sorry this all happened."

I do not know what answer he expects. I do not say anything.

"I never wanted . . . if it had been up to me, things wouldn't have changed—"

He is wrong. Things would have changed. Don would still have been angry with me. I would still have fallen in love with Marjory. I am not sure why he is saying this; he must know that things do change, whether people want them to or not. A man can lie beside the pool for weeks, for years, thinking about the angel coming down, before someone stops to ask him if he wants to be healed.

The look on Mr. Aldrin's face reminds me of how I have felt so often. He is scared, I realize. He is usually scared of something. It hurts to be scared for a long time; I know that hurt. I wish he did not have that look, because it makes me feel I should do something about it and I do not know what to do.

"It is not your fault," I say. His face relaxes. That was the right thing to say. It is too easy. I can say it, but does that make it true? Words can be wrong. Ideas can be wrong.

"I want to be sure you really are—you really do want the treatment," he says. "There's absolutely no pressure—"

He is wrong again, though he may be right that there is no pressure from the company right now. Now that I know change will come, now that I know this change is possible, the pressure grows in me, as air fills a balloon or light fills space. Light is not passive; light itself presses on whatever it touches.

"It is my decision," I say. I mean, whether it is right or wrong, it is what I decided. I can be wrong, too.

"Thanks, Lou," he says. "You—you all—you mean a lot to me."

I do not know what "mean a lot" means. Literally it would mean that we have a lot of meaning in us, which he can take, and I do not think that is what Mr. Aldrin is saying. I do not ask. I am still uncomfortable when I think about the times he talked to us. I do not say anything. After 9.3 seconds, he nods and turns to go. "Take care," he says. "Good luck."

I understand "Be careful," but I do not think "Take care" is as clear. Care is not something you can take and walk around with, like a box. I do not say that, either. Afterward I may not even think about that. I should start now to think what afterward is like.

I notice he does not say, "I hope you are cured." I do not know if he is being tactful and polite or thinks it will not go well. I do not ask. His pocket tagger bleeps, and he backs out into the hall. He does not shut my door. It is wrong to listen to other people's conversation, but it is not polite to shut the door on someone in authority. I cannot help hearing what he says, though I cannot hear what the other person says. "Yes, sir, I'll be there."

His footsteps move away. I relax, taking a deep breath. I take down my favorite spin spirals and take the whirligigs off their stands. The room looks bare, but my desk looks cluttered. I cannot tell if it will all fit in Linda's box. Maybe I can find another box. Soon begun, soonest done. When I get into the hall, Chuy is at the door, struggling to hold it open and carry in several boxes. I hold the door wide for him.

"I brought one for everybody," he says. "It will save time."

"Linda brought a box I am using," I say.

"Maybe someone will need two," he says. He drops the boxes in the hall. "You can have one if you need one."

"I need one," I say. "Thanks."

I pick up a box that is bigger than the one Linda brought and go back to my office. I put the manuals in the bottom because they are heavy. The colored pens fit between the manuals and the side of the box. I put the whirligigs and spin spirals on top and then remember the fan. I take them out and put the fan on top of the manuals. Now there will not be room for everything else. I look at the box. I do not need the *Employees' Manual,* and no one will be angry with me for having a copy in my office. I take it out and leave it on the desk. I put the fan in, and then the spin spirals and whirligigs. They just fit. I think of the wind outside. They are lightweight and might blow out.

In the last drawer, I find the towel I use to dry off my head when it is raining and I have walked in from the car in the rain. That will fit on top of the spin spirals and whirligigs and keep them from blowing away. I fold the towel on top of the things in the box and pick up the box. Now I am doing what Mr. Crenshaw was doing, carrying a box of my things out of an office. Maybe I would look like Mr. Crenshaw to someone watching, except that no security guards stand beside me. We are not alike. This is my choice; I do not think his leaving was his choice. When I get near the door, Dale is coming out of his office; he opens the door for me.

Outside, the clouds are thicker and the day seems darker, colder, fuzzy around the edges. It may rain in a little while. I like the cold. The wind is behind me, and I can feel it pushing on my back. I put the box down on the front of my car, and the towel starts to blow off. I put my hand on it. It will be hard to unlock the door while holding the towel down. I move the box to the passenger side of the car and rest my foot on the edge. Now I can unlock the door.

A first drop of icy rain flicks my cheek. I put the box on the passenger seat, then close the door and lock it. I think about going back inside, but I am sure I got everything. I do not want to put current project work in a stack for special storage. I do not want to see that project again.

I do want to see Dale and Bailey and Chuy and Eric and Linda again, though. Another flick of rain. The cold wind feels good. I shake my head and go back to the door, insert my card, and enter my thumbprint. All the others are in the hall, some with full boxes and some just standing.

"Want to get something to eat?" Dale says. The others look around.

"It is only ten-twelve," says Chuy. "It is not time for lunch. I am still working." He does not have a box. Linda does not have a box. It seems odd that the people who are not leaving brought boxes. Did they want the rest of us to leave?

"We could go for pizza later," says Dale. We look at each other. I do not know what they are thinking, but I am thinking it will not be the same and also too much the same. It is pretending.

"We could go somewhere else later," Chuy says.

"Pizza," says Linda.

We leave it at that. I think I will not come.

It feels very odd to be driving around in the daylight on a weekday. I drive home and park in the space nearest the door. I carry the box upstairs. The apartment building is very quiet. I put the box in my closet, behind my shoes.

The apartment is quiet and neat. I washed the breakfast dishes before I left; I always do. I take the container of coins out of my pocket and put it on top of the clothes baskets.

They told us to bring three changes of clothes. I can pack those now. I do not know what the weather will be or if we will need outside clothes as well as inside clothes. I take my suitcase from the closet and take the first three knit shirts on top of the stack in my second drawer. Three sets of underwear. Three pairs of socks. Two pairs of tan slacks and a pair of blue slacks. My blue sweatshirt, in case it is cold.

I have an extra toothbrush, comb, and brush that I keep for emergencies. I have never had an emergency. This is not an emergency, but if

I pack them now I will not have to think about it again. I put the tooth-brush, a new tube of toothpaste, the comb, brush, razor, shaving cream, and a nail clipper in the little zipper bag that fits into my suitcase and put it in. I look again at the list they gave us. That is everything. I tighten the straps in the suitcase, then zip it shut and put it away.

Mr. Aldrin said to contact the bank, the apartment manager, and any friends who might be worried. He gave us a statement to give to the bank and apartment manager, explaining that we would be gone on a temporary assignment for the company, our paychecks would continue to be paid into the bank, and the bank should continue to make all au-tomatic payments. I bounce the statement to my branch manager.

Downstairs, the apartment manager's door is shut, but I can hear a vacuum cleaner moaning inside. When I was little, I was afraid of the vacuum cleaner because it sounded like it was crying, "Ohhhh . . . noooooo . . . oohhhh. . . . nooooo," when my mother pulled it back and forth. It roared and whined and moaned. Now it is just annoying. I push the button. The moaning stops. I do not hear footsteps, but the door opens.

"Mr. Arrendale!" Ms. Tomasz, the manager, sounds surprised. She would not expect to see me in midmorning on a weekday. "Are you sick? Do you need something?"

"I am going on a project for the company I work for," I say. I have rehearsed saying this smoothly. I hand her the statement Mr. Aldrin gave us. "I have told the bank to make the payments for my rent. You can contact the company if it does not."

"Oh!" She glances down at the paper, and before she has time to read all of it, she looks up at me. "But . . . how long will you be gone?"

"I am not sure," I say. "But I will come back." I do not know that for sure, but I do not want her to worry.

"You aren't leaving because that man cut your tires in our parking lot? Tried to hurt you?"

"No," I say. I do not know why she would think that. "It is a special assignment."

"I worried about you; I really did," Ms. Tomasz says. "I almost came up and spoke to you, to express—to say I was sorry—but you know you do keep to yourself, pretty much."

"I am all right," I say.

"We'll miss you," she says. I do not understand how that can be true if she does not even see me most of the time. "Take care of yourself," she says. I do not tell her that I cannot do that, because my brain will be changing.

When I get back upstairs, the bank's automatic reply has come through, saying that the message has been received and the manager will make a specific reply very soon and thank you for your patronage. Underneath it says: "Safety Tip #21: Never leave the key of your safe-deposit box in your home when you leave for a vacation." I do not have a safe-deposit box so I do not have to worry about it.

I decide to walk down to the little bakery for lunch—I saw the sign about sandwiches to order when I bought bread there. It is not crowded, but I do not like the music on the radio. It is loud and banging. I order a ham sandwich made with ham from pigs fed a vegetarian diet and butchered under close supervision and the freshest ingredients and take it away. It is too cold to stop and eat outside, so I walk back to the apartment with it and eat it in my kitchenette.

I could call Marjory. I could take her to dinner tonight, or tomorrow night, or Saturday night, if she would come. I know her work number and her home number. One is almost a prime, and one is a nested multiple of pleasing symmetry. I hang the spin spirals in my apartment where they twirl in the air leaking past the old windows. The flash of colored light across the walls is restful and helps me think.

If I call her and she goes with me to dinner, why would that be? Maybe she likes me, and maybe she is worried about me, and maybe she feels sorry for me. I do not know for sure it would be because she likes me. For it to be the same in opposite directions, she would have to like me as I like her. Anything else would not make a good pattern.

What would we talk about? She does not know any more about brain functionality than I do now. It is not her field. We both fence, but I do not think we could talk about fencing the whole time. I do not think she is interested in space; like Mr. Aldrin she seems to think it is a waste of money.

If I come back—if the treatment works and I am like other men in the brain as well as in the body—will I like her the way I do now?

Is she another case of the pool with the angel—do I love her because I think she is the only one I can love?

I get up and put on Bach's *Toccata and Fugue in D*. The music builds a complex landscape, mountains and valleys and great gulfs of cool, windy air. Will I still like Bach when I come back, if I come back?

For a moment, fear seizes my whole being and I am falling through blackness, faster than any light could ever be, but the music rises under me, lifts me up like an ocean wave, and I am no longer afraid.

FRIDAY MORNING. *I WOULD GO TO WORK, BUT THERE IS NOTH-*ing in my office to do, and there is nothing in my apartment to do, either. The confirmation from the bank manager was in my stack this morning. I could do my laundry now, but I do my laundry on Friday nights. It occurs to me that if I do my laundry tonight as usual and then sleep on the sheets tonight and Saturday night and Sunday night, I will have dirty sheets on the bed and dirty towels in the bathroom when I check into the clinic. I do not know what to do about that. I do not want to leave dirty things behind me, but otherwise I will have to get up early Monday morning and do a wash then.

I think about contacting the others, but I decide not to. I do not want to talk to them, really. I am not used to having a day like this, apart from planned vacation, and I do not know what to do with it. I could go see a movie or read books, but my stomach is too tight for that. I could go to the Center, but I do not want to do that, either.

I wash the breakfast dishes and stack them. The apartment is too quiet, too big and empty suddenly. I do not know where I will go, but I have to go somewhere. I put my wallet and keys in my pocket and leave. It is only five minutes later than I usually leave.

Danny is going downstairs, too. He says, "Hi, Lou, howyadoin'," in a rush. I think that means he is in a hurry and does not want to talk. I say "hi" and nothing more.

Outside, it is cloudy and cold but not raining right now. It is not as windy as yesterday. I walk over to my car and get in. I do not turn the engine on yet, because I do not know where I will go. It is a waste to run the engine unnecessarily. I take the road map book out of the glove compartment and open it. I could go to the state park upriver and look at the waterfalls. Most people hike there in summer, but I think the park is open in the daytime in winter, too.

A shadow darkens my window. It is Danny. I open the window.

"Are you all right?" he asks. "Is something wrong?"

"I am not going to work today," I say. "I am deciding where to go."

"Okay," he says. I am surprised; I did not think he was that interested. If he is that interested, maybe he would want to know that I am going away.

"I am going away," I say.

His face changes expression. "Moving? Was it that stalker? He won't hurt you again, Lou."

It is interesting that both he and the apartment manager assumed I might be leaving because of Don.

"No," I say. "I am not moving, but I am going to be gone several weeks at least. There is a new experimental treatment; my company wants me to take it."

He looks worried. "Your company—do *you* want it? Are they pressuring you?"

"It is my decision," I say. "I decided to do it."

"Well . . . okay. I hope you got some good advice," he says.

"Yes," I say. I do not say from where.

"So—you have the day off? Or you're leaving today? Where is this treatment going to be given?"

"I do not have to work today. I cleaned out my desk yesterday," I say. "The treatment will be given at the research clinic, at the campus where I work but in a different building. It starts Monday. Today I have nothing—I think I may go up to Harper Falls."

"Ah. Well, you take care, Lou. I hope it works out for you." He thumps the roof of my car and walks away.

I am not sure what it is he hopes will work out for me: The trip to Harper Falls? The treatment? I do not know why he thumped the roof of my car, either. I do know that he doesn't scare me anymore, another change that I made on my own.

*AT THE PARK, I PAY THE ENTRANCE FEE AND STOP MY CAR IN* the empty parking lot. Signs point to different trails: TO THE FALLS, 290.3 METERS. BUTTERCUP MEADOW, 1.7 KM. JUNIOR NATURE TRAIL, 1.3 KM. The Junior Nature Trail and the Fully Accessible Trail are both asphalt-surfaced, but the trail to the falls is crushed stone between metal strips. I walk down this trail, my shoes scritch-scritching on the surface. No one else is here. The only sounds are natural sounds. Far away I can hear the steady humming roar of the interstate but closer at hand only the higher whine of the generator that powers the park office.

Soon even that fades away; I am below a ledge of rock that blocks the highway sound as well. Most of the leaves have fallen from the trees and are sodden from yesterday's rain. Below me, I can see red leaves glowing even in this dull light, on maples that survive here, in the coolest areas.

I can feel myself relaxing. Trees do not care if I am normal or not. Rocks and moss do not care. They cannot tell the difference between one human and another. That is restful. I do not have to think about myself at all.

I stop to sit on a rock and let my legs hang down. My parents took me to a park near where we lived when I was a child. It, too, had a stream with a waterfall, narrower than this one. The rock there was darker, and most of the rocks that stuck out were narrow and pointed on top. But there was one that had fallen over so the flatter side was on top, and I used to stand or sit on that rock. It felt friendly, because it did not do anything. My parents didn't understand that.

If someone told the last maples that they could change and live happily in the warmer climate, would they choose to do it? What if it meant losing their translucent leaves that turn such beautiful colors every year?

I draw in a deep breath and smell the wet leaves, the moss on the rock, the lichens, the rock itself, the soil. . . . Some of the articles said autistic persons are too sensitive to smells, but no one minds that in a dog or cat.

I listen to the little noises of the woods, the tiny noises even today, with the wet leaves mostly flat and silent on the ground. A few still hang and twirl a little in the wind, tip-tapping on a nearby twig. The squirrel's feet, as it bounds away, scritch on the bark as it catches and releases its footholds. Wings whirr, and then I hear a thin *zzeeet-zzzeeet* from a bird I never actually see. Some articles say that autistic persons are too sensitive to small sounds, but no one minds that in animals.

No one who minds is here. I have today to enjoy my excessive and unregulated senses, in case they are gone by this time next week. I hope I will enjoy whatever senses I have then.

I lean over and taste the stone, the moss, the lichen, touching my tongue to them and then, sliding off the stone, to the wet leaves at its base. The bark of an oak (bitter, astringent), the bark of a poplar (tasteless at first, then faintly sweet). I fling my arms out, whirl in the path, my feet crunching now the crushed stone (no one to notice and be upset, no one to reprimand me, no one to shake a cautionary head). The colors whirl around me with my whirling; when I stop they do not stop at first, but only gradually.

Down and down—I find a fern to touch with my tongue, only one frond still green. It has no flavor. The bark of other trees, most I do not know but I can tell they are different by their patterns. Each has a slightly different, indescribable flavor, a slightly different smell, a different pattern of bark that is rougher or smoother under my fingers. The waterfall noise, at first a soft roar, dissolves into its many component sounds: boom of the main fall hitting the rocks below, the echoes of that blur that boom into a roar, the trickles and splatters of spray, of the little falls, the quiet drip of individual drops off the frost-seared fern fronds.

I watch the water falling, trying to see each part of it, the apparent masses that flow smoothly to the lip and then come apart on the way down. . . . What would a drop feel as it slid over that last rock, as it fell into nothingness? Water has no mind, water cannot think, but people—

normal people—do write about raging rivers and angry floodwaters as if they did not believe in that inability.

A swirl of wind brings spray to my face; some drops defied gravity and rose on the wind, but not to return to where they were.

I almost think about the decision, about the unknown, about not being able to go back, but I do not want to think today. I want to feel everything I can feel and have that to remember, if I have memories in that unknown future. I concentrate on the water, seeing its pattern, the order in chaos and chaos in order.

MONDAY. NINE TWENTY-NINE. I AM IN THE CLINICAL RESEARCH facility on the far side of the campus from Section A. I am sitting in a row of chairs between Dale and Bailey.

The chairs are pale-gray plastic with blue and green and pink tweedy cushions on the back and seat. Across the room is another row of chairs; I can see the subtle humps and hollows where people have sat on those chairs. The walls have a stripy textured covering in two shades of gray below a pale-gray rail and an off-white pebbly covering above that. Even though the bottom pattern is in stripes, the texture is the same pebbly feel as the one above. Across the room there are two pictures on the wall, one a landscape with a hill in the distance and green fields nearby and the other one of a bunch of red poppies in a copper jug. At the end of the room is a door. I do not know what is beyond the door. I do not know if that is the door we will go through. In front of us is a low coffee table with two neat stacks of personal viewers and a box of disks labeled: "Patient Information: Understand Your Project." The label on the disk I can see reads: "Understanding Your Stomach."

My stomach is a cold lump inside a vast hollow space. My skin feels as if someone had pulled it too tight. I have not looked to see if there is a disk labeled: "Understanding Your Brain." I do not want to read it if there is one.

When I try to imagine the future—the rest of this day, tomorrow, next week, the rest of my life—it is like looking into the pupil of my eye, and only the black looks back at me. The dark that is there already when the light speeds in, unknown and unknowable until the light arrives.

Not knowing arrives before knowing; the future arrives before the present. From this moment, past and future are the same in different directions, but I am going that way and not this way.

When I get there, the speed of light and the speed of dark will be the same.

*L*IGHT. *DARK. LIGHT. DARK. LIGHT AND DARK. EDGE OF* light on dark. Movement. Noise. Noise again. Movement. Cold and warm and hot and light and dark and rough and smooth, cold, TOO COLD and PAIN and warm and dark and no pain. Light again. Movement. Noise and louder noise and TOO LOUD COW MOOING. Movement, shapes against the light, sting, warm back to dark.

*LIGHT IS DAY. DARK IS NIGHT. DAY IS GET UP NOW IT IS TIME* to get up. Night is lie down be quiet sleep.

Get up now, sit up, hold out arms. Cold air. Warm touch. Get up now, stand up. Cold on feet. Come on now walk. Walk to place is shiny is cold smells scary. Place for making wet or dirty, place for making clean. Hold out arms, feel sliding on skin. Sliding on legs. Cold air all over. Get in shower, hold on rail. Rail cold. Scary noise, scary noise. Don't be silly. Stand still. Things hitting, many things hitting, wet sliding, too cold then warm then too hot. All right, it's all right. Not all right. Yes, yes, stand still. Slurpy feeling, sliding all over. Clean. Now clean. More wet. Time come out, stand. Rubbing all over, skin warm now. Put on clothes. Put on pants, put on shirt, put on slippers. Time to walk. Hold this. Walk.

Place to eat. Bowl. Food in bowl. Pick up spoon. Spoon in food. Spoon in mouth. No, hold spoon right. Food all gone. Food fall. Hold still. Try again. Try again. Try again. Spoon in mouth, food in mouth. Food taste bad. Wet on chin. No, don't spit out. Try again. Try again. Try again.

SHAPES MOVING PEOPLE. PEOPLE ALIVE. SHAPES NOT MOVING not alive. Walking, shapes change. Not alive shapes change little. Alive shapes change a lot. People shapes have blank place at top. People say put on clothes, put on clothes, get good. Good is sweet. Good is warm. Good is shiny pretty. Good is smile, is name for face pieces move this way. Good is happy voice, is name for sound like this. Sound like this is name talking. Talking tells what to do. People laugh, is best sound. Good for you, good for you. Good food is good for you. Clothes is good for you. Talking is good for you.

People more than one. People is names. Use names is good for you, happy voice, shiny pretty, even sweet. One is Jim, good morning time to get up and get dressed. Jim is dark face, shiny on top head, warm hands, loud talking. More than one two is Sally, now here's breakfast you can do it isn't it good? Sally is pale face, white hair on top head, not loud talking. Amber is pale face, dark hair on top head, not loud as Jim louder than Sally.

Hi Jim. Hi Sally. Hi Amber.

JIM SAY GET UP. HI JIM. JIM SMILE. JIM HAPPY I SAY HI JIM. Get up, go to bathroom, use toilet, take off clothes, go in shower. Reach for wheel thing. Jim say Good for you and shut door. Turn wheel thing. Water. Soap. Water. Feel good. All feel good. Open door. Jim smile. Jim happy I take shower by self. Jim hold towel. Take towel. Rub all over. Dry. Dry feel good. Wet feel good. Morning feel good.

Put on clothes, walk to breakfast. Sit at table with Sally. Hi Sally. Sally smile. Sally happy I say Hi Sally. Look around Sally say. Look around. More tables. Other people. Know Sally. Know Amber. Know Jim. Not know other people. Sally ask Are you hungry. Say yes. Sally smile. Sally happy I say yes. Bowl. Food in bowl cereal. Sweet on top is fruit. Eat sweet on top, eat cereal, say Good, good. Sally smile. Sally happy I say Good. Happy because Sally happy. Happy because sweet is good.

Amber say time to go. Hi Amber. Amber smile. Amber happy I say Hi Amber. Amber walk to working room. I walk to working room. Amber say sit there. I sit there. Table in front. Amber sit other side. Amber say time to play game. Amber put thing on table. What is this, Amber ask. It is blue. I say blue. Amber say That is color, what is thing? I want to touch. Amber say no touch, just look. Thing is funny shape, wrinkly. Blue. I sad. Not know is not good, no good for you, no sweet, no shiny pretty.

Don't be upset, Amber say. Okay, okay. Amber touch Amber box. Then say You can touch. I touch. It is part of clothes. It is shirt. It is too small for me. Too small. Amber laugh. Good for you, here sweet, it is a shirt and it is way too small for you. Shirt for doll. Amber take shirt for doll and put down another thing. Also funny shape, wrinkly black. Not touch, just look. If wrinkly blue thing shirt for doll, wrinkly black thing something for doll? Amber touch. Thing lies flatter. Two things stick out bottom, one thing at top. Pants. I say Pants for doll. Amber makes big smile. Good for you, really good. Sweet thing for you. Touches Amber box.

Lunchtime. Lunch is food in day between breakfast and supper. Hi Sally. It looks good Sally. Sally is happy I say that. Food is gooey between bread slices and fruit and water to drink. Food feels good in mouth. This is good Sally. Sally is happy I say that. Sally smile. More Good for you and good for you. Like Sally. Sally nice.

After lunch is Amber and crawl on floor follow line, or stand on floor one foot up then other foot up. Amber crawl too. Amber stand on one foot, fall over. Laugh. Laugh feel good like shaking all over. Amber laugh. More good for you. Like Amber.

After crawl on floor is more game on table. Amber put things on table. Not know names. No names, Amber say. See this: Amber touches black thing. Find another one, Amber say. Look at things. One other thing same. Touch. Amber smile. Good for you. Amber put black thing and white thing together. Do like that, Amber say. Scary. Not know. Okay, okay, Amber say. Okay to not know. Amber not smile. Not okay. Find black thing. Look. Find white thing. Put together. Amber smile now. Good for you.

Amber put three things together. Do like that, Amber say. I look. One thing is black, one is white with black place, one is red with yellow place. Look. Put down black thing. Find white thing with black place, put down. Then find red with yellow place, put down. Amber touch Amber box. Then Amber touch Amber things: red in middle, Amber say. Look. Did wrong. Red on end. Move. Good for you, Amber say. Really good work. Happy. Like make Amber happy. Good happy together.

Other people come. One in white coat, see before, not know name except Doctor. One man in sweater with many colors and tan pants.

Amber say Hi Doctor to one in white coat. Doctor talk to Amber, say This is friend of his, on the list. Amber look at me, then at other man. Man look at me. Not look happy, even with smile.

Man say Hi Lou I'm Tom.

Hi, Tom, I say. He does not say Good for you. You are doctor, I say.

Not a medical doctor, Tom say. Not know what not a medical doctor means.

Amber say Tom is on your list, for visiting. You knew him before.

Before what? Tom not look happy. Tom look very sad.

Not know Tom, I say. Look at Amber. Is wrong to not know Tom?

Have you forgotten everything from before? Tom ask.

Before what? Question bothers me. What I know is now. Jim, Sally, Amber, Doctor, where is bedroom, where is bathroom, where is place to eat, where is workroom.

It's okay, Amber says. We'll explain later. It's okay. You're doing fine.

Better go now, says Doctor. Tom and Doctor turn away.

Before WHAT?

Amber puts down another row and says Do what I did.

*"I TOLD YOU IT WAS TOO SOON," DR. HENDRICKS SAID, ONCE* they were back in the corridor. "I told you he wouldn't remember you."

Tom Fennell glanced back through the one-way window. Lou—or what had been Lou—smiled at the therapist who was working with him and picked up a block to add to the pattern he was copying. Grief and rage washed over Tom at the memory of Lou's blank look, the meaningless little smile that had gone with, "Hi, Tom."

"It would only distress him to try to explain things now," Hendricks said. "He couldn't possibly understand."

Tom found his voice again, though it didn't sound like his own. "You—do you have the slightest idea what you've done?" He held himself still with great effort; he wanted to strangle this person who had destroyed his friend.

"Yes. He's really doing well." Hendricks sounded indecently happy with herself. "Last week he couldn't do what he's doing now."

Doing well. Sitting there copying block patterns was not Tom's definition of doing well. Not when he remembered Lou's startling abilities. "But . . . but pattern analysis and pattern generation was his special gift—"

"There have been profound changes in the structure of his brain," Dr. Hendricks said. "Changes are still going on. It's as if his brain reversed in age, became an infant brain again in some ways. Great plasticity, great adaptive ability."

Her smug tone grated on him; she clearly had no doubts about what she had done. "How long is this going to take?" he asked.

Hendricks did not shrug, but the pause might have been one. "We do not know. We thought—we hoped, perhaps I should say—that with the combination of genetic and nanotechnology, with accelerated neural growth, the recovery phase would be shorter, more like that seen in the animal model. The human brain is, however, immeasurably more complex—"

"You should have known that going in," Tom said. He didn't care that his tone was accusatory. He wondered how the others were doing, tried to remember how many there'd been. Only two other men had been in the room, working with other therapists. Were the others all right or not? He didn't even know their names.

"Yes." Her mild acceptance irritated him even more.

"What were you thinking—"

"To help. Only to help. Look—" She pointed at the window and Tom looked.

The man with Lou's face—but not his expression—set aside the completed pattern and looked up with a smile to the therapist across the table. She spoke—Tom could not hear the words through the glass, but he could see Lou's reaction, a relaxed laugh and a slight shake of the head. It was so unlike Lou, so strangely normal, that Tom felt his breath come short.

"His social interactions are already more normal. He's easily motivated by social cues; he enjoys being with people. A very pleasant personality, even though still infantile at this point. His sensory processing seems to have normalized; his preferred range of temperatures, textures, flavors, and so on is now within normal limits. His language use improves daily. We've been lowering the doses of anxiolytics as function improves."

"But his memories—"

"No way to tell yet. Our experience with restoring lost memories in the psychotic population suggests that both the techniques we'll be using work to a degree. We made multisensory recordings, you know, and those will be reinserted. For the present we've blocked access with a specific biochemical agent—proprietary, so don't even ask—which we'll be filtering out in the next few weeks. We want to be sure we have a completely stable substrate of sensory processing and integration before we do that."

"So you don't know if you'll be able to give him back his previous life?"

"No, but we're certainly hopeful. And he won't be worse off than someone who loses memory through trauma." What they'd done to Lou could be called trauma, Tom thought. Hendricks went on. "After all, people can adapt and live independently without any memory of their past, as long as they can relearn necessary daily living and community living skills."

"What about cognitive?" Tom managed to say in a level voice. "He seems pretty impaired right now, and he was near genius level before."

"Hardly that, I think," Dr. Hendricks said. "According to our tests, he was safely above average, so even if he lost ten or twenty points, it wasn't going to put his ability to live independently in jeopardy. But he wasn't a genius, by any means." The prim certainty in her voice, the cool dismissal of the Lou he had known, seemed worse than deliberate cruelty.

"Did you know him—or any of them—before?" Tom asked.

"No, of course not. I met them once, but it would have been inappropriate for me to know them personally. I have their test results, and the interviews and memory recordings are all held by the rehab team psychologists."

"He was an extraordinary man," Tom said. He looked at her face and saw nothing but pride in what she was doing and impatience at having been interrupted. "I hope he will be again."

"He will, at least, not be autistic," she said, as if that justified everything else.

Tom opened his mouth to say autistic wasn't that bad and shut it again. No use arguing with someone like her, at least not here and now, and it was too late for Lou anyway. She was Lou's best hope of recovery—the thought made him shiver involuntarily.

"You should come back when he's better," Dr. Hendricks said. "Then you can better appreciate what we've accomplished. We'll call you." His stomach churned at the thought, but he owed Lou that much.

Outside, Tom zipped up his coat and pulled on his gloves. Did Lou even know it was winter? He had seen no exterior windows anywhere in the unit. The gray afternoon, closing in to dark, with dirty slush underfoot, matched his mood.

He cursed medical research all the way home.


*I AM SITTING AT A TABLE, FACING A STRANGER, A WOMAN IN A* white coat. I have the feeling that I have been here a long time, but I do not know why. It is like thinking about something else while driving and suddenly being ten miles down the road without knowing what really happened between.

It is like waking up from a daze. I am not sure where I am or what I am supposed to be doing.

"I'm sorry," I say. "I must've lost track for a moment. Could you say that again?"

She looks at me, puzzled; then her eyes widen slightly.

"Lou? Do you feel okay?"

"I feel fine," I say. "Maybe a little foggy. . . ."

"Do you know who you are?"

"Of course," I say. "I'm Lou Arrendale." I don't know why she thinks I wouldn't know my own name.

"Do you know where you are?" she asks.

I look around. She has a white coat; the room looks vaguely like a clinic or school. I'm not really sure.

"Not exactly," I say. "Some kind of clinic?"

"Yes," she says. "Do you know what day it is?"

I suddenly realize that I don't know what day it is. There is a calendar on the wall, and a big clock, but although the month on display is February, that does not feel right. The last I remember is something in the fall.

"I don't," I say. I am beginning to feel scared. "What happened? Did I get sick or have an accident or something?"

"You had brain surgery," she says. "Do you remember anything about it?"

I don't. There is a dense fog when I try to think about it, dark and heavy. I reach up to feel my head. It does not hurt. I do not feel any scars. My hair feels like hair.

"How do you feel?" she asks.

"Scared," I say. "I want to know what happened."

*I HAVE BEEN STANDING AND WALKING, THEY TELL ME, FOR A* couple of weeks, going where I am told, sitting where I am told. Now

I am aware of that; I remember yesterday, though the days before are fuzzy.

In the afternoons, I have physical therapy. I was in bed for weeks, not able to walk, and that made me weak. Now I am getting stronger.

It's boring, walking up and down the gym. There's a set of steps with a railing, to practice going up and down steps, but that is soon boring, too. Missy, my physical therapist, suggests that we play a ball game. I don't remember how to play, but she hands me a ball and asks me to throw it to her. She is sitting only a few feet away. I toss her the ball, and she tosses it back. It's easy. I back up and toss the ball again. That's easy, too. She shows me a target that will chime if I hit it. It is easy to hit from ten feet away; at twenty feet I miss a few times, then hit it every time.

Even though I don't remember much of the past, I don't think I spent my time tossing a ball back and forth with someone. Real ball games, if real people play them, must be more complicated than this.

THIS MORNING I WOKE UP FEELING RESTED AND STRONGER. I remembered yesterday and the day before and something from the day before that. I was dressed before the orderly, Jim, came to check on me, and walked down to the dining room without needing directions. Breakfast is boring; they have only hot and cold cereal, bananas, and oranges. When you've had hot with bananas, hot with oranges, cold with bananas, and cold with oranges, that's it. When I looked around, I recognized several people though it took me a minute to think of their names. Dale. Eric. Cameron. I knew them before. They were also in the treatment group. There were more; I wondered where they are.

"Man, I'd love some waffles," Eric said when I sat down at the table. "I am so tired of the same old thing."

"I suppose we could ask," Dale said. He meant "but it won't do any good."

"It's probably healthy," Eric said. He was being sarcastic; we all laughed.

I wasn't sure what I wanted, but it was not the same old cereal and fruit. Vague memories of foods I'd liked wafted through my head. I wondered what the others remembered; I knew that I knew them in some way, but not how.

We all have various therapies in the morning: speech, cognitive, skills of daily living. I remembered, though not clearly, that I'd been doing this every morning for a long time.

This morning, it seemed incredibly boring. Questions and directions, over and over. Lou, what is this? A bowl, a glass, a plate, a pitcher, a box . . . Lou, put the blue glass in the yellow basket—or the green bow on the red box, or stack the blocks, or something equally useless. The therapist had a form, which she made marks on. I tried to read the title of it, but it's hard to read upside down like that. I think I used to do that easily. I read the labels on the boxes instead: DIAGNOSTIC MANIPULATIVES: SET 1, DAILY LIVING SKILLS MANIPULATIVES: SET 2.

I look around the room. We weren't all doing the same thing, but we were all working one-on-one with a therapist. All the therapists have white coats on. All of them have colored clothes underneath the white coats. Four computers sit on desks across the room. I wonder why we never use them. I remember now what computers are, sort of, and what I can do with them. They are boxes full of words and numbers and pictures, and you can make them answer questions. I would rather have a machine answer questions than me answer questions.

"Can I use the computer?" I ask Janis, my speech therapist.

She looks startled. "Use the computer? Why?"

"This is boring," I say. "You keep asking silly questions and telling me to do silly things; it's easy."

"Lou, it's to help you. We need to check your understanding—" She looks at me as if I were a child or not very bright.

"I know ordinary words; is that what you want to know?"

"Yes, but you didn't when you first woke up," she says. "Look, I can switch to a higher level—" She pulls out another test booklet. "Let's see if you're ready for this, but if it's too hard don't worry about it. . . ."

I'm supposed to match words to the right pictures. She reads the words; I look at the pictures. It is very easy; I finish in just a couple of minutes. "If you let me read the words, it'll be faster," I say.

She looks surprised again. "You can read the words?"

"Of course," I say, surprised at her surprise. I am an adult; adults can read. I feel something uneasy inside, a vague memory of not being able to read the words, of letters making no sense, being only shapes like any other shapes. "Didn't I read, before?"

"Yes, but you didn't read right away after," she says. She hands me another list and the page of pictures. The words are short and simple: *tree, doll, truck, house, car, train.* She hands me another list, this one of animals, and then one of tools. They are all easy.

"So my memory is coming back," I say. "I remember these words and these things. . . ."

"Looks like it," she says. "Want to try some reading comprehension?"

"Sure," I say.

She hands me a thin booklet. The first paragraph is a story about two boys playing ball. The words are easy; I am reading it aloud, as she asked me to do, when I suddenly feel like two people reading the same words and getting a different message. I stop between "base" and "ball."

"What?" she asks when I have said nothing for a moment.

"I—don't know," I say. "It feels funny." I don't mean funny ha-ha, but funny peculiar. One self understands that Tim is angry because Bill broke his bat and won't admit it; the other self understands that Tim is angry because his father gave him the bat. The question below asks why Tim is angry. I do not know the answer. Not for sure.

I try to explain it to the therapist. "Tim didn't want a bat for his birthday; he wanted a bicycle. So he could be angry about that, or he could be angry because Bill broke the bat his father gave him. I don't know which he is; the story doesn't give me enough information."

She looks at the booklet. "Hmm. The scoring page says that C is the right answer, but I understand your dilemma. That's good, Lou. You picked up on social nuances. Try another."

I shake my head. "I want to think about this," I say. "I don't know which self is the new self."

"But, Lou—" she says.

"Excuse me." I push back from the table and stand. I know it is rude to do that; I know it is necessary to do that. For an instant, the room seems brighter, every edge outlined sharply with a glowing line. It is hard to judge depth; I bump into the corner of the table. The light dims; edges turn fuzzy. I feel uneven, unbalanced . . . and then I am crouching on the floor, holding onto the table.

The table edge is solid under my hand; it is some composite with a fake wood-grain top. My eyes can see the wood grain, and my hand can feel the nonwood texture. I can hear air rushing through the room vents, and the air whooshing in my own airway, and my heart beating, and the cilia in my ears—how do I know they are cilia?—shifting in the streams of sound. Smells assault me: my own acrid sweat, the cleaning compound used on the floor, Janis's sweet-scented cosmetics.

It was like this when I first woke up. I remember now: waking up, flooded in sensory data, drowning in it, unable to find any stability, any freedom from the overload. I remember struggling, hour by hour, to make sense of the patterns of light and dark and color and pitch and resonance and scents and tastes and textures. . . .

It is vinyl tile flooring, pale gray with speckles of darker gray; it is a table of composite with wood-grain finish; it is my shoe that I am staring at, blinking away the seductive pattern of the woven canvas and seeing it as shoe, with a floor under it. I am in the therapy room. I am Lou Arrendale, who used to be Lou Arrendale the autistic and am now Lou Arrendale the unknown. My foot in my shoe is on the floor is on the foundation is on the ground is on the surface of a planet is in the solar system is in the galaxy is in the universe is in the mind of God.

I look up and see the floor stretching away to the wall; it wavers and steadies again, lying as flat as the contractors made it but not perfectly flat, but that does not matter; it is called flat by convention. I make it look flat. That is what flat is. Flat is not an absolute, a plane: flat is flat *enough*.

"Are you all right? Lou, please . . . answer me!"

I am all right *enough*. "I'm okay," I say to Janis. Okay means "all right enough," not "perfectly all right." She looks scared. I scared her. I didn't mean to scare her. When you scare someone, you should reassure them. "Sorry," I say. "Just one of those moments."

She relaxes a little. I sit up, then stand. The walls are not quite straight, but they are straight enough.

I am Lou enough. Lou-before and Lou-now, Lou-before lending me all his years of experience, experience he could not always understand, and Lou-now assessing, interpreting, reassessing. I have both—*am* both.

"I need to be alone for a while," I tell Janis. She looks worried again. I know she's worried about me; I know she doesn't approve, for some reason.

"You need the human interaction," she says.

"I know," I say. "But I have hours of it a day. Right now I need to be alone and figure out what just happened."

"Talk to me about it, Lou," she says. "Tell me what happened."

"I can't," I say. "I need time. . . ." I take a step toward the door. The table changes shape as I walk past it; Janis's body changes shape; the wall and door lurch toward me like drunken men in a comedy—where did I see that? How do I know? How can I remember that and also cope with the floor that is only flat enough, not flat? With an effort, I make the walls and door flat again; the elastic table springs back to the rectangular shape I should see.

"But, Lou, if you're having sensory problems, they may need to adjust the dosage—"

"I'll be fine," I say, not looking back. "I just need a break." The final argument: "I need to use the bathroom."

I know—I remember, from somewhere—that what has happened involves sensory integration and visual processing. Walking is strange. I know I am walking; I can feel my legs moving smoothly. But what I see is jerky, one abrupt position after another. What I hear is footsteps and echoes of footsteps and reechoes of footsteps.

Lou-before tells me this is not how it was, not since he was tiny. Lou-before helps me focus on the door to the men's toilets and get through it, while Lou-now rummages madly through memories of conversations overheard and books read trying to find something that will help.

The men's toilet is quieter; no one else is there. Gleams of light race at my eyes from the smooth curving white porcelain fixtures, the shiny metal knobs and pipes. There are two cubicles at the far end; I go into one and close the door.

Lou-before notices the floor tiles and the wall tiles and wants to calculate the volume of the room. Lou-now wants to climb into a soft, dark place and not come out until morning.

It is morning. It is still morning and we—I—have not had lunch. Object permanence. What I need is object permanence. What Lou-before read about it in a book—a book he read, a book I do not quite remember but also do remember—comes back to me. Babies don't have it; grownups do. People blind from birth, whose sight is restored, can't learn it: they see a table morphing from one shape to another as they walk by.

I was not blind from birth. Lou-before had object permanence in his visual processing. I can have it, too. I had it, until I tried to read the story. . . .

I can feel the pounding of my heart slow down, sink below awareness. I lean over, looking at the tiles of the floor. I don't really care what size they are or about calculating the area of the floor or the volume of the room. I might do it if I were trapped here and bored, but at the moment I'm not bored. I'm confused and worried.

I do not know what happened. Brain surgery? I have no scars, no uneven hair growth. Some medical emergency?

Emotion floods me: fear and then anger, and with it a peculiar sensation that I am swelling and then shrinking. When I am angry, I feel taller and other things look smaller. When I am scared, I feel small and other things look bigger. I play with these feelings, and it is very strange to feel that the tiny cubicle around me is changing size. It can't really be changing size. But how would I know if it were?

Music floods my mind suddenly, piano music. Gentle, flowing, organized sound . . . I squeeze my eyes shut, relaxing again. The name comes to me: Chopin. An etude. An etude is a study . . . no, let the music flow; don't think.

I run my hands up and down my arms, feeling the texture of my skin, the springiness of the hairs. It is soothing, but I do not need to keep doing it.

"Lou! Are you in here? Are you all right?" It is Jim, the orderly who has taken care of me most days. The music fades, but I can feel it rippling under my skin, soothing.

"I'm fine," I say. I can tell that my voice sounds relaxed. "I just needed a break, is all."

"Better come out, buddy," he says. "They're startin' to freak out here."

Sighing, I stand up and unlatch the door. Object permanence retains its shape as I walk out; the walls and floor stay as flat as they should; the gleam of light off shiny surfaces doesn't bother me. Jim grins at me. "You're okay then, buddy?"

"Fine," I say again. Lou-before liked music. Lou-before used music to steady him. . . . I wonder how much of Lou-before's music I could still remember.

Janis and Dr. Hendricks are waiting in the hall. I smile at them. "I'm fine," I say. "I really did just need to go to the bathroom."

"But Janis says you fell," Dr. Hendricks says.

"Just a glitch," I say. "Something about the confusion while reading sort of . . . made a confusion in the senses, but it's gone now." I look down the hall both ways to be sure. Everything seems fine. "I want to talk to you about what actually happened," I say to Dr. Hendricks. "They said brain surgery, but I don't have any scars that I can see. And I need to understand what's going on in my brain."

She purses her lips, then nods. "All right. One of the counselors will explain it to you. I can tell you that the kind of surgery we do now doesn't involve cutting big holes in your head. Janis, set up an appointment for him." Then she walks away.

I don't think I like her very much. I sense that she is a person who keeps secrets.

WHEN MY COUNSELOR, A CHEERFUL YOUNG MAN WITH A BRIGHT red beard, explains what they did, I am almost in shock. Why did Lou-before agree to this? How could he risk so much? I would like to grab him and shake him, but he is me now. I am his future, as he is my past. I am the light flung out into the universe, and he is the explosion from which I came. I do not say this to the counselor, who is very matter-of-fact and would probably think that is crazy. He keeps assuring me that I am safe and will be taken care of; he wants me to be calm and quiet. I am calm and quiet on the outside. Inside I am split between Lou-before, who is figuring out how that pattern on his tie was woven, and my current self, who wants to shake Lou-before and laugh in the counselor's face and tell him that I do not want to be safe and taken care of. I am past that now. It is too late to be safe in the way he means safe, and I will take care of myself.

I AM LYING IN BED WITH MY EYES CLOSED, THINKING ABOUT the day. Suddenly I am suspended in space, in darkness. Far off tiny chips of light, many-colored. I know they are stars and the blurry ones are probably galaxies. Music starts, Chopin again. It is slow, thoughtful, almost sad. Something in E minor. Then some other music comes in, with a different feel: more texture, more strength, rising up under me like a wave on the ocean, only this wave is light.

Colors shift: I know, without analyzing it, that I am racing toward those distant stars, faster and faster, until the wave of light tosses me off and I fly faster yet, a dark perception, toward the center of space and time.

When I wake up, I am happier than I have ever been, and I do not know why.

THE NEXT TIME TOM COMES, I RECOGNIZE HIM AND REMEMBER that he has been here before. I have so much to tell him, so much to ask him. Lou-before thinks Tom knew him better than just about anybody. If I could I would let Lou-before greet him, but that doesn't work anymore.

"We'll be out in a few days," I say. "I've already talked to my apartment manager; she'll turn the power back on and get things ready."

"You're feeling all right?" he asks.

"Fine," I say. "Thanks for coming all these times; I'm sorry I didn't recognize you at first."

He looks down; I can see tears in his eyes; he is embarrassed by them. "It's not your fault, Lou."

"No, but I know you worried," I say. Lou-before might not have known that, but I do. I can see that Tom is a man who cares deeply about others; I can imagine how he felt when I didn't know his face.

"Do you know what you're going to do?" he asks.

"I wanted to ask you about signing up for night school," I say. "I want to go back to college."

"Good idea," he says. "I can certainly help you with the admissions process. What are you going to study?"

"Astronomy," I say. "Or astrophysics. I'm not sure which, but something like that. I'd like to go into space."

Now he looks a little sad, and I can see he is forcing the smile that comes after. "I hope you get what you want," he says. Then, as if he doesn't want to be pushy, "Night school won't give you much time for fencing," he says.

"No," I say. "I'll just have to see how it works out. But I'll come visit, if that's okay."

He looks relieved. "Of course, Lou. I don't want to lose track of you."

"I'll be fine," I say.

He cocks his head sideways, then shakes it once. "You know, I think you will. I really think you will."

*I* CAN HARDLY BELIEVE IT, EVEN THOUGH EVERYTHING I'VE
done for the past seven years has been aimed at exactly this. I am
sitting here at a desk entering my notes, and the desk is in a ship
and the ship is in space, and space is full of light. Lou-before hugs the
series to him, dancing inside me like a joyous child. I feign more sobri-
ety, in my workaday coverall, though I can feel a smile tugging at the
corner of my mouth. We both hear the same music.

The identifier code on my ID gives my academic degree, my blood
type, my security clearance . . . no mention there that I spent almost
forty years of my life defined as a disabled person, an autist. Some people know, of course: the publicity surrounding the company's unsuccess-
ful attempt to market an attention-control treatment to employers
brought us all more notoriety than we wanted. Bailey, in particular,
made a juicy tidbit for the media. I didn't know how badly it went for
him until I saw the news archives; they never let us see him.

I miss Bailey. It wasn't fair, what happened to him, and I used to feel
guilty, even though it wasn't my fault. I miss Linda and Chuy; I hoped
they would take the treatment when they saw how it worked for me, but
Linda didn't until after I finished my doctorate last year. She is still in rehab. Chuy never did. The last time I saw him, he said he was still happy
the way he was. I miss Tom and Lucia and Marjory and my other friends
from fencing, who helped me so much in the early years of recovery. I
know Lou-before loved Marjory, but nothing happened inside when I

looked at her afterward. I had to choose, and—like Lou-before—I chose to go on, to risk success, to find new friends, to be who I am now.

Out there is the dark: the dark we don't know about yet. It is always there waiting; it is, in that sense, always ahead of the light. It bothered Lou-before that the speed of dark was greater than the speed of light. Now I am glad of it, because it means I will never come to the end, chasing the light.

Now I get to ask the questions.